Realm of Souls

CW00829555

By Shane Gostick

A special thank you goes out to friends and family who have encouraged me to finish this book and continue with the others shortly to follow.
And finally, thank you for everyone who buys this book.

CHAPTER ONE

The story begins

November 17th 2012, a dark and stormy night fell on the magnificent city of London, England.

The heavens opened to reveal dark drops of cold heavy rain pouring into the city streets soaking all beneath.

Thunder and lightning struck through the skies with a deafening rumble to follow the bright strobes.

The people of the city ran around the streets trying to stay out of the rain, but the weather was the last thing on one man's mind this night.

Deep in the woods of Hyde Park stood a man, his name was Jacob Rawn.

This man was known to very few in the world. He is a soldier fighting a war that has raged for thousands of years in the shadows.

For over seventy years he has fought Wars and battles which have never been seen by outsiders, in newspapers or on TV, with countless deaths on battlefields not of this world, and yet Jacob survived.

Survived and continued to fight this same war he has fought for most of life. and will do so till the day he draws his last breath.

Stood alone in the park his attention is focused on the open area around him.

His short blond hair now dark and soaked drips down his stern young face and into his blue eyes, yet he does not blink but remains focused on the open area.

His long grey trench coat fails to keep out the weather as the open front allows the rain to soak his white t-shirt and blue jeans.

The weather refuses to alter as he stands seemingly unaware of its effects.

His size and build well hid under his drenched coat are now betrayed by the see-through wet t-shirt, revealing a well-toned and muscular physique.

In a sudden and sharp swift motion, he spins around as his attention is caught by a faint sound behind him.

He readies himself as his eyes lock with that of his target.

A small black cat pushes through a bush trying to keep dry out of the wet weather.

A sigh bursts from him as he relaxes once more closing his eyes for a brief moment clearing his vision.

Opening his eyes and looking again to the open area his attention is grasped by a lone hooded figure.

Another sigh and a sharp flick of the head clears the rain from Jacob's eyes and dripping hair; he walks towards the lone figure.

Anger festers within him as he looks intensely at the approaching man.

Both men walk towards the centre of the open area until they meet, stopping within an arm's reach of each other.

The man slowly raised his arm and pulls back the hood hiding his face, to reveal long blood-red hair. He stared with a look of pure hatred towards Jacob.

"Well, well, the great man himself; the legendary Jacob Rawn, as live and breathe."

Jacob looked up towards the man's face stirring deep into his eyes and returning the look of pure hatred for him, as he listened to the man's husky deep voice.

Towering over Jacob by a clear 2 feet Jacob seemed not to be intimidated by his size or the anger directed at him.

"Been a long time Varamont," Jacob utters with firm hatred.

"Indeed it has." The red hair man replied.

Never removing their glare for each other both men seemed unaware by the heavy rain and thunder.

"I missed you in L. A. by a day."

The man's face let slip a smirking grin at Jacobs's remark.

"So you have been hunting me."

"Are you that eager to die, Human?" Varamont questions.

Jacobs gaze followed the man as he slowly walked around him as if measuring him up.

"Die" Jacob replied.

"I have died a few times, once by one of your minions, once I was nearly killed by your former master," Jacob added.

Jacob's fist clenched firmly as he remembered those dark days.

The tall man's face let slip a smile at the news Jacob revealed.

"Ha, petty humans are no match for the power of my kind." The husky voice of Varamont bursts.

"And we have no chance of besting one of you in battle, blah, blah, blah, I have heard all this a thousand times over, and yet, many of your kind have fallen to us."

Varamont's smile vanished and was replaced by a look of anger and hatred.

"That may be true." Varamont grunts.

Jacob now returned the smile with a gesture of confidence.

"You know it's true if the human spirit is trained and nurtured properly, as I was, then your kind is in deep shit!" Jacobs's words cut deeply into the man as if remembering some wrong Jacob had done to him.

"Humanities numbers greatly overpower even your hordes of hell, and in time they will be strong enough to fight for themselves," Jacob stated.

Both men stirred at each other, pure hatred running through them.

"We shall see, human, for when you fall tonight, no one will stop me summoning my lord, and laying waste to this stink infested backwater realm, and claiming the souls of every living thing in it!." Varamont's voice echos confidence and firm hatred.

Jacob stood motionless as the man almost screamed his last words; his hands lay still in his trench coat pockets as he watched the tall man in front of him.

Reaching into the folds of his cloak, a long black covered blade emerged as if from nowhere. The sword itself stood nearly three and a half feet in length and over three inches in width, the heavy two-handed sword was filled with blood-red rubies on the hilt and a black crystal at the pummel.

With one hand he pulled it from his cloak as if he was wielding a twig and brought it crashing down towards Jacob.

With his other hand, he ripped the cloak from his body revealing a blood-red silk martial art Gi suit, strange ancient golden silk symbols decorate the entire outfit.

Screaming with anger that burned within him he struck at Jacob.

"NOW DIE!!" Varamont screamed.

A quick jump back sent Jacob out of the danger zone of the mighty sword as it crashed into the muddy water and soil of the ground.

Regaining his footing he looked to his opponent, Jacob reached into this long dripping wet coat and pulled a fine silver blade from within.

Jacob's sword resembled that of the katana used by the mighty samurai in times past.

Both the blade and the hilt were made from some silvery blue metal that gleamed in the lights of the city.

The hilt had an engraving of a Chinese style dragon wrapping itself around a human, stood upright and arms stretched above its head, two blue gems were in the place of the dragon eyes, and in the hands of the human at the very pummel a large misty white crystal.

Holding out his sword pointing to the ground Jacob walked around his combatant never taking his eyes off him, finally he settled into a ready position with his sword raised high at the side of his head.

Both men return the hatred gaze to each other, as Jacob remained still, his opponent with a smirk on his face and a confidant walk slowly paced in front of him.

"You think you can beat me?" Varamont questioned.

With anger in his eyes and voice, the man continued, beating on his chest like an ape declaring his dominance.

"ME! A horned blood lord from the hell realm itself, do you think you have what it takes to kill me HUMAN!" Varamont shouts.

Once again the tall man swung with ease the massive two-handed sword, hurling the blackened blade towards Jacob thrusting towards his stomach, Jacob wastes no time and quickly parried with precision and skill.

Blow after blow, parry after parry the two men were locked in combat.

Jacob never losing his cool, managed to contain his anger and focus on his opponent, while his attacker relentlessly attacked.

His confidence was building as he noticed Jacob not returning his attacks and was fighting purely on the defence.

Letting the confidence get the better of him he steadily let his great strength wane slightly thinking he had this battle won.

Jacob's time had come; his attacker came in for a low stomach thrust with his mighty blade. Jacob patted down with his nibble blade and at the same time stepped in with his left hand aiming for his opponent's chest.

Summoning from within him a spark of his power, focusing on the centre of his open palm his hand glowed a bright blue, slightly shifting his hand out of view leaving only a faint outline surrounded in this hazy blue light.

At the same time as his pat down with his sword, the left open palm thrust into the open chest of his attacker striking true.

Jacob's palm closed on its target, but before actual contact occurred, the light from his hand hit its target, hurling the man away from Jacob, as if hit with a pressure cannon.

Lifting his opponent off his feet, his body hurled through the air some five feet, slamming hard to the muddy wet ground, sliding along the grass.

Looking to his enemy with surprise and pain, Varamont held his chest and noticed part of his fine silk suit now ruined, leaving a blacken exposed chest the size of a basketball.

Quickly Rising to his feet Varamont's anger swirled within, his grip tightened on the hilt of his sword, holding his chest with his free hand, he looked intensely at his enemy.

"Improvement I see." Varamont's voice echoed with rage

"I'm just getting started," Jacob replied.

Both men readied themselves for another burst, the wind and rain continued to fall, the thunder and lightning raged on relentlessly.

Finally, the peace was broken, both men moved in for the attack, blade clashed against blade, strikes aimed high and low, parries saved their owners flesh from devastating blows aimed to dismember or kill.

Jacob's eyes focused on his enemy, trying to find a weakness as his fatigue built within, yet showing no sign on the outside for his opponent to see.

Varamont struggled to match Jacob's sword skills, compensating with brute strength, overpowering Jacob's blows to shake him and knock him back slightly, giving him time for another strike.

Jacob pressed his attacks speeding his body beyond that of normal human beings, his arm and footwork become that of a fine dance.

His magnificent blade reaching out again and again, relentless for its target, only to be blocked by a now worried-looking enemy.

His arms becoming a steady blur, like something on film out of focus.

Striking towards his opponent Jacob finally connected.

The silver blade disappeared deep into the stomach of the tall man and then reappeared as Jacob continued his attack, spinning on the spot following through with another strike to his opponent's left upper thigh as the blade angled upward.

The attack continued, followed by a down angle strike to Varamont's left collar, down to his right hip as Jacob disengaged from the final attack and stepped back.

A flood of fresh crimson splashed from the now open wounds, the man let out no screams but mere grunts as if he barely felt them.

Holding back his anger and the small amount of pain he now felt he looked back to his stomach wound.

Pressing his hand to the wound and lifting to see the fresh blood flowing from him. His eyes turn to Jacob.

The tall red-haired man spun his mighty sword in his hand pointing the tip down to the ground; he slammed the blade deep into the ground leaving the blade alone as he stood up.

Reaching to his now ruined fine silk Gi he ripped the cloth from his body, never taking his eyes from his enemy.

The man's strong muscular build was well-formed and the slight flow of crimson upon him did little to hide his size.

Suddenly Jacob's eyes change from a focused steady look to a now curious slightly worried expression.

The tall man's body now seemed to grow in size, his eyes never leaving Jacob, but teeth gritted and a slow grunt come from him.

His skin colour changed to a deeper shade of red like the colour of blood itself.

Stood watching in amazement Jacob lowered his guard and watched in awe.

The now demonic-looking humanoid in front of him seems alien to the man that was standing before him mere moments ago.

Two large black horns curl out of his brow running around the top of his eyes round towards his ears then up sharply towards the sky.

The black and sharp-looking teeth are hard to spot in the blackness of his mouth.

The giant-sized demon was a huge 12 to 13 feet tall, with muscles to match his size; the creatures hand size could easily grasp Jacob's upper torso in one hand.

The large black sharp claws look like it could split trees asunder with a single stroke.

"Now, I'm pissed."

The large bellowing voice came from the towering beast looking towards Jacob with anger and anticipation.

Readying himself once more for the fight ahead Jacobs refused to let the size of his enemy affect him.

Reaching for his sword again the now huge beast swung for Jacob again and again.

Parrying barely, under the now even greater strength of his adversary, Jacob struggled to keep his footing, each blow staggering him from side to side.

The rage now felt by the beast allowed him to open a gap in Jacobs's defence with his mighty sword, following up he swings up with a back fist strike that could lift a truck from the ground.

Jacob's nimble blade clashes with the beast's blade, trying to stop the blow but the beast's strength was too great knocking back a few steps.

His sword knocked aside, the beast let fly his huge fist striking Jacob's head and upper torso at once.

The blow sent Jacob through the air flying backwards, his fine sword knocked from his hand. The tree some ten feet from his old position split in two, as Jacob's shoulder blades slam hard into it.

The tree taking the impact stopped Jacob's flight abruptly sending him straight down face first with a heavy thud.

Falling under the strain it took, the tree toppled over crashing to the ground.

Jacob barely heard the sound of timber splitting or the sound of the tree crashing into the now rain-soaked ground.

His body now throbbing with pain through his entire upper body remained still face down in the waterlogged grass as he struggled to catch his breath.

Walking towards his fallen prey the beasts smiled, letting slip the dark liquid from his mouth like a slavering predator about to feast.

"Your feeble human body is incapable of the power you need to defeat me," Varamont utters with pride.

Suddenly coming to his senses, as if a sudden electric jolt had run through him, Jacob heard nothing of his attacker's words, only feeling the heavy thuds as his massive feet closed in on him.

Staying where he lay, not attempting to move, Jacob looked fanatically for his blade never lifting his head continuing the rouse that he was badly wounded.

Locating the fine blade down in the grass some twenty or so feet from him, another plan came to mind, and the beasts mighty grasp picked Jacob from the floor like it would a piece of wet paper.

The beast looked to his prey with a smile on his face, pointing his mighty sword to Jacob's chest ready to run him through.

With a quick jolt, he thrust to end his prey.

But it was for nought, summoning some more of his mystical power; Jacob's body was now infused with unimaginable abilities.

Catching the black heavy blade between the palm of his hands like something out of some martial arts film the blade stops suddenly a mere three inches from his chest.

His body showed no sign of struggle or strain. Jacob's eyes opened and looked to his attacker, his entire eyes replaced by bright blueish-white crackling energy.

The beast's expression showed a small measure of fear, rumours of Jacob's kind and their abilities ran through Varamont's head.

The beast shoved the memories aside and applied his mighty strength to his current attack, dropping Jacob to his feet and charging forward, still pushing his blade into Jacob's hands. Jacob's body remained still as his feet tore into the soft ground until his movement was stopped by yet another tree.

Again the beast was held in a measure of fear and awe as yet his blade failed to penetrate Jacob's grasp and strength.

Jacob's arms and body shook violently under the strain, as he steadily but slowly managed to overpower the mighty demonic beast.

His blade lifted slowly towards his neck and finally to his head.

Unable to stop him with both hands, and all his great strength, the beast fear grew.

"Impossible!" The beast snarled as he pushed with everything he had, trying to ram the blade through Jacob's grasp and into his body ending his life.

A smile crept on jacobs face.

With a swift and sudden movement, faster than any soul could see, Jacob pushed the blade off to his left as he darted to his right; the mighty sword thrust forward slicing through the tree that pinned him.

Wasting no time the beast released his blade and spun around letting his mighty claws slice through the air as he swung his arm out, hopefully striking his target but none was found.

Jacob ducked the clumsy blow and countered with a solid left kick, swinging his hips forward and letting his body be the weight, his left leg hurled outward towards his enemies left leg at the knee.

With his enhanced abilities Jacob's leg smashed into its target knocking the knee out of position, forcing his enemy to fall to his right knee in pain.

The beast snarled as it dropped to its knee to take the strain off its other leg.

Another strike in the form of a tight right elbow broke into his enemy's uninjured knee.

Yet another howl of pain was heard from the beast, as now both knees collapsed to the floor, his body weight supported by his hands in the dirt.

The instincts within refuse to let up. Once again Jacob's deadly left leg snapped to life.

The strong hip movement taught to him, allowed his left leg to shoot up towards the beasts head, smashing hard into his targets face.

The sounds of bone-breaking were heard as the beast grunted in pain once more, his body now lifted slightly, allowed Jacob one more attack.

Using the beasts own hip, Jacob jumped onto his target lifting himself higher into the air, pulling back his right hand he let it fly.

Jacob's fists struck true and square onto his enemies jaw, as he fell towards the ground.

With the strange power held within him and the weight of his own body coming down to bear on the jaw of his target, causing the beast to grunt again as his own body fell to the floor.

Landing on his feet and looking to his opponent, Jacob watched, keeping his distance from possible retaliation from the powerful claws.

The huge body of the demonic beast fell heavily forward into the ground with a heavy splash of water and mud.

Jacob caught his breath, remained in a ready position, carefully watching his opponent.

The huge body moved only to breathe with grunts of pain.

Letting his better judgment escape him, Jacob let down his guard, looking to locate his sword again, taking his eyes from his target for a second, only to look back and find his enemy climbing to his knees again.

Jacob rushed in for the attack; the beast's eyes caught his oncoming prey.

Jacob let fly his fist towards his target only to be caught by the massive hands of his opponent.

Allowing no time to be wasted the beast blocked Jacob's attack, the two enemies locked up for a mere second till the beast followed through with his right cross.

Jacob's body remained stood, but staggered a few feet by the infusion of mystical energy within him, he pumped his physical abilities to inhuman states.

Allowing the beast a few seconds, he pulled forth his good leg and stayed in a kneeling position.

Jacob came in again with his deadly legs and with a right Thai style kick aiming for the now forward knee, the same kick that dislocated the first knee.

Placing his right arm down to block the kick, the beast countered with his left hand.

Jacob blocked the attack and returned the counter with a left snap sidekick towards the same knee.

Jacob's left leg lifted, his left hip doing the work, sending his leg firing towards its target. the kicks and strikes resemble the Thai boxing and karate style of fighting, striking with deadly precision and skill.

Once again the demonic creature blocked the attack. Its second counter struck Jacob.

The mighty claws slicing into Jacob's skin, tearing his t-shirt and jeans nearly spinning him round with the force from the blow.

Refusing to be beaten Jacob retained his position and attacked again.

Approaching inward closing the gap between the two combatants, with a right cross Jacob's fist flies towards the creature's chest.

Unable to find its mark as the creature blocked again, Jacob is ready and allows this block to continue as he lifts his right leg once more slamming hard into the muscle of the beast's good leg, and follows with a reverse elbow to the stomach.

Jacob's elbow flew back towards its target again striking true.

A small flow of blood comes from the now almost healed wound that was caused by Jacob's sword not moments ago.

The beast countered with a strong backhand striking Jacob hard in the head hurling him back towards the ground some five feet away.

A brief moment of silence enters the fry as the heavy rain continues to pour down on the two weary fighters.

Slowly the two enemies climb to their feet, Jacob's rolls over on to his belly allowing him to push himself up slowly.

The creature placed his hands on the floor and lifted himself onto his injured but sturdy good leg.

Hopping as he rises to a standing position, Varamont places some weight to the dislocated leg, still wondering how the puny body of the human could damage him so.

With a sudden twist and a howl of pain the dislocated knee of Varamont finds its right place.

Jacob looking now tired and fatigued watches patiently as his enemy corrects himself.

Both warriors look to their wounds and return there gaze for each other.

"How's the leg?" Jacobs's cocky tone fails to impress the beast, as does his now normal looking eyes.

"Strong enough to crush the life from you human, I underestimated you, a mistake I will not duplicate." Varamont spews with pure hatred.

Wiping the blood from his mouth Jacob smirks at his enemies remarks.

Walking towards each other, both now determined to end this battle forever, for neither could take much more than they have already.

The creature is the first to strike, throwing towards Jacob his mighty claws once more, ducking and weaving Jacob manages to evade the blows that are given and counters with devastating kicks and punches.

Blows and parries are exchanged by the two combatants, some striking their targets some merely glancing by. But neither will surrender the fight. The flow of blows is interrupted by the beasts cunning attack, with his right and left hands he throws his punches, Jacob block's or evades, quickly the beast swings his now solid knee once more into the battle, striking Jacob square in his torso covering his lower and upper body at once.

Lifting Jacob into the air slightly as the strike hits, a squirt of blood comes from his mouth.

Slamming his massive heavy hand into the back and neck of his target, Varamont blow rams Jacob's body into the ground.

With a solid football like kick the creature attacks with a blow to Jacob's ribs.

His body is hurled through the air some twenty feet landing hard with the last of his breath in him. Unable to move as several of his ribs are broken in bad positions, Jacob remains still, allowing the energies that are enhancing his body to heal or repair his body enough to breath and move. The creature basking in its latest achievement walks slowly towards his target, watching his opponent for any more trickery.

Hi preys now feeble looking body coughs up bloody spitting and rolling onto his back trying to get air in his lungs.

"You see now human, your kind is nothing but food," Varamont states firmly.

Jacob's ears pick up only a murmur of what is being said, the pain greatly affecting his ability to focus on his body healing.

"That's why so many of you were destroyed in the last battle"

The beasts words echo within Jacob, finally starting to make sense in his head he recognizes the words and there meaning.

Like a small fire being poured gasoline and erupting into a bonfire, the anger and emotions flare within him as memories of that day flash into Jacobs mind.

Opening his eyes and breathing heavily and sharply, Jacob's fist grips tight as the pain swells.

Slowly struggling to his feet the creature stops in his tracks with shock and surprise now on his face.

In his mind, Varamont begins to wonder what he must do to put this human down.

The creature still amazed at the sight of damage and energy his enemy has, and wonders how he can still rise.

The beasts anger festers and quickly overshadows the fear once more as he hurls his own body high into the air, his mighty claws lifted above his head ready to crash down upon his target below.

Jacob watches as the huge giant demonic creature flies through the air towards him.

Holding his right ribs which still seem to be broken and badly damaged, Jacob feels the rest of his body able to continue the battle, still injured but able.

Waiting for the last possible second Jacob remains still as the huge shadow of his attacker nearly reaches him, with the last of his strength Jacob summons his mystical abilities once more.

His eyes flare with a brilliant blue, and hurling his own body up, lifting high into the air, narrowly missing the claws of his opponent.

A pile of dirt, muddy water, and debris fly from the impact, as the nimble body of Jacob, flies over the head of his attacker, a trail of muddied water follows him like the smoke trail from a jet. Spinning into a somersault overhead; Jacob lands behind the creature. Turning into a spin he lifts his left leg and enters a kicking technique, his leg flies out at the end of his spin adding his strength and body weight square into the spine of the beast.

The beast's body slams hard into the tree ahead of him, his broad shoulders splinter part of the tree with the last of his breath the creature grunts with pain again.

Turning to the location of his sword Jacob holds out his hand and focuses his thoughts.

With a brief moment of concentration, the sword seems to spring to life, uplifting itself from its hold in the ground and hurling itself to its owner.

With a solid grasp, Jacob turns once more and thrust with all his strength.

The beast's roar of pain is heard nearly a mile away, innocent people walking or running trying to find shelter from the rain suddenly stop and wonder at the loud demonic roar they just heard.

The beast's eyes fail to focus, his head and chest pounds with pain, as does his heart, for the sight of a long silver blade covered in a hazing blue light protrudes from his chest.

Pulling the sword from its lodging within the creature's heart and chest, Jacob staggers back holding his ribs again looking at his soon to be fallen enemy.

Looking to his wound, which despite his best wishes refuses to heal, the beast turns to his attacker with terror and shock in his eyes, Jacob stands motionless struggling to catch his breath.

Falling to his knees holding his now gushing wound the beast looks to hi attacker.

"You think you have won human, I am immortal when I die my soul will return to my master in, hell, I shall return" The creature's words come as breath will allow.

Looking towards his magnificent sword and then to the sky Jacob lifts his sword slightly.

"Not this time, this is the blade of Shakarian, the soul reaper!" Jacob replies as if knowing his fallen enemy knew its meaning.

The creature's eyes open wide with fear as Jacob speaks the name, the beast's mouth trembles, his head drops slightly as if he were crying, and a sudden change comes over him.

"Mercy, please!" Varamont utters in fear.

Jacob seems taken back by his plea and wonders to himself.

"Why is it, those who beg for mercy, are the ones who never give it?"

The creature's slumps on his hands and knees the sounds of sobbing emerge from him.

Jacob raises his sword to the side of his head.

"Tonight, you die demon, for all the souls you have feasted upon in your time, in this or any realm, I now send you to meet those you have ended."

Jacobs swings his sword towards the neck of the demon ready to severe his head and life source.

Both the demon and Jacob scream as the attack flies, both suddenly silent as the final blow of the battle is struck.

The now lifeless body crashes to the floor, fresh crimson liquid mixes with the muddied water below.

Jacob's sigh comes with a wince of pain, his shoulders drop as his body relaxes, unable to hold his body up any more.

Collapsing to his knees and nearly falling face first, Jacob runs his blade into the ground, leaning on the sword for support, trying desperately to breathe.

The pain his body feels is immense, but Jacob has grown accustomed to pain over the years and seems to almost have an immunity.

Looking to the body of his now fallen adversary, Jacob closes his eyes and holds his hand over the body, reciting some incantation to himself, muttering almost aloud, he slowly climbs to his feet.

The fallen body starts to crumble like it was ageing a thousand years in a few seconds, steadily turning to ash.

With the final part of the body gone a brilliant bright red flash appears as the body is disintegrated, all that remains is a small golf ball-sized red light hovering where the body fell.

Rippling with electrical sparks the small light hovers with little movement, with the last few words of his incantation Jacob lifts his sword once more above his head spinning the blade up towards his ready position.

letting the mighty blade fall, striking the light below, as the blade lowers its mystical abilities comes to life, with a flow of bright blue electrical like energy.

As the light from the blade and the light from the creature touch a blinding flash erupts, as the red light is absorbed in the blade.

Watching as the light travels up the blade into the hilt the bright blue gems resembling eyes in the dragon carving flare with light.

The light travels up the carving and the roar of a mighty dragon is heard, eventually, the light is absorbed into the white crystal at the pummel.

A final flash erupts and all fall quiet, except the ceaseless rain and heavy wising from Jacobs injured lungs.

Jacob's body still aching with pain holding his ribs places his sword into his long trench coat now ripped and torn.

Slowly he makes his way to the tree housing the mighty black blade of his fallen enemy.

Reaching with pain in every movement he grasps the sword and pulls it from its resting place.
Walking away from the tree's, Jacob slams the black blade into the ground, once more he
steps back and again mutters to himself some strange words forming a strange incantation.
Raising his right hand, and holding it palm out to the blade, his hand glows once more, with a
flood of bright blue energy surrounding his hand, opening his eyes they now emanate the
same blue colour as his palm.
The blade slowly turns into a glowing version of itself, the once red rubies now glow a
brilliant white and start to sparkle.
The blade now a bright white infused with the energy from Jacob glows brightly.
Once more a brilliant flash is seen, a small smile emerges on his face as if he gains some
enjoyment from the light.
With a flash of light from the blade, it separates into a thousand small blues lights, like those
from the body of his fallen enemy only in brilliant white and blue.
The small lights swirl around Jacob, some slow some fast, he closes his eyes and opens his
other senses hearing the faint whispers from a thousand lost souls. These souls rush about
him like excited sparks; all saying their respects and thanks for the long-awaited freedom.
Slowly the souls finish their goodbyes and head for up into the sky for the stars and are gone
mere moments later.
Jacob stands alone, injured, once more the rain pours onto him and he seems oblivious to it.
"For absent friends!" Jacob's voice echoes sadness and regret.
With the lights gone and his enemy dead, its soul absorbed by his sword, Jacob's thoughts
run wild thinking to himself, this world is free from his kind, for a while at least.
Looking to the sky closing his eyes he wipes the blood from his mouth and brow in the rain.
Leaning against the tree for support, Jacob looks to his clothes and realizes they are ruined,
folding his long grey and torn trench coat around him, hiding the now healing bloody wounds
inflicted on him.
With a stagger and a wince he makes his way from the park, the storm above relentless,
quickly washes away the remaining traces of mud and blood on his coat.
Any passers-by would see Jacob appear no more than a humble tramp.
Approaching the end of the large park Jacob's wounds begin to let up, he stops suddenly in
his tracks as a familiar feeling comes over him, the feeling of being watched.
Reaching out with his senses his mind locates an energy source, a living being, to his far-left
hidden in the bushes following the path towards the city.
With a quick turn of his heals he reaches deep within the bushes, his mind guiding his hands,
as his eyes cannot penetrate the black of night or the bush.
"Err..." a shocked male voice erupts.
A whimper comes from within as Jacob latches his grasp to some cloth, pulling from the bush
and lifting into the air with ease, Jacob lifts free a large plump middle-aged man, his breath
heavy with fear and alcohol, his wet bald head shines in the night light from the nearby city
streets.
The rugged-looking man wears a brown suit and tie, his white shirt now dirty and soiled from
the wet ground and bushes.
"Ah, please, don't kill me." The fear erupts from the dangling man.
The man's voice is filled with fear as his back is slammed into a nearby tree while still lifted
into the air.
Jacob looks to the man, looking him up and down.
"Who are you? What did you see?" Jacob's voice harsh and firm.
"I didn't see anything, I had a few too many to drink and fell asleep."
The man's voice and eyes show to Jacob his captive is in shock and full of fear at the sight of
him.

"You must be a heavy sleeper, to sleep in this weather,"

Before the man could answer Jacob continues his interrogation.

"This is the last time I will ask, who are you and what did you see?" affirm tone utters from Jacob.

Struggling to hold onto his captor's arm as it holds him in the air against the tree, Jacob's strength inhuman for his size and build. The man's eyes open wider still, fear is all he can see and feel. Lowering the man down towards him, Jacob looks into his eyes.

Trying once more to pull away the man is unable to move as Jacob's grip refuses to loosen. The man looks back at his captor as if captivated by some magical wonder within his sparkling blue eyes.

calling upon the mystical abilities his mind allows him, Jacob looks deep into the man's eyes and beyond.

To Jacob's mind, a smoky vale like curtain lifts before him and the answers he seeks show themselves clear to him.

Dozens of fleeting images reveal themselves to Jacobs mind showing him everything he wants to know.

Mere moments pass by before his captors' silence is broken.

"Paul Simpson, you're a journalist." the voice now calm but still firm.

The man looks bewildered to his captor as if he had read the answer from some sign in his eyes.

The reporter's eyes wander once more to the last resting place of a small pile of black ashes now scattering to the wind and rain in the open field.

With a quick jolt Jacob pulls the man in close, their faces no more than an inch or two apart, Jacob returns his gaze once again to the man's eyes.

"You saw nothing eh?"

Without making a sound, the man shakes his head violently to the question.

Jacobs's eyes close, with a deep breath he looks back at the man in his hands, then returns his gaze to the resting place of Varamont's ashes, when slowly a smile appears on his face.

The reporter looks to his captors and fear swells within.

Another sigh follows from Jacob, his grip slowly lessens as he looks back to the man still smiling, placing a small amount of relief within him.

Before the man can run or speak Jacob lifts one hand to the forehead of the man, Jacob's voice emanates like a multitude of calm harmonizing voices overlapping each other in synchronisation.

"Sleep!" Jacob mystic tone utters.

As if a switch was flipped within his mind, the man suddenly collapses in a state of unconsciousness.

Jacob catches the falling man, all life seems gone from him as he sleeps.

Looking to the stars as if seeking answers, Jacob's eyes wander as does his mind before turning back to the man in his arms.

"Sleep this night, Paul Simpson, for tomorrow, brings with it many terrors, and for the first time in a long time, a possibility of hope."

With a final feat of strength, Jacob lifts the man onto his shoulders, like a fireman would carry a wounded man.

Walking into the night of Hyde Park, he gives a final look around for watching eyes, with a feeling of safety Jacob vanishes into the black of night with his new guest in tow.

***

What seems only moments later, Paul's eyes open, a warm comforting feeling greeted him.

His body felt rested as if he had slept for days on end, he was clean and dry, his eyes wander around the room in which he found himself.

The walls were made from wood, like the style you would find in a log cabin out in the wilds of America.

As he removed the covers from his bed he felt the rush of warm air, he soon realizes his body was naked, quickly his eyes locate the suit he wore last, it was placed neat and clean at the side of his bed.

Dressing he examined the room further, there were no windows and only one door located at the north of the room, one dressing table with a small mirror placed on a wall above it and a chest of draws is all that resides in the room.

Plucking what courage he had left he reached for the door, the door opened with ease as a flood of heat met him, followed by the smell of freshly made food.

Looking frantically around the room he looked for his host with a measure of fear in his heart.

The room had but one more door in the west wall and once more no windows, the walls remained the same, that of logs forming a two-roomed wooden cabin.

A large fireplace was roaring in the east wall, with two large sofa-like chairs in front of the fireplace, a blue rug donned the floor.

Paul relaxed with the sight of no one else in the cabin, looking around the room once more his eyes latch to the sight of a hot cup of coffee.

Laid next to it on the table to the north wall was a fried breakfast, bacon, eggs sausages and beans.

With his mind questioning what he saw he walked cautiously towards it, once again looking around the room for signs of life.

Paul's eyes keep wondering until they located many strange artefacts donning the walls.

On the east wall near the door, an old-world war one British service man's uniform and rifle were hung inside a cabinet.

Another wall housed swords and daggers of all sizes and types, some never seen before by Paul, the objects themselves would amass a huge fortune in an auction.

But once more the smell of fresh food seemed to invite him to eat as he sat at the table holding the fine food and finding he could no longer resist.

A strange sound cut through the air as he began to reach for the food; a sound like two large bits of wood sharply scraped together distracted Paul suddenly.

With a quick look around the room, his eyes and heart filled with fear again as he looked dead in the eyes of his host.

Jacob stood motionless in front of the fire; his now clean appearance did nothing to smooth the situation.

Jacob's grey sweater and clean blue jeans look slightly darker than they were, only illuminated by the firelight in the cabin.

His short blond hair clean and brushed, his smile seemed genuine as he looked back at Paul.

"I trust, err, us Brit's still loved the old fry up," Jacob questioned.

Pointing to the food before Paul, Jacob smiled and nodded, gesturing for Paul to eat the food.

Paul's eyes never left his host, unaware to all else around, his heart thumped with fear and seemed to be frozen to the spot.

"Relax Paul, I can call you Paul can't I?" Jacob's calm tone did nothing to sooth Paul.

With a quick sharp nod, Paul gave his silent agreement.

"Well Paul, my name is..."

"Jacob Rawn." Paul's interruption seems sharp and quick and was followed by the realization that he now had given away the fact he was not asleep in the bush the night Jacob found him.

Jacob smiled and lowered his head with a small chuckle to himself before returning his gaze to his guest.

"You can call me Jacob or Jay before you begin to have a panic attack, allow me to tell you, I mean you no harm."

Paul seemed unable to believe his host, his grip seemed firm on both the table and chair on which he sat looking at Jacob.

Another chuckle slips Jacob's mouth.

"OK, let me say it another way."

Again he looked into Paul's eyes, his own eyes flash slightly with bright blue energy, replacing the irises and pupils, with a soothing harmonising voice the same method used once before, the voice echoed like multiple voices overlapping together Jacob spoke to his guest in an attempt to smooth over his feelings.

"You are in no danger here, you are safe from harm, and you must relax, hear my words."

Paul's eyes latch onto Jacobs gaze, the blackness seemed to cover everything but his eyes. Jacob's voice seemed familiar; Paul's mind rushed back in time till it recognizes the tone. Finally, Paul remembers this it was his mother's voice speaking to him, giving him some strange impulse and guidance to which he felt compelled to obey.

Watching with a smile once more Jacob noticed his guest's grip lessen and a sigh emerges from him, his breathing returning to normal.

"That's better, now please eat it's fresh I cooked it only moments before you woke." Jacob's voice returns to normal as did his eyes.

Gesturing to his guest to eat, Jacob sat down in one of the chairs in front of the large roaring fire and waited for his guest to finish his meal.

Moments later Paul sat opposite his host with coffee in hand, he slowly lowered himself into the chair never taking his eyes from his strange host.

Sitting in the chair facing the fire, Jacob's head rested on his hands under his chin he sat with a smile on his face and watched Paul sit.

"Was the food OK," Jacob asked.

"Yes, yes thank you." Pauls frightened tone replied.

Jacob felt the fear still within him and tried to settle him with a few comforting words.

"You are safe here Paul Simpson, no one will harm you, this is my home."

A small soothing feeling seemed to come over Paul like a steady wave of heat he slowly begins to sit back in the chair looking at his host.

"Where am I, why am I here?" Paul cautiously asked.

"You are at my home, and I have brought you here to help me and yourself for that matter." Jacob states.

A bewildered look came across Paul's face, relaxing a little more Paul continued to listen.

"Well, you saw what happened in the park last night didn't you." Jacob looked to Paul as he spoke.

Paul's head nodded in agreement, a sorrowful look crept on his face.

"Well to answer your questions that thing, that creature was called Varamont and it was not human, as you might have guessed."

Paul's eyes opened wide with surprise and curiosity.

"There are thousands of inhuman creatures out there, just like him."

"And you?" Paul added sharply.

Jacob's eyes return from the fire to Paul after the quick question was asked, with a plain look on his face he quickly turned away.

"Yeah, I too am no longer human, well half human I guess."

Paul's reporter instincts seem to take over, the fear now replaced by a feeling of anxiety and curiosity.

"I was born in the year 1893." Jacobs's voice remained calm and slightly sorrowful.

Once again the bewildered look appeared on Paul's face, he looked to his host.

Holding up his hands as if in a gesture of bewilderment Jacob returned his look.

"I know, I look what, the late 20s and yet by that maths, it would make me a hundred plus right?"

Unable to answer either out of disbelief or amazement Paul sat and listen to Jacob's words as if his life depended on it.

"I was born in a city up north called Lincoln, I fought in the First World War, and that's where it all started really."

Unable to take his eyes from the fire, Jacobs fell silent as if memories flood back into his mind.

"How did you know I was a reporter, and how did you put me out like that?" Paul asks.

As if snapping out of a daydream, Jacob turned from his past back to the now and looks to his guest a build-up of tears lay within his eyes as a few drops fell down his cheek.

With a sniffle and a wipe of the face, Jacob brought himself round.

"Well through my years, I was taught many things, and that was one of them."

Paul relaxed further still, now content at the idea that the man before him seemed genuine, that he believed his tale to the letter, Paul seemed eager to find out what the story was.

"If you chose you can leave now, I will take you back to your house and you can live your life, wondering what the hell happened that night or, you can stay." Jacob smiled as he spoke, already knowing the answer.

"Stay, for what?" Paul asked.

"If you chose to stay, I shall tell you my story, the story spanning a hundred years, wonders you couldn't imagine, and most of all, the truth of your world."

His eyes showed no lie as Paul looked into them, face to face Paul's gaze refused to move from his host.

"The truth?" Paul asks not knowing if he wanted the answer.

"The world, in which you live Paul, is not the be-all and end-all like you think it is, as you observed last night in the park."

A sudden flashback of the battle replayed itself in Paul's mind, and the sudden strange reality stroke a nerve within him, quickly he looked back to Jacob who sat looking at him a smile on his face.

"So which is it to be Paul Simpson?" Jacob asked.

"I will stay to hear your story, but you realize that the story will be printed for the world to see, it will have to be told to others, your identity will be known all over the world," Paul asked hoping his host would agree.

"I know, but this must be done, for mankind's survival is at stake," Jacob replied with a heavy heart.

"Survival?" A worried feeling crept into Paul once more as Jacob continued.

"Yes, mankind is in danger, my friend," Jacob replied.

Jacob lifted himself from his chair unaffected by wounds it seemed and leant on the fireplace looking into the fire as he continued.

"Many, friends, I've lost in my time, only me and few select others have mourned for them, they deserve better, they fought, and died for mankind, without asking for anything in return." Jacob continued with tears in his eyes and sorrow in his voice.

"In the war, I knew soldiers fought and died for their country but."

Jacob caught his breath and painful memories haunted him.

"These people that I buried, most died fighting to keep the world free from the enemies like those you saw last night, we try to spare mankind from these horrors, but our numbers dwindle more each day."

Silence fell on the pair; only the roar of the fire could be heard as if the sound were pulled from the room.

Jacob broke the silence with a harsh tone.

"Now, only I remain."

"You! Just you!" paul questioned sharply.

Paul asked both with curiosity and now a concern.

Jacobs looked back to his new guest, a sorrowful look upon his face.

"That's why I need you to tell this story, tell it to who will ever listen, mankind must be warned before it's too late."

Paul sat back in his chair, a sudden feeling of responsibility coming over him, and a heavy burden seemed to be now upon his shoulders.

Watching Jacob lowered himself back into his chair, Paul lifted from his jacket a large notepad and pen, flicking the lid the point appeared ready to write.

"ok then, I am ready," Paul states positively

Jacob looked to his guest a smile on his face and a feeling of relief came over him, like a small portion of the responsibility had been lifted, shared even.

Both men looked to each other in the fire lit cabin, silence on both of them, Paul sat ready to write and Jacob recalled how it all began.

And finally, the story began.

CHAPTER TWO

A Brave New World

During the First World War, I was stationed on the front lines, lost somewhere in the trenches of France.

I was still a young man at the time, nothing special just a man trying to serve his country and do his part.

In my battalion, I grew very close to two men, Paul Jones and Simon Kenny.

We did everything together, eat, slept, and shat together, you could say we were best of friends, and each of us would take a bullet in the chest for the other.

One dark and gloomy day we were awoken by a single shot firing across the battlefield, we guessed one of our sharpshooters spotted a nice new helmet and decided to dent it.

From the moment we woke we all had this feeling, not just the cold and wet that surrounded us, but a feeling of dread, as if something was going to happen today, we knew it was going to be a bad day.

The morning past but the feeling remained, a gut feeling stirred within us all.

During the afternoon the odd shot was fired across the battlefield, more to see if anyone was out there than to hit a target.

An occasional firefight broke out now and again, sometimes we lost men we lost a lot of men during these firefights.

Day after day we lost men due to some reason or other, whether they were hit by stray fire or pot shot from a sniper, but they were lost and no reinforcements arrived.

Sometime after lunchtime, we were called into a briefing, because there were only a few men left in our battalion so we were all called in.

Our commanding officer or C.O. for short was giving the briefing, he was a captain in rank, and god knows how he got it, to us he was as stupid and wet behind the ears as you can get. But there he was in charge of a small ragtag battalion of men on the front lines somewhere lost in the war.

The C.O. drew up this plan, he wanted a small group of men to go over the top, run the distance to the enemy lines, and drop in a few grenades at the machine gun bunker that we knew were there.

After that, we were to hold the position from the enemy until reinforcements arrived, and we could take the enemy trench during the night.

Simon burst into laughter at the hint of such a thing.

"You serious, sir." Simon continued with a sarcastic tone.

"You want a small group of men, to charge over the wall, across the minefield to the enemy trench." gesturing to the enemy trench direction as he spoke.

"Take out a machine gun placement, and then hold it from counterstrike, till the rest of the unit manage to make it across." Simon's tone increases with anger.

"And then what's left of us take the trench."

Simon stood up and looked around at the men in the unit, he let out a sarcastic laugh, a few others did too, but they soon saw the C.O. was not joking, he meant to do it.

Simon always spoke his mind, no matter who it offended, but the captain this time was not impressed, the stern look on his face was a clear sign of that.

The rest of the briefing was spent in disbelief, listening to this crazy plan.

During planning, it was decided that it would be a three-man team that would charge the machine gun placement, and hold it once taken.

The fact that I, Paul, and Simon were chosen for this attack, did little to reassure me, that the C.O. didn't have it in for Simon for his outburst, and I and Paul were just plain unlucky.

We were to wait till nightfall, leaving our webbing, and most of our equipment behind, we managed to slip over the top without being seen.

Our rifles in hand, bayonets fixed, and guts swirling, we slowly crawled over no man's land. Now and then we came across a body, the stench with dried blood and rotten flesh was unbearable, unrecognizable features, and a lifeless look made us question whether they were bodies or dummies, we held our courage and dinners down and pushed on.

The smell and rotted corpses did nothing to help focus on the job at hand, but still, we had a long way to go, Simon was on point, me and Paul behind him, we were spread out slightly trying not to make us easy targets.

The cold wet mud beneath us was freezing in the night, the rain came down as it always did, making things slower.

After what seemed an eternity, we made it to what we thought was the minefield that the Germans had placed.

Unfixing the bayonets, we followed our training and dug the tips into the ground in front, then crawled a small distance and repeated the procedure.

Simon and I searched for the mines while Paul had us covered at the rear with his rifle.

At last, the Germans trench was in sight, and so was the machine gun nest, from our hiding place some thirty or forty feet away, we saw three soldiers laughing and fooling around. Drinking what we presumed was ale; the soldiers were a little worse for wear.

Simon was still on point, followed by me and Paul at the rear.

Simon and I crawled forward passing the small minefield, in which we managed to find several, and cleared a small path through the field for our troops.

The machine gun nest was slightly elevated from ground level, surrounded by sandbags and earth.

Paul watched as we approached, never taking his eyes from his target, he laid motionless in the cold wet mud, like part of the land itself.

Simon was a few feet away from the nest; I was still at least 20 feet away when one of the Germans in a drunken state fell over the sandbags laughing so hard.

Simon dropped his head in the mud, pretending to be dead, I did the same, and Paul kept his rifle sights on him, ready to end him should he spot us and try to raise an alarm.

Luckily the German picked himself up, looking only on the wet mud on his long jacket in disgust; he climbed back over laughing with his two friends.

Wasting no time, Simon was up and ran the remaining distance with his bayonet in hand, he jumped and cleared the sandbag wall, and shocked by the sudden move by Simon I was stunned for a moment.

Thrusting his bayonet into the closest soldier, while covering his mouth with his spare hand, Simon tried to keep our presence quiet.

The remaining soldier's laughter was suddenly interrupted, whether, by their drunkard state or pure luck, they didn't scream or raise an alarm.

Mere seconds after Simon landed in the nest, I was up and closing the distance, I noticed an enemy soldier climbing to his feet after grabbing his rifle.

Acting on instinct, I threw my bayonet at him, like something out of an action movie, as I continued running to the nest, out of pure luck it struck its target, striking the neck killing the poor soul almost instantly.

Simon made short work of the other soldier in the nest, throwing the corpse of his comrade on to him as a distraction; Simon closed the gap then struck.

Seconds later I arrived, Simon was covering the entrance to the nest, and his bloody bayonet in hand, and he watched and waited.

Paul climbed into the nest a minute later, Simon stripped the long coats from the dead German soldiers, and we wrapped ourselves in them trying to steady our nerves and warm ourselves.

"So much for the grenades!" Simon chuckled to himself as he spoke."

"Would have alerted the entire trench, it's better this way," Paul replied rubbing and blowing on his hands trying to warm them.

The three of us were freezing, scared, and in enemy territory, yet Simon still managed to laugh it off.

Looking over the dreaded field we had crossed, in the distance, we could see our small force crossing under the cover of darkness, and crawling over the bodies.

Unbeknownst to us, a few soldiers had seen our forces crossing, and had raised the alarm quietly.

Without warning we were being shouted at in German, Simon and I both spun round bayonets in hand, Paul's rifle was quickly rising ready to silence the enemy.

A soldier of some rank was in the main trench lower than us, screaming something and waving his arms around gesturing towards our approaching forces.

Simon looks at the soldier, a bewildered look on his face and tries to keep calm; he lowers his bayonet and throws a quick clueless look my way.

"Ya! Ya!" Simon replies waving his arm in a gesture to move along.

Simon Turns back to the machine gun in front of us, we pretended to setup fire positions, preparing to fire, as such we didn't know this gun, but we were pretty sure we could operate it.

However, the soldier behind must have been convinced as he left us to our pretend preparations.

Waiting as our forces closed in we could do nothing to help as a barrage of fire opened up from the Germans behind us.

The sudden eruption of gunfire and flashes stunned us; rapidly turning from side to side we were struck by terror.

Gunfire was all around us, both sides were returning fire.

Our forces were caught out in the open; they wouldn't last long if we did nothing.

We watched in terror, as we saw our friends fall on the cold wet body filled field, filled with fear we dropped behind the sandbags.

Shedding the German coat, Paul was the first to come to his senses, shaking Simon from his transfixed stir out into the field, and with a grab on my arm, he looks me in the eye.

"Time to be heroes, or our friends die." Paul's comments hit me like a brick.

The realization that if we do not act, not only will we die but so will all our friends, suddenly filling us with courage and conviction.

Paul climbs down the ladder into the trench and covers us, as I and Simon followed.

The enemy was oblivious to our presence as they focused on our attacking forces, they were positioned on the side of the trench firing into the open field, or reloading on both the left and right of us.

Simon was last into the trench as he had unhooked the heavy machine gun from its resting place, using some makeshift sling he made, he slung the weapon and carried it like Rambo.

I fixed my bayonet back to my rifle; with a nod of agreement to each other we took positions and opened fire.

Paul and I opened fire on the left side, and Simon with his back to us opened fire with the heavy gun on the right.

Our enemy was again off guard, and bodies fell from the walls like leaves from a tree in winter, screams of pain and horror filled the trench, but it was not enough, more and more men filled out of tunnels and other trenches.

Round after round we fired, bodies fell in a heap before us. Screams and the sound of gunfire were all we could hear for what seemed to be an eternity.

Every soldier I fired on fell from the wall, the look of pain and surprise on their faces still haunts me today.

Shortly after the start of our assault, the enemy rushed over the top themselves, trying to avoid the slaughter.

Some soldiers stayed and tried to take us out in a counter strike, but most jumped the trench and took their chances with our forces.

Over the sound of battle, Simon screamed to us that his ammunition was out, and was now using his rifle, our advantage was gone.

Paul rushed up the ladder to the machine gun nest, then covered as Simon raced up the ladder next, followed by me.

However the Germans had not forgotten us, and several soldiers opened fire on us again. Simon was hit in his right shoulder, Paul was hit on his left hand by a ricochet, and I was hit in the leg.

Simon pulled me back up into the nest, we managed to hold on for a few more minutes after tossing down a grenade or two.

Paul was first over the nest wall, with a wounded hand he continued to fire at the now onrushing enemy.

I covered the nest entrance till Simon was over the wall and back up to cover me, before leaving I pulled the pin on my last two grenades, and threw them down the trench below, and leapt over the nest wall.

A loud explosion threw the three of us to the ground in a heap, our ears ringing and our wounds blistering with cold wet mud rubbed in them, we climbed to our feet slightly dazed and ran for it.

As we looked at our comrades we could see nothing but smoke. Grenades, mines, and gunfire had created a blanket of thick smoke.

Gunfire and the sounds of battle echoed through the night, sudden quick bright strobes of light, and a loud explosion rumbled the air, screams of agony echoed through the smoke.

The three of us tried to find our bearings helping each other forward, trying to make it back towards our lines, Paul the least injury took point with his rifle as Simon helped me walk.

The smoke covered our retreat but the stray fire was still flying through the air, but we stayed on our feet and staggered back to our friends.

Our journey was interrupted once again, a grenade exploded nearby some twenty to twenty-five feet away, again all three of us were thrown to the ground.

I was the least affected by the grenade, as Simon body must have shielded me some, looking around my vision still blurry I found our attackers, a small number of men came into sight from the smoke, it was the enemy.

I was the first to my feet trying to aim at the charging soldiers, I fired, and fired again, killing one oncoming soldier, but the others kept coming, two more fell to Paul's careful aiming, while Simon was still laid on the floor, holding his head from the grenade attack.

Four more enemy soldiers reached us, their bayonets gleaming and anxious for blood, they charged in.

Responding with our rifles ready, Paul and I even slightly dazed and wounded, found our adrenaline was pumping and keeping us going.

Blocking a killing blow to my stomach, I pushed the enemy's blade from me with my rifle, and sent the butt of my weapon into the face of the German soldier, he fell to his knees, and I responded with a bayonet into his chest.

Paul dealt with his attacker more swiftly, with just a dodge to the side of a thrusting attack and placed his bayonet into the throat of his enemy.

Simon was not so lucky, still dazed and groggy he used the last of his ammunition and fired wildly at the attackers, realizing he had missed; he climbed to his feet and charged.

Two trained soldiers proved they were too much for Simon in his wounded condition, one blocked his attack while the other pushed his blade into Simon's stomach.

Watching in terror, my wounds were suddenly forgotten as were Paul's, both of us rushed the remaining two soldiers, rage in our hearts, and revenge on our minds, we charged screaming at our enemy.

Paul threw his empty rifle at one soldier as he approached, as the soldier blocked it to the side with his rifle, Paul thrust his blade into the stomach of his attacker, again and again as he fell on top of him to the muddy floor below.

The last soldier was mine, he opened fire on me, one round sailed past me, the other struck me in the right arm, I felt the impact but no pain, my only thought I was closing on my prey. Like some wild animal about to closing in for the kill.

I knocked the rifle aside with my hand, as he thrust his bayonet at me, with my bayonet in hand I thrust it into his side and twisted it.

I heard his scream but I wasn't finished, pulling the blade from its resting place, I inserted it into the back of my enemy into his heart.

Staring at the man before me, I watched and noticed him turn in to the dead man before me, his lifeless body fell at my feet.

The sounds of battle still around me, I stood motionless in the middle of no man's land, as if taking in the scene.

I was disturbed from my trance, the sudden feeling of pain in my arm and leg; I struggled to turn to find Paul holding onto Simon.

Simon was still barely alive, blood was coming from his wounds and his mouth, with every struggle of breath, blood poured from him.

As I rushed to his side almost panicking from the sight, he grasped my hand and Paul's, he looks to each of us and tries to speak, the blood prevents what would be his last words, as his eyes lower from me and stair into the open smoke-filled field.

Suddenly filled with anger, grief, and what seems every emotion I could think off tears drop down my face, as look to my now gone friend.

Paul looked to me, tears in his eyes and a gritted jaw he nodded, with a nod of my own I knew what he meant, I closed Simon's eyes and removed his tags, Paul went through his upper pockets trying to find his last letter.

Lifting Simon's body on my shoulder, I was suddenly reminded of the pain in my arm and leg, Paul found a useable rifle and ammunition from the dead Germans and took point, as the two of us tried to find our forces.

Walking for what seemed hours in the smoke, we passed bodies of both enemy and friend, the smoke seems to take on a life of its own, never able to see more than twenty feet from us, it whipped around like a smoke machine pumping out fresh smoke.

The smoke continued, and so did our walk, the sounds of battle were all around us but we could see no one, it was like something out of a bad dream, battle all around us, vague shadows appearing and disappearing in a flash.

After probably a mile or so, the bodies we came across were freshly killed, both German and British alike, they were killed not by bullets or blades, but by what seemed like large animal claws.

Finally, we could make out our trench, on the very top laid the body of our C.O. he was killed by a shot to the head; it seemed the Germans took his orders less seriously than us.

The C.O.'s body was again clawed badly, his chest was cracked open, as were all the wounded we found near our trench.

Still the sounds of battle raged on, no matter how far we walked we could see no one or nothing, but bloody covered bodies laid in the cold wet mud, and no end in sight.

We searched our area of the trench, looking for medical supplies and ammunition, patching up our wounds as best we could, we decided to search for survivors and head back to our territory.

Staggering from exhaustion and our wounds, helping each other as we went, we could not help but have the feeling that we were being watched, stalked, the feeling became more apparent at our trench, but in hindsight, it was always there.

Paul continued to search for ammunition as we encountered numerous dead British soldiers.

Finally, it seemed our dream was about to end in a dreaded nightmare, through the smoke and battle sounds, we could make out a faint figure in the distance.

Paul raised his rifle as a precaution as did I after lowering Simon's corpse; we closed in on the figure.

As we approached the figure was kneeling on the ground holding onto another body, the figure bent over the body, feeding on the corpse it seemed, like out of some vampire movie.

As our distance closed our fear grew, the man bent over a corpse in German uniform, was chewing at its neck as if eating him, the man in his arms was dead from the claw-like wounds he had received.

The man stood slowly his attention was caught by our approach, he turned to face us still part of the dead soldiers' flesh hanging from long sharp teeth in an oversized mouth.

His brilliantly bright red eyes turned and locked on us, he glared as if looking straight through us, the blistering red light in his eyes and the blood around his mouth did little to stop our terror.

A large smile emerged on the man's face, followed by a long snake-like tongue wiping his mouth, the sudden surprise look on mine and Paul's face amused him.

Suddenly Paul and I were even more shocked, as he walked quickly towards us, his arms open at his sides, with a larger than humanly possible smile filled with huge teeth on his face.

Instead of hands and fingers, he held out large oversized paws with large claws on each end, the five fingers replaced with long blade-like objects, his uniform although a German officer, was mainly covered in fresh blood from the collar down to his waist.

Paul and I opened fire on our target, round after round blasted into his chest and stomach, suddenly realizing this was not working as the man continued towards us, Paul managed a shot to his head, clasping the man to the floor.

Stood with fear and disbelieve we stayed for a few moments, a large sigh revealed Paul's relief, followed by my own.

I plucked up the courage to investigate, keeping my rifle on the target I closed in.

With my bayonet almost touching the freaks throat, I was about to fire another round into it, to make sure it was dead when its arm rose and knocked my rifle aside.

Jumping to his feet, it closed its massive paw around my throat and lifted me into the air with ease; before I could blink I could feel the sharp metal like claws slowly cutting into my skin.

Paul opened fire again this time the creature stood there, a slight nudge moved him as each round hit him, its red eyes turned to Paul while holding me some two feet into the air.

Throwing me hard to the ground in a heap, the wind knocked from me, I managed to turn round only to see the creature knocking the rifle from Paul's arms.

A sudden fear and scream came from me as I could do nothing but watch, as the creature raised its might claw in the air, then brought it slicing down across the face, throat and chest of my friend.

Paul's body fell to his knees as if in slow motion, the creature just stood and watched as his prey fell, Paul flopped to the side, then to the floor, still screaming at the creature to stop, I watched in horror and disbelief.

Paul's body was then lifted into the air by the creature blood pouring from his wounds as if demonstrating some sort of trophy.

Once again adrenaline filled my veins as I picked myself up and lifted my rifle once more; I charged in, the bayonet dug deep in the back of the creature dropping him to his knees.

Paul's body landed limply on the floor, with a gasp of relief I see Paul's eyes blinking as his hand grasps his throat trying to stop the flow of blood.

The creature rose like a demon rising from the grave, a greedy smile on his face as he turned towards me pulling the blade from his back.

Looking to me once more, his mighty arm came swinging back and smashed into my face hurling me through the air, landing some feet away in a heap, I am reminded once more of my wounded condition.

As I turned over and looked for my attacker, I watched as the creature lifted Paul to his mouth and feasted, blood poured from both his existing and new wounds.

The wound on Paul's throat pulsed fresh crimson, his body convulsed as he tried desperately to reach out to me.

I scream at the creature with terror and despair, unable to do anything but climb to my knees and watch in disbelief.

Moments later the creature throws the body of my friend to the floor, seeming satisfied at the meal, he then turned to me, licking the blood around his mouth.

My body throbbed with pain, my mind could focus on nothing but Paul and Simon's death, and how helpless I was as I knew my death was coming soon.

A sudden strange feeling came over me, my body cramped up, every muscle seemed to stiffen, my fists and teeth clenched with pain, and the air in my lungs seemed light as if I was breathing in high altitude.

I opened my eyes only to be horrified at the sight of a blue haze covering my body, small electrical discharges were whizzing around me.

With a sudden jolt the blue haze hurled towards the creature, my body fell limply to the ground, exhausted and unable to move.

The blue haze shot through the air like a large blue electrical ball striking the creature in the chest, sending the creature hurling back some ten feet.

The creature collapsed on the ground convulsing with the electrical energy running through its body.

With a last look at my enemy, I watched in terror and disbelief as the electrical energy dissipated, the creature lifting its head with a look of pure surprise on its face.

Quickly it lifted itself and charged towards me as I fell into unconsciousness expecting the end.

***

Jacob's head lowers as he looks back into the fire, tears in his eyes the memories flood back to him of his old friends.

"Forgive me, my memories of that time are, still a little hazy Paul," Jacob stated.

Paul Simpson looks back at his host, still in shock of the tale he has been told, he looks back to his notepad even now more than a few pages have been filled.

"I take it, the pain of their loss haunts you still Jacob," Paul asks.

"still," Jacob replies.

"But then I have lost so many friends, their loss will be with me till the day I die," Jacob adds.

Never taking his eyes from the fire and leaving the tears welling in his eyes he continues his story.

***

My body fell to the ground exhausted, unable to move at all, I felt so heavy, I waited for and expected the end.

But at that last moment, before his strike should have finished me, there was an eruption of light, a brilliant white light from behind me, then another light struck the creature square in the chest.

What seemed like a bolt of lightning struck the creature in the chest and burnt straight through him killing him instantly.

I saw his body fall as I fell once again unconscious, I kept slipping in and out, my body was exhausted, still unable to move or able to speak even.

I awoke again moments later, I could see several people from where I laid, I could hear voices but I couldn't make the voices out, but I knew there were a few of them.

In and out of darkness, throbbing pain in my head and my wounds awoke me once more, I looked about me, and I was crossing what seemed a desert.

Sand-filled dunes were everywhere, little vegetation was seen and yet my body was cold, my vision was still blurry and unable to make most things out.

I was being carried by six men on a makeshift stretcher, hooded in black cloaks with blue trim, I couldn't make out any other features.

They were being led by a short grey-haired man, dressed strangely but familiar, then finally my body gave up and once more I collapsed into unconsciousness.

CHAPTER 3

Rehabilitation

What seemed like only moments I awoke, my eyes blurred and pain coursed through my body, my wounds were bandaged with a clean dressing and neatly done.

Lifting my upper body slightly I looked to my surroundings; I was laid on a thin straw mattress on the floor, with a single round soft pillow.

I was covered in a soft blanket and was laid in a single one-room hut, the roof was of a thatched type, and the walls were solid wood.

There was a small round table in the middle of the room no higher than knee height with several small cushions surrounding it.

There were no windows to the room and only one door.

struggling to lift myself on the bed I noticed I was dressed in a crude lose baggy white top and bottoms tied with cords, every muscle in his body throbbed with pain as it felt like every muscle had been ripped and re-ripped again.

The movement was slow and painful.

Struggling to my feet I narrowly managed to miss the table in the centre of the room, as my legs gave out from under me, slamming hard to the floor in pain and gasping for breath as I collapsed.

Reaching the door, my body again fatigued, was struggling as I slide the wooden bolt back opening the door.

A flood of colour rushed in the room, nearly blinding me, lifting my hands to try and block out some of the light I struggled to see the world beyond.

With the light blinding me, I tried to adjust, but my eyes were unable to cope, I closed the door again and struggled to bed.

With a measure of fear in my heart and mind, I struggled to cope with the situation fearing I had become a prisoner of war by the Germans.

Again consciousness evaded me, for most of the day I seemed to be in and out.

The following morning I awoke, this time by a voice and not just the pain, struggling to come round, my eyes slowly creeping open, only to be forced open with fear at the sight before me.

Looking down to my now semi-naked body, there were hundreds of small three-inch needles pieced in my skin, with small smoking bubbles at the other end, unable to move anything but my neck and head, I was paralyzed.

My body throbbed, but not just with pain as before, but with a rushing feeling, as if water was running up and down inside me, I looked fanatically for those responsible.

An old white-haired man stood in the room, his shoulder-length hair was windswept but still neat, his long white beard was trimmed and neatly kept.

The man's appearance was defiantly Asian; he was dressed in a long black cloak covering a black and blue samurai-like uniform.

"Who are you, people?" I demanded.

My chest hurt with the pain, I could not help but feel a small amount of fear from the shock of all the needles currently placed in me.

"Rest easy Jacob Rawn, you are safe now." the old man replied.

His voice was calming and gentle, and somehow managed to calm me slightly.

"Well you don't seem any worse for wear, considering." a smile crept on his face as he spoke.

"Considering what? Fighting a war, losing my only friends, and then being beaten senseless by god knows what that creature was." my chest hurt as I spoke.

"Oh and I got a hole in my leg and arm, plus a thousand needles sticking in me."

The old man smiled.

"Yes, considering that, yes," the old man replied.

"Who are you, people?" My voice was frail as I asked.

"My name is Takami, and I am the master and protector here." the old man walked around me as I lay on the bed.

"Your name is Jacob Rawn, you are a soldier in her majesties armed service, yes?"

The old man was still smiling, trying to be comforting as he spoke.

"And no you are not a prisoner of war, you are not a captive Jacob Rawn, you are my guest, and you are safe."

I couldn't help but look to my host with yet more surprise, the old man knew just what I was thinking at that moment.

The old man came and sat on one of the cushions by Jacobs's side and started to remove the smouldering needles.

"How did you?" I tried to ask him how he knew what was in my head, but my frail form wouldn't allow it.

Again the old man smiled.

"Never mind that now Mister Rawn, we have more important things to do and discuss." again his tone comforting.

"Such as?" I asked.

"Such as the creature which attacked you on that battlefield," my mind rushed back to the memory of the creature and the death of my friends.

"Is it dead?" my whole body tensed as I asked.

"Oh yes, it's dead," the old man replied as he tries to comfort me.

"He was not a demon as you thought, but what we call a devourer; they come from another realm, but enough of that later."

I couldn't help but think of my friends as the old man removed the remaining needles.

"You have healed well Mister Rawn, but your body is still tired, you better rest a little more I think." again the old man smiled as he comforts me.

As the last of the needles is removed I tried to get up, the old man pushed me back down.

"No, no stay Mister Rawn, there will be plenty of time for questions and answers."

The old man pushed me down and laid me out straight, and then with a quick touch to my forehead with his finger he uttered a word.

"Sleep."

The voice that echoed from the old man was calming and commanding at the same time, like a multitude of voices speaking at once, I felt I had no option but to obey.

The old man placed a telepathic command into my mind and placed me unconscious again.

***

"You passed out again."

Paul's voice was inquisitive and a little mocking at this part of the story.

"What do you mean again? you try fighting a war, watching your friends die, a strange energy bursting out of your body, then being carted off to god knows where, wake up with fifty thousand odd needles with some black shit burning on them placed in your body, I think that might just might, deserve a little blackout don't you?"

Jacobs's harsh voice made Paul a little edgy, lowering his head and eyes to the notebook he waited till Jacob continued his story.

***

What seemed only moments later I came to; with a glance to my body I was relieved to see no needles or any evidence that there ever was any.

My wounds were redressed and clean, I was once again clothed in a loose white baggy top and bottoms tied by a large cord at the waist.

Looking around the room my eyes focused on the table in front of me, a large bowl of steaming white rice and what appeared to be vegetables, along with a large bowl of fruits.

Slowly struggling to my feet my wounds gave me some pain, as did every muscle in my body, slowly moving to the table some strength had returned as my footing was slow but steady.

Gulping down the rice and vegetables, followed by the gulps of water from a large pail provided, my stomach ached with joy as it felt like it hadn't eaten in weeks, the crystal clear water washed down the food.

I relaxed by returning to sit on the bed leaning against the wall content for the time being.

Biting into a fresh juicy apple for dessert, I relaxed in the quiet, only to be startled again.

"Your appetite has returned I see." A smooth voice stated, suddenly.

Quickly turning towards the table and the sound of the voice, my mouth still filled with half-eaten apple, my eyes locked on the old Asian man. He was sat on a cushion at the table that I had eaten from not more than a few minutes ago.

Sitting crossed legged and hands on his knees he sat with a smile on his face looking at me, my surprise was clear.

"HOW THE HELL DID YOU...?" I tried to ask.

The old man's hand rose quickly as if to stop me finishing the sentence, and then gestures to his side at the table.

Struggling in pain with every move I made, I managed the distance to the table but never taking my eyes off my strange host.

"Well, well Jacob Rawn, I wonder what sort of man you will become?" the old man again smiled as he spoke.

The confusion on my face must have been clear, as to my mind I was already a man, I was 21 years old and old enough to fight for my country, yet to this old bugger, I was not yet a man.

Again the old man smiled and chuckled to himself.

"You seem confused young Mister Rawn, to me you are a very young man, in earth years, I would be somewhere in the region of 600 years old, give or take." the old man seemed unsure himself.

My confusion grew as I looked to the old man, and yet a mere 50 years is all I would guess to be on him, my mind began to wonder if this man was mad, and yet something inside felt it is true.

Stroking his trimmed beard again a small chuckle crept from the old man as he looked at me, his gaze seemed to be looking straight through me.

My mind ponders on thoughts of fear, capture, and the wonder of why I am here.

"You are here young Mister Rawn, because you have a rare gift, a gift of great power, a gift like few others possess, and a curse to carry it forever." the old man seemed to pull the questions from my mind before I finish thinking them.

"What gift? What curse? What, who are you, old man?" I was compelled to ask.

"As I said young Mister Rawn, my name is Takami, Master Takami to you." I noticed for the first time at this point his slight Japanese accent as he spoke normally.

"This is my home, my school." the old man walked around the room as he spoke.

"School?" my curiosity getting the better of me.

"Yes school, where I teach people with the same gifts as you, well not quite the same as you but, I teach them how to use their gifts and skills, and direct them to help and defend those who are unable to defend themselves." the old man seemed proud of the task he did.

"In time, you will learn how to use your gift." he gestured for me to follow him as he continued, still eating my apple, I was suddenly filled with awe and confusion, the apple still in my mouth half-chewed, seemed to be hard to swallow along with the story I was being told.

"Yes young Mister Rawn, you do have a choice, you can stay here learn, train, and live a new life, one of service and difficulties, and full of challenges, or you can return to your world, and your war."

"You make it all sound so appealing." my sarcastic remark was wasted on the old man as he reached for the door to the hut.

A sudden realization of what the old man just spoke to me stopped me in my tracks.

"Return to my world, you mean, I'm not on my world?"

Again Takami the old man smiled at me and pulled open the door.

My mind suddenly seemed to slow to a crawl, trying to cope with this new information, looking back to the old man he now stood outside, a strange purplish light flooded into the room, almost blinding me.

"No my young friend, you are no longer in the earth realm, you are in what we call a pocket realm, one roughly the size of your London city I suppose, no one can find you here, and no one can leave unless I let them."

I stood in the doorway just far back enough not to be able to see anything outside but the strange purplish skylight, paralyzed it seemed with the new information.

"Rest young Mister Rawn, tomorrow we shall talk again."

The door closed in front of me, a strange man wearing the same black and blue uniform as those who I saw carrying me here, reached in and pulled the door shut, the sound of a bolt sliding across the door, and I was alone with my thoughts.

Looking around the room and rubbing gently the wound on my leg, my mind wondered at the latest news my host gave me, impossible, I thought to myself, but I could not help but feel it was true.

Unable to sleep that night, I sat in the same position on the bed leaning against the wall, my thoughts past through the events of the last few days, from the war to the night mission with Paul, Simon and myself, to the strange happenings of late.

The light slowly crept into the hut, through cracks in the walls and roof, the bolt on the door outside slid open, the old man standing in the doorway; he walked in carrying a tray, holding more rice and vegetables along with a fresh pail of water and more fruit.

"Good morning young Mister Rawn, how are you feeling today?"

Trying to be welcoming, I smiled and nodded, but I couldn't bring myself to speak or rise from the bed.

The old man placed the food on the table and sat opposite me at the table, looking straight at me with his piercing blue eyes; it felt like he was peering straight through me once more.

The purplish light flooded into the room once more through the open doorway giving everything a strange hue.

"You speak in riddles old man, you spoke of different worlds, gifts and curses, and my head is in pieces," I said pulling myself to the edge of the bed.

"The last few days feels like I been through hell, my best friends killed in front of me, I was shot twice, then taken to a strange place by strange people."

The old man just sat and looked at me.

"You have been through more than you know Mister Rawn; there are very few people in any of the realms, which can harness the power you did without training." the old man replies.

"Harness the what?"

The old man interrupted me with the rising of his hand, and once again I felt compelled to obey.

"Jacob, you have a gift within you, a gift that allows you to harness the power of your very soul, in time you can learn to focus them into a powerful weapon, for all mankind." the old man's voice suddenly serious.

"With time and training, you can be capable of incredible feats."

The old man continued speaking as I just sat on the bed, trying to take it all in.

"When you released your bio-electrical energy, towards that devourer, you taped into a part of the human soul, which is almost impossible to reach without years of training; it has been lost to mankind for thousands of years."

The old man's genuine tone told me that he believed what he was telling me to be the truth, but my head was unable to take it in.

"I don't understand what you're talking about old man."

The bewildered look on my face must have compelled him to try explaining it again.

"Bio-electric energy is the electrical energy within your body, it sends messages from the brain to the muscles and tells them to move, with training you can control it to do much more."

"And the devourer?" I interrupted.

"Ah yes, the devourer well, it's a creature from another realm, it feeds mostly on flesh and blood, they come from a realm similar to ours, they are an unnatural creature in our realm."

"How do you expect me to believe all this old man." Again my disbelief getting the better of me.

The old man looked at me with a smile on his face, he rose to his feet and reached from behind the open door a wooden walking crutch.

As I climbed to my feet both my legs and arms ache and complained, taking hold of the walking aid and supporting my weight under my good arm, I looked back to the old man and saw him stood outside in the bright purplish light.

The old man gestured for me to follow him; the bright light seemed to make my head throb, as my eyes struggle to cope from the brightness.

Lifting my bad arm trying to shield my eyes, I managed to walk outside on to the porch, after a few seconds my eyes adjusted; suddenly I was amazed at the sight before me.

The sky was not blue, but purple, the clouds were deep blue, as I watched for a few seconds, I saw them merge creating large flashes of lightning as they raced across the sky.

Two moons shone high in the sky, one was typical of our moon only a hundred times bigger, it filled almost half of the horizon, and the other moon was of a faint red colour, hidden slightly behind the first as if casting a shadow in the sky.

After a few moments spent in total awe by the moons and sky, my eyes lowered to the ground before me, again suddenly taken back at the sight.

For what appeared to be miles of rows of straw huts twice as large and long as mine reached into the distance, men and women numbering into the hundreds, ran around wearing similar clothing to myself.

They were spread out in separates groups like you would expect from a military training ground, several groups were training in some form of combat, some were armed some not, other groups were running around what appeared to be this very large camp, while others were running an assault course.

Looking from group to group I noticed several large huts with no walls to them, just a roof, and a polished floor, held up by large wooden columns, inside sat students listening to a teacher or training in some form of exercise.

The camp itself was massive, with a quick estimate I counted into the thousands of warriors in training, several large huts with several stories to them lay to the west of the camp, guessing these were the barracks for the students; I paid little more attention to them.

A small hut similar to my own was to the east, sat on its own on a small hill overlooking the camp; another smaller hut was just off to the right of the hut on the hill.

The old man slowly walked along with me, allowing me to keep pace with him, everyone in the camp who saw us coming would stop and bow low, paying their respect to the old man.

As I watched it reminded me of a general walking around some military base, every soldier suddenly struck with fear as the general passes by, jumping up straight and standing to attention.

I was taken back a little as I realized, it was not out of obligation, but respect that they did this, and once we had passed by, they would continue with their training.

Sight after sight I saw, each one more impressive than the last, men and woman were locked in combat with each other, they fought with speed, precision, and grace, each technique was executed flawlessly.

Some sights stopped me in my tracks, unable to grasp what I just witnessed; some students showed abilities unnatural to humans, the speed in which they moved was not normal.

The arms and legs became a blur, they were strikes thrown at an opponent, and yet they were evaded in the same manner, with blinding speed.

Other students I saw, sat calm and serene in a small hut, they had no expression save for the crossed leg position they were in, watching for a few moments I was again in amazement, and they started to lift from the ground, floating before my eyes, some a few feet from the ground.

The old man just stood and smiled at me; as I was stood mouth open in disbelief.

"That's, not, possible," I said to him.

He just smiled and continued to walk on.

More amazement, caught my eyes as we walked on, this time in the form of a student armed with a fine sword, his stance was in a ready position his blade in front of him.

His grip tightened slightly on the hilt as his eyes closed, my eyes were drawn to his blade, a faint blue haze and a small electrical pulse started running up and down the blade as if he were holding a Tesla coil in his hands.

With a single stroke, the blade sliced through the air, the electrical energy and the blue haze continued forward arcing itself into some sort of wave, tearing through the air towards a large timber pole some 5 feet away.

"Wow!" I scream.

A sudden solid thud and the sound of splitting wood echoed in the air, I suddenly staggered and fell to the ground with a sudden thud myself as it impacted.

I looked back at the old man from the floor in shock.

"How?"

The old man helped me to my feet and back onto the wooden crutch, I looked to the now slightly split timber pole with astonishment.

"All in good time young Mister Rawn, now come we shall return to your hut you need your rest."

The small hut suddenly seemed very small compared to what was happening outside, my mind wondered on all the things I had seen, my familiar four walls didn't help to contain my imagination of the world beyond.

A fresh meal sat on the table ready for me as I entered the hut, but my apatite was gone.

My attention was suddenly drawn to my bed were a freshly washed British infantry uniform lay, the bloody stains could still vaguely be seen.

Taking only a fresh apple, I sat back on the bed back against the wall, my mind filled with images from today's experience, a sudden feeling came over me, I thought to myself if I could do some of the things theses students could do back in the war, Paul, and Simon might still have been alive.

My dreams that night were filled with horrors, of my fallen friends, the creature I fought, and the training of these men and woman in the camp.

Finally, one dream stood in my mind, an image of myself stood on that battlefield back in the war, armed with a fine sword like the one I saw the student in the camp holding, and in front of me was the creature.

The battle commenced, I beat the creature with the training from the old man, and Paul and Simon were still alive.

The morning came and the memory of the dream stayed with me, sitting on the edge of the bed I couldn't shake the dream from my mind.

"So I take it you will join us then, young Mister Rawn?" Came a familiar voice from the door.

The old man stood in the room, the door was closed and no other sign of entry gave his presence away, his tone was soft again and welcoming.

"Join you? You think am capable of those things that you showed me yesterday?"

The old man let slip a smile on his face, then walked up to me and looked me in the eye, a serious look back on his face.

"Do not except this lightly young Mister Rawn, for if you agree, your life will change like you cannot imagine, you will for the rest of your life hunt and be hunted, the enemy will know you, and you it, and you will forever be alone in the world, one way or another."

"Can you teach me to stop those creatures, like the one that killed my friends on the battlefield?" gritting my teeth, as I spoke.

"I will teach you, to defend all peoples of the earth realm, the ones you love, and the ones you don't, all have a right to life, no matter their transgressions."

I thought about what the old man had said, I stretched out my hand to seal the deal, the old man took it and smiled.

"You will be a great warrior young Jacob, a bright light against the coming darkness." both his words and his eyes seem to pass through me.

Unsure of what my new master meant, I trusted that in time I would soon find out, rising to my feet, I endured the pain and bowed to my new master.

"So, how do we start?" I asked.

The old man's face lit up, he gestures for me to sit on the bed again.

"Your training will begin tomorrow my friend, but we have a few things to do first." the old man said with a smile.

"Now hold still and try not to move." the old man suddenly serious again.

Holding his hand a few inches from my chest he closed his eyes, my chest suddenly felt tight, as if my lungs were being squeezed, I looked down to his hand at this uncomfortable feeling, my eyes grew wide with fear and surprise.

The old man's hand glowed with a white haze, followed shortly after by light in my chest steadily glowing brighter, with the same strange blue haze I saw on the battlefield.

Suddenly stricken with fear I tried to move, the old man's firm grip held me in place with his hand on my shoulder, slowly the lights in both my chest and the old man's hand start to dim, as did the tight feeling in my chest.

"You should rest another day young Jacob, however, I am very interested in seeing what you are capable of." the old man said, with an inquisitive look in his eye.

"Follow me," he said.

Turning towards the door the old man waited for me to get up, with my trusty wooden crutch in hand and eagerness in my heart I followed him.

Master Takami took me to an outdoor training area, the floor was marked by a large thick rope, laid out into a large twenty-foot diameter circle, and several students sat kneeling around the rope.

Takami walked to the centre of the circle, and bowed to the students, in unison the students respond with a bow of their own, the old man then gestured for me to enter the circle.

A quick look around the area alerted me to the purpose of the ring, several other circles littered the area, and each circle had students facing each other in unarmed combat.

Suddenly both fear and adrenaline coursed through me, now aware of what the old man meant, by seeing what I was capable of.

"This is the training circle, or as the students call it, the circle of pain," Takami stated.

Stood in the centre of the circle his arms open at the sides, Takami smiled and slowly started to walk around.

"Attack me."

"What?" I replied, shocked.

"Attack me, Mister Rawn, as fast and hard as you can, do not stop till you have hit me." Takami's voice was now serious.

"OK."

With a damaged leg and arm, my fighting abilities were severely limited, throwing a right cross, followed by a left cross, I fell to the ground.

"Mister Rawn if you are going to fight the creature in your dream, I would suggest you do it quicker, harder, and mean it." Takami's voice now firm and unimpressed.

My mind suddenly filled with images of the devourer on the battlefield, my stomach began to twist, and my chest tightened like the moment Takami made it glow before I knew it I was swinging wildly at Takami, like a wild animal.

Punch after punch I threw at the old man, none landed as Takami moved like a graceful cat evading them, the swiftness at which he moved, all to unnatural for a man his age.

My arm and leg begin to throb with pain in a complaint, but I pushed through, again I attacked, none of my flimsy punches manages to go anywhere near the old man.

Takami finally grabbed my right arm at the wrist after I throw a right cross, taking my arm with him as he steps under my arm and behind me, I flipped through the air landing hard on my back where I was once stood.

"You're doing well young Mister Rawn," Takami says, without loss of breath.

"I haven't touched you yet," I replied as my breath would allow.

Panting heavily I tried to strike my target, Takami was ready each time, finally, the old man grabbed my attacking hand, he twisted it out to the side, and swept my good leg from under me, landing me in a heap on the floor.

Takami must have been expecting me to stay down after the last sweep, I climb to my feet gasping for breath, I found the old man stirring at me, his gaze seems to look through me again, a smile and an impressed look crept on his face.

Managing somehow to stand up, and ready myself for another attempt, Takami held up his hand gesturing for me to stop.

"Enough young Mister Rawn, we don't push you too hard too fast."

Panting heavily, I attacked without warning, my attack aimed and fast for an injured man, speed towards the old man.

With ease my attacks were evaded and ducked, out of no were a stray attack came from Takami spinning me over in the air by my arm, without a thought my good leg flew out a reactive instinct, Takami was forced to block his first attack.

Landing hard face down, I winced in pain as the air was knocked from my lungs, turning myself over holding my leg as the wound was throbbing.

The old man offered me his hand, he pulled me up to my feet with a strength that he should not have had, once up the crowd around us stood and bowed in unison.

Leaving the circle, crutch underarm and Takami helping, we made our way back to my hut, the going was slow and painful.

"One day, master, one day," I said while trying to gather the breath between limping and wincing.

"Ha, one day Jacob, one day." the old man smiled with a chuckle.

Knowing I meant with respect, one day I would land a blow, I remembered that fight for the remainder of my time in the school.

After a solid nights rest in the hut, I awoke to the sounds of combat, the normality of the camps everyday routines, echoed through.

Lifting myself to my feet, I tried a few simple stretches, to my surprise there was no further damage to my wounds, they were redressed and clean as per normal when I awoke, however, my body complained about aches and pains in other areas, due to the exercise the day before.

With a steady walk around the hut without the aid of my trusty crutch, limping and wincing I tried to get my leg to work, finally moving outside I stood on the porch looking out to my future home.

The camp was full of life and busy happenings my fellow students training in the hazy light of the twin moon sky.

Without warning my peace was disturbed.

"Good morning, young Mister Rawn." Takami's familiar voice says loudly.

Nearly jumping out of my skin, I turned to face master Takami walking out of the hut behind me, with no evidence of entry or of being seen.

"Jesus master, you nearly gave me a heart attack."

Holding my chest over my heart I tried to steady myself, the smug look on the old man's face gave away his joy for doing these tricks.

"Are you rested Mister Rawn?" Takami asks smiling.

"Yes, thank you, I feel much better now that I have had my ass kicked by a six hundred-year-old man."

Both of us laughed at the remark.

"Well that's good because your training will begin at once." a stern tone now replaced the smile and happy go, lucky master.

The cocky smile was wiped clean from my face I looked to my new master with a bewildered look, hoping he was kidding.

"But, but my arm, my leg?" I asked.

Aiming for sympathy, none was returned from my harsh new master.

"Your enemies will not show you compassion for injuries; they will take advantage of it, now up Mister Rawn."

The pain in my leg must have heard the conversation and complained in pain grabbing my trusty walking aid and loose white top I followed the old man to the training grounds.

Walking through the busy camp all stopped and bowed in respect to their master, walking behind Takami, I looked at my fellow students, but none returned the look, their eyes and heads down in the bow.

After a short walk we stop at another outdoor training area, a small group of students were stood in a line formation practising unarmed combat techniques.

As we approached, the normal bowing routine commenced, both students and teacher turned and bowed to Takami, patting the instructor's shoulder a tall brown-skinned man stood up and smiled at the old man, they shook hands and a genuine feeling of friendship emanated from them.

"Mister Rawn, I would like you to meet your first instructor, this is Mister Siynth." Takami gestured.

The large stocky man walked forward wearing a black ninja-like suit and boots, a blue trim finished the edges, shoulder, and elbow pads, his small black-trimmed goatee suddenly sparked a memory in me.

A memory flashback suddenly hit me, the encounter with the black-hooded men back in the earth realm, the memory of six of these same dressed men carting me to my new home as I slipped in and out of unconscious.

The tall man held out his hand in a gesture of friendship, taking his hand I could feel the power he had, his hands had scars running all along with them on both sides, lines like small train tracks running across his skin.

"Thank you for helping to carry me Mister Siynth."

With a small head bow and a smile he gestured to a place at the side of one of the students, taking my place I was eager to get started, the old man smiled and nodded to me, Takami then walked away leaving me with the class.

Siynth returned to the front of the group, he shouted in some strange language I have not heard before, he placed himself into a combat position followed sharply by the students. Following the techniques as best I could, watching Siynth and the students, I spent the next five hours in solid combat training.

Technique after technique I performed, my wounds pulsing with pain, sweat pouring from every pore of my body, the fatigue started to kick in.

Siynth continued till every move, every word spoken was performed over a hundred times, punches, kicks, elbows, and knees flawlessly done by the students.

Five hours of gruelling exercise passed and Siynth called an end to the session, barely standing, resting my hands on my knees bent over gasping for breath, I welcomed a break.

"Well done Mister Rawn, that wasn't bad, for the first lesson I didn't expect you to last even half of what you did." the man's voice was deep and bellowing.

"Ha, thanks." Speaking as my lungs would allow.

Patting his hand on my back, Master Takami surprises me once more, appearing out of nowhere again.

"Time for your next lesson young Mister Rawn." Using his smiley friendly voice again.

Takami Smiled with a gesturing hand back into the camp, unable to speak or complain, I followed my master limping as I went and desperately trying to catch my breath.

A short walk from the last session area, I was led to a small wooden hut with no walls; large wooden columns held the roof at bay in the four corners of the hut.

A small group of students sat on cushions with a teacher at the head of the group, both the students and the instructor's eyes were closed, their faces were expressionless.

As we approached the instructor's eyes opened and turn straight to us.

Master Takami signalled for the teacher to approach.

"Mister Rawn this is Carl, a graduate of the camp, and now a fellow instructor like Mister Siynth."

Dressed the same as Siynth, Carl was in the black uniform; I guessed this was their combat dress, much the same as our military uniforms.

Shaking Carl's hand, again I could feel something inside twist and turn, the feeling of power coming from this man was immense.

Takami smiled and nodded and left me alone once more.

"So Mister Rawn, how are you, are your wounds fairing." a strong Scottish accent emerged from the new instructor.

"Were you with those who brought me here?" I asked.

"Aye, I was, you were lucky that Master Takami managed to open the porthole quick enough to kill that Tongue Whipper."

"Tongue Whipper?" I asked.

"Aye, the devourer, most of us grads, have our nicknames for the different species of unnatural, you'll get used to it," Carl replied.

Carl smiled with a little chuckle, putting his arm around my shoulders he took me into the hut and sat me down with the other students.

Returning to the front of the class Carl continued his lesson, the students remained still.

"OK, we have a new student with us today, Mister Jacob Rawn."

Pointing me out to the whole class the other students turn to me, a smile, a nod of the head, or quick hello we became acquainted, suddenly been put on the spot was not a comfortable feeling.

"OK, back to the realms, as I said before this is not your homeworld, this is what we call a pocket realm."

My wounds complained about sitting on the hard wooden floor, but listening to Carl about the realms, and managing to catch my breath from the morning exercise was a welcome trade.

"Our realm, the earth realm, is one of the countless others within the multispanning universe of existence."

As I watched the other students as well as listening to Carl, I was relieved to see I wasn't the only one having trouble taking it all in.

"Surely the purple sky and twin moons are more than enough evidence, that this world is not yours eh," Carl says pointing to the sky.

The class smiled and laughed with Carl as he broke the news to the class carefully.

"This wee pocket realm you're in was created by Master Takami and another race called the Drakeions."

Some of the students looked as confused as I was.

"Drakeions sir?" An Italian accented woman asked.

"OK, the Drakeions will be covered in a sec, let me finish this before I draw a blank and forget it myself," Carl replied.

"OK, the pocket realm was created by master Takami and the Drakeions like I said they created it to house and train those with the gift to be defenders of our realm, hence you guys."

"This realm, although it's not on earth itself, it is located on another version of the earth; we are in another dimension, only we call them realms." Carl continued.

Carl's class was stunned, as was I, still, it seemed a little too far-fetched.

"So we are now in another dimension?" another student asked.

"Aye, you are." Carl smiled as he spoke.

"To get back to the earth realm, you must open a porthole in this realm to a place called the nether-realm or shadow for short."

The entire class was hung on Carl's every word, transfixed on the thought of dimensional travel.

"In this place are countless portholes, most invisible to the untrained eye, but they are all over this realm, think of it as a crossroads, from here you can travel to any other realm in the entire multiverse."

"Wow." the word escaped before I realized.

"OK, in the shadow world you must be careful, there are usually travellers from other realms in there, creatures we call the unnatural, these creatures although not all evil are still dangerous, and possess abilities, not of this or any other world but their own."

"Cool, so you mean aliens master?" a student asked.

Unable to hold back his laughter his loud voice echoed through the hut.

"No son, not aliens, the unnatural are creatures from another realm, not a planet."

Carl still laughing continued.

"Some realms are capable of inter-realm travel some not, some are evil some not."

"So how do we know which ones are evil?" The Italian women asked again.

"When you're ready to graduate from this school and return home you'll know," Carl replies.

"So, once you're in the shadow, you experience strange things, for instance in this realm time is different, it's a lot slower than the earth realm, but in the shadow, there is no time at all, it does not exist."

"Also the air there is thinner like you were high up in a plane or on Mount Everest, so if you end up in combat there you'll tire very quickly, never stay there if you can help it."

"Sir, will we have the ability to travel through the realms as well?" A Chinese looking student asked.

"Aye, in time you'll be taught the language of the Drakeions and their ways, the ability to open the portholes, however travelling to another realm is strictly forbidden to us Sentinels."

"Sentinels master?" I felt compelled to ask.

"The Drakeion mystics gave us this name thousands of years ago," Carl replied.

"These warriors from another realm, who have schooled us in advanced combat, mental and physical training beyond anything you can imagine, they also have taught us the power of the soul, and trust me you'll use it." Carl continues.

"Their purpose is to train men and women to defend all life on earth, the population of the earth must never know the truth, we cannot and will not disrupt the flow of their lives, is that understood." Carl's harsh tone demanded an answer.

"Yes sir." the students replied.

"But why would they give us all this knowledge and power, what's in it for them?" I asked. Carl looked at me and smiled.

"Well, Drakeions are an ancient race, one of the oldest we think, they and few other races took it on themselves to educate and prepare the less fortunate realms."

The class sat and listened as Carl continued.

"The Drakeions came to another realm, a realm full of mage's, humans who can manipulate the four elements at will, and shape them into whatever they see fit."

"Magic is real?" a student asked.

"They are an aggressive species, they look and act human, with subtle differences depending on their element, and they managed to trick the Drakeions into teaching them their knowledge of the soul."

"After learning the secrets of the Drakeions their power was amplified a hundredfold, and they attacked their former teachers."

The class fell silent at this news, we continued to listen.

"Now with many conquered realms under their belt, they have been fighting the Drakeions for thousands of years, if they were to take this realm and the souls therein, they would be unstoppable."

"And so they taught us to defend ourselves, it was either that or wipe us out and use the power here for themselves."

"So by defending our realm, we are thereby helping them as well master?" I asked.

"Aye, but this knowledge has a price, we are forbidden to wage war on other realms, like the mage's have done, we are defenders, sentinels, guardians only, not warlords."

Carl's lecture filled us with as many questions and it did with knowledge before we knew it the chill of night was upon us.

"Your duty, once you return to the homeworld is to seek out and destroy all evil unnatural life forms, for there are some unnatural life forms on earth that are there to help, like the Drakeions." Carl continued.

"OK, back to the Drakeions, these creatures are the stuff of legends, their races have visited earth many times, and we would have known them in their ancient form."

The students seemed bewildered and Carl was forced to explain.

"In our history or mythology, there is a creature called the dragon, well the Drakeions are those creatures of myth, but in humanoid form."

"Humanoid form sir?" The Chinese student asked.

"Thousands of years ago, the Drakeions came to earth in the natural form and taught us the ways of combat and their power, the power of the soul is what they use."

"The soul is the ultimate fuel source, it has no limit, and if harnessed properly, its uses are limitless." Carl stood and walked back and forth in front of the class as he continued.

"Mage's were at war with the Drakeions, and were travelling the realms conquering them for slaves, and souls to fuel their magic."

"You mean there were dragons and magic in our world master?" Another student asked.

"Aye, a long time ago there was, the Drakeions taught the disciplines to us, but the human mind was too fragile to cope, we only learned the ways of combat, so the Drakeions took it upon themselves to defend us, till we were capable of doing it ourselves."

"But sir there has never been tales of dragons fighting battles for humans in our history that I know of anyhow," I asked.

"Very true, the Drakeions had their powers, they were able to change their appearance and transformed into the closest thing to us they could, they look like us, except they are always tall and slim, their eyes cat-like with huge irises."

"The mage's pressed their war against the Drakeions, in both their and our realms, however, pushed to their limits it was only with the power of the human soul that they were pushed back."

"So humans did help fight them off." Another student asked.

"Some humans developed under the tutelage of the Drakeions, they learned the power of the mind and soul, and fought alongside the Drakeions."

"After a few centuries past, the Drakeions forgot their true forms and were trapped in their humanoid forms."

"Trapped sir, couldn't their magic do something?" The Italian women asked.

"No I'll get to that in a minute lass, they accepted their fate, well some did, however, their eyes gave them away for what they were."

"While trapped in this form, they developed a sense of energy, they could feel the energy in all its forms, for every move we make there is energy generated, every beat of our hearts pulses with energy, and they can see it."

Carl moved over to the Italian woman as he continued.

"OK, back to your question lass, the Drakeions on earth couldn't use their magic to transform back, because the earth realm is a natural battery of energy, the raw energy in the air the ground everywhere was too overpowering to them, it forced their change to be permanent, after only a few weeks on earth."

"So they all remained in human form master?" I asked.

"Aye to this day, well the ones that came here anyway, but even in human form they have great power, they can move faster than the eye can see, they can bend a steel bar, or crush a man's skull with their bare hands, they know where everything is around them even if they can't see it."

"Then there is their mental powers, all of which you will be taught how to do."

My mind was pulsing with images of these magnificent creatures known as the Drakeions, the shadow world, earth, and my future role in all of this.

"Err, master," I asked.

Carl looked with a smile.

Sat as best I could, holding up my hand like a schoolboy in class, I waited till I could no longer hold back my question.

"Why do the mage's, the Drakeions and all the other unnatural fight for the earth realm?"

"Good question Jacob," Carl replied.

"The earth realm with its abundance of natural resources has an incredible amount of raw energy within itself, it also has one more vital ingredient which pulls all other unnatural to it…..the human soul."

"Sir?" I asked.

All the students looked puzzled at Carl's latest statement.

"The human soul is pure limitless energy, if we could plug a human soul into the electricity grid back home, it would light England up like Black pool illuminations."

Again my mind was wandering with possibilities, Carl suddenly brought me back to the lecture.

"One more thing boys and girls, in all the realms the Drakeions, have visited, the human soul remains the most powerful they have encountered, just a thought to leave you with."

Carl dismissed the class, we all wandered back to our beds for the night wondering about the future.

Limping back to my small wooden hut, I could not help but wonder what good I could do for the earth realm, after facing one of the creatures Carl spoke of and almost dying from it.

"Give it time, you will learn Jacob." Carl's rough Scottish voice echoed from behind.

I spun around expecting to be greeted by Carl, instead, Master Takami stood in his place, and he looked at me with a smile on his face.

"Master, I respect you greatly but, DAMN! Will you stop doing that to me; you'll put me in an early grave." I stated.

A small chuckle emanated from him as he began to walk with me back to the hut, for a few steps we enjoyed the night air.

"You will learn to use your mind, the power of your soul, and you will do great deeds defending the earth realm from the unnatural invaders that threaten it." Takami's voice now his own.

Takami, walked with his head lowered as if contemplating something important, unaware of how it would turn out.

"How did you enjoy your first day Mister Rawn." he suddenly asked.

"Err, different I'll say that much, but I stand by my decision to stay and learn," I replied.

"And so you shall Mister Rawn, so you shall, goodnight."

Before realizing we had arrived at my hut, I looked to my door then back at the old man ready to say good night, nothing was there but an empty camp at night.

CHAPTER 4

A New Life Begins

The training continued, the same classes with the same students and instructors, after a few days I started to get to know them better and even started to enjoy them.

A few days more and I was capable of copying the basic combat techniques of the first class without watching instructor Siynth.

Both some of my strength, and fitness was returning, I was still limping and I was aching after each session but it felt good.

In the evening class I was taught more of the unnatural, the enemy I would face, and the Drakeions and their language, along with the history of my new profession.

During this time master, Takami paid me many visits, more than any other student had received in their entire stay at the school, so I was told.

Each time I saw master Takami he would seem friendly and ask me how I was doing, I concluded he wasn't just checking on my health, but something more was bothering him.

After a few weeks of training master Takami visited me before my first session, he asked me to sit on the bed and remain still.

He placed one hand on my shoulder and one in front of my chest again, the tightness in my chest returned as did the glows of light in the old man's hand and my own body.

As quickly as it started the tightness faded but the light remained, after a few seconds more Takami suddenly pulled away from me staggering backwards, the look of shock on his face.

"Are you OK master?"

"Fine, fine, Jacob," Takami replied shaken at something.

His face and response hiding his true feelings, he regains his composure and gestures for me to stay sitting.

While checking my wounds master Takami found they were almost healed which did little to ease the old man's mind that something was different.

"Incredible." Takami states.

Looking down to the leg wound I to was surprised to see nothing but a scar and a small amount of swelling, as if the wound were months old, my arm to had healed at the same rate.

"OK am guessing you used some magic medicine on these wounds right?" I asked.

Takami lifted his gaze to mine, looking me straight in the eye he shakes his head side to side slowly, claiming no.

"How is this possible, it's been what, three or four weeks maybe?"

Takami looks to the wound and probes it with his mind, placing his palm over it and closed his eyes as if his hand was some sort of scanner.

"Nothing remains of the bullet hole, or its path through your leg, the muscles have almost repaired the damage, save for the scars and swelling that remains," Takami replies.

"Most impressive young Mister Rawn."

"But how master?" I asked again.

"I don't know Jacob, you should not be able to heal like this until you have gone through the awakening, and then had the training to focus it, and I have no answer to give you my young friend." Takami's voice sounds concerned, and excited.

"The awakening?"

"A small ritual that awakens the soul within, it allows you to use the powers of the sentinels, and the Drakeions," Takami replied still looking to my wounds.

The following months progress rapidly, my training increased in both time and difficulty, instructor Siynth increased the number of techniques we did, Carl started to teach us meditation as well as history, and language.

Physical training now including total body fitness, push-ups, sit-ups, pull-ups, long-distance running, and of course swimming, all the things you would expect from a military soldier or professional fighter.

The morning started with a steady five laps on a sandy track around the camp, with a rough guess I would say the camp lap was at least three or four miles each.

Combat training followed the morning run, Siynth was drilling us on single strike techniques with heavy rocks attached to our limbs.

Strength training consisted of push-ups on elevated blocks, sit-ups with a bamboo staff wrapped in rags slapping into your lower abdomen, your feet were held by a block and your whole body was left hanging from the knees.

Pull-ups with rocks attached at the waist, skipping while carrying rocks, this was added after a month or so.

Though I was still fairly fit from my soldiering days, my body complained endlessly every day to the new treatment, my wounds although painful were still healing faster than they should.

Although every night I staggered back to my hut and bed in agony, the following morning I was fighting fit and rearing to go, no aches or pains that normally accompany physical exertion wounds wasn't the only thing my body could fix quickly.

In my fourth month at the camp, my wounds were completely healed leaving nothing but a faint scar. Takami continued his daily visits, and Siynth had decided to give us a surprise fitness evaluation.

We walked out of the camp to the north, after a small group of bushes and trees the view opened up to a massive open sandy assault course, it was like looking out into a Huge abandoned stone quarry.

My jaw dropped when my eyes find the track in which we must run, clearly marked out with red flags, the course starts with a straight run for two miles, then turns downhill to the left into a swamp for a mile, a sharply rising hill then follows.

Following the course in my head, I am suddenly devastated as a further sandy straight lead into a fast-flowing river that flows over a portion of the track, the course ends some two miles after the river.

"Each lap is almost six miles long, consisting of swamps, sand, rocky hills, and a river." Siynth states.

As I looked at the other students I could tell they were as devastated as I was, Siynth walks to the starting line, gesturing for us to join him; I was taken back as it seemed Siynth was going to run the course with us.

The students and I walk to the starting line, they shook their heads and not looking forward to the task ahead.

"OK folks, I want three laps minimum, you have two hours until breakfast, and I suggest you hurry," Siynth says.

"Go!!"

With a fast pace, Siynth starts down the track and is quickly out of view, the other students and I run at a more slower cautious pace.

The first leg of the track is hard gravel, after a mile or so it then leads downhill easy enough I thought to myself, my cocky remarks were suddenly dampened as I look into the distance to see Siynth, waist-high in the last part of the swamp.

My speed suddenly slowed as did the other students as knee-high swamp water and boggy footing followed, the further in we went the deeper it got, towards the end of the swamp we were buried up to our waist.

The swamp turns to heavy dry sand, and an uphill hike, our now wet clothes cling to the sand making us tire more quickly, my heart sinks as I look to find Siynth swimming through the river beyond.

The sand passes to water from a rough flowing river some twenty meters wide at the crossing point, speed is again greatly reduced as we emerge from the water like drown rats, and fatigue hits us hard now running on dry sand once more.

Siynth finished probably ten minutes before, stood as a model for composure, fitness, and endurance he watched as I passed him among the front runners of our group.

As the front of our group carried on onto the second lap, Siynth stopped the last of our eight-man group leaving us only six, the two left behind collapse in a heap on the floor by Siynth feet.

The second lap seemed to last forever, by the time the main group had hit the swamp I was just halfway down the slope of gravel, and I was knackered beyond belief.

Wading through the swamp I could see others just dropping on the hill, collapsing from fatigue they just remained till they could gather the strength to walk home.

The students who remained on the track dwindled as body after collapsed body I passed, pushing on I hit the river, the cold seemed to shock me, and wake me up for a burst to finish the second lap.

The third lap seems to take everything out of me, my pace was down to a slow jog, my head was spinning, my lungs were gasping, suddenly I was shocked as I caught up to another student.

Only three of us remained in the race, I was the last of the three, the front runner was making his way up the hill as me and the other student hit the swamp.

Clearly, in better shape than me, the second runner pulls away once again, leaving me in the swamp as he makes his way up the hill, gritting my teeth and pushing through I was determined to finish.

The final uphill run nearly killed me off, now staggering with exhaustion instead of jogging I was struggling to stay conscious, suddenly I was shaken from my daze; I could hear someone screaming.

Looking to the river the second runner was in trouble, struggling to stay afloat the river was pulling him along and under, his strength failing I acted without thinking.

With a deep breath and a sudden clarity my fatigue subsided, as if a fresh breeze blew it away, I broke into a run as fast as my body could allow, willing myself to move faster with each step.

My vision shifted slightly as if everything but what I was focusing on blurred, like a tunnel I was charging down towards the other end.

With a jump and a dive I entered the water, the rough current above swirls overhead, holding my breath I dove into the depths trying to find the drowning student.

Failing to find him with my eyes I started to panic, finally listening to my instincts I shot up to the surface, look fanatically for the student, I found him clinging for dear life to I broken tree branch Siynth found and held out for him.

I swam to my comrade, taking him under his arm holding his head above water I managed to push against the current back to the crossing point, the other students in the race had come back down to help drag him out the water.

Collapsing once more on the riverbank I watched as Siynth quickly joined us, checking the troubled student over he grabs my shoulder and looks down to me as I try and catch my breath.

"Incredible." Siynth was as shocked as I was.

Helping the poor boy I rescued clear his lungs of water Siynth lifts him to a sitting position, a few coughs and splutters later the boy sits smiling and panting for breath.

Seconds later master Takami and several black-robed sentinels appear, quickly they see to the boy making sure all are OK, looking through the flurry of people I found the boy looking straight at me.

With a nod of his head, he mimes a thank you, smiling as my breath will allow, I nod in return before he is carted off the track by several instructors.

The wet sand below me cools me down, it helps me centre myself trying to catch my breath, the fatigue I had in the race had returned, mere moments later I could feel my muscles give me some control back.

Siynth stands above me, his eyes and smile show his mood of amazement, holding out his hand to me I take it as he hurls me to my feet.

"Incredible Jacob, you were as fatigued as that boy was, and yet you swung it aside like you would a dirty shirt and dove in, you saved that boys life."

Still unable to speak as the breath was scarce, I smiled and nodded as a gesture of appreciation, Siynth pats me on the back shaking his head and smiling in disbelief he walks up the hill to the camp.

The morning after breakfast passes, a few well done and pats on the back as I walked to my lesson, Siynth stood waiting fresh uniform and all.

The students in Siynth's class all turned to me as I approached, the sound of clapping echoed through the camp, I looked around to see it spreading to other training circles.

Siynth looks to me with a huge smile on his face, with his arms held out the side and an unknowing look was all he offered before he too was clapping, I couldn't help but be humbled by it all.

I continued to walk into the circle only to see master Takami also clapping as he walks from behind a cluster of students.

A smile on my face and a few nods of thanks to the students I took my position in the class, the other classes returned to their routines shortly after.

The training continued despite my actions at the river, no more was said of the issue, as if it was now just another thing that happened Siynth's training was still as harsh and gruelling as ever.

Carl s evening class was still a mental trial, the Drakeion language was a complex one to learn, depending on how you used certain words, some had to be hushed and stretched out as if speaking with a long reptile-like tongue, and others had to be sharp tones almost shouted.

That evening, however, was not spent on the language or history but focused on the meditative arts, Carl once told us, once we have gone through the awakening, meditation was the way to focus the soul energy to do tasks.

The group sat around Carl in a circle, we sat crossed legged with the right over the left, back straight, head up and hands grasping our feet at the toes.

"OK folks, time to move on, till further notice we will be working on the meditation art of calming the mind." Carl states.

A simple breathing procedure is explained and demonstrated by Carl, followed by ourselves, after a few attempts we all managed to breathe correctly, pushing our bellies out as we draw air in and shrinking it in as we exhale.

The meditative technique that followed was hard to understand, we were to close our eyes and focus on our chest area, imagining our heart pulsing, as it did it would radiate the soul's energy through the body.

Hours passed, and some of the students enjoyed little success with their visualizations, I found the whole experience a soothing relaxing time, however, I could see my heart pulsing with energy, I choose to just sit and calm myself.

Carl continued to describe the next step, from the heart radiating out into the whole body, we should feel, relaxed, warm, and after the awakening ritual, we would be able to feel our bodies healing.

The energy from the heart should surge through our bodies and repair any damage, in time the sitting position wouldn't be necessary, in time a mere thought would be enough, and we could continue to fight on.

Some of the students grew angry at themselves as they failed to grasp the calming feeling I reached, settling into my comfortable state I simply relaxed, the image in the mind of my heart pulsing with energy.

As I sat relaxed I could feel my chest tighten slightly, similar to the time master Takami stirred the energy within me only not as profound, a second later it was gone.

Suddenly I began to panic, I could feel my heart rate slowing, hearing each beat like drum steadily slowing, I jump back to consciousness with a scream of fright; I came too only to notice the hut was empty.

Stood with master Takami, Carl turns to me as I come too, quickly he reaches down to me and shakes me gently.

"Easy lad, easy, focus your attention on me."

Master Takami walks into the hut shaking his head, he can't help but laugh at this new development.

"That's the first time I have seen a student go into the trance that quick," Carl says.

"What trance?" I ask trying to calm myself.

"The trace is a state you place your body into, in that state you can sustain your life in harsh conditions, such as the extreme cold or thin air."

I looked as confused as always climbing to my feet with Carl's aid, Master Takami walks over chuckling to himself.

"You calm your mind and soul with this technique, your energies sustain you, your focus increases and your intuition improves, but if you go too deep you enter the trance," Takami says.

Trying to steady myself, I noticed it was now dark out, but mere moments ago it was still early evening.

"How long was I under?"

"About three hours, you were under deep my young Jacob, I wanted to see how deep you would go," Carl replied.

"I heard my heart beating, I felt it slowing, and then I got scared."

Carl looked to master Takami, with a look of acknowledgement and a smile, returning there gaze back to me both Carl and Takami shake the heads and laugh.

"Well Jacob, you just exceeded the other students on your first attempt, am impressed," Carl says placing his arm around my shoulders.

"How deep can you go with this technique?" I asked.

Carl looks back to master Takami as if asking for approval.

"If you enter the trance, your body can remain sustained in a death-like state almost indefinitely," Carl replied.

Looking out into the night sky, the single small red moon illuminates the camp below my mind suddenly fascinated with the new skill I just learned.

"Can we try it again?" I asked.

Once more Carl looks to Takami for approval, the old man nods in response, Carl gestures to the floor a smile on his face, he was as excited about this as I was.

Carl guides me to the relaxing state, a few moments later I was back into the trance, my heart rate slowed, my breathing almost stopped.

With more guidance and practice I could enter or awaken myself from the trance state at will, each time the feeling of being refreshed grew.

Left alone in my hut, my mind still running through the last lesson in my head,

Questions run across my mind, what-ifs, maybes, and how is this possible.

Finally, I gave in to desire, sitting in the centre of the room on top of the table, I enter the trance, my mind slowed a steady stream of thoughts and memories flash before me, once again I could hear and feel my heart slowing.

What seems only moments later I could hear footfalls from outside my door, with a little effort I brought myself round to consciousness, I felt utterly refreshed, energetic, and my mind seemed sharp and clear.

The door opened letting in the purple morning light, my eyes winced at the rush of daylight into the room, the light fell on my skin, it felt amazing as if the first time I had felt daylight on my skin.

"Good morning young Mister Rawn did you sleep well."

A few more steps into the room and the door closed behind master Takami.

His usual samurai type garb was replaced with a set of silver and white silk sentinel style clothing, strange blue symbols littered the arms, legs and chest of this outfit, I soon realized they were Drakeion in nature.

"No, I couldn't sleep, so instead I practised the meditation techniques again."

"Aha, and do you find it as easy as you did the first time you went under?" Takami questioned.

"Yes master, but I feel rested, refreshed even, and yet I didn't sleep at all last night."

A small chuckle emanates from the old man as he slowly paces around the room.

"Good, very good," Takami replies.

Without explanation, he turned and left, a little baffled by his sudden appearance and swift disappearance I decided to get ready for the morning class.

Days passed, I grew in strength and fitness, during the day my body being pushed to the limits, in the evening my mind being trained in knowledge and meditative techniques.

Finally, the day came for me to join my fellow students, master Takami took me from the one-room hut and escorted me to the barracks where the other students stay.

"These are your new quarter's young Mister Rawn, and these are your fellow students and friends."

The old man left me looking around the room, rows of bunk beds line the east wall, a single small locker and set of draws stands next to each bed.

The Students looked at me, like some recruit joining the military, some nodded with a smile some ignored me and returned to their activities.

"Well, well, finally decided to join the big boy's eh?"

I turn round to face the voice, only to be surprised by Carl stood in nothing but shorts, suddenly it seemed strange to see him without his uniform on.

With a shake of the hand, I looked to Carl a little bewildered.

"Well guess I can't expect special treatment forever can I?" I replied.

"Well, how else you gonna get to know the others eh?" Carl sniggers.

Carl turns to the rest of the students as he swings his arm around my shoulders.

"Listen up," Carl shouts.

The whole barracks suddenly pay attention, stopping whatever they were doing.

"This here is Jacob Rawn, some of you already know him, some don't, but no one here is a stranger or alone right."

A loud shout of voices in unison reply no, student after student come to welcome me to my new home, introductions done Carl pulls me towards the end of the barracks several beds lie empty save for the top bunk at the very end.

"That be your bunk fella." Carl points to the bottom bunk below his at the top.

"I thought they would house all the instructors together, you know away from the students?" I asked as I place my old uniform on the bed.

"Aye, they do, but I never been one for all that tradition lark, am just one of the boys, know what I mean. Carl replies as he jumps onto the top bunk.

Sitting on my new bed, testing the comfort, I notice the locker and draws assigned for me, grabbing my old military uniform I go to place it inside, suddenly surprised to find several more sets of training gear inside.

The drawer's houses washing materials, spare cloth and sewing materials lie in another draw.

"Ow that's just in case you need to make some undies or something, I know how that white stuff irritates the nads," Carl says with a wink.

The following months fly past, my improvement grew in leaps and bounds, and my combat skills were starting to excel over the other students as did my mental capabilities.

Master Takami took great interest in my training, I always knew when he was around watching from the shadows, the swirling energy and tightness in my chest flinched when he was around.

Carl and I became good friends, after class we would sometimes spar, with Carl merely playing along with me, or correcting my technique, sometimes we would talk to the early hours of the morning, needing only an hour or so meditating to make us wake fresh as daisies for the next day.

In the following few days, master Takami takes the morning combat class, watching the students closely with Mister Siynth.

Our normal routine is suddenly interrupted, Master Takami orders us to surround the circle, Mister Siynth steps into the centre.

"Jacob!" the old man shouts.

I looked to master Takami with a shocked expression.

Takami pointed with a stern face and his gesture for me to enter the circle of pain, the students kneel around the rope circle they watched with interest as this appeared to be new for them too.

A sense of anxiety and a little fear filled me as Mister Siynth turned to the old man and bowed, following the procedure I to bowed, Siynth then turned to me and bowed, fear raced in me as I now knew what was going to happen, I was to fight Siynth.

After rising from my bow to Mister Siynth I caught him lowering himself into a ready stance, his hands and guard up he nodded to me, again following my instructor lead and assumed the same stance.

Both of us stood ready for combat in the circle of pain, a stillness came over us for a time, suddenly the peace is broken with sharp sudden strikes towards me, blow after blow is thrown with me totally on the defensive.

Siynth presses his attack with quick strikes and harder blows, he pushed me back towards the rope, kicks, punches, elbows, and knees all seem to come from nowhere.

Although struggling to defend at first, I begin to settle into the fight, I began to read my opponent, seemingly getting easier his attacks were avoided or blocked.

Siynth, continues his relentless attack, the strength and precision could easily cripple with a single blow, this was serious, my instincts suddenly kicked in due to a feeling of reality.

My counter-attacks were blocked or evaded with ease, both of us now locked in combat, we must have looked like something out of one of those old Shaolin Kung Fu movies.

Unable to compete at that pace for long my lungs and muscles already began to complain, I realized I need to stop this fine dance of strike and parry, pushing everything I had I attacked with tenacity.

Siynth must have been impressed, the smile on his face as we fought was seen, suddenly my comfort feeling in this fight was shattered, and Siynth suddenly doubles in speed and strength.

Each attack from my instructor knocks either my block or my stance aside, barely able to see his attacks coming I tried to keep my distance, both evading and even somersaulting out the way completely.

The manoeuvres failed to work, several strikes land, and each one hitting me as if hit with a sledgehammer, the ground felt suddenly safe as I laid there on the sand.

Siynth wasn't finished, charging in at me I felt my chest tighten and a surge like feeling pumped into my body.

I pushed myself up and began our Frey again, our speed and our strength suddenly felt matched, both of us attacking and defending at a lightning pace.

Managing for a second to look outside our fight, the world outside seemed to move in slow motion, each punch, kick, block or parry seemed to create a percussion-like effect as they connected, releasing a blast of air from the sudden impact.

Small trails of sand followed each kick or knee, suddenly blasted away from the sudden block air percussion effect.

"Enough!" Takami shouts.

The Frey stops in unison as if someone had just hit the pause button, we both stepped out of our combat stances and bowed to each other, Siynth lifts his head chuckling to himself as he looks to me.

Master Takami claps as he walks in the rope ring, placing a hand on both mine and Siynth's shoulder.

"Well fought gentleman," Takami offers as he paces around us both chuckling to himself.

"Well, Mister Siynth your decision?" Takami asks.

Siynth smiles and looks to his master.

"yes, master." Siynth replies.

Suddenly he stops walking and looked me straight in the eye.

"Very well, congratulations young Mister Rawn, you just graduated basic training," Takami says smiling.

Confused as ever, I tried to recover my breath and comprehend, the students all jumped to their feet cheering and applauding as did Siynth.

Master Takami, gestures for me to follow, leaving the circle and my fellow students and instructor I was escorted back the main huts in the north.

CHAPTER 5

The Awakening

Two huts sat in the north of the camp, the largest sat on top of a small hill was master Takami's residence, a smaller one was just to the side slightly lower down the hill, roughly double the size of the hut I was in when I first arrived.

As we walked side by side still trying to catch my breath I was bursting for answers, the silence as we walked was too much to bear.

"Master Takami, how did I graduate? I didn't even strike Mister Siynth let alone win the contest." I asked, stopping us in our tracks.

"You were not meant to win Jacob Mister Siynth could have beat you easily."

I was taken back at the old man's comments, not due to pride, but I couldn't understand why Siynth would let me get so close when he could have stopped me easily.

"Then why did I graduate?" I asked.

Looking confused, the old man tried to put my mind at ease.

"Mister Siynth was testing you, Jacob."

"Testing me for what?" I replied.

"To see if you could access what you have learned from him, to see if the energy within you would work when needed."

The old man points to my chest as he spoke.

"And it did." smiling at me he continues to walk towards the huts.

"You see, even with all potential, you had no chance of beating him, he has abilities you do not possess yet."

"Yet?" I replied.

Gesturing towards the huts I noticed the smirk grin on his face, we continued to walk towards our destination, both the grin and my anxiety made me uneasy.

"Graduation to the next level, only comes when both your instructors and I agree that you have mastered, all that they can teach you, and you have," Takami says.

"So what will I be learning now?" I replied.

"All in good time, first there is a little something we must do, you and I."

confused and worried, I followed Takami up the hill to the left hut, inside the old man lights several candles within the room, the pale light illuminates a alter holding the candles and a large solid wooden table along the opposite wall.

The table stood upright stretched from ceiling to the floor facing the alter, noticing a lever on the side of the table I figured that it could be lowered to a flat tabletop, noticing hand and foot straps made me feel uneasy.

Takami gestures to the table, swallowing my fear I turns my back to the table and places myself in master Takami's care.

With the straps tightened around both feet and hands I laid arms by my side and legs outstretched, the table falls back slowly and lays flat in the room facing the ceiling.

"Relax Jacob, you're not a sacrifice." laughing as he spoke.

"Master, what's this going to do?" I asked.

"Try and relax, you will feel some discomfort, but trust me."

the old man places on his silver and white robes with the Drakeion blue symbols on, returning to the alter Takami began muttering under his breath a ritual of sorts in Drakeion.

The alter starts to glows from a Hugh crystal at the centre of the stone structure, the blue and white light swirls around sending strobes of bright light in all directions. Blue Drakeions symbols emerge on the stone altar as if tearing into the stone itself, the sound of stone cracking can be heard.

Takami's eyes suddenly opened, replaced entirely by a bright blue light, no pupil or iris could be seen, he lifts one hand and hovers it a few inches over my head, the other slowly runs the length off my body at the same height.

After a few moments I started to notice tingling all over my body, a slow feeling of burning followed, moments later a harsh cold rippled through me, this cycle continued growing in strength each time.

Trying to watch and ignore the feelings within my body, my attention is grabbed by a now loud hum like noise building in the distance, like that of a choir humming.

The feelings increase in intensity, Takami's hand began to shake slightly, followed by an eruption of bright white light from within his hand.

The distant noise continued, the light in the old man's hand gets brighter, suddenly my body begins to cramp up as it did that dark day on the battlefield, the day my friends died.

Trying to hold back the memories, and stop the cramping in my body, my body started to shake violently, the tightness in my chest suddenly dissipates and is replaced by a full, bursting feeling.

The old man's hands were held above my heart and head, suddenly the bursting feeling in my chest gave out, and a pulse of light erupted from my heart.

My entire body now engulfed in a strange pale blue and white aura, an electrical current coursed over my skin and through it, as if it belongs to me.

Seconds later the light seemed to dwindle and the electrical current through and around me seemed to settle back in my body, all went quiet, my mind, my body, and the humming sound from beyond.

The crystal in the centre of the alter dimmed, Master Takami withdraws his hands and opens his eyes to reveal they're normal colour.

The feeling of exhaustion was all too familiar to me, I could do little else but lay there as the old man flipped the lever on the table and I was once again stood upright.

Reaching for the straps to my arms, Takami and I both were suddenly shocked, the feeling returned, I suddenly cramped up again, worse than before.

Bright silver and white light emerged in my chest, Takami stood back and watched in confusion. He looked at the alter to see it quiet, unable to grasp what was going on he could do nothing but watch.

The light grew in my chest, the pain I felt was immense, my body arched with blistering cold, my muscles convulsing, I screamed out in agony.

Rushing to help Takami tried to push me back onto the stood up table, another eruption of light and energy throws the old man back against the far wall in a heap, the table I was on vanishes leaving me hovering slightly in the air.

The pain and the convulsions stopped as quickly as they came, once more able to open my eyes and breathe, I looked to my master sat on the floor against the wall where he was thrown.

Suddenly I realized my clothes had gone, the blast that knocked Takami against the wall also incinerated the table I was on and the clothes I was wearing, a small amount of the floor where I was stood on was also gone.

Master Takami mouth was open as if witnessing something in disbelief, his eyes shifted to my gaze but were unable to speak, I looked around to try and find what he was so shocked by, and the wall behind me was flash burnt.

There was an unburnt area where I was stood, out to both sides of my body two large long wing-like appendages were also flash burnt onto the wall.

Takami rose to his feet still looking at the outline on the wall he shakes his head in disbelief, I turn to face the marks on the wall also in disbelief.

"Err, master."

"Yes Jacob?" he replied.

"Is that normal?" I asked pointing to the burned outline on the wall.

"No," Takami replied shaking his head.

"Didn't think so."

A few moments were spent in silence, the old man lowered his head from the wall and started walking around the room deep in thought.

"Master?" I asked unable to hold my curiosity at bay.

The old man just turned to me his eyes looking worried.

"What happens now?"

"Now we carry on training, and I look into this new development," Takami replies.

"OK."

Both of us worried about the events inside the hut, Takami slowly started to calm down his pace and then sort to reassure me.

"How do you feel Jacob?" the old man asked.

"I feel tired, drained, my head, my whole body aches, and yet I feel, good, I feel different as if something within me is free."

Takami suddenly looking worried again he turns me to face the burnt wall once more.

"Ow, there's something free alright my young friend," Takami replied.

"The first part of the ritual that I performed freed the energy within you, your soul has been awoken."

"But what about the second part, and this?" I asked gesturing to the flash burnt wall.

Takami takes off his outta silver and blue robe and covers me in it, suddenly the realization I was still stood there naked hit him it seemed.

"I don't know Jacob, I have never seen anything like it, and I need time to find the answers, for both of us," Takami said.

I nodded in agreement as again we just stood and looked at the wall.

"We must not mention this to the others, not until I know what we are dealing with."

"Yes, master," I replied.

"But not tonight, time to rest, regardless of what else happened here, you still had your awakening, tomorrow is a new world for you."

Takami helped me back to the barracks, the journey was a short one but the silence and the activities of the night made it seem an eternity of walking.

Before reaching the door to the barracks Takami stops and turns to me.

"Jacob, did you know your parents?" Takami asked out of the blue.

Trying to lean on the wall of the barracks to remain standing, once again I was confused, I looked back to my master to find him once again in deep thought pacing slowly about the porch.

"Well my father was a simple man I suppose, very religious, strict, he was a joiner by trade, I barely knew my mother, and she died when I was 5."

"Why do you ask master?"

"How did your mother die Jacob?" Takami replied.

"There was a fire, an old church, a ruin if truth be told, she was always there."

Takami still deep in thought looked as confused as I was.

"Why, was she trying to restore the ruin?" Takami asked.

"Master is there something wrong?" I replied.

"No, no, not at all, just curious, now go in and get some rest, we have a lot to go through tomorrow."

With a final smile and a shut of the door, I walked inside the barracks leaving Takami to his thoughts.

I struggled too my bunk helped at the last minute by Carl.

"Easy lad, quite a day you've had."

Laying on the bed still wrapped up in Takami's silver robe, exhaustion almost took me.

"I heard you graduated to soul training, Siynth told me you did well, he's proud of you."

I struggled to turn myself around on the bed to face Carl, he stood leaning on his top bunk looking down to me smiling.

"My body hasn't hurt this much since that day I first awoke here, what did he do to me?"

Carl laughed as he lowered himself to sit on my bunk leaning against the footplate and looking at me.

"You just had your awakening mate, your soul is your greatest weapon, and also the reason the unnatural won't our world," Carl said.

I was struggling to stay awake, let alone listen to one of Carl's lectures.

"Unnatural, ow yea, our enemy you said," I replied.

"It's the nickname the students have given to the invaders, I think it's kinda catchy," Carl replied with a chuckle.

A sudden realization of what had happened hits me.

"So, your saying master Takami touched my soul?"

"You don't believe me, fine, but it's true, he touched your soul, it hurts like hell doesn't it? I remember when I had it done, I thought I was going to die."

"So what's going to happen now?"

"Wait till tomorrow boyo, you'll find out."

With a last smug grin, Carl climbed into his bunk, leaving me to my thoughts of the night's activities.

The following day brought both fear and wonder, new instructors and lessons tested my mind and sanity, and the morning began with more physical training, both harder and more intense. Barely managing to keep up with the rest of the class, I struggled through five laps of some assault course I never saw before with combatants attacking at regular and surprising intervals.

The afternoon consisted of combat training, two or more opponents was a warm-up, weapons followed, and body conditioning to finish.

My new arena was split in two, the first was the familiar rope circle, the second was filled with small stumps around 15 inches in diameter, pushed up from a 6ft pool of water.

The evening classes had me filled with frustration at first, followed by some sleepless nights, The mediation techniques I was taught by my friend and former instructor Carl, taught me how to calm and slow my mind and body allowing me to rest.

Due to the awakening, my energies were running wild and amplified a thousandfold, finding it hard to focus due to so much energy I struggled to control my mind internal energy.

Eventually, after a few hours of practice I managed to enter the trance, my energy pulsing but still I remained under, feeling the energy coursing through every cell in my body I relaxed into the feeling, I was shocked and amazed to find how pleasurable it was.

Within mere minutes of meditating the fatigue, I held from training during the day vanishes, entering the trance, within moments I could feel the energy within rushing to an injured area of the body and start to repair it at alarming speeds.

After a few days I settled into the new routine, back at the barracks one evening I felt no need for sleep, sitting on the small wooden porch looking up to the strange configuration of stars in the sky.

Enjoying the cool night air, I closed my eyes, my mind still with no thoughts of anything just peace, it's been so long since I felt at peace with things I thought to myself.

"You OK lad?" a familiar Scottish voice asked from the barrack door.

The energy within swirled whenever near an unnatural creature or fully trained sentinels due to their training, after a time I began to distinguishes presences, Carl's presence was one of the strongest in the camp next to the old man.

"Yea am fine, better than fine actually," I replied.

Carl lowered himself beside me on the bench, looking to the stars, before turning to me.

"Good, so why you sat out here?" Carl asked.

"no reason, just enjoying a bit of quiet time I guess, I felt the soul thing swirling around when I was in the trance, it started pulsing through me."

Both of us looked at each other, Carl looked slightly shocked and awed at this.

"You felt it, you felt your bio-electrical energy flaring this soon," Carl stated.

"Bio what?" I asked.

"The energy that's released inside you, is called bio-electrical, basically when you move any part of your body, a small electrical charge shoots from the brain to the muscles involved and tells them to move right?"

"Yea," I replied.

"Well the ritual that we go through, released the rest of that small electric charge, which in turn is powered from our core, our soul."

"OK, I think," I answered with a confused look.

"Well in time, you'll learn to access more of it, allowing you to do amazing things, the name for that energy is called bio, meaning biological, electric, hence bio-electric energy."

"Don't worry, your instructors will explain it all to you in your classes, but it's the first time I have heard of anyone being able to feel its presence this soon."

Looking back to the stars we just sat in silence for a moment, with a gentle pat on the back Carl lets out a small chuckle as he walks in the barracks.

"Wow." Carl lets slip.

The days that followed were as hard as my first in this realm, both physically and mentally, every day I found myself hurting in new ways.

The morning assault course nearly killed me every time whether due to fitness or the surprise attackers managing to catch me nearly every time.

The combat training in the afternoon saw me being knocked senseless by both unarmed and armed opponents, whether in the rope circle or on the stumps that always break my fall before the soft water below.

The evening session was less painful but equally strenuous, as my bio-electrical energy seemed to be out of control, every time I was told to call upon the power for even the most meagre tasks, both my concentration and focus seemed unable to call it forth.

The barracks seemed to empty quickly during those days, students seemed to disappear, one night they would be bedding down with the rest of us, in the morning they were gone.

A letter to their friends who remain was all that was left off them, revealing they have been chosen for the next stage of training. The black warriors came in the night and took them to their new home.

After a time I began to miss the ones who have gone, even though we were not close they were my training and fellow brothers and sister in arms, my mind wonders if I will ever reach the next stage would the black warriors ever come for me.

At that moment a sudden longing for home came over me, I longed for England, for Lincoln, for my home, a strange thought entered my head, asking if I will ever see the earth realm again.

"Of course you will see it again lad." From nowhere Carl's voice a sympathetic tone and pleasure to hear in my loneliness.

Turning to see my friend putting away his long black hooded cloak, I wondered if I will ever get the black tunic and cloak, the sign of final graduation.

"One day you will lad, why having second thoughts?" Carl asked sarcastically.

Over the last few months sharing the barracks with both the students and Carl, I had become accustomed to Carl's regular mind probes and thought-reading, which came to him as easy as breathing it seems.

"no of course not, it's just, it seems we lose more and more students to the next stage these days, and am stuck here, and it looks like I'll always be here the rate am going," I replied.

Leaning on one of the bunk beds, Carl looked at me with a confused expression on his face, he waited silently as if expecting to hear the rest of this problem.

I could see the inquisitive look in his eye, and felt I should explain myself.

"How long did it take you to graduate Carl?"

"A long time, it took me nearly two years just to graduate from the first stage."

"No please tell me how long till you finally graduated?" I pressed.

"I can't remember exactly, but the day we came for you, the world had changed so much, even in the brief moments we were there, the things I saw were so different."

Carl's gaze lowered, I guessed a flood of memories hit him.

"When I was a wee lad, I grew up on a farm in highlands, just a normal family really, I used to get up with my father and help out on the farm." Carl continued as memories came to him.

"I was 12 or so when I was brought here, I couldn't tell you what year it was."

"Do you know what year it is now?" I asked.

"No, I've only been to the earth realm a couple of times since, and they were on collections like yours, but soon my time as an instructor is up."

Suddenly confused and worried at Carl's comments I was compelled to ask.

"What do you mean your time is up?"

Carl looked at me a slightly worried look crept on his face.

"When you graduate from this camp, you'll be taken to another place, another realm, there you'll be taught everything, the unnatural, history, weapons, tactics, survival, and how to be a true sentinel." Carl slowly starts to walk around the empty barracks as he continues.

"When you graduate, you're given the uniform and the rank of instructor."

Carl turned to the window and looked out into the black of night as if trying to see the future.

"Finally after several years of teaching, you're sent to the earth realm where your life as a sentinel begins, fighting to protect those who can't protect themselves, defending the earth realm from the unnatural who threaten it," Carl states as if the verse is burned into his mind.

Suddenly the air in the room turned freezing, a sudden realism hit us both.

"Anyway, what makes you think you're never going to see the earth realm again, you've been doing great haven't you?" Carl asks.

The mood suddenly lifted by Carl's uplifting happy tone and smile.

"No I haven't, I can't seem to focus either strong enough or long enough to call on my energy," I replied.

"What do u mean?" Carl asked puzzled.

Reluctantly I shared my failure with my friend.

"Well tonight, for example, we were meant to use our energy to empower our bodies, making us stronger, faster and all that but, I couldn't do it."

Carl nodded in agreement slowly walking back and forth listening to me.

"Every time I try, I can feel it start to course through me, then it's gone, and I can't seem to get it."

"Ah-ha, OK I got it," Carl replied.

Nodding his head he walked towards the door gesturing for me to follow, the other students in the barracks take no interest as they continue either sleeping, eating, or meditating.

I walked outside onto the porch, I turned back to face Carl as he closed the door, without warning Carl spun on the spot lifting his leg and thrusting it out at his side entering a spinning sidekick.

Striking me square in the chest, my body flies through the air some twenty feet landing in a heap, hard on the dusty ground.

Struggling to breathe and holding my chest I looked for my attacker, Carl stood some three feet away, apparently waiting for me to climb to my feet.

Climbing to my feet, I looked to Carl with shock and pain, my body feels like my chest is caving in, I tried to speak.

"What?"

Before I could finish my question another strike hit, several more strikes followed before I finally hit the floor in a beaten heap.

Gasping for air my lungs still deflated from the stunning kick I sustained, I barely managed to remain conscious.

Carl grabbed me by the back of my training shirt, lifting me into the air like he would a twig.

"Is this! what you want! to be meat for something out there hunting you?!" Carl snarled.

my body drops hard on the ground as Carl throws me aside with ease, finally, a gulp of air entered my lungs, breathing heavy and hard I managed to hear the footfalls of Carl slowly walking up to me.

Climbing slowly to my feet holding my chest I stood in front of my attacker, looking him in the eye I saw Carl's distaste, he was not enjoying this.

He's doing it for a reason and not just for spite, I suddenly thought.

"Is that it? you're done? you're not going to even try and fight back?" Carl asked.

Standing not three feet from his me, Carl's arms held out to his sides as if questioning, tempting me to try something, my body throbbed and ache with each breath I could do little but stand there and bleed.

Carl shakes his head in disappointment.

"What would your fellow dead soldiers think of you now?" Carl asked.

BOOM! An explosion went off inside me, my mind flashes imagery of my fallen friends back in the war.

My body and soul flare, the swirling whirlpool ripples with life within, my left-hand clenches tight and hunger's for contact.

A roar and a charge is all the warning Carl received, my leg is the first to come to life, bring my knee-high in front of me and slamming the heel of my foot into the chest of a friend.

Carl sprawls backwards through the air, the air knocked from his lungs I thought, with a quick twist of his body he entered a backflip and lands on both feet safely.

"That's my boy, let's see what you got now," Carl says with a smug grin.

With purposeful walk towards Carl, I attack again,

My body now a fine-tuned fighting machine I forgot my injuries and attacked, strike after strike is hurled at Carl, easily evaded at first Carl's smile never fades but grows as my speed increases.

The fight continued, my mind saw every move Carl made whether a strike or defend and still neither of us land a blow, forcing myself harder with the image of my fallen friends in mind I pushed my focus to force the bio-electric energy to empower my body further.

Again Carl seems impressed, my body now moving more quickly than any human could do and growing faster still, my arms and legs become blurry and out of focus with speed.

"Good lad, very good, now come and get me."

Thrusting himself up into the air and over my head, Carl enters a somersault in the air and lands some twenty feet from me, running deeper into the camp.

Without thinking I followed at speeds I wouldn't have thought possible mere moments ago. Another devastating thrust kick that would have floored a rhino struck, I was hurled back through the air again thrown some thirty feet from my opponent.

Carl watched eagerly as the blow he gave me would have almost killed a normal human being, with huge satisfaction he watched as I hurled myself back towards him at great speed. Carl with a quick sharp thrust of his legs hurls his body up into the air, spinning as he goes landing on his feet on the roof of a second story hut.

Approaching the building I didn't even think I just acted, I jumped with everything I had for the roof, landing a few feet from Carl my mind still in battle mode, without noticing the feat I just performed I continued my attack.

Carl abruptly ends the battle with several swift strikes with his hands to my body and neck, unable to block or evade due to their incredible speed even beyond my enhanced state.

The impact from Carl's strikes in certain areas of my body suddenly knocks me to my senses, the energy within suddenly shuts down as if Carl's attack had flicked a switch inside me and shut down the power.

Suddenly aware of my situation stood unbalanced on the roof edge, I struggle to hold my footing before falling back to the safety of the sloped roof.

"Can't focus eh, can't control it." Carl laughs.

"What, what the hell just happened?" I asked suddenly gasping for breath.

"Well, basically you managed to find your focus."

"You hit me.!" I replied suddenly holding my chest as the pain had returned.

"aye, kinda had to, I had to get you riled up enough for your training to take over, which it did, and it did you proud boyo," Carl replied.

"I got you so worked up with anger and frustration your mind took over your body, you were still in control sort of," Carl added.

The confusion on my face must have encouraged Carl to explain further.

"You had a mission, a purpose to spur you on, you had to beat me for what I said, and by the way, your friends, they would be proud, just like me."

Overwhelmed and fatigued by our little bout, I struggled to take in all that just happened, Carl was jumping for joy at this turn of events.

"OK now all you need to do is remember what triggered it, but don't use a bad memory of your friends, use a good one, one you can carry with you forever, the bio-electric energy will do the rest," Carl stated.

Shaking off the fatigue I watched as Carl hurled himself off the roof headfirst, falling the first 10 feet he entered a somersault and lands firmly on his feet, turning to look up to me he gestures for me to follow.

"You're going to have to empower yourself again to make the jump without injury." Carl states with a cocky smirk.

I focused my thoughts back locating a fond memory of my fallen friends Paul and Simon, a memorable time enters my head when we shared a beer in the pub after basic training.

I closed my eyes as the feeling of a storm erupted within me, Muscles tensed then release suddenly, the feeling of strength returned.

Imitating Carl I flipped my body through the air landing on both feet on the ground in a crouched position.

Carl looked impressed as I walked up to him, the same cocky smirk filled his face, I looked at my hands as if they were new ones, clenching them into a fist and feeling the strength ripple through me.

A strange feeling came over me, the thought of my friends although gone from my side, were still with me, pushing me on, giving me strength, I was suddenly filled a joyous and happy feeling as the power settled down.

"You know I once heard my father say if we remember someone, then they're not gone, if you remember your friends and they give strength, then that's your trigger." Carl states.

I nodded in agreement, still looking to my hands in amazement.

"I'll always remember them, but this way it feels like they are still with me, helping me," I replied.

"Maybe they are lad, but don't see them as helping you Jacob, instead see them as fighting alongside you, as they did during your time together, they will never leave you, my friend." Carl Throws his arm around my shoulders and chuckled as was his custom.

"Come, you need some time in the trance to make sure you're ready for tomorrow."

Gesturing again for me to follow, we walk back to the barracks, chuckling at our little bout.

Days passed after Carl's and my special sparring session, my training continued but unbeknown to me at the time a witness to the bout was seen.

Master Takami always watching had seen our fight that night, ordering all the instructors to push me harder in an attempt to see how far I could go.

Both mentally and physically I slowly climbed back towards the front of the class, my combat skilled excelled once again, defeating single and multiple opponents.

The weapons class was my favourite, all sentinels choose a weapon to focus on, My weapon of choice, the sword, after a short time it seemed to be a mere extension of myself.

With my trusty wooden weapon in hand, I could defeat more than four attackers at once it was clear this weapon was to be mine.

My mental abilities vastly increased, both my instructors and master Takami were impressed with the ease and speed at which the energy inside me swirls to life on command.

Most nights were spent talking and training with Carl, enjoying our training with our practice weapons made of wood, Carl and I both shared affection for the sword.

One such session was interrupted, Takami walked to the barracks recruiting Siynth, Carl and other instructors on a hasty mission back to the earth realm.

Running towards the back of the camp near the assault course master Takami summons forth a rip to appear in the air.

A massive swirling whirlpool of energy almost ten foot in diameter bursts into being, the familiar sound of wood scraping on something sharply as it tears into the air.

bright blue and white energy erupts from the porthole with bright strobes of electrical energy arc outward, a strong wind blows forth form the rip as does the sound of rushing energy, like that of waterfall ripples through the air.

The seven men including master Takami walk through the porthole in full battledress, the warriors in black gi suits and long black outer hooded coats, disappearing one after the other.

With a sharp flash, the rip is sealed and all grows dark and quiet, I stand alone outside our barracks with no company but my thoughts.

Not ten minutes pass before another flash of brilliant light erupts, nearly blinding me and staggering me back in surprise, and seven men emerge from the porthole, carrying another.

Another flash and all is dark except for master Takami leading the other six men carrying a wounded man to the very hut that I awoke in that first time I entered this place.

Moments later the six sentinels leave the hut with one remaining outside the door stood looking like some statue.

Carl approached lowering his black hood he looked saddened and shaken.

"I think am going to call it a night lad," Carl said nodding and trying to fake a smile

"What's wrong, is that guy OK? Are you OK?"

"Aye, we're both fine, it's just..."

Carl unable to say what bothered him turned and walked to the barracks.

"Carl! Wait up, what's wrong?"

Quickly following my friend I caught up only to see both fear and excitement on his face.

"I'm leaving Jacob, my time has come."

"What?" I replied.

"Master Takami told me, I leave for the earth realm tomorrow."

Carl put on a brave face, a fake smile as he turned to the barracks and disappears inside.

The following day arrives quicker than both Carl and I wish, we shook hands for a moment before he left the barracks, the door opened letting in the early morning light.

The brave face Carl put on was but a lie, his bag drops to the ground he walks to me and throws his arms around me as if he would never see me again.

"I'll see you out, lad, don't make me wait too long. Out there without company." Carl states with a saddened tone.

Without another look, he grabs his bag and walks towards master Takami and the other instructors waiting at the bottom of the camp.

With handshakes, hugs, the instructors and master Takami say their goodbyes, the old man gives Carl a fine sword, a katana of great craftsmanship holds a blue crystal in the hilt.

Carl bows in respect and takes the weapon in both hands, with a blast of light the porthole appears once more, Carl turns to the school where he has lived for most of his life.

With a final look around the camp satisfied he will remember, his gaze finds me in the crowd, a simple nod, and a familiar smile he turns to the old man, both master Takami and Carl disappear within the light.

Suddenly I felt alone once more, Carl was my only true friend in the school realm, even among so many friendly students and teachers.

many days since passed, as they do, I couldn't help but think of my friend as he said goodbye, the feeling I would never see him again rested heavy on my mind.

The barracks seemed empty and quiet, laying on my bunk I watched the other students, their bodies breathing steadily as they dream away, I reached out with my senses, and all were asleep.

My loneliness grew as memories of my old war comrades came to mind, Paul, Simon, now Carl, how many more would I say goodbye to I wondered.

"You may see him again you know."

With a jolt, my loneliness is shattered, nearly jumping out my skin with fright,

I looked to where the voice originated from, master Takami sat on the side of Carl's bunk.

It appeared The old man had a few more tricks up his sleeve, managing to hide his presence from me, once again he could play his old game of scaring me half to death as he suddenly appeared.

"Just because he's not here anymore, doesn't mean you will never see him again." Takami continued.

"I know master, but I can't help but feel I shall never see him again, and I owe him so much."

"You owe him your friendship young Mister Rawn, that is all, what Carl did for you is worthy of friendship, and we as sentinels will honour and need such friendships."

"Get some sleep young Mister Rawn, tomorrow is a new day."

Takami left me to my thoughts, leaving this time by the door and not his strange appearing or disappearing act.

Training continued as per the norm, my progress was still advancing I was determined not to let Carl's teaching go to waste on me.

As the days training ends, I was travelling back to the barracks with fellow students laughing and joking at the day's events.

Takami walks to our group, all stop and bow as was the custom, with a responding bow, the old man asks the other student to leave us to talk.

"You have done well young Mister Rawn, your training has improved greatly once again."

"Thank you, master," I replied.

"Tonight, pack your things!" Takami said with a stern voice.

"What?" I asked.

"Pack your things, write a letter to those who remain, you have graduated to the next level." Holding out his hand Takami smiles at me, my face must have shone with anxiety and joy, I shook his hand suddenly feeling like I was doing lost friends proud.

"Yes master, thank you."

"But do not tell the others, bed down tonight as normal but have your things packed and ready to go, understood?"

"Yes, master of course."

With a bow of respect I ran into the barracks, closing the door behind me I looked to the other students, some reading, some training on techniques they learned today others were nursing injuries.

The other students detected nothing and bed down normally as did I, all my few belongings were packed and hid in my locker ready.

Unable to sleep I decided to meditate until the black warriors came to get me.

Finally, the energy within me swirled, a familiar feeling of a powerful soul approached, the door opened and in walked a man dressed in the black uniform.

The man approached, his hood up covering his face, his uniform hid the rest of his features, he looked to me and gestured for me to follow.

Jumping from the bunk already dressed I grab my bag, with a last look to the other students I left the letter on my bunk and closed the door behind me.

The black warrior stood on the porch waiting for me, behind him another black warrior emerges this one from the size and body language reveals it to be a woman.

A small group wait for the porthole to appear at the bottom of the camp, with a blinding flash it arrives and Takami walks through first, I walked to the porthole but found myself afraid.

"Do not be afraid, only your destiny awaits on the other side." The woman speaks softly.

Swallowing my fear I griped my bag tight and pushed through.

The brush of the energy particles on my face felt like walking through a spider's web, a cold feeling rushes over me as electrical current ripples the air and my skin.

With a brief moment of light, the journey is over, the other side of the porthole lays a desert. The air is thin a dark blue haze falls on the desert below, the sky races overhead releasing pulses of strange energy, like the Aurora borealis in the arctic.

Takami stood by waiting for me, quickly walking towards me the old man catches and supports me, I was feeling dizzy, and struggling for breath.

I felt like was walking through water, movement is hard and slow, my breathing gets heavy and the dizziness continues.

Managing to get a grip and pull myself to a focus my energy to breathing, moments later I recover, with a nod of the head I tell Takami am OK.

Moving through the desert everything illuminated by the strange dark blue haze we walk up a small rough hill towards a cliff face.

A large rock sits three feet away from the cliff's edge, master Takami runs his hand across the front from left to right across the stone, a strange sound echo's from the rock, the sound resembles wood scrapping on wood and then all goes quiet.

Master Takami nods to me then walks to the left of the stone around the back between the cliff and the stone, upon reaching the far side of the stone he vanishes as is he walked through an invisible door.

Suddenly shocked and awed I followed the old man's path, a quick sharp pulling feeling and a quick heatwave the surroundings change dramatically.

The air is sweet and filled with the fragrance of strange flowers, the sky clear with bright shining stars, all about me men and woman walk about their business, most wearing the black and blue uniform of the sentinel, some in the plain white training garb that I wore.

Looking about I was suddenly startled by a powerful sight, sat high in the sky slightly phased out by the pale daylight sat six planets, each one reaching further back than the one before sat in a celestial alignment.

The first planet so close and huge it seems almost touchable, unable to see the whole of the first planet due to it being eclipse by the horizon.

Takami walked over and laughs.

"I know, I felt the same way when I first saw it," Takami said.

Following master Takami I continued to look around my new home, the new encampment was massive measuring around three times the size of the previous camp.

The black warriors were everywhere now, I lost count as my attentions were caught by a small group of students stood practising a slow set of techniques called kata's only their bodies were covered in bio-electric energy.

Different sized huts and tents littered the place, my senses were overwhelmed due to the amount of soul energy here.

Finally, I was taken to a hut only slightly bigger than the one I had first arrived in all that time ago.

Bowing to Takami before entering the hut, I couldn't help but feel sorry to see him go.

"Ow I'm not going to be leaving you young Mister Rawn, I shall be training you personally." Takami once again pulled the thought from my mind.

Shocked at the news I rose from the bow.

"What about the other students? Back at the other camp?"

"I believe I am the master here young Mister Rawn, do you mind if I make a few choices as to what's best." Takami Laughed as he spoke.

"It will be an honour and a pleasure to be your student master Takami."

"Good, then go inside and get some rest, you'll need it."

Retreating inside the hut I looked about the place, there were four beds, a small table in the middle, a weapons rack with a selection of wooden weapons, and four small lockers sat next to each bed.

I walked to one of the empty bunks and unpacked my things.

Finally, I rested into my new bunk and waited for tomorrow to arrive.

CHAPTER 6

The Training of a Man

The training Takami gave me, forced me to my absolute limit, both mental and physical strength was tested again and again, each time pushed further and further.

Takami taught me how to harness the powers of the mind, telepathy, empathy, and finally telekinesis.

By using the energy of the soul and focused by trained and an able mind I was able to call on exceptional abilities.

Within months my mind was a powerful weapon, I was able to enter another man's mind to read his most intimate secrets and intentions, with nothing but eye contact needed.

With the mind sharp and clarity of thought, my telekinetic abilities were astounding, with little effort I could control objects around me, able to lift and move great weights with ease.

By infusing my body with bio-electric energy I was taught how to heal myself and others to health.

With little effort, I could shrug off fatigue, with concentration I could seal open wounds, and mend bones in a short amount of time, with full concentration merely minutes.

With nothing but the passing of time my body would recover from almost any injury, including lost limbs if placed in a deep meditative trance, although luckily I never had to test this myself.

By forcing my body to absorb more bio-electric energy, I could push my body beyond human limits, strength, speed, agility, and stamina were enhanced to amazing levels.

Roughly a year later in the new school, I awoke as normal, fresh and ready to go, but something swirled within me, a strange feeling that today was going to be another one of the days I would remember forever.

my first class was combat training followed by physical and mental fitness, by now my combat prowess was unmatched above all students, I was even giving instructors a run for their money.

Finally, it came to an evening class, the hut was filled with my instructor and fellow students, the lesson began with the usual discussion on the unnatural, different known species, habits, strengths and weaknesses.

Suddenly my stomach and chest went tight, a sharp pain hit me in my old war wounds, and I felt both sick and uncomfortable as the energy within swirled to life, my mind flashed back to the terrible day on the battlefield.

"Jacob are you OK son?" the instructor asked looking at me across the room.

"Yes, sir am just, feeling weird sir."

The instructor smiled at me.

"Good."

Suddenly shocked at the answer I watched with bewilderment.

"You may come out now master Yevelle.

From behind the door walks a stranger to the camp, his frame tall and slim, too slim even for the most extravagant model of the day.

The man stands almost seven feet tall, his walk seems to glide almost across the floor as he walks, he turns to face the class, and his long silver robe covers all other detail about his build as does the hood over his head.

Moments later the students suddenly feel the same as I, a sickness and a pain strikes their stomachs and chests, their energy suddenly awakens, as a form of natural readiness.

The student's shuffles back towards me at the back of the class away from the tall stranger, all seem to be in awe at the size and build of this man, and they were all unclear what to make of him.

Unlike my fellow students, my first impulses were not of shock and awe but tactics, I noticed he was unarmed, my mind then thought of unarmed combat tactics to subdue him should the need arise, shaking away such urges I returned my attention to where it belonged.

The strange man lifted his hands to his silver hood, the long white and slightly glittery fingers seem oversized for his slim wrists, the hood drops behind revealing the strangers face.

Shocking gasps and awe trembled through the students, his long-drawn face was smoothly featured with high cheekbones, and his large eyes were cat-like, large horizontal slits for pupils with irises of a bright sky blue.

His silver-white skin intensified the colour of his eyes and reflected the reflection of the torch flames lighting the hut.

"Students, this is master Yevelle." the instructor stated.

The tall stranger lifted his right hand and places it across his chest above where his heart would be, bowing slightly showing us respect, as is the formal bow of the Drakeions and the sentinels.

"The feeling you have now is going to be a very common one for you, as your training continues, you will now be interacting with more of the unnatural and the Drakeions." the instructor said.

"Sir Will it always hurt and make me feel as sick like this?" one of the students asked.

The student lowered himself back into his seat after asking still clearly uncomfortable.

"No son it won't, the more you encounter the unnatural the easier it gets until it becomes just a bearable ache and groggy feeling."

"In time you will use this feeling to track the unnatural in the earth realm."

After a short time in the presence of the Drakeion the class was split up and sent out into the camp looking for the unnatural, the feeling we encountered in the classroom was our guide and our only way to find the future enemy.

Searching the camp the class managed to find four more Drakeions hiding within the camp, after returning to the instructor the Drakeions were introduced and began interacting with their new students.

Shaking hands and trying not to stare the students were still in awe of these fascinating creatures, students began asking questions about their race and others about the enemy.

Without realizing I somehow managed to walk through the students and the Drakeions towards master Yevelle, I moved across the hut as if in a daze, arriving next to him I looked him up and down, his height a clear few feet above mine, the man was huge.

Swallowing hard and pushing away my sickness and the sudden realization of where and what I was doing I locked eyes with master Yevelle.

"Err, hi," I said rather shyly.

Yevelle smiles and bowed deeply.

"Master Rawn I presume, I have heard many good things about you," Yevelle said smoothly and deeply.

"You have?" I replied shocked.

I looked to my instructor who stood close by, a quick nod of the head confirmed master Yevelle's statement.

"What sort of things have you heard?" I said.

The tall slender figure lowered himself onto one of the class tables, his gaze now lowers almost level with mine, clearly an attempt to put me at ease.

"Well the rumour is your nearly ready to graduate, and a full 2 years ahead of schedule."

"You can't be serious?" I replied shocked and suddenly fearful.

Yevelle smiled and placed his hand on my shoulder and offers comfort.

"it's true, master Takami told me himself, as of tomorrow you will all be training alongside me in combat, and master Takami of course."

"But am not ready," I replied shaking.

"Hah modesty, very good, all students fear their graduation day, but don't worry your time here isn't over, your graduation is real combat training is all I meant."

Suddenly sighing with relief I listened on.

"And once that is done you will still have to remain for another few years to help train the next generation of students."

once relived I began to talk of Yevelle's race and the war that they have fought with the mage's for centuries, and why they chose to train both mage's and humans.

As the class finished the students returned to their bunks, sleep or meditation awaited them, but my mind could not be calmed, thoughts ran through my head of the magnificent Drakeions, finally, I was to see them in training.

The following day came and was filled with struggle and pain, through physical and combat training, and finishing with mental training, I was exhausted and beaten.

Months past at the hands of both master Yevelle and master Takami, combat training was with live weapons, unarmed combat was brutal and full contact, broken bones and organ damage was a common occurrence.

Sometime later that year my progress was clear to all, combat whether mental or physical was tested against Drakeions, after a time I even managed to come close to beating one or two of them.

One evening after I had finished training and finally managed to beat one the Drakeion masters with a sword, a female student runs up to me and delivers an urgent request for me to visit master Takami's hut.

As I walked to the old man's hut, I noticed all the instructors watched as I went past, a sudden feeling something wasn't quite right struck me.

I knocked on the door and waited for the old man to ask me to enter, a few moments of silence later I felt the energy inside me swirl and shift, the old wounds flinched and my mind was flown back to the demon creature on the battlefield.

A sudden fear entered my mind, I couldn't feel master Takami inside, hidden within there was another presence, something very powerful waited for me inside.

I swallowed my fear and cautiously entered the hut, mind and body filled with adrenaline and bio-electric energy ready for combat.

The hut was dark and lit only by few candles spread throughout the room, a large conference table filled most of the front area of the room followed by a bed and several large book shelf's lining the walls.

Slowly I walked around the table Looking around the room I finally lock eyes on a tall figure kneeling facing away from me praying at what appears to be a shrine.

He's tall and slim figure gave him away as a Drakeion, his long sliver hooded robe covers his frame, my gaze shifted to his right-hand side, laid at his side like some ceremony piece was a finely crafted katana sword.

"Err excuse me, master, I was told to report here to see master Takami," I asked.

"I am afraid he is not here, you will have to settle for Me." a deep serious almost angry voice replied.

Rising slowly to his feet picking his sword up as he stood he turned to face me, his bright green eyes stare straight through me as if I wasn't there, just like Takami used to.

"Forgive me master but I do not remember you, I am JA..."

Suddenly interrupted the voice hard and stern vibrates towards Jacob.

"I know who you are Jacob Rawn of Lincoln, I am grandmaster Shakarian, and I am here to test you."

"Test me sir but I don't understand I thou…"I tried to reply.

"I don't care what you thought Jacob Rawn, defend yourself, or die." the stranger replied harshly.

Stunned at those words I watched in disbelief as the strange man hurled towards me fist flying.

Fist, feet, knees, and elbows, all but a blur to the eyes as the Drakeion attacked relentlessly, using only one arm to attack as the other held firm his mighty sword, I was relieved as the speed would have been too much for me if he had used two arms to attack.

His precision flawless, his timing impeccable and yet not a single strike landed, struggling to hold back the onslaught of attacks purely on the defensive, I managed to watch my attacker, reading his moves.

Suddenly my defence was broken, a rapid bunch of attacks and a final executed butt strike from the sheathed blade landed square in the chest hurling me through the air landing hard on my back on top of the conference table.

With a gasp of air that is forced from my lungs as I slammed down hard, I quickly jump up onto my feet with a quick flip searching for my attacker.

Across the room still stood in the attack posture of the strike that lifted me in the air, the Drakeion returns to an upright position and waited for me to approach, shaking off the blow, I jump back down to the floor holding out my hands in surrender.

"Please sir I don't wish to fight you, you are a mas…" I tried to say.

Again interrupted I was forced on the defensive once more.

Strike after strike flies towards me still unable to place a counter strike I opted for another method, Allowing the overpowering strength and speed to come in closer to my body and not to spend precious energy trying to fight it I waited.

The attacker presses his advantage thinking the human is weakening under the pressure of the attacks, pushing harder and faster the Drakeion continues waiting for his blow to land.

Finally, my moment arrived, I summoned my bio-electric energy within and focused it as I sidestepped a punch to the head, forcing the bio-energy to life, a hazy blue light fills my body as I urge into being a psychokinetic thrust to my hands and hurl it towards my attacker.

The Drakeion blocks the incoming blast of force by crossing his arms in front of the impact area and charging his energy to absorb the blast.

The energy slams into his arms and pushes his firmly planted feet along the floor some few inches.

Finally stopping still both men exchange glances, I watched as the Drakeion reached up and lowered his silver hood.

His long white hair dropped back and his gaze lifted revealing a smirking grin.

"Nicely done Jacob." the Drakeion replied.

Without warning, he charged into battle once more, now with more than fist and foot but with telekinetic force strikes and pushes.

Blast after blast slammed into the ground and walls, few strikes hit my defence due to my dodging and evading, my confidence starts to wane as the pull of fatigue and the drain of my bio-energy starts to kick in.

Still, we fought, finally, I had to risk a strike of my own or this fight would continue in his favour, summoning my last bit of bio-electric energy I focused on the table and chairs, one by one they flew at him like ballistic missiles.

With ease, the Drakeion either hurls them aside with his telekinetic ability or evades them with pure grace like that of a leaping cat, a welcome reprieve from relentless attacks arrives just in time as I took advantage of the distraction and launched a powerful spinning hook kick at my attack.

I stood both gasping and fatigued, as the strike landed spinning him in the air but somehow managing to land back on his feet.

A look of impressiveness crawls on the Drakeions face as he looks over to me who looks barely able to stand.

"Impressive, for a human, you should be unconscious by now with the amount of energy you have used."

Barely able to catch my breath I embraced the small break.

"I... had ...a good teacher," I spoke as breath would allow.

"No Jacob, you had the best."

Again the peace is broken the battle rages on, with constant attacks, I summoned every ounce of energy I had and empowered my body with speed and strength, and finally, I started to push back at my attacker.

Blows are flown and countered by both of us, finally, I felt myself slipping, my energy depleted, the fatigue starts to steadily drop my speed and power.

Again my defence is broken and I am sent flying through the air in pain,

Blood flies from my mouth as the Drakeion lands a perfect sidekick into my left ribs.

I landed hard on my back, remaining flat but conscious, I quickly scanned my body in my mind, at least three broken ribs I found and internal bleeding.

Slowly walking towards his prey the Drakeion examined me before going in for the kill.

Barely able to remain conscious a sudden flashback entered my mind, my long-dead friends on the battlefield in the war, a fresh memory then erupts of his friend Carl telling him to hold onto the thought of his friends and they will help to carry him through whatever ordeal he faces.

My body suddenly goes numb from pain as if shut off by a switch, my energy flares to life within me, and a freshness swims through my muscles as if waking from a good night's rest.

Watching with surprise and admiration the Drakeion smiled as I approached. Looking to my attacker, we both nod in agreement and readies ourselves for another round.

The sounds of battle flood the room as we fly at each other to the surprise of the Drakeion and myself several blows land on him, as several lands on me.

Both of us unwilling to stop we continue to battle on, the hits come and go both of us struck over and over but nothing remains but a dull sound.

Now the Drakeions nose is broken as are several ribs, a fractured wrist and broken toes but still, he continues as if nothing is wrong.

My body feels nothing as if numb and my brain is on autopilot, a broken jaw, hand, ribs, shine bone, punched lung, cracked skull and dislocated hip and foot didn't stop me from fighting on.

Finally, the Drakeions own power began to wane, fatigue began to creep slowly towards him and he decided to end this battle suddenly.

Summoning his great strength enhanced by his bio-energy he pushed his strength further, enhancing further his telekinetic ability, he spun to the side of me evading my attack.

Sidestepping attack after attack creating a small amount of distance between us he jumped into a spinning sidekick, the kick barely touched me but the telekinetic force projected from his leg did.

Smashing several more ribs and almost snapping my spine in the process, the kick drives into my stomach bending me in double.

I flew through the air at great speed and smashed through the wall of the hut into the Drakeions own room beyond.

I could barely see him with the one eye I had open, my body was broken I was paralyzed, mere breathing took all my concentration.

Finally giving in to his injury's and fatigue his body-powered down and he collapses to one knee gasping for breath, using his still sheathed sword to hold his body up he struggled for breath.

Just before I lapsed into darkness a sudden bomb went off inside me, just like the awakening ritual with master Takami, a pulse of light engulfed my body, not blue like I have come to know, but of brilliant white with a tint of silver.

I screamed in pain as the energy ripped through my body I could feel bones repairing muscle rebinding, blood flowing to where it should.

After mere seconds the light was gone, although not fully healed I was able to move, I felt like I had a small amount of energy left and I was determined not to let master Takami down.

Unable to hold back his disbelief the Drakeion shakes his head at the sight of me struggling to walk with such damage, still struggling for breath slightly and tending to his wounds he stands up to face me.

I managed to hobble on one leg, the other was unable to withstand the slightest pressure, lifting one arm to hold in a guard position I looked to my attacker with pain all over my face and one open eye.

"Co...Come on, that the best… Best you got."

My voice barely audible over the raspy breath.

The Drakeion looked at me in disbelief, he lifted his hand out towards me and urges his telepathic powers into action.

With a strong jolt to my mind, the Drakeion commands it to shut down and recuperate, with little or no resistance my mind obliges, falling to the floor in an unconscious heap, the battle was over.

Several days passed before I awoke, I was deep in a healing trace placed there by Takami himself, the infirmary medics kept me alive while the old man repaired the damage with his healing abilities.

After I awoke I was surprised to see my attacker in the bed next to me, his wounds almost healed by the time I saw him, suddenly on edge I flinched when I saw him looking and smiling at me.

"How is he?" a familiar friendly voice asked from the side of me.

"Alive, and healing, the injuries I gave him should have killed him five times over, and yet he came at me again and again." the Drakeion replied with pride in his voice.

Takami walked from behind me and over to the Drakeion placing his hand on his shoulder, both men looked at me strangely, as if I had accomplished some great feat.

"He is an incredible adversary my friend, he wouldn't quit." the Drakeion stated.

"So what is your final decision grandmaster?" Takami asked a hesitant tone in his voice.

The Drakeion looked up to master Takami.

"This had to be done Takami, you know that." the Drakeions tone now firm and serious.

"Did it? You could have killed him." Takami replied.

"Make no mistake about it my friend I nearly had to, to stop him." the Drakeions voice sharp.

Takami and the Drakeion stood looking at each other then back to me, I was still laid out on the bed unable to grasp the full meaning of what they were discussing.

"We only just got to him in time Shakarian, both of you were only minutes from death, was all this pain you caused and took worth it?"

The Drakeion turned back to the old man and a smile filled his face.

"Yes, every bit my friend, it was incredible, he was like an unstoppable force of nature, at one point he was outlasting my abilities, you should be proud of him Takami."

"I have always been proud of him master, from the moment we recruited him, there has been nothing but greatness, humility, compassion, and pure strength of character."

"I believe you Takami, he will be our greatest weapon against the unnatural, I could not be more proud of what you have done with him, he's your greatest achievement, my friend, I just wish he had been ours."

"Thank you, master." Takami bowed as he replied.

The Drakeion rose to his feet and placed his hands on the old man's shoulders.

"His training is over Takami, graduate him, give him his rightful place in our ranks, I will welcome him as a brother, and look forward to the day we may fight side by side together."

Unable to keep listening or remain conscious any longer my body returns to its healing trance.

the following day feelings of pain rush to my attention, my eyes straining with the light I slowly came to, as my vision cleared my eyes focused on master Takami stood at the bottom of my bed, the strange Drakeion warrior I fought was still recovering in the bed next to me I slowly tried to lift myself to a sitting position and was quickly helped by the Drakeion warrior, every breath and movement was a painful experience.

"Welcome back young Mister Rawn," Takami said.

"Did I, go someplace master."

"Very nearly," Takami replied.

Still keeping my eyes on the Drakeion attacker I was uneasy.

"How long was I out?"

"Nearly a week my friend." the Drakeion replied.

I looked to the Drakeion with suspension, I couldn't help but feel threatened by his presence.

"Easy Mister Rawn, I mean you no further harm, you have nothing to fear from me."

The Drakeions voice calming and gentle is reinforced by a genuine smile.

Slowly moving to the side of my bed and lowering himself down to my eye level, the Drakeion placed his left hand on my shoulder, his right hand went across his chest and bowed to me.

The Drakeion rose to his feet still looking at me as master Takami joined his side.

"you have earned my admiration and respect, and I ask you not to forget our battle, but cherish it, for that, is how hard I will fight to protect our new friendship." the Drakeion stated holding out his hand in time-honoured human custom he waited for me to take his hand in mine.

I took his hand with what little strength I had left, my uneasy feeling had been lifted and replaced with admiration.

With a quick grin to master Takami, the Drakeion replaces his hood and turns to leave.

"Master, wait," I shouted.

Turning slightly to face me, the Drakeion looks with interest.

"Sorry, for wreaking your hut, I'll try not to damage the walls and furniture next time you kick my ass," I stated.

Another smile crept across the Drakeions face, and a small chuckle is heard as he leaves the hut.

"I think you have made a friend for life there Mister Rawn." Takami chuckled.

"Next time master, I'll try an easier way to meet your friends thank you."

Both of us laughed, only my ribs objected to the idea.

A few days later I was up and healed, my training resumed and the lessons intensifying, the fight with the Drakeion had a huge effect on me, my entire body seems to flow in combat, my moves become as a dance, strikes and parries merged into a blur.

Every technique came as easy as breathing, my bio-electric energy totally in tune with my mind, I was able to call any ability to flow at will.

With my soul open my powers become incredible, rivalling or besting all the instructors, grandmaster Shakarian joins master Takami in continuing my final training.

Sometime during the next few days, I was in the circle of pain with four opponents one of which was one of my current instructor, unable to match me I evaded and counter struck each in turn.

"impressive." the strange feeling of the Drakeion was felt within, I turned to lock eyes with grandmaster Shakarian.

I bowed in respect as did everyone around the circle.

"Let's see how much you have improved shall we?" Shakarian said with a smile.

I smiled back and bowed, following the grandmaster to the weapon stand, my weapon of choice a sword resembling a Japanese katana.

Shakarian pulls from his robes the fine katana sword made of a hazy blue and silver metal, the same blade he held during our battle, its hilt was wrapped in dark blue leather, the silver metal underneath shining in the light of day. this katana was a masterpiece.

Passing his outta cloak to a bystander, we both entered the circle and readied for a fight, both of us were aware of the pain we caused each other the last time we fought.

Master Takami stood by and watched, I could see the worries in his eyes, without warning we charged, blades blurred out of existence it seemed, both moving at incredible speeds.

Both blades clashed a thousand times, blows from kicks, punches, and sweeps are blocked and yet neither one of us seemed unable to land a strike.

The battle raged on, grunts and screams emerge from us both as we attack, the clashing of blades echoes through the camp, the whole camp ceased their training and ran to the battle to watch.

Blasts of bio-electric energy pulsed from the fight slamming into blocked guards, blades or unlucky bystanders watching.

Finally, a break in the fight appears, both of us pull away from the Frey to catch a breath and examine each other of injuries, none were found.

Shakarian lowered his blade to his side, he rose from his combat stance, unsure if this was a ploy I remained in mine ready.

With a twirl of the blade to a resting position at his side next to his belt Shakarian smiles and bows indicating the fight is over.

I lowered my blade and walked to Shakarian, bowing deep to the grandmaster, I waited a few moments and lifted my eyes.

I was suddenly taken back at the sight of Shakarian stood now holding arms out towards me the magnificent katana sword, the scabbard made of pure white oak.

Smiling and indicating for me to take the weapon Shakarian waits for me to do just that.

I called for a fellow student to take my practice weapon with a quick bow and thank you I reached for the magnificent sword held by Shakarian.

Taking the weapon in both hands and examining every inch of it like a small boy receiving his toys at Christmas, I felt a connection to the weapon immediately.

"It's made from metal on my home realm, twice as strong and as light as your strongest steel" Shakarian stated.

"What… what do I you want me to do with it?"

I was genuinely confused by this turn of events, Takami moves to the side of me holding a pile of black clothing with blue trims.

"The sword is yours now Jacob, I made it myself, from metal on my lands back home." Shakarian said.

"And these Mister Rawn are your new uniform."

Turning my attention away from the weapon, I looked to master Takami with surprise at the gift.

"I graduated," I replied.

Master Takami stayed quiet and nodded in agreement, the whole camp suddenly erupted in shouts, claps, and celebration.

Friends rushed in to congratulate me and look to my new weapon.

"Well JA, that's a new one, I ain't ever seen grandmaster Shakarian do that or make something for a student himself." one of the instructors said.

As the celebration continues I watched both master Takami and Shakarian walk away from the crowd.

that night my mediation is interrupted, my excitement and feelings swelled in me, unable to calm myself I stepped outside to a training area, still dressed in my training garb I took my new sword with me.

drawing my weapon from the scabbed, I listened to the bright sharp ring of the blade echo as it was freed from its resting place. After a moment I entered a sword kata, the blade cuts through the air with harsh slicing sounds, my bio-energy runs down the blade leaving a trail of hazy blue light for a split second where I have struck.

suddenly the strange feelings and images of his enemy on the battlefield that day flood into his mind as my stomach began to turn slightly, my energy within had been disturbed.

"Evening grandmaster," I said without turning to find him.

Shakarian walks up to the training circle and places himself out of reach on a log.

"I never got to congratulate you on your graduation Jacob."

Finishing my kata I settle down both my mind and body and join Shakarian on the log.

"Thank you, grandmaster, but I don't think am ready."

"Hah modesty, good, you're as ready as you ever could be Jacob, you're the best master Takami has ever trained."

"Mas..."

"Please, call me Shakarian, I never did like titles." he interrupted.

"OK, Shakarian the sword is..."

Again I was interrupted.

"Is now an extension of you, and as such will be well looked after, used for the right reasons, I do not doubt that." Shakarian stated.

"Master I don't feel I deserve this, not yet."

Shakarian laughed out loud.

"You're the finest warrior ever to come from this camp or any other, save for master Takami, of course, you are ready."

"Thank you for the sword, it's amazing," I replied.

"Yes, I am proud of that one."

"So, what happens now?"

"Now, myself, master Takami and you will train the others until your time has come to return to the earth realm."

I returned to the barracks both sleep and meditation avoided me, my thoughts were of the role I would now assume.

The following morning the sun awoke me shining in through the open window, I rose to gather my things trying not to awake the other students.

I grabbed my few belongings and my weapon, a last look around the room watching as the students still sleeping or meditating I was filled with a feeling of lonesomeness again.

I walked from the barracks, meeting up with Shakarian and master Takami, we walked to the site of the portal, the last look back at the place I called home for the past months, filled me with sadness.

Passing from the second camp to the first meant travelling through the shadow world, my body felt weird as it did the first time travelling through this place only this time I was in control.

The dizziness and sickness passed, the hot and cold feelings washed away and finally, we are through into the first camp.

The blackness of night greeted us as does another sentinel instructor, bowing low to both master Takami and Shakarian and then finally to me, the instructor looked at me strangely as he was now aware of my black and blue GI uniform.

Master Takami and Shakarian retired to their huts, the other instructor leads me back towards the barracks, before entering I turned to the far end of the camp and was relieved to see the welcome hut still standing and occupied.

The barracks were dark and quiet, the students again asleep or meditating, finding a spare bunk I climbed into it resting, letting my thoughts drift until finally, I slept.

The morning arrived, I awoke as the sun rises with all the other instructors, quickly filing out of the barracks to a meeting in the centre of the camp.

master Takami and Shakarian stood giving instructions to the others and me telling them their roles within the camp, a series of changes were made to the order of things like the new arrival of myself made things a little easier to teach more classes.

My assignment was physical training, conditioning, basic combat techniques, and history in the evening, settling into these roles was easier than I first thought.

Within weeks I enjoyed and became a patient instructor, teaching with passion, and an attitude of feeling is believing, and learning by doing.

Students seem to swell under my tutelage, their progress rapidly increased both mentally and physically, my relationship with the students blossomed as well as becoming friends with many of them.

Training students by day, trained by Shakarian at night in better sword handling, and advanced healing by master Takami, my life was full, and I was finally content.

Late one evening sometime after training with both masters my meditation was suddenly broken, I felt the presence of master Takami and several other awakened souls approaching.

Walking to door I could feel an uneasy and hasty mood emanating from the other side, I opened the door to be greeted with master Takami stood with five other sentinels ordering me to accompany them.

Grabbing my weapon and outta robe, we walked to the river were Takami opened another portal.

passing through into the shadow world we continued to the barren wasteland ahead, travelling several meters into the sandy wastes and passing a section of large rocks Takami stops and raises his hand ordering us to stop.

watching with interest I monitored every move Takami makes, holding his hand forward Takami walks around a set of rocks maybe 3 meters high, finally he climbs up the large boulder onto a larger rock.

Looking out into the open wastes before him he takes a step forward as if he were stepping into thin air, vanishing leaving nothing but the sound of wood scraping on wood and a sudden gust of harsh wind.

Myself following the other five men one by one copy every move Takami just made, a sharp pull and a bright flash later I was through into another realm.

looking around Takami walked forward towards what seemed a city street, tall buildings stretched up to the sky's, large metal stairways ran down theses building, large piles of rubbish and big metal bins laid in this alley, the place humid and filled with rotten smells.

Strange noises surrounded us, what sounded and look like futuristic cars rushed past the dark alley, people wearing strange fashions walked past completely oblivious to the seven men walking around in the alley.

The so-called peace is broken, all seven men began to feel sickly and my mind flashes of my old adversary on the battlefield all those years ago.

In unison, the sentinels respond to the sudden feeling by pulling their weapons, save one, the old man.

Takami walked deeper into the alley ahead of everyone, we followed cautiously, looking fanatically around looking for any signs of the unnatural.

Takami ordered us to hold, standing some twenty feet ahead, the old man waited patiently, looking around the alley we could see and sense everything, somewhere in this alley an unnatural creature lays in wait.

Suddenly the sentinels jump into action as the training dictates, as leaping from the rooftop of a nearby building a large grey creature lands in the alley, his massive size holds a large man under one arm as if it were a doll.

The creature's skin was a rough dark grey and bulges with muscles, it's head humanoid-like except for a large rhino-like horn protrudes from his forehead and nose.

I and the sentinels avoid the impact area as the creature lands and crumble the ground under his massive weight.

Both Takami and the rest of us focus at the job at hand, waiting for the old man's order we stood ready.

Takami pulls back his right hand to his waist, summoning forth his bio-energy into a large telekinetic jolt, a split second later he sent it flying into the chest of the beast.

With a grunt and a smirk grin the creature shudders under the blow but nothing more, all present were suddenly shocked and began to let fear grow inside.

The creature throws the man in his arms to the side like a rag doll, and hurls himself towards Takami, without thought I hurled myself through the air aided by my telekinetic ability I caught the unconscious man's body landing in a heap in a large collection of disused cardboard boxes and rubbish.

Checking him for injuries I could senses life within the man, placing his body safe on the cardboard I dusted myself off and looked back to the creature.

Pulling my blade from its sheath I was suddenly stunned at the new sight I was witness to, standing motionless with his back to me some 30 feet away the beast remains still.

As a deafening roar rips through the alley from the creature, small hazy blue lights envelopes it, finally its huge body explodes into whispering dust.

Standing in a combat stance looking to the floor, his right hand held out at what would have been the creature's stomach Takami stands motionless.

The light in his hand dims and finally fades out, rising to his normal stance Takami looks to the others and smiles as he locates the innocent man unconscious laid in a heap of boxes.

The only remaining thing from the creature was a small yellow light the size of a golf ball, whipping around Takami. Closing his eyes and whispering some texts from the Drakeion teachings, within a few moments the small yellow light flies up into the sky vanishing from sight.

The journey back to the school realm went without incident and the unconscious man is taken to the welcome hut and healed, returning to my bunk within the barracks my mind ran through the night's events.

Remembering how and why I was brought here, I felt for the poor soul within the welcome hut, what he will be faced with, and the choice he will have to make.

The following morning life began as it always did in the school, training, followed by more of the same.

I was summoned to Takami's hut, as he approached the door I felt the presence of Shakarian inside, entering the hut my two masters stop and look to me both smile, bow and follow through with a strong embrace.

"Good morning masters, you summoned me," I said.

"Please Jacob sit." Takami gestured towards a chair

We sat at a table filling most of one end of the room, a quick look around the room reminded me of the other hut me and Shakarian fought in.

"What can I do for you masters?" I asked again.

Shakarian stayed quiet and looked to master Takami to answer.

"Jacob we have a situation that arisen, our last few remaining sentinels have disappeared."

"Disappeared?" I replied.

"Yes, nearly all of them that have gone before you have vanished or been destroyed."

Suddenly I was filled with concern, as I could also feel an uncertain, worried mood coming from both masters.

"We have no answer as to how or why all we know is they are no longer there." Shakarian's words are cold and harsh.

"But how can this have happened?" I asked.

"We have no idea my friend, which is why we have summoned you here."

Again my emotions betrayed me, my heart and face filled with shock and concern.

"We are sending you home my friend, normally you would remain here for another few years before we would send you back but our need is great."

"But master I car..."

"You must Jacob, you are the only one who can, we drakeions would raise to much attention now in your modern world. It has to be you, you're the only one who is ready." Shakarian interrupted.

"Your abilities, your heritage, and your past make you the only logical choice," Takami said.

"What do you mean?" I replied.

Master Takami looks to Shakarian with a look of shame, walking towards one of his many bookshelves in the hut he returns to the table holding a huge book wrapped in a silk cloth.

"Jacob we...we need to talk about your past." Master Takami stated.

Now totally confused I sat with a look of worry on my face.

"OK master, what about it?"

"You rescued me from the middle of a war if you remember."

"Yes we did, but I want to go a little further than that if we may," Takami asked.

"Not much to tell was born in a city called Lincoln in England, father was a joiner, and mum was a groundskeeper at an old church or monastery."

"Your mother, Jacob, was she religious?" Shakarian looked on with interest.

"Yea both my parents were, what's that got to do with anything?" I asked.

Both masters look to each other, with a nod of agreement master Takami uncovers the book under the silk wrappings.

A large black leather book with a single symbol in gold on the front cover emerges, the symbol resembles a humanoid figure with what look likes wings on its back.

"This book, tells a story over many a thousand years old it's the first encounter of the unnatural on our world and many others," Takami stated.

"It looks like an angel on the front master." I tried to say seriously.

"It is, the story tells of angels and demons that come from another realm, thousands of years ago they fought through the many realms." Shakarian said.

"They fought on our realm too?" I asked Takami.

"Yes, according to the book they freed the evolving species of man from the demon hordes, then were ordered home, or to another war somewhere."

"However, not all returned home, some of the angels decided the human soul was to rich a resource and too powerful to leave unchecked and undefended, some chose to stay, to defend, to nurture. "Shakarian said.

My stomach sank as I looked to my too masters.

"Surely you don't think..."

"We think you are a decedent of one of these creatures," Takami interrupted.

"Angels and demons exist, Jacob, so does their war, to this day they fight on, much like my peoples and the mages continue to wage war. So do these creatures.." Shakarian added.

Confused and believing nothing at this juncture I tried to take it on board.

"But what has this got to do with me? Why do you think am one of these creatures?"

"Not an angel or a demon but a descendant, a half breed if you will, one of your parents must have been one of the fallen."

"Fallen?" I asked.

Both Takami and Shakarian look to each other before continuing.

"The fallen is the name given to an angel when it chose to stay in the earth realm, they gave up the war and stayed to protect the human race."

"I don't understand," I replied.

Shakarian jumps to my aid.

"The story tells of seven angels who remained on earth, they were called the fallen, that's the name the other angels call one of their own who rebels, and they are exiled."

"But why me, how?"

"The story's all so tells us they bread with humans and had kin of their own, theses half breeds had exceptional ability's similar to the angels themselves and were capable of defeating or banishing demons."

"master Takami told me of your awakening, there was a massive discharge of bio-energy that formed a faint glow of wings-like appendages from your back, that and the subject of the other abilities you poses" I replied.

"What abilities, I only know of the ones you have taught me."

"No Jacob, you have much more, when you first came here you were able to heal faster than any I have seen without training, you were able to release a force of bio-energy into the devourer in the earth realm," Takami replied.

My mind wonders with doubt and possibility, trying to find a handle on the moment.

Shakarian jumped to my aid once more.

"Jacob when you and I fought, you were able to call on more power than even master Takami has access to at any one moment, you should have been killed four or five times from the blows I gave you, and yet you fought on, fought on and nearly beat me, that's impossible for someone without something extra inside."

"But I don't under...."

"Jacob the energy inside you is endless, like all human souls, but as a fallen, it's twice maybe three times as potent, which explains how your mental disciplines are stronger than any of the others in this camp instructor or no."

All three of us fell in silence, thoughts rush through my mind unable to process all this.

Rising to my feet I walked away from the table-turning away from my masters trying to calm myself.

Takami was the first to break the silence..."

"That is why we have to send you, you are the finest warrior to emerge from this camp or any other, and with your even greater gifts you have a better chance at survival."

"Master, I don't, know, how to...."

"When you return, you will look for the others, once you find any trace of them return to us, and hopefully we will piece things together and return some measure of security to the earth realm." Takami interrupts again.

Shakarian stands and looks at me.

"It's time you returned home, you will leave in the morning for the earth realm and your destiny."

Shakarian pats me on the shoulder before leaving the room leaving master and student alone.

"Master, I…"

Takami interrupts me.

"It's time Jacob, in your travels you may even find some trace of your heritage."

"Tomorrow when you return, you will feel out of place at first, time moves slower here than in the earth realm, it will be very different for you."

"And remember through the opening of your soul you will age slower than normal humans, but old age will catch you eventually, unless."

"Unless what master?" I asked.

"as a fallen, you may never age, no one knows of their powers and abilities, but it is known they travelled the world for centuries, healed rapidly when injured, and even returned from the dead, however, I suggest you don't put the later to the test."

I fell silent, deep in thought, my fear starts to show.

Turning away from the table and my friend and master I start to leave.

"Jacob, the book tells us, the fallen were hunted from time to time, by demons and angels alike, they were captured and taken home or killed were they lie, the fate of the fallen is lost in history, but maybe you can find their present."

Rising from the table Takami holds out his hand to me and gestures me to take it.

"Master, am scared."

"I know my friend, but the earth realm needs you, we can keep things going here, tomorrow you will leave for the earth realm, no one here knows your heritage nor will they, only Shakarian and myself know of this, and I suggest you keep it that way."

"Yes, master."

Walking to the bedroom of his hut Takami stops suddenly and turns slightly to meet my gaze. "You know, if the tales of the fallen powers are true, then your mother may be still alive, for I believe it is her who walked with the fallen," Takami spoke with a smile.

Closing the door of the hut behind me I walked out onto the porch my thoughts and emotions a mess, suddenly I was taken back a little as I had not noticed Shakarian outside looking to the stars.

"You still doubt what we told you?"

"Yes master, but some of it feels right," I replied.

"In your travels, you may find the answers to the questions we could not answer."

Shakarian turned to me placing his hand on my shoulders.

"Do not fear Jacob, your skills and abilities will be more than a match for anything you come across, and if it is not, then return for me, we shall face it together."

"I can return once I leave?" I asked.

"Of course, this will always be a haven for any who need it, and I shall be here for any reason you need me."

We shook hands before going our separate ways, I returned to my class training my students, my mind always elsewhere.

The night seems to race by, my meditation unable to place me at ease, my thoughts a mess through the night, I chose instead to wander the camp.

Returning to my hut and packing my few belongings before the others awoke, I looked over my sleeping or meditating comrades, I was filled with lonesomeness and fear at the coming events.

Swallowing my emotions I emerged from my hut to be surprised by the presence of several of the Drakeion masters, Shakarian, master Takami and several of the instructors.

All those awake in the camp stand in two single lines leading down to the river stood Shakarian and master Takami.

Swallowing hard, and pushing forward I slung my large bag on my shoulder my magnificent sword attached to the side I walked on.

Walking down the row of warriors towards my masters I looked to each face, each one looking on with pride and regret.

"Good luck j."

"Give em hell my man."

Words of encouragement and salutes off my friends, I felt tears well in my eyes and fall down my face.

Approaching my masters, I wiped the tears and swallow down my fear.

"Young Mister Rawn, Jacob, today you take your rightful place amongst us, do not accept this lightly, for your life is now bound to every other on earth," Takami said.

Shakarian stepped forward taking my hand in his and embraced me, stepping back he bows and steps to the side nodding to master Takami.

"Your path will lead you on many roads, many battles, you will fight to survive in a world that does not know you exist, you will fight to protect those that cannot protect themselves."

Shakarian places his hand on my shoulder.

"We shall meet again my friend, if you need me, you know where to find me."

I bowed and turned back to master Takami who seems in deep concentration.

Without warning an eruption of wind and light bursts into the space behind master Takami.

The porthole swirls with energy and life, master Takami turns away from it and gestures for me to face my destiny.

"The earth realm awaits you sentinel Rawn, your destiny beckons you."

The crowd behind burst into cheers and praise.

Adjusting the bag on my shoulder and one last bow to master Takami and Shakarian I walked on.

A few steps more and I was no longer with them, the porthole closes rapidly behind me, leaving me with nothing but the wind.

The shadow world greets me as it always has, hot and cold sweats, dizziness and thin air, adjusting to the new conditions I was greeted with two more sentinels.

Gesturing to follow them they lead me to a small path leading into the barren wastes,

A few meters into the wastes we arrived at a single small tree.

With a bow of the head, one sentinel remains still, the other gestures for me to walk around the back of the tree.

"When you wish to return to us, follow the same path back and there will be a guard waiting." One of the dark sentinel's states.

"Good look Jacob." The other man shouts.

As I drew near the back of the tree a sharp gust of wind picks up walking forward a blinding flash erupted and I was pulled through.

CHAPTER 7

The Hunter

The roaring fire crackles as the timbers split and fall in the fireplace, the heat emanates from the hearth warming the two men in the room.

Paul's hand starts to crap from constant writing of notes from the story he has been told.

Paul turns the last page of his note pad and is suddenly taken back at the lack of fresh paper. Taking a deep breath trying to take everything in, he closes his eyes and runs through the story in his mind.

A feeling of the burden Jacob carries hits him, followed by the sudden realization that he now carries this burden, his mind swells to the responsibility Jacob has placed on his shoulders.

"I need to take a break," Paul says shaking his writing hand.

"Am also outta paper."

Jacob turns his attention from the fire back to his guest, nodding his head in agreement he turns back to the fire and just sits.

"Maybe it's for the best, we've covered a lot so far," Jacob replies.

"Did you do something to me? You know while telling me the story?" Paul asks.

Jacob smiles and nods in agreement.

"I didn't just hear it, I felt it, and I saw it playing like a movie in my mind as you spoke." Paul states while rubbing his forehead.

"A simple telepathic trick, it explains things easier," Jacob replies.

Paul watches as his host rises to his feet and walks to the door of the wooden cabin they are in.

a fresh breeze blows in from outside as Jacob stands to lean on the door frame looking out into the world beyond, Paul's mind continues to wont to know more about this man.

"How long were you gone, I mean, in the other realm?"

"Oh, around ten years or so, but back here around seventy years had passed, at any rate long enough for everyone and everything I had known to be gone," Jacob replies without turning away from the open door.

Paul rose to his feet and walked closer to Jacob before speaking again.

"I'm sorry Jacob," Paul says with a heavy heart.

"Why?" Jacob replies.

"I know what it's like to be alone, and you have been alone a long time, losing everyone around you in one way or another."

Jacob returns to his seat in front of the fire.

"I wasn't always alone." Jacob smiles looking into the flames as he continues his story.

******

Travelling the world over Jacob marvels at some of the new technologies, but despairs hits him at the suffering in third world countries, cultures have grown and diminished the world was once again filled with suffering, we are losing Jacob thinks to himself.

Encountering Unnatural in all countries some good and some evil Jacob deals with them as he has been taught, sometimes staying with the helpful and learning a few things about the world around him from these unnatural.

Finally, after a few years Jacob realizes one country seems to be amassing all the world's attention, America houses one of the biggest populations and it seems likely as they are one of the world's superpowers that's where the remaining sentinels if any would be.

Sometime later Jacob arrives in LA, the city of angels he heard it called, Jacob was amused by its nickname, and maybe the city of the damned he thought to himself.

Although Jacob had visited America in his search for the sentinels, he was always amazed at the depth of change in his short time back on earth.

Governments were full of petty squabbles, fighting for bits of power over one another, wars everywhere, hunger and suffering in other countries plagued on, the environment was damaged possibly forever.

How did things go from one extreme to the other Jacob thought as he walked through busy streets from city to city, state to state, country to country.

Walking through the busy streets of LA Jacobs hunger returned his attention to the fact he hadn't eaten in days.

It wasn't long before Jacob found a local diner, finding a windowed seat he sat and looked at the menu.

A sudden embarrassing feeling crept on Jacob as he soon realized he had little or no money, settling instead just for something hot inside he ordered a cup of coffee and just relaxed listening to the troubles of the world from the commuters of the diner.

The sudden peace was shattered by screaming and shouting, three men armed with modern shotguns burst into the diner, one darted for the till one stayed by the door and the other took the waitress as a hostage screaming at the other punters of the diner to lay face down on the floor.

The gunman at the till was screaming at the waitress behind the desk to fill his bag with cash as he was quickly looking around for signs of opposition, the one by the door was the calmest, he stood gun pointed at the ceiling looking both in and out the door.

The gunman holding the other waitress was dragging her around with him, as a shield and screaming at the rest of us to stay face down on the floor.

A deep sigh and flash of anger flared within Jacob before lowering himself to the floor, looking each gunman over, in turn, weighing them up and thinking tactics Jacobs's attention then lowers to people on the floor.

Both men and women were crying and shaking with fear, Jacob reached out to a woman and took her hand, clearly panicked she flinched before allowing her hand to be taken.

"It's alright, calm down, it will be alright."

Jacob lets his mind slip a little telepathic control into her mind easing her fright.

The gunman holding the waitress as a shield saw Jacob trying to calm the panicked woman on the floor, walking over he dragged the screaming woman with him and stood in front of Jacob lowering the barrel of the gun to his head.

Jacob looked up at the armed man directly into his eyes making sure the man knew he wasn't afraid.

"What the hell are stirring at buddy?" the gunman said.

The man trying to affirm his power overall in the room stood protected behind the waitress, unable for Jacob to reach with normal means.

"You gonna try and be some kinda hero, eh?"

"No, I was just wondering, do you even have the stomach to fire that thing?" Jacob replied in a cocky tone.

The man's cocky smile suddenly dropped as he looked at Jacob in surprise.

"Shut up! You're gonna get us all killed." the former hysterical woman on the floor said.

The gunman now filled with anger that a mere unarmed man has the balls to stand up to him pushes the waitress he held hostage aside and cocks his shotgun pointing it back to Jacobs's head, standing in an open but cocky stance.

A quick smile creeps on Jacobs's face as his ploy to clear the innocent woman from harm's way has worked, with split-second thinking and timing Jacob reaches up with his left hand taking the end of the gun and pointing it away from him into a safe position.

The reactions from the gunman although amazingly slower than Jacobs instantly takes over and fires the weapon, the blast smashes into the very seat Jacob was sat in before this began. The shot echoes through the diner, before the gunman can react again Jacob spins his left leg up slightly and smashes it into the legs of his attacker.

The gunman's legs knocked from under him starts to fall shoulders first towards the floor, continuing to turn in the direction of his first kick Jacob brings his now free right leg up and to bear on the falling gunman.

Slamming hard into the ribs of the gunman his body fails to hit the floor as expected but hurls out through the glass window landing in an unconscious heap covered in broken glass.

The whole attack smooth as if practised in a fine dance happened with such speed it was as if the gunman was moving and falling in slow motion while Jacob moved freely.

The gunman at the till turns his attention to bear on the sound of the commotion, Jacob realizes he cannot use his abilities here in public and has to run the distance at normal speed.

Taking the risk Jacob allows the two gunmen to see him moving to take the risk from the innocents on the floor, he quickly moves to cover as both men open fire into the diner.

Seconds later the till gunman is screaming at his weapon as he out of ammo.

Wasting no time Jacob acts, emerging from cover and hurtling towards the gunman.

Knocking the weapon easily aside with his right hand he grabs the man's head and rams it into the till he was trying to rob, knocking him unconscious instantly.

A little added extra strength was added to the attack, to make sure the gunman remembered the scar he would now have on his forehead, would remind him to stay away from an armed robbery in the future.

Turning to the last gunman Jacob was filled with anger, the man had adapted quickly and took a hostage of his own.

The same waitress Jacob had previously tried to calm was now wrapped up in the gunman's arms with a large shotgun pointed at her head.

Realizing the bad position he was in Jacob was growing angry he could not use his abilities here, the gunman smiles cockily in the comfort he now has power over the situation again.

"Yeah boy! Now, what the hell are you gonna do?"

Jacob raises his arms in a surrender position and slowly walks from behind the counter.

"Let the woman go," Jacob says firmly.

"NA! The hell with that man, am gonna keep the bitch, just in case eh."

Lowering his head he licks the waitress's neck up to her face, the poor woman cringes and cry's as he does so, never taking his eyes from Jacob in torment he smiles as he can see the anger and hatred flare within him.

Slowly walking towards the gunman Jacob festers to get hold of the man, quickly reacting as Jacob starts to approach the man suddenly returns the gun to the woman's head.

"BACK OFF! Or this bitch's head gonna be part of the stew over there."

Stopping dead in his tracks Jacobs's anger grows.

"OK tough guy am back, just let the woman go."

Thinking of possibilities Jacob realizes he has to use his ability's or this man will getaway, and the woman will be dead.

Reaching out with his mind Jacob forces the door behind the gunman to open slightly then slam shut suddenly, the gunman jumps into action throwing the woman aside and spins round shotgun ready to blow a hole into whomever just walked in the door.

The man quickly realizes there is no one there and returns his gun to bear on the helpless woman, suddenly taken back at the sight of Jacob stood not six inches from him looking him in the eye.

"How the Fu…?"

Before he could finish his question Jacob grabs the top of the gun with his right hand pulling him forward slightly then sent it flying back into his face at speed, the long barrel slams into his head hard.

Dazed, and hurt the man staggers back releasing the weapon, quickly gathering his sense trying to see straight he swings a punch at Jacob.

With rapid speed Jacob parries the punch with his right arm and returns the attack with a left uppercut straight to the man's chin, flying through the air the man was unconscious before smashing through the door and landing on the hood of a parked car outside.

Stepping outside the now broken door, the waitress staggered slightly, looking first to the unconscious man on the car then the other two, in turn, she turns her gaze to Jacob.

"Are you OK?" Jacob asks.

Without warning, she flings herself at him slinging her arms around him and hugging him as her life depended on it.

"Thank you, ow god thank you," she said when crying would allow.

A Hugh overweight middle-aged man emerges from the diner a little disorientated and confused he turns to see the woman hugging Jacob, dressed in chef's attire and holding one of the shotguns at the top of the barrel he nods his head in agreement and pats Jacob on the back.

Jacob nods and smiles trying not to look uncomfortable still being hugged by the very grateful waitress, the other people in the dinner rise from the floor cautiously and shaken.

The sound of sirens could be heard in the distance as more people emerge out of the diner.

"It's OK miss, it's over now," Jacob says to the hugging woman.

Slowly lifting her head from Jacobs's chest still crying she looks around to see the others still in shock the same as her.

A few moments later the police arrive, arresting the gunman and questioning everyone, a few little telepathic slips allow Jacob to explain his antique sword, and why he is not needed down at the station for more questioning.

Hours later the sun has gone down and the cold breeze leaks into the broken windows and doors, Jacob helps the large chef put up boards and nail them in place, till they can be replaced by repairmen later.

The customers and waitress all drift away one by one, all thanking Jacob for his help and offer if there is anything he needs in return before leaving, his telepathic abilities allow him to see they were genuine in there thanks alone not the offers they gave.

As the two men work to patch up the holes in the windows and doors, Jacobs mind wonders, helping the people here felt good, better than any of his achievements in training.

Realizing this was his calling, he would not just protect humanity from the unnatural, but from the darkness within humanity own heart.

With the door and windows fitted with temporary wooden boards, Jacobs returns to his belongings, putting on his coat the waitress and large chef look on with admiration, turning to the two Jacob places his pack on his pack.

"Am sorry again for the window and door, I don't have anything to help pay for it either am afraid." Jacob states.

"It's fine honestly, doors and windows can be replaced, people Cant." the waitress replied smiling.

With a quick nod, Jacob turns to leave.

"Wait!" the chef says loudly.

Jacob stops and turns to the two, the chef smiles and moves towards Jacob holding his kitchen towel in hand.

"At least let me cook you something, you been here for hours with the police and then helping with the repairs, it's the least we could do."

Both the waitress and chef alike were genuine in the offer, their mood elevated when Jacob accepted their invitation.

Jacobs hope in humankind was kindled, he had found two good people surrounded by a world of suffering, his mood improved as he sat at the bar lowering his pack to the chair beside him. The waitress rushed around the other side and poured fresh hot coffee for him with a huge smile on her face.

"What would you like dear? Anything on the menu, it's on us." the waitress said.

"Anything is fine to thank you,"

A loud snigger came from the open kitchen behind the waitress, the large chef lifted his head looking to Jacob.

"Typical Brit, full of pleases and thank you's, no need to stand of ceremony here boy, this here is our way to say thank you."

"You recognized my accent, you know many British?" Jacob replied.

"Am an army brat, family all military, my old man was stationed in England just after world war two, made a few friends over there a long time ago?"

Jacobs's heart sank once more, his mind flashed back to the time he was in the army, the loss of his friends, the pain and suffering of those times in the trench and a sudden realization that horror had repeated itself.

Jacob realized he knew next to nothing about the world since he left it in during world war one, he decided there and then when the opportunity arose he would study the history and state of the world.

"So what brings you to the states?" the chef asked.

"Err, just travelling, taking in the sights," Jacob says as he snaps back from his horrid memories.

"Well there plenty to see over here, but something tells me you're looking for something particular"

The waitress turns to the chef with a look on her face to warn him to stop prying into their guests business, Jacob smiles at them both.

"Maybe, yea, am trying to find some old friends I lost touch with a while ago."

The chef smiles and looks to Jacobs's meal.

"Am Marie, that's my husband frank." the waitress continued.

"Jacob," he replied.

"It's getting pretty late Jacob, you got a place to stay tonight?" she asked.

"No, not really, I normally just find somewhere on the road," Jacob answered while looking at the now dark sky outside.

A sudden flurry of rain opened up and soaked the city outside, Jacob looked on in disapproval shaking his head and then return to his coffee.

"Ow no, not tonight you don't, we have a small apartment next to the cellar here, you're gonna stay there tonight, and for as long as you need." Marie's tone and expression gave Jacob the feeling this was not open for discussion.

"I don't want to be a problem." Jacob states.

"Better just do as your told Jacob, she gets real cranky if try to argue with her." Frank interrupted.

Jacob eats well that night, feasting on a full English roast, as best as frank could remember. Walking round to the back of the diner to the cellar door and then into the small apartment Jacob was pleased to have a roof over his head for a change, along with a real bed.

The following months seemed to fly past in the blink of an eye, both Marie and frank became like family, the diner provided a bit of income as he helped out with chores, and the apartment below became a new home.

The apartment although only a small place comprised of a bathroom, kitchen, bedroom and dining room, Jacob spent most of his time here studying.

Many hours were spent reading about the world he left behind when he was taken to the school realm, the first and second world wars, the technologies developed, medical wonders, and a man on the moon.

Jacob spent time in the diner helping Marie and Frank, in payment for food and lodging, even learning a few recipes from Frank.

During this time Jacob would use his telepathic abilities to listen to conversations and thoughts of the customers, learning first-hand about the world around him now.

Many thoughts and theories past his mind's eye, many thoughts on greed and corruption, it dawned on Jacob that to protect mankind from both unnatural and itself was going to be a never-ending struggle.

During the long nights, Jacob wandered the streets of L.A. Doing what he could to help, a subtle telepathic imprint here and there, changed a corrupted bought and paid for judge to suddenly re-evaluate his positions, a sudden burst of speed and nimble hands, left a would-be armed robber holding nothing but air pointing to a cashier behind a counter.

The city papers started printing stories of strange blurs caught on cameras, of the robbed stores and banks, city law enforcement has given strange anonymous tips to drug locations and there dealers.

Armed gangs and even stolen goods were sometimes, dropped on the police doorstep by truck or stolen car, the men unconscious or bound in some way, leaving a note and photo evidence of their wrongdoing.

It wasn't long before the city was alive with rumours of some kinda vigilante on the prowl, no sooner was Jacob enjoying his new line of work and feeling he was making a difference it was swept from him.

Merely days went past and criminals were back on the streets doing what they do best, corruption seeped back into the system wearing a different face, it soon became apparent no matter what he did Jacob would never free the world from the devils grasp, until he could start at the top of the corruption and work his way down.

Following his upset he turned his attention to the law itself, he must understand it if he is to fix it he thought to himself, the local library was open the following day and allowed Jacob to study this strange set of rules.

Hours past, his mind absorbing almost every page as his mental clarity produced a photographic memory, his attention suddenly shifted.

His mind flashed back to the day on the battlefield, the devourer, his friends, the energy inside swirled, sending a shiver straight up Jacobs's spine, sudden returning his mind under his control he turned to try and find what he had sensed.

The library that day was pretty quiet, only a few people remind inside as Jacob walked around the place looking for the unnatural he had sensed, examining every person he came across, he soon found his target.

Located down one of the aisles pushing a trolley of books placing them back into the shelves in proper place stood a human-looking male, he was dressed in a brown monks robe, his tall thin frame was well hidden within his garb.

Jacob slowly started walking towards him trying to recognize his species, the monk stopped suddenly as if he had suddenly felt something stir within, he turned slowly to face Jacob.

The monk's face was mostly hidden by his hood, as he turns his attention to Jacob he slowly lowered the hood to reveal a pale white slim face, his eyes were huge as was the iris and instead of a circular pupil, his were cat-like.

"Drakeion," Jacob spoke allowed.

The monk stood looking at Jacob a worried look, and an uneasy feeling crept from him, Jacob stopped moving and raised his arms in showing him he wasn't armed trying to put the creature at ease.

"Easy, am not going to hurt you," Jacob spoke in fluent Drakeion.

The monk let slip a smile at the sound of his native language confirming the man approaching him was not a threat, his sudden relief swept over Jacob.

"You are a sentinel?" the monk asked.

"Yes," Jacob replied returning the smile as he slowly started to approach.

"I thought you to be a hunter, as the coloured man."

"A hunter? The coloured man?" Jacob asked.

"He..."

The monk stopped abruptly as both he and Jacob suddenly felt another presence, this felt different, a presence almost like that of another sentinel but not as refined, raw almost.

A loud bang echoed through the library as the two large wooden doors slammed shut, Jacob and the monk turned to the door to see a large black man dressed in leather trench coat smoking a large cigar.

His bold head revealed scars on his face and atop his head, his huge frame made it clear he is in peak physical condition possibly better from the feelings Jacob gets from him.

The man looked straight at the monk and let slip a cocky smile, suddenly his pace quickened as he marched toward him, the monk looked back to Jacob before he bolts down the aisle towards an emergency exit.

The dark man unaware of Jacobs's presence chases after the monk, like an eager predator closing in on his prey.

Jacob quickly followed the two, running a little further back from the large black man Jacob scanned him mentally, his mind was closed off as if he was trained to resist mental probes.

Jacob continued to follow behind and opted to watch as the dark man pursues his prey, the monk increased his speed to that of a world champion sprinter, followed still by the large leather-clad man, and keeping pace.

The three men hurdled through shops and houses, street after street they ran until the monk decided to go to high ground, bursting into a hotel he reached the stairs and started to climb at an even faster pace.

The dark man reached the stairs and stopped leaning on the railings for support as he catches his breath and looked to the monk currently hurtling up the stairs, with a grunt and burst of strength he peruses his prey.

Jacob reaches the stairs mere seconds later, looking up at the pair he decides he has to stop this before someone gets hurt, wiping the fatigue from his body he surges his bioenergy to life energizing his body.

Both the monk and the dark man suddenly stop in their tracks and look down to the sudden sense of power below.

The dark man looks down at Jacob.

"What the fuck?" he whispers to himself.

With the last glace Jacob hurls up the stairs, the dark man refuses to let go and pushes himself beyond normal human levels after his prey.

Reaching the top of the hotel building some ten or twelve floors up the dark man kicks open the door to the roof access and rushes out, not paying attention to his instincts and feelings he is suddenly struck in the head by a large metal bar.

The monk laid in wait, with a perfect hit to his pursuers head, dropping his weapon he ran on across the roofing content that his attacker will remain on the floor for a few hours.

Seconds later Jacob emerges from the same doorway, stopping in his tracks he looks to the man on the ground unconscious, with a glance Jacob watches as the monk disappears from the site across the rooftop.

Jacob bends down and starts to examine the fallen man, reaching out with his mind he senses for injuries, other than the large cut on his head.

A sudden shock hits Jacob as he scans up to his head and senses he is conscious and playing possum.

The fact is reaffirmed by a cold steel pistol of some sort placed under Jacobs's chin,

"Don't move freak." a deep husky voice speaks.

Jacob looks down to the man and lifts his arms in a surrender position.

"Where did it go?" the dark man demanded.

"Where did what go?" Jacob replied.

"Don't toy with me boy, that thing would have ripped you a new one given half a second."

The man pushed Jacobs head up with his gun and rose to his feet as if nothing had happened to him.

The man kept his gun posed on Jacob as he looked around the roof for his prey, Jacob reached out with his feelings and found the monk hiding on a small platform just off the side of the building used for cleaning windows.

The man lowers his gaze for a second as if listening or trying to sense for his prey.

Walking around the roof while still keeping his gun trained on Jacob he finally walked towards the edge of the building and finds the monk cowering on the platform below.

Once again the cocky smile returned on the dark man's face, keeping his pistol aimed at Jacob he pulls a large shotgun with a laser sight from within his trench coat and takes aim at the monk.

"Nice run freak, you would have been a good athlete, if you were born on this world."

Jacob listens to comments and realizes this man knows of the unnatural, he can use abilities not normally known to the untrained, there is more to this man meets the eye.

The monk closes his eyes and accepts his fate, the dark man starts to pull on the trigger but is foiled at the last second.

Jacobs boot comes from out of nowhere and kicks the shotgun aside.

The round bursts into the hotel roof leaving a smouldering burnt hole, the dark man drops his weapons and grabs Jacob with both hands lifting him in the air with ease.

"What the hell is wrong with you boy, that thing don't belong here." the dark man shouts.

Throwing Jacob down hard to the floor some few feet away he reaches for his weapon again, the monk climbs to the top of the roof and stands on the edge.

"I won't let you kill him, he's an innocent being, a monk for god sake." Jacob states.

The dark man looks back to the monk and shakes his head and starts to aim once again.

Jacob rushes to the man pulling the barrel away from its target and lifting it into the air with his left hand and slams his right into an open hand strike to the man's stomach knocking him back and down the floor.

Jacob threw the weapon aside and stood before the dark man on the floor.

"My name is Jacob Rawn, I know of the unnatural like you, am a sentinel, if that means anything to you."

The dark man looks to Jacob with a little shock on his face before climbing to his feet and looking down into Jacobs's eyes.

"Well, I'll be, a sentinel here in LA."

"Yes I am, and I will not let you destroy an innocent."

Once again the dark man turned his gaze to the monk stood motionless on the side of the build, held in his hand a wooden cross as if he was praying, once again he shook his head as if disagreeing himself.

"It don't belong here Rawn, and frankly neither do you."

Without warning the man draws another pistol from his left side under his trench coat and aims the monk, Jacobs training and instincts take over.

Jacob moved at lightning speed, Taking the weapon arm in his left hand he steps in and round going back to back with the dark man, Jacob pulls his arm around and in front of him keeping the weapon barrel away at all times.

The speed at which Jacob moves makes the tall leather-clad stranger look like he is in freeze-frame as Jacob moves normally, the man's body follows the pull of his arm round to face Jacob, he steps in right arm up and over the man's chest like a clothesline and brings it crashing down to the floor.

The man hits the floor with a loud crash the air knocked from his lungs as he crashed down, Jacob turns to the monk and smiles as he nods for him to leave.

"I'll find you again freak." the dark man's voice emanate from behind Jacob.

Jacob spins round to see the man stood holding his chest a smirk on his face, as shock fills him.

"Time for some sweat and bad breath punk." the man states.

The two men erupt into combat, punches and kicks emerge from nowhere at lightning-fast speeds, Jacobs training takes over and soon has the upper hand as multiple strikes land hard on vital striking zones on the man.

Kidneys, liver, knees, nose and eyes all struck with precision make the man withdraw to compose for a second, shaking off the effects as if he had an off switch Jacob watches and realizes the man has had some training in the same physical techniques as himself.

A large smirk creeps on the man's face as he slowly removes his long leather trench coat, the mans rippled muscle structure is complemented by a host of webbing belts holding two more pistols a large knife up his back and a large broadsword laid within the trench coat.

Quickly loosening his shoulders and neck the man smiles and lowers himself into a fighting position, and gestures for Jacob to attack, removing his hoody top and throwing it aside Jacob also lowers into a ready position.

"Please stop, there is no more need for violence, please not for Me." the suddenly appeared monk states as he jumped between the two men.

The large man suddenly looks in anger at the monk.

"It ain't bout you no more scumbag, you just got yourself an extension on life now get!" the man shouts and gestures for him to scram.

The monk looked to Jacob with a look of sorrow as he expected him to be beaten.

The man suddenly grabbed him by the arms and starts to push him away with a swift boot up the ass to help him along.

"Scram, I'll see you soon enough."

Without another second the man charged in, fists were flying back and forth, kicks were thrown and blocked, Jacob increased his strength to compensate for the man's strength along with his speed which his attack seemed to be increasing steadily.

Again Jacob had the upper hand his combat training was paying off as strikes rippled through the man, relaxing slightly and to soon Jacob was suddenly surprised by a sudden burst of speed and increased strength smashing through his defence and into his stomach with a huge size 12 boot in the ribs.

Landing some three of four feet away Jacob quickly jumps to his feet and allows his healing abilities to take over, the man charges in again both men increase their strength and speed to human limits and beyond.

Jacob senses the fatigue building in his attacker and the power he is using is quickly draining, deciding to bring this battle to end Jacob empowers himself further to the height of his power.

Again and again, Jacob hit the man each hit would smash through brick walls with ease or bend steel bars as they struck but yet this man stood, blood emerged from his mouth and cuts on his face left by Jacobs attack.

Finally, minutes later the man's power faded, he's fatigue had taken over, barely able to move under the pain and injuries Jacob had given him.

Again Jacob attacked but with lower speed and power, with a shock to Jacob the man parried and changed tactics, opting instead for his natural strength to carry him through the fight.

Slipping a right cross from Jacob he reached under his arm and round his upper body and lifted him into the air and over his head, a perfect wrestling suplex smashed Jacob through the floor into the room below.

The room below was an empty storage unit, jumping down to continue the fight the man grabbed Jacob from the floor and threw him into the wall, followed by a huge side kick knocking him through the wall into the next room.

Shaking off the pain and injuries Jacob waited for the strong grasp of his attacker to take hold, the large hands grabbed Jacob neck but didn't hold on for long.

Knocking the arm aside with his right hand Jacob launches his left hand into the lower ribs of the dark man smashing at least three, with his right arm still held up in a guard he lifts the elbow swiftly into the chin of his attacker.

Wasting no time Jacob continues his attack lifting his left leg into a perfect roundhouse kick to the head sending the man flying back through the wall back into the cleaning unit.

Following holding his wounded ribs Jacobs looks for his attacker and finds him climbing to his feet, both men look at each other and are unwilling to give in, blood pours from wounds bruises pulse with pain and bones rattle as they move but still they fight on. Slow punches and kicks with huge amounts of effort attack on striking their target with little or no defence on either side, the battle come to a sudden stop as the pair both attack and strike, knocking each down once more.

Gasping for breath both men try and hold themselves in one piece, lying spread out on the floor.

Jacobs's body suddenly pulses to life, broken bones and injuries rapidly mend as his energy levels return, still not fully healed but more than capable of continuing.

Looking up to face the hole in the ceiling that he came through while his attacker lays out on some boxes to his left looking at Jacob and holding his ribs.

"Ah man, you fight like a rhino demon, hit like a sucker too." the husky deep voice rasps.

"Thanks, I think, you're not too bad yourself," Jacob replies as breath allows, slowly climbing to his knees.

Jacobs body starts to repair itself, a few bones suddenly snap back into place allowing him easier breathing and movement, Jacob decides to keep up the act of his serve injuries just in case.

Both men try to climb to the feet and wince in pain as they do, they stand looking at each other and try to ready for another round, the battle is interrupted by a small lump of roof cement falling from the ceiling onto the man's head.

The lump the size of a tennis ball does no damage but is enough to make the man grunt and look up, as his gaze lifts he struggles to find balance and falls back into the boxes.

Jacob begins to snigger and laugh but is in too much pain to do so as he falls to his knees holding his wounds and trying to snigger in the interim.

Both men look to each other and seem to come to an unspoken truce. The piece is suddenly broken as the sky's up ahead erupts into a flurry of dark rain.

Both men start to laugh at their current situation both in agony and unable to move in the rain.

The laughter grew as their bodies ached for them to stop but laugh they did still.

"Typical, my target gets away, I get my ass kicked and it pisses down, what a night!" the man rasps.

"What's your name?" Jacobs asked between laughs.

"Steels, Steels Jackson," he replied between giggles of laughter.

"Pleased to meet you Steels."

"You to Jacob."

"Are we done?" Steels asked slowly climbing to his feet holding his wounds.

"God I hope so," Jacob replied.

Helping each other to their feet they collected their things from the roof and tried to dust off.

"You hungry, I ain't ate all day, and I heal quicker on a full stomach." Steels asked.

"I know a nice place, I live there too."

"That'll do."

Both Jacob and Steels walked through the dark wet streets limping and winching in pain, Jacobs's wounds healing quicker allow him to help Steels carry himself to the diner.

Passers-by freaked at the sight of these two weary combatants walking with each other, covered in bruises and cuts, blood still soaked in their clothes.

By the time both men reach Jacobs diner, the blood had washed away from their faces leaving them only bruised and battered.

As they both walked in Marie screamed and rushed to Jacob holding his face and looking at his cuts, blacked eyes and broken nose, like a mother checking over her son that's been in a fight.

Frank came running out of the kitchen with a huge carving knife as if expecting trouble, steels reacted in kind and pulled out one of his pistols and took aim.

"Back off tubby, or ill pop you and watch you fly all over this place as the fat gas releases."

Jacob quickly lowers steels gun and laughs it off as a joke, looking to steels and sternly gestures for him to put the gun away.

"What, sucker comes out with a big ass carver." steels says to Jacob cockily, placing his gun away.

"These are family steels, why don't you go sit down and ill order us something eh," Jacob states with a smile and gestures to the seats.

"Family or no, sucker comes at me with a blade I'll go with a gun, problem solved." Steels mutter to himself as he limps to one of the seats away from everyone.

Jacobs calms over the situation with Marie and Frank and joins steels at one of the tables.

Jacobs major wounds were almost healed by the time he sat down but he noticed steels was clearly in a lot of pain and still struggled with his breathing.

"So where did you get your training steels?" Jacobs asks.

"Thought we came to eat man? Steels replies.

Jacobs sits in silence with a stern look on his face at steels expecting an answer.

"I was recruited by a guy called Simon's, john Simon's, bout eight years ago."

"Recruited?" Jacob asked.

"Yea, recruited, he found me, trained me, I whooped ass." steels replied.

"I never knew there was anything other than my order in the realm protecting mankind," Jacob states trying to search his memories.

Steels light a huge cigar and take a deep breath of the smoke, letting out a large sigh and cloud of smoke his lungs are almost repaired.

"Yea we hunters protect mankind, by killing those freaks, not holding hands with them, like you sentinels." steels states.

"So tell me about you JA, you train at the school realm dint ya?"

"Yes, I was trained by master Takami and Shakarian in the school realm, I was there for ten years or more." Steels suddenly cough on his cigar.

"You trained under that jap for ten years?" steels asked.

"Yea, why how long did your training take?" Jacob replied.

"Not that damn long, ha, you got hustled JA."

"Ya old man Simon's told me about them, and the little school, said Takami was a stubborn son of a bitch and a misguided fool."

"He was stubborn at times, but not misguided, he trusted some of the unnatural like the Drakeions, he doesn't trust them blindly."

Steels take another large puff on his cigar and let out several loud coughs as his lungs seem to complain to both injury and smoke.

"Simon's trained us in a warehouse in New York took bout three to four years, and he told us all unnatural are evil and to be destroyed, all of them."

"Not all of them are evil or killer's steels, the monk tonight was an innocent I couldn't let you kill him, he's heart was good."

Steels sniggers.

"You use your Jedi mind trick crap on him eh?"

"My what?" Jacob replied.

"You know star wars, Jedi's special powers and shit, mind tricks?" Steel's comments fell on deaf ears.

Gesturing for Jacob to forget it and carry on with their other discussion, Steels' thinks it best to forget the jokes.

"Yes, I read his mind, his memories, he's never taken any life not even in his realm."

"Yea Simon's never taught us any of that mambo jumbo crap, just the useful stuff, like the arts of combat, healing, and how to turn our bodies into effective killing machines."

"That monk was a Drakeion, the same race that came to our realm centuries ago and taught us those very useful arts, to defend ourselves, and remain to teach us to this day." Jacob states.

Steels fall quiet and seem to contemplate what Jacob has just said.

"That mental training would come in useful for you, but you need to understand your prey, take my word for it, my friend, there not all evil."

"You may be right, you might be wrong, guess we'll see won't we." steels states.

"You better not use that Jedi shit on me JA or we gonna go for round three, you hear me?"

"What is a Jedi?" Jacobs asks a little bewildered as steels keep referring him to one, Steel's just shakes his head in disbelief but remains quiet.

Both men sit quietly for a few moments till their food arrives, tucking in they both continue their conversation

Chapter 8

The long road ahead

Several months had passed since Steels and Jacob fought on the roof, during that time the two friends got to know each other well.

Together they agreed to help each other in their mission to protect humanity, strength in numbers so they told themselves, in truth they needed each other's company more than either one would admit.

Steels would visit every day to the diner, he and frank grew close, they would argue constantly about anything, the two would look like they were going to tear each other apart then laugh uncontrollably all of a sudden.

During the nights both Jacob and Steels would go out on Patrol, Steels had also agreed to help Jacob stop the crime and corruption in the city, a lost course if you asked Steels but he humoured Jacob, and any excuse to let Betty his trusty shotgun lose always made him smile.

Night after night they would venture out into the dark, and each evening they return to Jacobs's humble abode satisfied they had done some good in the world, Even Steels began to like the work they were doing.

During those nights the two saw humanity at its best, and it's worse, but still, they would struggle on, for any life, any soul is worth saving if possible Jacob would drill into steels.

The crime rate dropped dramatically in those months, all manner of crimes were all turning up with similar evidence, descriptions of blurred figures knocking people senseless or weaponless.

The police were at a loss, no forensic evidence were found at any of the incidents, and only blurred imagery if any showed up even on time-lapsed cameras, the police decided amongst themselves to just be great full for their avenging angels they called them.

The police came up with the name when two police officers were saved from going over a cliff thanks to a bunch of armed thugs trapped them in their car and started to push the car over.

Out of nowhere came two figures one black one white, the largest black figure landed in front of the car and stopped it with his bare hands from moving any further forward, the white one landed behind the car and quickly made thugs unconscious in the blink of an eye, with no physical injuries on the thugs.

The large black angel pushed the car back while remaining hidden in the shadows as if they were clinging to him, the white one appeared by their side with a quick slash of silver light their bonds were cut and they were free.

Jumping out the car to thank their guardian angels they were gone, only their handy work of unconscious thugs and the stumped police officers remained.

The time the two spent together allowed them time to train, they would spar for hours and try and help each other in ways the other seemed to be lacking in.

Steel was both naturally stronger and when empowered with bio-energy, he was the strongest thing Jacob had ever encountered, surpassing his abilities.

Jacob taught Steels how to meditate and regulate his energies allowing him to hold on to his empowered state for longer, also allowing a calmness Steel had never known before.

Steels in return would try and educate Jacob in the ways of modern weapons and tactics, for a muscle head grunt soldier from the Bronx, steels had such a grasp of military tactics and military history it amazed Jacob.

Steels stole the show when it came to firearms, his arsenal was impressive and he carried a lot of hardware wherever he went.

Steels always carried a pistol under each arm and one on each leg, his shotgun was modified with a laser sight and placed on a sling on his shoulder, his large sword sized kukri went up to his back with the handle at his right hip,

Jacob also trained Steels in better sword techniques with his oversized kukri, although he would never best Jacob with the weapon his skill did improve to make him a competent swordsman, easily ranking at least world national standards.

One night the two were out on patrol, nothing out of the ordinary so it seemed they struggled to find anything to do and opting to sit on a high spot all over the city they would watch and wait.

Jacob enjoyed times like this as it gave them more time to talk, Steels seemed to loosen up when he was out on Patrol, his mind to the job at hand and wasn't paying attention to what was being said.

"Hey Steels, tell me more Bout Simon's, your Teacher," Jacob asked.

"What you want to know?" Steels replied looking through his binoculars out into the distance.

"Well did he ever say how long he's been here, or why he never thought to complete your training?"

"He did complete my training JA, just didn't see the need to baffle my swede with all that mental crap." Steels stated.

Jacob could sense steel starting to take a little bit of interest in the conversation and opted to change subjects, he was always protective of his master and his training.

"OK tell me how you were recruited," Jacob asked.

"I told ya." Steels replied.

"No, you said you would one day, but you haven't told me yet."

"OK, OK." Steels stated while he turned to face Jacob putting down the binoculars.

"Was bout nine years ago now, I was a ranger in the US army, we were on an op, in Afghan."

Steels seem to drift off, locked in harsh memories, his left-hand start clenching making a fist while his right slowly and gently starts rubbing lower left abdomen as if stroking an old wound.

Jacob knows steels is replaying his memories and reliving his pain from those days, same as he does when thinking back to the days with his friends in the trenches back in the war.

"Anyway, we were ambushed by a group of the local militia, I managed to keep them pinned down while my team managed to clear an exit route for us, and I followed when they gave me the signal to follow."

Jacob watches his friend as tears start to well in his eyes.

"I leapt over a metal fence they had gone over before me not a few seconds before, when I got on the other side, they were dead."

Steels stop and wells up clenching his fists he turns away and leans on the small wall surrounding the roof they were on, he looks out into the city below as if looking for relief.

"they were torn to shreds, the thing that did it stood in front of me as if expecting me, a huge bear looking thing standing nearly eight feet with four huge green eyes and claws that looked like long daggers covered in blood and guts from my friends."

"A shapeshifter," Jacob responds.

Steels nod his head in agreement, Jacob can feel steels pain and understands it all too well.

"I ripped into that thing with everything I had, my m4 unloading while I fired a grenade from my launcher into it at almost at point-blank range, I managed to jump back before the blast knocked me through the fence I had jumped, and out into the open courtyard."

Steels rub his abdomen again, the pain comes flushing back to him.

"The militia came running out and surrounded me, my head was pouring blood from shrapnel from the grenade I didn't know where the hell I was, the militia were screaming at me at first till that thing came out and started on them."

Jacob walked up to Steels turning to face him and lean on the wall.

"How did you escape?" Jacob asks.

Steels suddenly smile and look Jacob square in the eye.

"I didn't, I blew that suckers head clean off." Steels replied.

Jacob looks confused at Steels.

"I knew I couldn't pierce its skin with the weapons I had so when it was dealing with the militia, I pulled two grenades from my belt, reloaded one and kept the other at hand and waited for it to come and get me."

Steels sniggered and looked back to Jacob.

"it bounced me around a bit, throwing me through walls and shit, I think it wanted to tender me up a bit before it ate my ass when it had enough it grabbed me and lifted me to start chewing on me."

Jacob listened with amazement as steels now sniggering as he spoke.

"I rammed that grenade in that suckers mouth using the butt of my rifle, I smacked its jaw shut, as I started to fall back as it staggered, and I fired the other grenade at its face."

Steels turned to face Jacob and gestures to the scars on his face and head with a smug grin.

"I woke up a few days later in an army hospital, I was wrapped up like a mummy, and the doc said I was lucky to be alive, I must have been made of steel, hence the name stuck."

The two friends laughed.

"Anyway, I was in the hospital when my man Simon's approached me, offered me a chance at payback at the things that killed my unit, the rest you know."

The night drew on, nothing seemed to be needing their special attention, both the police were in fine form and the rumours of some crazy vigilantes roaming the streets seemed to have the crime rate staying low.

Walking back towards Jacobs's apartment both men discussing the news as steels read in the paper, Jacob stops dead.

Steels turn to look at his friend with a look of bewilderment, Jacob's eyes lowered to the floor his spine-tingling and thoughts and feelings cast back to the dark days on the battlefield and the devourer all those years ago.

Moments later Steels catches on to Jacobs situation, looking to his friend lowering his newspaper he approaches.

"We got company?" Steels ask.

"Yes, something is near, something I have never felt before, it's dark, twisted, and hungry," Jacob replied with a sour look to his face as if tasting the very essence of this creature.

Steels looked around rapidly trying to find Jacobs target, the city street buzzes with cars, buses and people.

Finally snapping out of the still state he was in Jacob looks to his right down yet another alleyway leading into the darkness, the back of the unlit alley gave it a menacing look.

Jacob slowly turned down the alley, Steels follows closely behind scanning both forward and behind, checking for an ambush.

Slowly walking down the alley both men begin to feel a cold, uneasy presence emanating from the darkness before them, steels lift a hand to one of his pistols under his coat to ready himself.

The noise of the city drains away as does the light around the two friends, the alleyway now a dim greyish light seems silent and cold, lifeless.

A low whispering laugh emanates all around them, both men stop in their tracks steels readies himself lowering his posture and draws his pistols, Jacobs remains still, his gaze lowered seems to pierce the darkness locking onto an unseen presence beyond.

"They won't help you here, hunter." the whispering voice remarks to Steels guns.

"Well they sure as hell make me feel better pal, why don't you stop with all this wizard of Oz crap, come out here and well see how helpful they can be huh?"

Jacob remains still never moving his gaze or his senses from the located unseen target in the black.

From the blackness echoes footfalls approaching the two men, a tall slim man dressed in a black suit and wearing black sunglasses emerges.

His sleek black hair gelled back gives his chiselled face a menacing look, his posture confident with arms held behind his back he stands just on the brink of the dim light, his smirk cocky grin does nothing to ease the two friends.

The three men stir at each other, steels continues to look about him waiting for an ambush that doesn't seem to be coming.

"LA's two hunters, I have been wanting to meet you." the cocky man states, in his whispering voice.

"Ah you hear that JA, were famous among the freaks, al send them the number to my fan club." Steels replies while still looking for the ambush.

"You have caused me a good deal of trouble of late." the whisper replies.

"Glad we could be an inconvenience dude." Steels once again replies hastily.

The cocky man's face suddenly drops his smirk and a flash of red eyes slowly gains in brightness through his glasses and then fades once more.

"What are you?" Jacob demands sternly.

"Beyond your understanding human, he replies.

"OK." Steels states.

Suddenly springing to life, Steels turns his two loaded Glock pistols to bear on the man and opens fire, round after round smashes into the black suit of the man shaking him slightly as they hit.

Jacob suddenly was taken back slightly by his friends attack he readies for a return attack.

The pistols click repeatedly as Steels continues to fire even after they have emptied, the man steadies himself and brushes down his suit as if he had gathered dust.

The many holes made by Steels bullets rapidly close leaving no mark not even a crease in the suit, the man looks back to the two men his cocky smile develops into a scream and a face of anger as he charges in, with a black blur of speed.

His eyes bright red shine through the black glasses, his mouth now black with sharp black fangs, and his skin shows black veins under the pale whiteness of his flesh.

Reaching the two friends the man reaches for Steels and Jacob grasping them by their clothes lifting them into the air with ease and throwing them some distance into the walls either side of the alley separating them.

Landing hard first into the walls then falling to the floor below both Steels and Jacob land with a thud.

Jacob is the first to his feet and running back at the now deformed man in the alley, his height had increased and his skin had tinted red slightly his frame had also grown to a muscular powerlifter size.

Unaffected by his new appearance Jacob attacked, both speed and strength would have been enough to smash through concrete walls and yet this creature stands, smiling at his attacker.

Blow after blow crashes into the body of the creature and still, he is unaffected, Steels returns his attention to his attacker after shaking off his slam into the walls.

Reaching into his long leather coat he releases Betty his trusted sawn-off 12 gauge shotgun from its resting place and let's rip.

The creature staggers with each round that is fired into him, once again the wounds seem to close on their own with no blood loss.

Turning to face Steels the creature reaches out with hand and grasps Steels throat through telekinesis, still some distance away the creature lifts Steels into the air choking him without even touching.

Jacob watches for a mere second as he ceases his attack and focuses within, the powerful soul awakens within once more, his bioenergy flares to life rippling through him and out into the world beyond showing as a bright blue glow around his body and filling his eyes.

The creatures attention is suddenly drawn back to Jacob in front of him, a look of bewilderment creeps onto his face removing the snarl he once hard.

"A sentinel." the creature snarls.

Wasting no time Jacob summons all his energy to his hands and slams them both into the upper and lower body of the creature releasing the bio-energy simultaneously.

Steels drop back to the floor gasping for breath, the creature hurls backwards through the wall in the alley to the world beyond, the dim light is now replaced by more natural nightlife and sounds of the city.

Jacob runs to Steels side checking on his friend, Steels gestures he is OK but still unable to speak as he breaths heavily, Jacob runs to the hole in the wall and watches as the now normal looking man leaves the laundrette he was blown into through an elevator heading to the roof.

Jacob springs into action and hurls his body up the stairs next to him after his prey to the roof. Kicking open the roof door smashing the lock to bits Jacob jumps out searching for his target. Finally finding his enemy at the roof's edge smiling back at Jacob waiting for him to approach.

"We thought you all dead sentinel, my master will be pleased I found you." the man says with a now normal voice.

"What master? Who's we? What are you?" Jacobs demands as he approaches slowly.

"You will know soon enough human, my master is coming, you and yours are doomed, this is our world now."

Jacob pulls from his coat his magnificent silver katana and readies himself still slowly walking forwards.

The man's gaze shifts from Jacob to his weapon and drops his grin for a second before returning to Jacob.

"You cannot stop us human, your order is both powerless and weak, the hordes are waiting, and the master comes."

Without warning the man turns and leaps from the roof, Jacob runs to the roof's edge and watches as the body falls towards the concrete below.

The taxis windows are blown out as the roof collapses under the blow of the body smashing into it from some five stores above.

Steels appeared beside Jacobs and nods in agreement at the sight of the bloody mess below, "Discreet." Steels states.

Jacobs turns to Steels and checks him over quickly before his senses are brought to bear back to the body below.

An invisible entity emerges from the body below, the people on the street below are stricken by the body and blood but unaware of the twisted demonic-looking creature pulling itself from the corpse.

The creature stands some eight feet high a twisted muscular build with tinted red skin and black veins, its eyes blood red and mouth black and filled with sharp teeth.

Jacobs looks to Steels who also seems unaware of the new development and then back to the body and watches as it runs off into the night.

The following days were hard for Jacob, searching his memories from his training trying to recognise the species of unnatural he had encountered, although in his gut he thought he knew what it was and feared to admit it.

Training with Steels had increased, Jacob was determined to teach Steels how to sense the unnatural to give him the advantage in a combat situation as well as teaching him more of the mental side of the dragon forms.

Steels mind seemed unable to perform such acts, it seems the teachings he had received in the past that blocked his mind against mental probing and telepathic commands also prevented his mind from grasping such abilities.

No one was more annoyed at this than Steels, although he would never admit to wanting such knowledge even he knew how much it would help him in his fight.

Jacobs mind was focused on the words of his recent encounter, his mind flung back to the conversation of the hordes, and his master is coming, but none stung him more than the words we thought you all dead sentinel.

Steels would sit and watch Jacob training after the ordeal, he cannot help but be in awe as Jacobs seems to grow in strength, confidence, skill and power with each encounter of the unnatural.

Realising the last encounter stirred something in his friend, Jacobs wants to find others like himself, his fellow sentinels, Steels had decided to remain in L.A and carry on the work he and Jacob had started.

Jacob finished his last routine and approached Steels sweating and panting heavily.

"Ready to get started?" Jacob asked forcing a fake smile.

"Not today J." Steels replied.

Jacob looked at his friend as if questioning his decision.

"I know the freak last week got you thinking dude, I know you wanna go find others hoping he was spieling a load of bull, bout them being dead."

Jacobs smile drops as does his gaze, he nods in agreement, unable to say the words out aloud.

"You need to get going." steels states while holding out his hand waiting for Jacob to take it.

Jacob pushes past his friend's hand and closes in for a strong bear-like hug, the old familiar feelings of losing someone and being alone creep back into Jacobs being.

Steels squeeze back and smiles, he too feels the same emotions as Jacob but seems to hide his better, as the two men pull away they let out a large sigh.

"Will you stay in L.A?" Jacob asks.

"Ow hell yea, plenty for me to do here, besides who'll keep Marie from killing frank at the dinner." Steels replies with a smirk.

Jacob sniggers as he dresses into his travelling clothes and packs his old backpack, with a last look around the place he locks the door and gives the key to Steels.

"Tell Marie and Frank I'll miss them, and never forget them."

"They know dude." Steels replied.

"But I'll tell them." he continued.

Jacobs hugs Steels one last time and turns to walk away down the long road into the unknown, refusing to say goodbye Jacob buries those old familiar feelings and marches on.

Steels stood and watches as his friend disappears, once more both men face the unknown alone.

"Stay safe my friend, I hope you find them." steels mutters to himself.

Jacob once again travels the world, continuing his mission given to him by his masters, searching every continent and major city, following rumours of strange happenings wear ever he went he found nothing.

A bad feeling began to work itself into his heart, he was lone out here, knowing the world is too much for him he feels he must return to the school realm and inform his masters to the situation.

Making sure he is alone in the wilderness Jacobs meditates for hours running the ritual he was taught in training to open a porthole to the shadow.

Following his training precisely the whirlpool bursts into being, grabbing his belongings he walks through, the shadow greets him once more, the same old feelings run through as he walks the desolate land.

Travelling from his entry position to the sight of the school realm takes days following only his powerful senses guiding him towards his destination.

Finally emerging at the locating to the school realm Jacobs's eyes widen at the sight, two bodies in the sentinels garb littler the floor.

Running as fast as his legs will carry him he approaches their bodies, both members dead their bodies partially chewed on and both soulless, their eyes plain weight no iris or pupils remain.

Trying to determine when this happened is impossible in the shadow as time does not exist here, Jacob pulls from his pack his fine blade and summons his courage as he runs for the door to the school realm.

The bright light erupts with the strong wind for a brief second before suddenly ending and the school realm appears, Jacobs eyes once more widen this time in horror.

The school realm is ablaze, students scream in agony and run as huge red skin demonic looking figures ravage their flesh and souls, the creature tall at least six or seven feet tall with twisted and muscular bodies, their black eyes looking for their next targets.

Students are struck down by the black short curved stone-like blades or claws, the creatures themselves resemble the invisible creature that threw himself from the roof before himself and Steel's a few years ago in LA.

Jacob watches for a brief moment looking in shock he witnesses students being ripped open, their souls drain as the demonic creatures bend over them drawing the soul from their mouths into themselves.

Without a second to waist Jacobs powers flare to being his bright blue Aura covers both him and his blade, strike after strike he makes, slicing through the massive hordes of enemies.

The creatures take note of a sudden eruption in their blissful slaughter, one man wrapped in his bio-electric energy is cutting a clean path through their army towards the huts on top the hill.

The creatures take exception to this intrusion and run to attack this upstart, Jacobs mind and fury will not be stopped, enemy after an enemy is cut down, some sliced in two others beheaded and their very chests blown open as bright blue Bioenergy rips into them exploding both mind and heart.

Jacob continues to work his way up the hill facing down many enemies in his path, sweat pours from his brow, and his nose releases a small amount of blood showing the strain in his mind.

Jacob refuses to be denied, finally reaching the top of the hill to his masters home he pulls the door from the hinges with but a thought and walks inside his bioenergy strobes out like electricity at the proximity of the door frame.

The slaughter rages on outside Jacob run around the rooms only to be greeted with a mess of books and furniture as the place was the sight of a recent battle.

His anger grows as he turns outside once more, stepping from the hut porch an army of demonic creatures starts to encircle him like insects swarming towards him.

His gaze is suddenly caught by a flash of energy as a porthole is brought into being at the bottom of the school, a large man with long red hair dressed in a suit accompanies a man in a long black trench coat and a black hood.

The man in the hood turns towards Jacob surrounded by the creature's some few hundred feet away, dragging into view the man pulls a beaten and barely conscious master Takami.

The man with red hair gestures to the hooded man, with a single swift motion a blade appears through Takami's chest piercing his heart.

Jacob screams at the sight before him his aura flares in agreement anger festers in him, jolting forward a few steps before realising he is surrounded by maybe a hundred or more foes he stops and looks back to the porthole.

The long red-haired man holds a hand over Takami's body as a small bright white light erupts from his chest into the man's hand, he walks through the porthole a cocky smile on his face, the hooded man turns and bows to Jacob before following.

The porthole closes behind them, Jacob's hands shake with anger his bioenergy flaring like solar flares from the sun, his eyes completely enveloped by the bright blue colour of his aura. The creatures sliver and slowly approach, their black stone like short swords and claws eager for more blood.

Jacob waits patiently as his breath fast and shallow as if the anger is taking up the rest of his lung space he waits for the attack.

Finally, it comes three demons attack from the front, with lightning speed Jacob parries and counters, parries and counters his blade slicing through the creatures either through the heart or beheading as he goes.

As the three lifeless bodies fall to the floor others charge in, Jacob enters a spins charging his soul into his blade, more than he has ever done in the past, remembering the exercise he was taught to perform on the wooden log, sending his bioenergy through the air at a target.

The blade leaves a cut through the air as his spin taking him from left to right, finally finishing the cut in less than a Nanosecond the energy takes flight and grows as it travels.

The pulse from the blade erupts into a massive twenty-foot long arc of pure power striking the front ten or twelve demons, their bodies were flown back as if the wave were a concussion blast from a grenade.

Landing away from the main ground those creatures stuck convulse and tremble in agony as the energy works its way through their systems shorting them out.

Jacob falls to one knee panting, his sword still held out to the side from his last cut, his last attack drained him his bio-energy flares the last time before fading completely, the beasts look on hungry.

"COME AND GET ME!" Jacob shouts.

The creatures oblige, one after another they charge in, and one after another they fall, Jacobs mind Maybe be tired and out of Juice but his body is a highly developed combat instrument. Blow after blow hits Jacob his body complains in the form of pain but his mind pushes those thoughts away. Small and large cuts from claws and weapons now litter Jacobs's body but he fights on as if they are but scratches.

Finally, Jacobs fatigue catches up with him, his body hurls through one of the barracks walls smashing some of the furniture inside under the might of one of the demons.

Trying to shake off the blow and climb to his feet he barely manages to grab his sword as the creature pounces through the same hole and charges him.

Grabbing Jacob by his torn and sliced Trench coat the beast pics him up and slams into the wall trying to strangle him and hold his weapon arm pinned against the wall.

The six-foot creature had Jacob pinned and can choke the life from him comfortably with his strength, the pain suddenly subsides as another burst of light ripples outside.

The creature still holding Jacob looks to the new disturbance, Jacob uses the distraction and uses his last mental energy and pulses a stunning telepathic command to the creature, a simple command.

"Sleep" the creatures grasp let's go dropping Jacob to the floor, landing on his feet he watches in surprise that his command worked, the creature looks drowsy and falls to its knees.

"Who would have thought you had a mind to reach," Jacob states as he thrusts his blade into the creature's heart.

Reaching the window Jacobs's heart lifts, the sight of warriors dressed in black, some already wounded and battle-worn flood through the porthole at the demands.

The cries of battle, not slaughter echo out into the world beyond, more and more still flood through the porthole, Drakeions follow the sentinels into war including a familiar grandmaster.

Jumping from the window Jacob evades the odd attack and darts for his fallen friend, finally reaching his body Jacob lifts him and walks him away from the fight.

Laying him down on the barrack's porch he ignores everything else around him, the old man's soulless eyes look out into the field.

Jacobs's ignorance is one demons gain, a large black blade protrudes through Jacobs's chest glancing his heart, and he screams in agony as the beast lifts him on the blade before flinging his limp body back through the wall into the barracks once more.

Barely able to breathe Jacob can feel the life leaving him, watching his dazed eyes as the creature approaches to claim his prize Jacobs mind sudden takes over, another part of him seems to want more, lifting his upper body to a sitting position Jacob waits for the beast to approach.

The blade still lodged in his chest, the creature reaches for it snarling with content at Jacob, reaching for his arm as the beast latches onto the blade, Jacobs's body suddenly pulses to life with energy once more, his eyes flare pure bright white energy as does his hand.

The creature suddenly screams in pain at the mere touch, his own eyes and heart seem to glow with the same colour, a loud sound like energy building to a climax is heard before the creature's body drops to its knees silent.

Jacob collapses suddenly as the creature now dead body flops on top of him, the pain seems to dull as Jacobs mind slowly starts to drift, blackness and death take him.

***

Pain racks his body, his eyes barely able to open, noises rush back to his ears waking him from his slumber, his mind unable to grasp what's happening he falls unconscious once more.

What seems only moments later the sound of the wind blowing through trees, of birds of some unknown nature sing in what appears to be a blue sun shining light onto this face.

Slowly his eyes open, Jacob is suddenly aware he is alive, looking around the place it resembles one of the medical huts in the school realm but flapping tent above and skies outside alerts him otherwise.

A single bright swirling sun in a white sky shines down, neither of the school realms had just one such sun.

Slowly lifting his upper body he notices the bloody bandages covering his chest and abdomen, the pain pulses through him, ignoring it as he always as he struggles out of bed.

Looking about the room, his heart suddenly drops, more than forty beds filled with students and sentinels alike, some will never heal, some will. Still dressed in his blue jeans and bandages alone he ventures from the infirmary holding his left ribs, walking out into the world, he is surprised at the new sight.

Sentinels and Drakeions walk around fully armed, tents instead of huts range far into the distance, students are out training as they did in the school realm.

Leaning on a crate of supplies Jacob rested for a moment.

"It's not the school, but we're safe for now." A familiar voice states from behind.

Turning to face his old friend and grandmaster, Jacob sits on the crate for support.

"How many...?" Jacob tried to ask.

"We number less than eighty." Shakarian's voice sternly states.

Jacob suddenly feels like his heart has just skipped several beats as the pain of the loss hits him.

Shakarian jumps to his side trying to hold Jacob as he seems to fall due to injury and weight of the loss.

"I thought I lost you too for a moment when I found you." Shakarian's voice said coldly.

"Feels like you did," Jacob replies wincing in pain.

"In truth, we did!" Shakarian's voice interrupts Jacobs's pains as he tries to walk back to the infirmary.

"What?" Jacob asks turning back to his friend.

"You died Jacob!" again his cold voice sternly states.

"That's impossible, am stood right here."

"That blade cut into your heart, almost severed it in two, no sentinel not even my race can heal such a wound." Shakarian states while pointing to Jacob's heart and closing in on his friend.

Jacob looks to his friend a worried look on his face, but the pain is too much and he needs rest, turning back to the infirmary Shakarian helps him to his bed.

"What happened, in the attack how did they find us?" Jacob asks while laid flat out on the bed.

"I wish I knew my friend, but they hit both camps at the same time, I was at the second camp when the attack happened, master Takami was at the first," Shakarian says while looking out at the sentinels and Drakeions.

"I saw you arrive with the remaining sentinel's, I guess you fought them off at your school," Jacob replies.

"Yes, master Takami believed having all our eggs in one basket was too risky, and how right he was, the other school housed the student with further training remember?"

Jacob nods in agreement but then his mind flips back of the attack and the death of master Takami.

"Master Takami?" Jacob suddenly blurts out as he quickly rises sitting look straight at his friend.

Shakarian shakes his head in a saddening gesture that he did not survive.

Jacobs's eyes close as he flops back down to the bed, not caring for the pain he feels from his wound only the one in his heart.

Shakarian walk's to his friend's side placing a hand on his shoulder.

"Am sorry Jacob, he was an incredible man, he would have fought bravely till the end if he could, just as you did, he would be so proud of you and the defence of the school you showed."

Jacob cannot bring himself to speak as the pain he fills wells up.

"Gets some rest, my friend, we have a lot of work to do when you are well." Shakarian states as he leaves his friend in peace.

The following morning Jacob would try and help in the infirmary with the wounded, still wounded and bandaged himself his wounds are healing rapidly, helping as he can he grows to know the remaining sentinels and students.

Merely four days later Jacob rose bright and early in the morning and once more with a trusty walking aid he began to walk the camp, remembering back to the early days when he first arrived he drew comfort from those thoughts.

Walking among the inhabitants of the camp struggling a little with his walking aid every sentinel and student would stop and bow deeply, even the Drakeions would bow showing respect.

Jacob returned their bow with a look of bewilderment on his face, he was no master and yet they are showing their respects, the students who past him would stir in awe at him as if he were some rock star passing by a parade.

Most nights Jacob would return to the barracks tents watching as the students would relax for the night, telling them stories of the world beyond and his struggles, the students were soon joined by the other sentinel's, all would come and listen to his tale.

A week later Jacob rose from his bed, his body seemed to pulse with strength, slowly gripping his hands together he could feel his muscle ripple with power and an eagerness to be tested.

Walking from the infirmary Jacob scuttles with his walking aid to one of the training circles, standing in his blue jeans and bandaged up to his neck he drops his t-shirt and lets his walking aid fall to the side as if a symbol he no longer needs it.

Slowly he lowers himself into a combat position, following his training and ignoring his wounds, he proceeds into an unarmed kata.

His body twists and turns, strikes and blocks are put into play against an invisible foe in his mind, unbeknown to Jacob he has gathered a few observers, looking from the window of the barracks or their assigned tents, both students and sentinel's alike watch on with pride.

All in the camp know who Jacob is, and what he did in the attack, they also heard rumours he was slain trying to save master Takami's body, whether true or not, they all look on him as a hero.

They knew he was sent on a mission to the earth realm and returned at the right moment to help defend the school, they know he stood alone against perhaps a thousand demons and wouldn't give up.

The fact is right now before them they have a new master Takami, a warrior both tried and tested, true to his beliefs and the order, a man who slew demons and fought alone against unbeatable odds.

Shakarian's walks from his tent as his senses alert him to a growing power out in the camp, finding the source of the disturbance he watches from the side, he also feels nothing but pride and respect for this man.

dust from the floor flies into the air under jacobs sweeping leg strikes and swift movements. The air is punctured by percussion blasts reaching out into the distance as Jacobs form dictates. Louder and louder they grow, more power pumped into his flawless moves.

Suddenly Shakarian's gaze is averted as a student merely days from an operation on his arm to save it walks besides Jacob, breaking his concentration Jacob looks to the small woman who approaches.

She takes up position beside him ready to join him in morning exercise, Jacobs's heart swells with pride as a tear reaches his eyes, slowly they start the young woman also holding back tears as her hero has accepted her to train with him when others would not.

Merely a few simple moves are finished before several more students run from the tents and bow to Jacob before taking positions at his side.

Jacob feels honoured as his heart suddenly glows, he cannot help but feel humbled by these brave noble warriors honouring him.

Finally, the rest of the students, whether injured or not rush out to the training area, followed by the sentinels themselves.

The kata is performed in perfect unison, Shakarian looks on tears flow down his cheek as he thinks of his fallen friend master Takami.

"Look, my friend, look what you have created!" he speaks as if Takami were stood there.

Walking from his tent he approaches Jacob at the front of the class, tears also swell in his eyes as he looks to his friend.

Shakarian smiles to him and joins his students in kata, the Drakeions emerge from their slumber and walk down to the camp training area, their senses detecting a massive amount of bioenergy flare into being., watching in shock and awe as the humans have once more risen against the darkness, they are not beaten yet.

Day after day Jacob would be the first one on the training grounds, now wearing his sentinel uniform he would train endlessly with whoever wanted, teaching both fitness, unarmed and armed combat, his evening filled with discussions of the unnatural of what he's fought and teaching new mental disciplines.

Each morning would begin as it did that last day were all would join in morning kata, after a few days even the Drakeions would join him and master Shakarian.

Shakarian felt as if his friend had taken some of master Takami's responsibilities on himself doing as much as he can.

The students flourished under Jacobs's tutorage, their minds were sharp and their wills were strong, Jacobs own skills had improved also weather from his recent death and resurrection or pushing his powers to their limits in battle he was stronger.

The camp was being rebuilt on this new location, from there the second camp would be chosen and the Drakeions would take over training from there, roughly a year had gone since the attack, Jacob was considered to all as the most senior sentinel, even the Drakeions had started to call him master, a point Jacob asked them to stop using over and over.

Jacob and Shakarian would train together constantly as well as training other students, never letting their skills become complacent.

One night the two friends were sparring as normal, their weapons although real would never seriously injure the other should either land a strike.

Sweat poured from Jacob as he continued to spar with his master, Shakarian species could not sweat and was growing slower after a good few hours of sword work.

Both men opting to stop for the evening the two friends leave the training circle laughing and joking with each other, Jacob wipes the sweat from his face with one of his old training tops used for a towel.

Shakarian invite Jacob to his tent for a drink, accepting they both walked the camp, both student and sentinel bowed in respect as they went.

Sitting in the tent looking out the front at the slow moon rise as if watching over the camp the two friends sit at a small desk.

"What's bothering you, Jacob?" Shakarian asks, clearly sensing Jacobs's mood.

"I need to leave master," Jacob replies.

Shakarian's head lowers as he smiles.

"Earth!" he states.

"Yes master, I left only to report back that the other sentinels are gone, I couldn't find them, and since I have been here I have tried to help as best I can but…"

Shakarian rises to his feet drinking from his cup still looking out into the camp.

"I need to do something when I left the realm was a mess, I might be able to make a difference even a small one until some of the other students are ready to join me."

Walking up to his friend looking at him seriously Jacob waits as if he was asking permission.

"What of your duties here, the students and instructors look up to as they did master Takami?"

Jacob sniggers as the comment he feels is well above him.

"I'm no master Takami," Jacob replies.

"Never the less they look to you as you did him, they are moved by you, and your struggles."

"Then I shall lead by example master, let me return to my realm and continue what you and master Takami trained me for, I will do what I can till the others are ready."

Shakarian finishes his drink and looks to his friend placing his hand on his shoulder.

"Very well, I'm sure myself and the other instructors can manage, the others of my people have agreed to stay and help as needed, they too were impressed by what you have done here."

"you're the grandmaster Shakarian, you taught master Takami, am sure with your tutelage the students will flourish, and I'll be in the earth realm waiting for them."

The friends bid each other good night and Jacob returns to the barracks, as he walked in several students rushed in asking him questions and riddles to certain problems, Jacob feels like the big brother.

Talking with the students he beds down for the night, he helps everyone who needs him with one problem or another before bedding down for the evening.

The following morning Jacob was up before the rest of the camp, his gear packed and his dress back to the earth realms clothes he had now mended.

Walking quietly from the barracks he closes the door behind him before walking off the porch to be surprised at an amazing sight before him.

The camp was already awake and formed in front of him, mere seconds later the students in the barracks behinds' him flooded out of the tent and formed around him.

Jacobs's heart sank, his eyes welled up once more, the students and instructors alike would not let him simply slip away without a proper send-off.

A sharp whistle and the students run towards the end of the camp forming a long tunnel waiting for Jacob to pass by, each student reached out and touched Jacob either on the shoulders or shaking his hands.

Some had tears in his eyes as Jacob did, finally, he came to the sentinel's, each one bowed in unison and stayed bowed as they would have for master Takami.

Jacob bows back as the students close in around him, walking on the Drakeions also bow as the sentinels did, Jacobs feels his heart pumping and an overwhelming feeling of respect falls on him.

Swallowing his tears and walking on Jacob finally appears next to the whirlpool of energy in the form of a porthole to the shadow, stood before is Shakarian.

Walking up to his friend Shakarian places a hand on Jacob's shoulder smiling.

"You didn't think they would just let you slip away did you?" Shakarian says.

"I had hoped master, it hurts too much to say goodbye again."

"Well, I'm afraid they insisted." Shakarian adds.

Turning once last time Jacob looks to each student and sentinel remaining, the Drakeions are next and finally, he turns to Shakarian.

"Look after them master, and call if should you need me," Jacob asks.

"Likewise my friend." Shakarian states.

As Jacob steps forwards towards the porthole all burst into a cheer as he marches on.

The sound is soon drowned out as the shadow emerges.

Travelling the distance to the door to the earth realm, Jacob suddenly notices how easy is coping with the wastes of this land, his normal dizziness and the cold feeling never appear.

Finally reaching the door Jacob jumps through, arriving back in the same place he did when he first returned to earth, he stops closes his eyes and takes in the sweet air of his home realm.

The Forrest around him tweets with birds, he can feel life all around him as he did when first appeared all those years ago.

Walking slowly onwards he finds the sun in the sky and feels the warmth on his face, pushing past the feeling he's currently enjoying he emerges from the Forrest and looks down on Tibet from the height of the Himalayas.

chapter 9

Beings of light and dark

New York City, August 12th 2005, this great city pulses with life, its roads rush with vehicles, like blood vessels within a vein, carrying materials and people where needed.

The people walk about the streets like zombies completely unaware of what happens around them unless something out of the ordinary were to occur.

One such occurrence happens in the form of a lone young man struggling to remain in control and sane, he slowly walks through the streets desperately trying to avoid physical contact with any passers-by, causing a commotion as he travels.

This young man rapidly dodging people and waiting for openings to appear in a large group has the look of a mad man on his face, his nervous eyes and expression hide a man struggling to remain in control.

He dashes through the crowds heading home never taking his eyes off the oncoming traffic of people, avoiding all as if his life depended on it.

Finally, the young man makes a break for a small doorway giving him a second of peace away from people, he gathers his senses and takes a breath.

Placing his backpack on the floor in front of him he crouches down and runs his hands through his rough long blonde hair and enjoys a moment of peace.

The masses once again pass by unaware to this man, just the way he likes it, thinking of his route home he takes comfort he's only a block or so away.

"Nearly there, just hold on a little longer." he thinks to himself.

Once again this young man's fears are realised, a familiar pain shoots through his brain, he squints and falls to his knees holding his head, the pain pulses through his entire mind, his eyes flash on and off with bright purplish light and fade once more.

Fighting back the pain, the young man reaches into his hoody pocket and grabs a small whiskey flask within, gulping down the rusted liquid his pain dulls slightly.

Returning the flask and reaching to his other pocket and pulls a small flask of pills, tipping the contents of the tub out into his hand paying no attention to how many tablets there are the swallows them enjoying the small amount of relief he now has.

Leaning against the wall and gasping slightly he grabs his pack and forces himself out into the street, once again dodging and avoiding contact he struggles to make his way home.

Once more fate reveals her cruel face from out of a small shop to the young man's right a man emerges, the young man is caught off guard as he evades a small group of young women on a night out, merely falling into the man briefly and for but a moment the contact is made.

The shopper feels nothing but a mere shoulder rub across his back, but the young man feels much more, his mind rips into being, random memories, thoughts, ideas, emotional moments good and bad, all played into this man's mind like watching a movie in his head and rapid speed.

The stranger turns to face the now staggering man holding his head in agony.

"What's your problem dude?"

The young man waves back at him as he continues to stagger on.

"Am sorry man." his young English tone echoes the pain he is in.

"Freak!" the strange man replies.

Finally making it home the young man bursts through the door replacing the locks, staggering into his one-room apartment he rushes to the only sink he has and splashes fresh cold water on his face as if the cool water would cool the pain in his mind.

Looking up to the small mirror above his sink the man looks over to his light switch on the other side of the room, reaching out with a gesture and his mind the switch is flicked with but a thought.

A sudden shock appears on the man's face in the mirror, his nose drips fresh crimson into the bowl below, with a quick wash and wipe the blood is gone, walking over to his bed the young man collapses upon it wishing this was nothing but a bad dream.

Once again fate intervenes, slowly voices creep into his head, and thoughts that are not his own, secrets, passwords, all thoughts are open to his mind from the passers-by and the other tenants of his building.

The pain stops but the thoughts remain, more and more pour into his mind's view.

Unable to block them out the young man reaches for the fridge with his mind, the door flies open and a bottle of bells whiskey flies from its resting place to the man's hand.

Taking large gulps as if he were drinking for the first time after running the desert the bottle empties.

Once more the voice quietens, the pain dulls, he is alone for a few moments, using the time he walks towards his answering machine, before pressing the play button he resists the urge to touch it as if remembering a bad experience.

Swallowing his fear he reaches for the machine, as his fingers make contact his eyes close and images flood his mind.

The first was of a group of women sat at a desk in suits talking on a headset and filling out documents on a computer.

The second image was of his friend and foreman at his place of work telling him bad news about his job and something about his paycheck.

The last thought was of a businessman in a phone box, making some kind of mistake.

In the brief half a second for the images to play in the man's mind he pressed the button, snapping out of his trace and staggering backwards holding his head he collapses once more to the bed, gasping in pain.

The answering machine rewinds and starts to play the messages.

"You have three messages, the first message." a robotic famine voice echoes from the machine.

"Hello this is the neurological research institute, am trying to reach Kyle Thomas, we have received and reviewing your application for our research material and will respond to you shortly, thank you."

"typical." the young man Kyle responds while still on his bed holding head in his hands.

"Second message."

"Hey Kyle is Henry, bad news dude, the company's lost a few contracts last few months and they got to make some cutbacks, with you being on the sick these last few days they told me I got to let you go, am sorry Kyle, let me know if you want me to drop your paycheck at home yea?"

"Third message."

Ow crap sorry, think I got the wrong number, my mistake."

Slowly the pain started to ease, Kyle took this opportunity to get some rest and just listen to the sound of silence as the voices to start to fade.

Taking no chances Kyle slowly made his way to his kitchen area and found his last remaining bottle of whiskey, returning to the bed he opened and drank.

Slowly the voices were gone as was any will left to stay awake, as he drifts unconscious.

Mere hours later that same night the city was alive and pulsing with life, however, another being had emerged to join the populace of New York.

Not far from Kyles home, a strange phenomenon was occurring, the street lamps started to fade and go out over a full block, the people below in the street watched in bewilderment and carried on their way.

Invisible to the untrained eye the shadows started to form together, moving like black smoke they merged twisting and turning, a large black mass started to form, its black form twisting like pulsing black smoke from a thick fire.

Slowly two fiery red eyes opened from within the blackness, a whispered roar slowly builds as does the wind, people still baffled at the dim light and cold feeling they now receive from this area quickly go about their business and move away.

Finally, the shadows start to return to the original places leaving behind a large black human skeleton with burning red eyes, his waist down is a whisp of black smoke like substance never-ceasing to move.

The wind dies down and the lights return to normal, a new creature has emerged in the night, The creature looks around him taking in a large breath as if he hand lungs to breathe.

Deciding to take in the sites he floats along the city streets still unnoticed by the people, occasionally coming across an interesting specimen of a human being he examines them looking deep into their soul, none seem right for his new host.

Floating from street to street none appealed to its tastes, realising his time is running out he had to find a host before the sun rises or he will be cast back to his realm he rushes through buildings and cars alike desperately searching.

Finally, a presence nearby catches his attention, the creature turns towards it as if sniffing him out and looks up towards Kyle's room in his apartment block.

The creature lets out a moan of excitement at the sense of this human, his soul stronger than a 1000 other humans would make a perfect host, with the host's powers under the control of the creature it knows he would be invincible.

Lifting from the ground and floating through the walls like a ghost the creature emerges into Kyle's room, the young man lies unconscious on the bed twisting and turning as if having a nightmare.

The creature approaches slowly his jaw drops as if he were slaving anticipating its next meal, within the creature grasp is probably the most powerful human soul he has ever known in thousands of years of watching and waiting.

Mere inches from his prey the creature hovers over Kyle looking deep within peering into his souls and relishes what it sees, finally, Kyle awakes, his eyes lock with the demonic-looking thing before him and gasps fear takes over.

The creature floats back slightly as Kyle pulls himself from under it, and hugs the wall, fear holds him as his eyes give clear notice.

"Be still Kyle Thomas." a deep rattling voice emanates from the creature.

"I am here to grant your wish, I am here to make the pain stop, to silence the voices, to give you back your life and more." the creature holds out his black skeletal hand as if gesturing for Kyle to take it.

"Your kind of a screwed up fairy godmother aren't ya?" Kyle responds without realising.

The creature lowers his hand shaking his head slowly in disappointment.

"Have it your way." the creature replies.

With a sharp thrust, the creature lunges for Kyle as if he were to dive into him, a purely reactive instinct takes over as Kyle throws his arms forward gesturing to stop, turning his face away screaming in fright.

The creature is suddenly struck by a bright purplish light bursting from his body, Kyles own powers seem to reject to having another host as much as Kyle himself does.

The light crackles with bio-energy and rips through the creature hurling it through the wall out into the world beyond, the creature phases through the wall harmless though the bio-energy doesn't.

Stopping himself some thirty or so feet away in the air the creature shakes off the pain and his disbelief, he examines his body for injury and notices his missing left arm at the elbow, the creature snarls, slowly more black smoke from around his lower body creeps up his twisted shape and forms a new limb in place of the old.

***

high up on the rooftops another interested party has been taking note, the seven-story building reaches high into the night making the watcher unable to hear what is said but his senses tell him it's not good.

Piercing the night sky with bright sparkling blue eyes he watches intently,

This lone figure watches as this dark ghost creature approaches a powerful human soul if they were to merge there would be little anyone could do to stop it.

Still, the man watches crouching on the building's ledge waiting.

***

Kyle still shocked at what just happened suddenly falls to his knees grasping his head, his nose drips fresh blood again as the pains shoot through his skull, his mind feels like his head is about to explode.

Working through the pain Kyle runs from his apartment out into the open street, quickly looking for his attacker he watches as the creature slowly lowers to the floor among the people unnoticed.

"Look out! Run!" Kyle shouts at the people around the still invisible creature.

The creature starts to approach with a snigger only Kyle can hear, another pulse of pain hits him as he takes to his senses and runs as fast as his feet will take him.

The creature follows at a comfortable pace letting Kyle make mistakes in his haste as he bumps into people and falls over due to the head pains and images running through his mind due to contact and his out of control abilities,

Collapsing on the floor in agony, grasping his head Kyle doesn't hear the remarks from the people passing by, finally, he manages to crawl into a close-by alley, the creature approaches laughing.

"This is pointless Kyle, there is nowhere you can go, nothing you can do to stop me, surrender and it all stops."

Kyle manages to climb to a sitting position leaning against the alley wall, looking at the demonic creature before him.

"What the hell are you?"

Kyle gasps for breath watching as the creature approaches, trying to hold back the pain and exhaustion he tries to summon his abilities holding out his hand towards the creature.

The approaching creature sniggers as it grabs Kyle by his hoody lifting him into the air with ease, he looks deep into his eyes, slowly it lets Kyle go and holds him still in the air as he opens his arms wide and floats towards him as if he were to embrace him.

Kyle lets out a last-ditch attempt at freedom, screaming as loud as he can ignoring his pain and focusing on his abilities he is rewarded, another burst of purplish bio-energy erupts from his body into the creature.

Knocking him back a mere foot or two the eruption was nothing like before and the creature watches and laughs as Kyle falls to the floor exhausted.

Trying to crawl away exhausted and fatigued in desperation the creature continues to laugh loudly, Kyle realises he cannot escape now, turning over he looks to the creature, tears fall down his cheek as he begs for mercy.

"No Kyle Thomas, you and I will join, and become the most powerful entity in the realm." Again the creature approaches, Kyle closes his eyes waiting for the end.

The creatures laugh is suddenly taken from him as a lone figure lands before him as if falling from the sky, the man lands cracking the concrete below him into a small creator, and yet remains unharmed as he rises to a combat posture with a silver katana sword raised above his head in a strike position.

The creature all though taken back and silenced neglects his instincts and common sense and wonders how this human can see or sense him, let alone fall from a multi-storey building and remain unharmed.

"Who the hell are you." the creature demands.

Without a word the man's body is enveloped by bright blue energy, his eyes flash with the same energy as if a lightning storm was held within his eyes, the magnificent blade glows and crackles with energy, with a single strike through the air the blade releases its energy towards the creature.

The energy travels with lightning speed through the air and slams hard into the creature, howling in agony as the attack rips through the ghostly figure erupting small parts of his body in bright blue crackling light the creature erupts into a large cloud of dark shadowy smoke.

Kyle gasps at the sight, the pain and exhaustion have left him only leaving pure shock and awe, still lying on the floor he watches as the man turns to him shouting at him.

"Can you walk!" the man shouts.

Kyle shakes his head in agreement sharply but is unable to speak.

The man quickly looks around as if searching for something, Kyle looks down to the blade in the man's hand and back to the man, his open grey trench coat flaps in the wind as does his shoulder-length blonde hair, his white t-shirt and blue jeans give him a normal look, but the man's eyes show pure sparkling power,

"OK there's a church not far from here just a few blocks up, do you know it?" the man demands more calmly.

Again Kyle nods in agreement as he is lifted one-handed onto his feet by the man, Kyle's flinches in preparation for the sudden flood of thoughts and images he will get from the man touching him, but none come.

Taken back by the surprise Kyle smiles and looks to the man in awe once more, as they start to leave the alley in the opposite direction, with the man holding onto Kyle's arm escorting him slowly.

Kyles turns his gaze back to the point in the alley the creature last stood, his sudden gasp at what he sees alerts the strange man.

Stopping in his tracks his senses alert him to the same position, slowly turning his gaze round to see for himself the man remains calm but lets out a sigh of disappointment.

The shadows from the alley start to merge, gathering in a central plume of black smoky like substance, from within the twisting blackness two burning red eyes emerge.

"Go!" the man states as he turns back to Kyle.

Kyle obeys his saviour and runs as best he can for the church, following at a distance never taking eyes from the creature the man follows at a steady pace placing his sword back within the folds of his trench coat.

Reaching the church Kyle bursts inside holding the door open for his new friend, once inside the man pulls him away from the door and deeper inside towards the main altar.

A loud screech echoes through the halls and the building begins to shake as if in a small earthquake, Kyle looks around in amazement but still terrified expecting to see the creature burst through the walls any moment.

"Don't worry your safe here." the man states in a calming tone as he lowers himself to the alter step, and sits relaxing.

"Thank you, thank you for saving me from whatever that was," Kyle replies.

"You're welcome Kyle, the man replies.

"How did you know my name? Who are you?"

"My name is Jacob Rawn, and I know a lot about you, my young friend, including why that thing was after you."

"What was it?"

"I'm not sure I've only encountered one thing like it before, am starting to think there actually is a hell realm in this universe, and that thing is from it."

"Demons?" Kyle replies.

"I think so, kinda fits the description doesn't it?"

Kyle nods in agreement, as he joins Jacob on the alter step.

"Are we safe in here then, will this lot keep it out?" Kyle gestures to the crosses and the windows.

"I believe so, guess some of the old legends are true."

Kyle takes a deep breath and suddenly realises his mind is quiet, no pain, no blood and no voices echo within his mind, letting out a sharp snigger he falls back smiling enjoying the first bit of peace in a long time.

"What's so funny?" Jacob asks.

"This is the first time since as long as I can remember since my mind was at peace."

Kyle continues to tell Jacob of his tale and his abilities, Jacob knows all too well of the problems Kyle is facing.

Jacob joined the conversation explaining a few truths of his powers and abilities and a method of how to quiet his mind and slowly gain control of it, after all that what the creature was targeting him for.

"So you're saying you have these same abilities? And you can control them?" Kyle asks.

"Yes, but my mental abilities are no way near the level at which you can use them,"

"But that thing you did with the sword, with that glow, what was that? I can't do that." Kyle asks.

"no that's a different set of skills and abilities merged into an effective weapon, part of it is mental of course but the rest, well that's gonna take a while to explain."

Again he nods in agreement, suddenly Kyle is half-blinded as a single ray of bright sunshine bursts into the church.

"It's morning already?" Kyle asks in disbelief.

Putting on his long trench coat Jacob agrees, with a quick scan with his senses outside he finds no trace of the creature and deems it safe to venture out into the world.

Emerging from the church and squinting at the bright sunlight Jacob once again scans the area, finally his enhanced senses locate the creature hiding from the sunlight in a basement across the street, and Jacob smirks as he now knows a weakness to these creatures, sunlight.

Back at Kyle's apartment, Jacob enters first sword and senses at the ready, Kyle follows scanning the area with his eyes, as Jacob sheaths his blade putting Kyle is immediately at ease.

"Thank god." Kyle states.

Looking around the place Jacob is reminded of his small apartment back in L, A, Kyle wastes no time in starting to pack his few belongings, Jacob notices and turns to him.

"Going somewhere?" Jacob asks.

"You're damn right, where ever the hell you're going," Kyle replies.

"Ha, that's not going to happen, I have my problems right now, I can't have some kid, even one as powerfully gifted as you tagging along, it's not safe." Jacob sniggers.

"Look Jacob this is the first time anything like this has happened to me both the demon thing, and my mind being calm, you expect me to last alone."

Jacob shakes his head and turns to the window searching for answers.

"it's too dangerous, I have no idea where I'm going or what will happen, I need to find someone and some answers before I bring anyone else into this."

The news is not taken well by Kyles mind, the pain shoots through his whole body, grasping his head and falling to his knees his body pulses with glowing bright purple energy.

Jacob watches in bewilderment, unclear on what to do he approaches cautiously.

"Kyle, what are you doing?"

"It's not me! I can't stop it." Kyle screams as the gasps allow.

Jacob tries to touch Kyles shoulder, with rejection in the form of a small electric shock, refusing to just back away Jacob searches Kyles mind for a way to calm him down.

Kyles mind takes over, feeling as though Jacobs mental probes as an attack, retaliates in kind, a pulse of energy slams into Jacob knocking back across the room slamming into the wall.

Shaking off the attack Jacob realises Kyle powers are purely instinctual based and will need to be shut down or he would be a danger to anyone around him.

"Kyle you need to calm down, this is gonna get someone hurt or worse," Jacob shouts while climbing to his feet.

"I can't stop it, the pains are getting worse," Kyle screams.

Jacob slowly moves around the apartment never taking his eyes from Kyle screaming in agony on the floor, something inside urges Jacob to help this boy, to protect him, as he slowly realises that this boy could be the future.

Kyle's bright purplish aura erupts again and expands from his body, the energy reaches a few feet from his body and seems to be expanding, Kyle screams in pain.

Jacob watches in awe as if looking at the human evolution itself before his eyes, Kyles screams snap him back to his sense he cautiously approaches Kyle again, the bio-energy flares slightly towards his position making him back off again suddenly.

The realisation hits Jacob that he has to be cruel to be kind and must close Kyle down before he damages himself or others.

Summoning his formidable bio-energy the blue haze returns around Jacob, extending a few centimetres from his body, the difference in size is like David and Goliath, a position Jacob has been in and beaten many times.

Kyles own bio-energy flares once more erupting a large blast of raw power towards Jacob, raising his arms in front of his face and leaning into the attack the powers collide, Jacob's feet slide across the floor as he is pushed back by the force.

The bright eruption of sparks fade leaving Jacob unharmed but some five or six feet further away from his last position, lowering his arms Jacobs eyes flash with sparkling power as his arms lower to his belly and placed together as if in prayer position.

Slowly drawing them apart from a flurry of bright blue electric streaks between them until a small sphere of pure bio-energy erupts into being between his hands.

The sphere grows in size to that of a small football, his eyes open and locate his target still lying in agony on the floor, Jacobs pours his telepathic might into the sphere of bioenergy with one purpose, to overload Kyle's synapsis and shut him down, unconscious.

With a swift jolt from his right hand, the sphere flies towards Kyle, its targets own bioenergy field erupts towards its incoming attack trying to defend itself.

Both bio energies erupt into a flurry of sparks but the telepathic sphere flies true, bursting through the bright purple energy striking Kyle in the chest.

Kyle's body is wracked with more pain as he convulses uncontrollably on the floor as if having a fit, an electrical current runs up and down his entire body, the bioenergy field covering him dissipates and fades.

Kyles body stops still, a small amount of smoke emanates from his body as if he were singed, Jacob wastes no time and rushes to the boy on the floor, checking his pulse and with his senses feels the life from him.

Relaxing with a loud sigh his bioenergy field fades harmlessly away, his eyes return to the natural blue, Jacob lifts Kyles body off the floor and places him onto the bed.

Examining him closely with his mind Jacob places a mental block into Kyles mind through telepathic hypnosis, although it would only be temporary it will hold Kyles higher abilities at bay till he has time to control them.

"I'm, sorry, JA," Kyle mumbles as he comes to for a mere second.

Jacob looks with surprise to Kyle's persistence before smiling and placing his hand to Kyle's head and placing a mental command to sleep in his mind.

CHAPTER 10

A Dark Union

Night had fallen on the magnificent city of New York once more, a night indeed as one of hell's own had come to the big apple.

The large black ghostly figure of the demon who mere hours ago attacked Kyle Thomas wonders unnoticed by all but curious animals.

Pet owners suddenly turn to their pets in bewilderment as they whimper and hide in fear behind their masters trying to avoid the gaze from this creature.

The attempt to claim Kyle as a host has weakened this fiendish creature dramatically and desperation has claimed him, instead it found a temporary host in the form of a stray kat to see out the day.

the warrior who foiled him forever burned in its memory will be dealt with in time, but a new host is at the front of its darks desires.

Searching the city streets unseen for a new potential candidate, the demon looks deep into the souls of bystanders, police officer, and criminals alike.

***

Daniel lance is a young man, his long black hair blows lightly in the wind, and his old badged and frayed leather jacket and torn jeans give him the rough rocker and biker look.

This looks hides his dark ambitions, twisted evil habits of robbery, murder, and theft are just means to an end as he has his sights set on the big leagues of the criminal underground, maybe one day to run it all.

Walking the city streets with a cocky untouchable swag he barges past all in his path without thought or guilt.

The fiery red eyes of an onlooking demon finally catch a glimpse of a potential candidate as it watched Daniel walking through the street as if this world was made for him alone.

Following for a short time, the fiend watched as Daniel walks straight into a local liquor store, pulling from its hiding place tucked into his jeans Daniel pulls his black colt 45 that belonged to his father and takes aim at the cashier.

Demanding a bottle of his finest whiskey and what remains in the till Daniel walks out with his prize and walks on without a care in the world.

The demons appetite and interest grow as Daniel walks on, the man has no fear of any man or even the laws of man.

Staggering out of yet another bar still holding his now almost finished stolen bottle of whiskey the demon watch intently, wondering on towards his home Daniel realises his lack of money for another bottle.

Unhappy at this turn of events he shakes his head and slaps his cheeks repeatedly in an attempt to sober up.

Looking around for potential other sources of income his attention is caught by a beautiful young woman elegantly dressed with her escort walking towards there rather expensive BMW car.

As the man places his key in the car door Daniel jumps up from behind grabbing the woman and smashing his almost empty bottle over the head of the man, knocking him unconscious.

The woman yells in panic and fear before Daniels places his hand over her mouth and pulls his gun showing it to her in all its glory.

"Easy babe, shut that pretty mouth of yours or lover boy down there gets one in the head," Daniel says in a mocking soft tone pointing his gun to the unconscious man on the floor.

The woman goes quiet while the fear emanating from her is palpable, Daniel savers it as he sniffs her perfume from her neck, dark sexual thoughts run through his mind until his eyes lower to the pearl necklace around her neck.

Spinning the woman round to face him and pushing her up against the car he rips the pearls from her neck, opening the car door he gestures for her to get in.

The demon watches with delight at Daniels handy work, only hoping it ends with the more primal delights for him to watch.

As the woman sits in the car with the door open, Daniel reaches for the man on the floor, taking his watch wallet and rings.

A closer examination of the man's wallet reveals a hearty sum of cash.

"Score!" Daniel states as he smiles at the woman.

Turning his attention back to the man he lifts him so the woman can see his face and holds the gun to the back of his head.

"Give me the rest, or I redecorate the inside of your car with what's in his head."

The woman removes her earrings and jewellery and begs him to leave the man alone.

Daniel looks to his new acquisitions with approval, a dark thought creeps into his mind and he crouches next to the woman who's currently crying and gasping at the sight of him.

Reaching for her head he grabs her long blond hair and pulls her head towards him, kissing her gently on the lips the woman tries not to respond as Daniel lets go licking his lips with a smile.

Slowly rising from the car and leaving the couple with a finale kick to the man's gut Daniel walks away, the woman's screams at her male friend on the floor echoes through the night as Daniel laughs.

The fiend watched the entire event with intent and has made his decision, Daniel lance is to be his new host.

Following his latest score, Daniel finds the nearest pawn shop and trades in his finds, emerging with a wallet full of cash for the jewels, Daniels smug grin illuminates his face as he slowly heads home.

Almost home walking down a few more side streets and alleys Daniels cocky stagger is suddenly halted in its track.

"Daniel!" a voice whispers as if coming behind him.

The man turns around his smug grin wiped clean and replaces with a serious look, the alley behind bellows steam from a vent and shows no signs of life save for the odd passer-by on the street at the far end.

"Here." The voice whispers once more.

Daniel spins around pulling his gun and looking frantically for source to the voice, nothing stands out except the fact he is alone, the alley before him ends in a dead-end and the fire escape leading to his apartment three-floors up.

Still looking for his target Daniel's curiosity slowly changes to caution and a little fear, walking towards the fire escape he continues to look around trying to find were the voice comes from.

"I'm right here." The voice whispers as if in his left ear.

Spinning to face that direction Daniel's fires his weapon, the bullet encounters nothing but a brick wall some few feet away.

The voice laughs which seems to echo all around him, Daniel's fear grows, so does his anger.

"Show yourself you chicken, shit son of a bitch," Daniel shouts forcefully.

"Did you enjoy that, back at the car, I was watching you." The whispering voice claims. Daniels face now shows his concern as does the several rounds he fires from his gun in random directions.

"You can't hurt me with that." The voice replies.

"Ow ya, show yourself you son of a bitch and I'll show you how much it hurts."

The voice once again laughs, Daniel continues to look around as he reaches the fire escape, the ladder before Daniel suddenly starts to twist and turn as if some invisible giant creature were squeezing it in its mighty hands, Daniel jumps back pushing against the wall as he watches the metal twist.

Finally panic takes Daniel, his cocky interpretation of the world belongs to him has gone as again he fires in random directions and runs for the alley entrance some forty or so feet away. Daniel once again suddenly stops dead in his tracks his arms held out at his side he is unable to move as if he were paralysed stood up, his body lifts into the air a few feet and turns around facing the darkness that now inhabits the dead end of the alley.

All the shadows of the alley seemed to have formed together making a jet black void filling almost a third of the alley.

Daniel watches in terror as a long black skeletal arm protrudes from the blackness its arm turns and gestures that of single bony finger pointing up moving side to side as the whispering voice toots in unison, gesturing disappointment.

"What the hell are you?" Daniel shouts.

"I'm your future, Daniel, if you choose it." The whisper replies.

"Choose what?" Daniel replies.

"I can give you what you won't Daniel, all your dreams rolled into one, money, power, and of course the perks that go with it."

Daniels mind is suddenly intruded with flashes and images of the dark thoughts he had of the beautiful woman he robbed earlier.

"What makes you think I need you for that?" Daniel replies still trembling in his voice.

The voice once again laughs, then suddenly grows quiet as Daniel's fear grows as the creature emerges from the blackness.

Screaming wildly and desperately trying to move as the large black figure bursts from the shadows his burning red eyes locked on Daniel.

"I'm talking real power, over this world and the next, a power that will allow you to control men, the power to live forever, the power to have everything you want when you want it," The creatures rattling deep voice states.

The creature approaches Daniel and turns his head so his gaze looks straight into his burning red eyes.

"What is your answer?" the demon asks.

Daniel struggles to look at the creature but managed to answer out of fear alone.

"Screw you, whatever you are?"

"You're disappointing me Daniel, not a very wise move on your part, I could bring the world within your grasp." The demon replies.

Daniels is suddenly dropped to the floor in a heap, the creature looking on as if expecting a response he will enjoy.

Daniel reaches for his gun, replacing a fresh clip inside he fires continuously into the creature, the bullets pass through him as they would smoke into the wall behind.

A deep loud rattling laugh echoes all around Daniel.

The creature holds out his hand towards Daniel once more, through the distance a psychokinetic grip latches around Daniel's neck and lifts him into the air once more.

Both creature and man fly high into the air, passing the great skyscrapers with ease the creature continues dragging Daniel choking behind him.

Finally stopping some few hundred feet higher than the towering heights of New York Daniel is brought to face the creature.

"Last chance Daniel, join me or die." The creature screams.

Daniel looks frantically as best he can with an invisible grip around his neck down to the fall below him then back to the creature.

"If I agree, what will happen to me?" Daniel asks as gasps allow.

"You'll become a god, immortal, powerful, and able to control powers beyond your imagining." The creature shouts throwing his arms aside and spinning around as if excited and revelling in his strength.

"Now choose!" The creature shouts.

Daniel nods and speaks a single word.

"Ok"

Without wasting a second the demon circles Daniel's body before diving full force into his chest as if he were diving into the water.

Two beings become one as Daniel's body convulses with pain, the black smoke bellows from his mouth, nose and eyes, his hands grasp at his heart as if he were trying to contain it in his chest as he curls up in the air.

Violently his body is thrown left then right as if he were a rag doll in the hands of a child, its limbs flop around wildly as if uncontrolled, still conscious of all that happens Daniel screams, his voice now deeper and rattling as the demon merges with every part of him.

Finally, the convulsions and movement stop as the body just hangs lifeless for a moment before falling to back to earth, its body lifeless it seems as it hurtles towards the ground.

The impact from the fall shatters the concrete below, another mysterious crater for the engineers to fix, the body within the crater a bloody mess, organs and blood spread out and open to view.

The body remains lifeless and still for a few moments before the blood seems to flow in reverse, the organs follow its blood lead back into the body as if in rewind.

A sudden gasp of life and breath are taken by the body of Daniel as a mere moment ago he was a giant bloody mess, slowly rising to his feet he looks to his hands which clench into fists, a smug grin takes over his pale face.

"This will do nicely." The now deep smooth voice states.

Within the man's eyes for a moment is an image, swirling around as if in a whirlpool Daniel's soul screams for freedom as he slowly swallowed by the current of the pool within.

The new man, made of Daniel lances body and the demon, takes in his first breath and savours it, he looks back to what he is wearing in disgust.

"Well now, this won't do, we shall have to change that." the new Daniel states.

Slowly he walks towards the city lights knowing that they will soon belong to him as will the rest of the world, and then every world fuelled by the souls that will dwell here.

"Time to introduce new management." The man states with his now confident dominance.

CHAPTER 110

Back To School

Hours have passed in Kyle's apartment since Jacob placed the mental command in his mind for him to sleep.

Sitting and watching Kyles breathing Jacob wrestles with his conscious, his duty, and his heart, what to do with Kyle.

Left alone he is a danger to both himself and others, innocents could be put at risk and that is unacceptable, let alone unfair to this poor boy before him suffering in pain instead of living his life.

Jacob's thoughts interrupted as his senses alert him to Kyle slowly coming to, with a gentle touch to his forehead and another mental command placed within his mind Kyle returns to asleep.

Jacob walks to the window and looks out to many people walking below, the hole which Kyle blew the demon through the wall allows a gentle night breeze to blow through.

Feeling the chill Jacob wraps his coat around him and covers Kyle with his quilts, a sudden feeling of responsibility creeps over him, a single thought echoes in his mind, what if master Takami had left him to the devourer on that fateful day back in the war.

Jacob watches Kyle sleep for hours still toying with different possibilities, unable to make up his mind his eyes are suddenly hit by a bright ray of sunshine as morning breaks.

Looking to the sun and watching it illuminate the dark cold world below, Jacob feels the rays on his skin, the warmth reaches deep within, and the light makes his heart lift as if an instant shot of happiness was injected.

Suddenly a new wave of thoughts pierce his conscious, Kyle could be the hope the world needs, and he could be the very future of humanity, their ultimate potential.

The thoughts continue flooding into his mind, grandmaster Shakarian could train this boy to be the best there has ever been, all Jacob has to do is teach him to control the power fluctuations and get him to the school realm, the master would know what to do.

Removing his coat and sitting beside Kyle, Jacob places his hand on his forehead once more, summoning his bio-energy and telepathy he pushes through Kyle's remarkable mental defences and into his subconscious.

Jacobs telepathy pushes through Kyles mind clearing away fear and doubts and replacing a feeling of strength and control over his abilities, installing a few mental blocks, and opening others Jacob makes Kyles mind easier to control for himself and Kyle.

Morning turns to afternoon, to evening, and back to night.

Its morning before Jacob wakes from his trance, a deep sigh follows his awakening, Kyles eyes slowly open as he stretches and yawns as if he has been sleeping the best sleep he ever had.

Jacob looks on with a smile.

"Morning," Jacob says.

"Good morning, how long was I out?"

"Only a day or two."

"A day or two! What about that thing, it could have found us again?" Kyles tone worried as he jumps off the bed and looks about frantically.

"It didn't, your safe." Jacobs tone was forceful at first then smooth.

Kyle relaxes and looks around his apartment, before realising his mind is once again quiet, no voice, no pains, and complete silence.

Jacob smiles as its clear Kyle is shocked by the new stillness in his mind.

"It's ok, their still there, I just calmed it down for a while."

Kyle rubs his head a huge sigh erupts from him as tears well up in his eyes.

"Thank you, you have no idea how much I missed the quiet," Kyle states, as tears allow.

"I think I can guess," Jacob replies with a smile.

Kyle struggles to hold back the tears as he walks around the room touching things as if for the first time, slowly he comes to the answering machine, his hesitance is clear as he forces himself to touch the play button.

"No saved messages." The robotic voice echoes.

Kyle's eyes open as more tears run down his cheek, no pain, no images, nothing but the stills of a calm mind like the calm after a storm, and the cold touch of the machine on his fingers.

Kyle flops onto his sofa his hands shake slightly in front of his face as he weeps with joy as if his entire world was suddenly wiped clean of worries and debts.

"Kyle, we have to go." Jacob states.

Looking up to his new friend Kyle wipes the tears from his eyes and nods in agreement, rising to his feet he finds his backpack across the room and begins to pack.

"Where we heading?" Kyle asks while still packing.

"First we head to L.A, talk to an old friend, then I'm talking to you meet some special people."

"Special people?"

"The masters of my order." Jacob states.

Kyles grin is hard to ignore as he continues to pack furiously.

"Will they take me? I mean train me to be like you?" Kyle's voice betrays his excitement.

"Ow, they'll take you." Jacob sniggers.

Walking to Kyle he interrupts his packing and turns him to face him looking him in the eye, clearly a serious moment.

"Kyle listen to me, they will train you, it will be hard, there will be times you'll wish the demon did take you, but it's all worth it, you'll be the best the order has ever seen, better than me, better than grandmaster Shakarian I'm betting."

Kyle feels the burden Jacob meant with his words, a sudden realisation of being Jacob's hope for the future weighed heavy on his heart and mind, a hope Kyle was determined to see realised.

His bag packed, he looks to Jacob waiting by the door his own pack back slung on his shoulder, the last look around his apartment makes Kyle feel he is saying goodbye to an old life as he steps into a new one.

Kyle takes his first step on his new journey, in his mind a secret promise is made to both himself and Jacob, I'll make you proud of me Jacob, I promise.

Jacob gestures to Kyle to leave the apartment with a smile and a nod, watching as Kyle does so, Jacob smiles as he passes him and walks down the stairs, slowly following him Jacob is filled with a feeling of hope renewed as his telepathic abilities secretly hear everything Kyle is thinking.

Leaving the city of New York behind the two new friends wonder the roads heading to L.A occasionally hitching a ride here and there the two spend most of their time alone, the days are for travelling and training at night.

Resembling his own training Jacob teaches the physical training during the day in the form of walking and hunting for food and water, and the evenings for mental and theory work.

The night's instruction was as hard for Jacob trying to explain the unnatural and their reason for coming to our world, to trying to explain Kyle's powers bit by bit as it was for Kyle to learn it.

It took days for Kyle to master the basics of meditation properly as his mind would suddenly wake up as he started to focus, the mental blocks Jacob had placed were gone, burnt through by Kyles raw power.

Unknown by Kyle he was now keeping his powers at bay by continually training them and releasing the built-up power in training, the meditation techniques were helping to keep his powers in check as he would spend most of the night in the meditate state instead of sleep, just as Jacob did.

Merely a week later Kyle didn't need Jacob to hold his powers in check, both meditating and allowing his built up power to be released allowed him to find a balance he had been lacking all his life, learning how the disciplines of bioenergy release the most dangerous of all mental powers, Jacob slowed his learning to a crawl.

Days and nights spent honing his skills as to form a defensive shield around himself and to stop it just acting out of instinct.

Jacob would release small amounts of his bio-energy in the form of pure psychokinetic strikes from his blade at Kyle, the shield would bend and flex but never give under the strain. Confident in his new ability Kyle would joke around from time to time flicking little psychokinetic jolts at Jacob taunting him cockily, as Jacob was unable to perform such feats unless it was charge into his blade and released as a strike.

Jacob would retaliate by empowering just a little more power into a strike or sword strike than Kyle could absorb safely, knocking his shield down leaving him a red-faced and flat on his back.

Only three months into the cross country trek Kyle was suddenly getting tired of the sand, the dust, and the wind off the open road.

"J, I don't want to sound like a broken record or ungrateful, but Jesus man, couldn't we just catch a bus or something?"

"How can I teach you what you need to know if we're surrounded by people on a bus eh?" Jacob replies sniggering at Kyles request.

Kyle stops and drops his pack and collapses to the floor in the hot desert heat, leaning on his pack for support.

"What about just catch a train at next town, just shave a few miles of the journey, you know?" Jacob stands next to Kyle sniggering at his young student.

"I got to stop J, my feet are killing me, and I hate the heat," Kyle states as he collapses spread out on the floor.

"Whoever is teaching phase 1 physical training, at the school these days is going to have a field day with you, Kyle." Jacob sniggers as he looks to his friend laid flat out on the side of the road.

Kyle waves in hand in response as if waving off a school of flies.

"Whatever" Kyle gasps.

"I suppose we could camp here for today, it's getting on a bit and its nearly time for training," Jacob states as he gives Kyle a jokingly soft kick in the leg ushering him further off the road.

"Great, first walk me to death, now lecture me to death, I love my life." Kyle jokes.

Jacob drops his pack and begins gathering firewood, using a small little dune as cover from the cold blowing wind they light a fire and face the road some fifty or so feet away.

Training that night consisted of usual mental focus training and telekinetic training, Kyle would lift objects into the air with ease, and through them around as if juggling.

Jacob would interrupt him through throwing random thoughts into his mind disrupting his focus or giving him little jabs with a stick.

By now his abilities far exceeded Jacobs's mental abilities, all except his telepathy ability and the ability to mix bio-energy and physical abilities.

Kyle was growing increasingly unhappy with his lack of progress in this area, Jacob could feel his disappointment and tried to comfort him.

"It's probably just the lack of physical training you have had Kyle, but that will change when we get to the school."

Returning to their normal routine the friends mediated for several hours, fatigue and hunger were wiped from their bodies as they both awoke refreshed and energised.

Both men exchanged stories from their past as they always did after training, share both laughter and sorrow, Jacob always had more stories but they were always sad.

Kyle wondered how one man can have gone on through so much pain and suffering and yet still has the will to fight on, possibly forever.

The night dwindled on, Kyle stayed awake looking to the stars and wondered if there are other dimensions there must be other creatures up out there too.

He turns to his friend who he observes snoring away deep in a dream, Kyle shuffles over and looks at his friend and can feel nothing but respect, friendship, and pity.

Running through his mind again are the stories Jacob told him, thoughts begin to form how he must feel, being alone for so long, fighting the same fight year after year.

Suddenly Kyle's eyes are drawn to the fire, as images blast into his mind, unlike before where contact was needed these images seem different, they seem distant somehow as if they are things that have yet to come to pass.

Images of a towering red-skinned demon with black horns, mouth and burning red eyes with a huge black sword attacking Jacob.

The images twist and reform into a well-dressed businessman with gelled short black hair and dark eyes, the image twists and a glimpse of the demon ghost who attacked him replaces the man.

His vision then widens as he looks down onto a battlefield, the two sides consisting of large slender beings and men and women dressed in black, against huge towering demonic looking figures.

Jacob stands in the middle blood pours from a wound on his forehead, he is dressed in the same black uniform as the other humans and slender creatures, a fire rages all around him as bloody spit falls from his mouth he is injured.

His weapon held out at his side he looks to an unknown enemy in this battle, as he holds his right rib with his other hand.

The images twist once more and are replaced with a vision of himself lost in a sea of screaming people, the image red as blood, swirls around as if in a whirlpool.

Finally, Kyle snaps out of his trance as a piece of burnt wood falls in the fire, Kyle gasps for breath and panics as if he had witnessed his worse fear.

Jacob remained asleep during Kyles short-lived panic attack, calming himself down Kyle wonders around the fire rubbing his hands through this rough shoulder-length hair startled at these new images.

Finally calmed and relaxed a few minutes later Kyle walks to his sleeping bag, before climbing into his bed a strange feeling creeps up his back, a feeling he knows all too well, the unnatural.

The feeling grows steadily, Kyle looks around searching both sky and ground for a reason, and the feeling grows stronger still and seems to be coming from over the dune they were using as a windbreak.

Climbing up the dune Kyles eyes follow a small movement in the distance, finally realising something is coming for them, and something unnatural Kyle looks to Jacob still sleeping on the floor and chooses not to wake him.

Watching from the dune a single well-dressed man in black jeans and a long black trench coat with a red silk shirt seem to hover some ten to twenty feet in the air as if flying.

Slowly landing a few feet away the white-faced man's eyes are dark blood red almost black his gaze never leaving Kyle's eyes.

"Nice trick." Kyle states.

The strange man nods in agreement.

"And you are?" a smooth and mellow Italian accent asks.

"Kyle."

"Ah, you know of my kind Kyle?" The man asks as he slowly walks around in front of Kyle.

"Some of you, ya."

Again the man nods in agreement as he continues to pace.

The creature looks Kyle up and down as if measuring him up for a fight, then stops and sniffs the air like a dog picking up a scent in the wind.

"You have power young one, but are you capable of using it." The man asks with a smug grin.

Kyle smirks and focuses for a brief moment as his entire body is surrounded by his bright purplish bio-energy reaching a few feet from his body.

"Ah." The man replies to Kyles display.

He turns to face Kyle holding his arms out to the sides opening up his in an open gesture.

"Then let us begin young one." The man states.

"Fine with me," Kyle replies firmly.

Without wasting a second Kyle takes a step and lunges his arms and bio-energy forward, the blast the size of Kyles shield hurtles forward towards the pale man striking him square in the chest.

The body of the man is lifted some ten or so feet into the air and knocked back landing thirty feet away in a heap as he twists and rolls further away in the sand.

Kyle watches as the body lands and lets a smile creep on his face, a short smile lived as the creature rises and dusts his now slightly singed shirt off as if he felt nothing.

"impressive, you do have power, and now so do I." the man states as his dark eyes now crackle with the same bright purple energy as the blast Kyle just gave him.

Kyles face mirrors his shock, the man's walks swiftly towards Kyle hurling himself a few feet away and leaping over Kyle's head landing on the opposite side, as he lands the creature reaches across his body and brings a back fist slamming into Kyles face.

The attack empowered with Kyles own bio-energy knocks him flying away at speed, he lands hard a short distance away, shaking his head after landing his mind struggles to focus on where he is let alone defence.

Without a second passing the creature appears in front of Kyle mere millimetres from nose to nose the man opens his mouth now revealing two large canine fangs like that of a vampire.

"Were not done yet young one."

The creature grabs Kyles hoody and lifts him into the air hurling back into the dune with a thud.

Kyle grunts with the impact and pain as he lands, again barely a second passes before the creature is upon him.

sharp pains rush through Kyles left shoulder as long sharp nails like long thin black daggers from the creatures fingernails pierce Kyles flesh, Kyle screams and struggles under the massive strength this creature has.

"Mm your blood reeks of power young one, I shall enjoy your soul and your blood."

The creature bends over Kyle mere centimetres between them, the man opens his mouth wide-bearing his huge fangs as if to take a bite out of his prey.

The quick reflexes of the creature stop him from being nailed to the floor as a silver streak flies towards his chest and slams into the floor a few feet away, leaping out of the danger area the creature lands safely away from Kyle.

Looking to the weapon now standing dug into the desert floor takes the form of a beautiful katana sword, looking to were the attack ordinated the creatures gaze watches as another man slowly walks up the dune.

The light from the fire hides the man's features, in the dark of night but not his powers as the man held out his hand towards the sword as if answering its masters call the blade wiggles free and flies to his hand.

The creatures looks on a now concerned look crosses his face as this man all through senses less raw power than the young one, this man carried himself a tried and tested warrior, his powers refined, and there is something buried deep within him.

"Leave the boy alone nightcrawler, pick on someone your size."

A familiar voice to Kyle echoes to his ears and sounds just like a friend called Jacob.

"As you wish my friend, I'll settle for you tonight, your young friend later." The creature's voice rasps.

"I don't think so," Jacob replies.

Spinning his sword in his grip he turns the blade up to the sky and backs down in front of him summoning his bio-energy field as he does so, the blade glows and crackles with raw power.

"Ha! I should have known he didn't wipe you all out." The creature shouts.

Jacob hears the creature's words but forgets them for the moment as he focuses on the job at hand.

"A mistake I will rectify tonight."

"You and whose army?" Jacob replies with a smile still stood in a battle-ready position.

Both the creature and Jacob jump high into the air carried by their mental abilities, the sword and claw clash as if steel crossed steel, both land on opposite sides and lunge back into the air at each other without looking.

They hang in the air as they clash longer than they should normally, slowly falling back to earth multiple strikes are exchanged before they both land next to each other and continue to fight.

It isn't long before Jacob gains the upper hand his speed and strength more than the unnatural can match ends with a sword strike to the neck which is blocked as expected, Jacob follows the attack with a spinning hook kick from his left leg continuing his turn from his sword strike.

The blow lands hard on the creature's face spinning him rapidly in the air and hurling some three or four feet away.

Jacob stops his attack and follows up with a rapid double eyebrow raise, as a cocky taunt, the creature's watches from the floor as he pushes himself up and dusts himself off again.

"Most impressive sentinel, but not good enough."

Hurling himself into the air once more he falls towards Jacobs's position, waiting patiently Jacob waits for the attack, lifting his blade to block at the last second, following immediately with a sword swipe across the chest.

The creature reacts and drops to the floor avoiding the strike and flips himself back to his feet only to be met with an empowered front thrust kick from Jacob to the chest.

Staggering back slightly the creature takes in a deep breath and throws his arms forward as Kyle did to form a bright purple bioenergy blast.

The blast tears up the ground as it hurtles towards Jacob at speed, a burst of light and sparks erupts and the sound of metal clashing on a hard substance as Jacob brings an energised blade down on the blast at the perfect time slicing through it.

The energy dissipates almost instantly but passes Jacob harmlessly, wasting no time Jacob follows up the creatures attack, leaping slighting into the air as if he were to perform a slam dunk with a fist his attack lands hard on his enemy's face.

A shocked face erupts on the creature as a sharp blade punctures his body running him through and bending him over as it enters his stomach and protrudes out the back.

The creature looks to Jacob gritting his teeth blood pours from its mouth, Jacob returns the look with another cocky double eyebrow raise.

Altering his grip on his sword hilt to that of a reverse grip he spins round pulling the blade from its resting place and following with yet another left hook kick.

The body flies through the air landing hard on the sandy floor and slides some few feet before stopping.

Flipping the sword in his grip he wipes it clean from a piece of cloth held in his pocket and watches as the creature slowly rises to his feet.

The unnatural looks to his wounds and smirks.

"Not bad human, let's see how your ancient techniques deal with this."

From under his jacket, the creature pulls two black desert eagle model pistols and begins to fire at Jacob.

His instincts take over moving Jacob at the height of his unnatural speed, his magnificent silver blade brought to bear on each round as it hurtles at him.

From Kyles and the creature point of view, Jacob is but a blur, as if multiple versions of him exist in one space moving this way and that, sparks fly from the impact of blade and bullet.

The creature continues firing confident at least some will hit, the sparks cease as does the silver glean of the blade as the last few rounds seem to force Jacob to move more than that block.

The final round seems to send Jacob spinning on the spot before finally sending him spinning through the air as a horizontal flip before he lands and finishes his spin facing the creature his blade held in an up position up the back of his arm in a reverse grip.

Looking Jacob up and down both Kyle and the creature are shocked to see not one round and hit its target, Jacobs smug grin is suddenly dwarfed as he lifts his left hand and opens his hand to several smouldering bullets.

Once again Kyle and the unnatural shock is all over their face, Jacob takes advantage and runs towards his attacker dropping the bullets, spinning towards his prey Jacob goes for a reverse grip decapitation.

The creature ducks wisely but is then surprised once more as Jacob continues to turn and spin on the spot bring the blade into a piercing attack striking true through the creature's heart. The fight ends.

Jacob still in a combat position facing away from his enemy with his weapon lodged in his chest. A final twist of the blade lowers the unnatural to his knees holding the blade in his hands.

Jacob pulls the magnificent unscathed blade from where it is lodged and cleans it once more, the creature gasps as the blade is withdrawn.

Kyle now standing holding his ribs in discomfort looks on with shock and awe.

"Before I send you on your way nightcrawler, what did you mean when you said wiped us all out?" Jacob asks sternly.

The creature coughs up blood as he laughs.

"You find out soon enough sentinel! You'll be joining them soon enough." The creature replies as his breath will allow."

"Have it your way," Jacob replies.

Lifting his sword above his head in a ready position Kyle and the creature both in shock watching as Jacobs's blade crashes down with precision dropping both head and body separately to the floor.

Breathing a sigh of relief Jacob seems to shrink in size and anger as he turns to check on Kyle.

"You ok?" Jacob asks not even out of breath.

"Yeah man, just a bruised pride I guess," Kyle replies with a smile.

Jacob cleans his blade once more before digging into the ground and shaking his left hand rapidly, a look of discomfort on his face.

Kyle grasps Jacob's hand and is shocked to see several deep red pressure and heat marks wear the bullets were caught by his still human skin.

"What the?" Kyle asks, with a worried tone.

"It's ok it will be gone in a few minutes'," Jacob replies, pulling back his hand and resuming shaking it.

"I guess that hurt after all?"

"Yea!" Jacob replies smiling.

"Then why do it?"

"Look good didn't it?" Jacob replies cockily.

"Ow yea defiantly."

"Well, there you go."

Finally, the pain eases in Jacobs's hands as he grasps his sword and walks to the fallen body.

"Anyways speaking of dumb things to do, what's the idea taking on this thing alone," Jacob asks while giving the body a swift kick.

"I didn't want to wake you, I thought I could handle it."

"Kyle listen to me fella, as powerful as you are you have no experience, these things take time and I need to teach you of the different types of unnatural and their weaknesses."

Kyle nods in agreement but cannot help feeling as though he has let Jacob down, sensing his turmoil inside Jacob walks up to him placing a hand on his shoulders.

"Listen, I admire you for trying, but you're far from ready my friend, give it time ok?" Jacob asks.

Again Kyle nods in agreement.

"In time there will be nothing that can stand in your way, not even me," Jacob states with a smile.

Walking back to the body Jacob stabs his blade in the ground before him in-between him and the corpse.

"This is what's known as a nightcrawler, there from an almost identical realm, they're responsible for the legends of the vampire in our world."

Kyle looks back to the head its eyes flickering slightly as the nerves die, unable to watch anymore he turns to face Jacob now kneeling next to the body.

"Their absorbers, we nicknamed them sponges, they can absorb energy, whether blood, souls, bio-energy and use it to fuel them or fuel their powers." Jacob states.

"So when I blasted that thing, it recharged him?" Kyle replies.

"Yeah pretty much." Jacob sniggers.

Kyle disappointment shows on his face and in his posture as he kicks a small rock in anger.

"Patience Kyle, you'll learn, just not everything at once."

Returning his attention to the corpse Jacob closes his eyes, and begins muttering some ancient Mystical language as his body flares with the bright blue bio-energy.

Lifting his hands over the corpse he waits patiently muttering some prayer till the body itself begins to glow with the same colour.

Mere moments pass before the body seems to rapidly decompose before Kyle's eyes, as if ageing thousands of years in mere seconds, finally the wind scatters what remains leaving only a blacken patched of sand.

Walking back up the dune sword in hand Jacob turns to Kyle still looking to the final resting place of the creature.

"You coming, mate?" Jacob asks.

Kyle turns and follows his friend up the hill to the camp and they rest for the remainder of the evening.

Sunrises wake the two friends both a little sore from last night's action the crack and moan as they rise from their beds and stretch.

Kyle debates still whether to confront Jacob about the vision he had before the unnatural attacked, finally giving in to his curiosity he tells of his visions.

To Kyles amazement Jacob knew what he was seeing was visions of the future, informing Kyle he also has clairvoyant abilities and they will manifest at times.

Unsatisfied by Jacobs answer he makes a mental note to pester him further once they reach the school realm.

Travelling back on the open road the two friends encounter no more unnatural or adventurous situations, the training Kyle endured allowed him to control his powers.

His abilities now equal or beat Jacobs in all area except combat enhancement bio-energy empowerment, only the experience kept him ahead of Kyle.

With each step Kyle progresses on his path, Jacob congratulates him on every advancement of himself and cannot help but hope for the future of the human race.

CHAPTER 12

The Reunion

For the past year, the two friends Kyle and Jacob have travelled the wilderness of the Americas, remaining away from populated areas as much as possible while Kyle learns control of his amazing gifts.

Only two days walking remains before they reach the great city of L.A, where Jacob hopes to catch up with an old friend before taking Kyle to the masters in the school realm to continue his training into a sentinel.

The sun rose to wake the friends and alerting them to their morning rituals, for Jacob he would spend the next few hours in a physical and mental training routine called kata, his bio-energy charges and coursing through him the entire time, followed by calming meditation.

For Kyle his morning was simpler but no less important, meditation and focus exercises would be his way, these exercises allowed his mind to stay clear and bleed off small amounts of built-up energies, keeping him in control of his devastating abilities.

Morning fades away as the two finish their routines and cook breakfast.

"You know those focus exercises kill me in the morning JA, I feel drained for hours after them." Kyle states.

"Good that's their purpose, it keeps your bio-energy at a manageable level until I can get you to the masters," Jacob replies still cooking the last of their bacon.

Kyle shakes his head in disagreement while nibbling his bacon butty.

"It's ok for you JA you had decades to practice, and no offence but a master with years of teaching experience pulling you along."

Jacob continues to cook while lifting his gaze and a small smile to Kyle.

"None took, but your right I did have a decade to practice, I had the best teaching me, and soon so will you, but for now you'll have to settle with my limited teaching experience." Jacobs mocking tone snapped.

"All am saying is there's got to be an easier way or a faster way to keep me from frying myself?" Kyle states.

Jacobs smile drops as he starts to eat his bacon butty and looks to Kyle a little disappointed.

"You think it's that easy, I trained my heart, mind and soul each day from sun up to sun down and beyond, nearly ten years of my life battling those better than me till I became the best." Jacobs tone was a little angry as he throws the remains of his butty and starts packing his belongings.

"After a decade of struggling I was thrown back to the wolfs, fighting in a world I no longer knew, once again people I knew and cared for taken from me, my life became one long hard battle, facing creatures with amazing powers, time and time again."

Jacob continues as Kyle now feels Jacobs anger welling inside as he realises his comments were out of line and disrespectful.

"Ja, I didn't mean." Kyle's voice was frail as he speaks but is soon shutdown as Jacob continues.

"Your right I had it easy, an easy life filled with friends dying around you, knowing somehow how you survived and they didn't." Jacob's eyes begin to well up as his mind remembers his hard times and losses back in the school realm and before.

Kyle walks to his friend placing a hand on his shoulder as he continues to pack.

"Am sorry Ja, I didn't mean to." Kyle's soft voice is unable to finish his sentence.

Jacob stops packing holding his pack and sword in hand, he stirs to the sun as if looking into the future.

"It's ok Kyle, I know you didn't, it's just," Jacob replies but also seems unable to find the words.

"Just what?"

"I was taught, never to take the easy road, all the training, all the pain, is earning the right to go on when others can't, never let your powers be enough, never let the training be enough, never let pain stop you, so you have earned the right to go on."

Kyle's feels Jacobs pain and tries to manage a smile.

"And so I'll go on, fighting this war that started thousands of years before any of us existed, till the day I die, alone." Jacob's head lowers and a quick sniff and a wipe of his eyes.

Swinging his pack onto his shoulder he shows Kyle a quick smile as he slowly starts walking down the road, quickly packing his belongings Kyle runs to catch up with Jacob slowly walking down the road hands in pockets as if cold.

Kyle walks alongside him with glances at Jacob as if he were shy.

"You're not alone any more J." Kyle's states with a smile.

Jacob sniggers and smiles back as the uncomfortable silence is broken and the two walk on together.

Finally, the huge city of Los Angeles spans the horizon as they approach the buzzing city, as they draw near both men feel the uneasy feelings emanating from before them.

The city seems rife with evil as if the city were a creature itself swallowing those insides, Kyle's stomach churns as if here were going to be sick.

"Ow man, what the hell is that?" Kyle asks stopping holding his stomach.

Jacob stops and turns to his friend, his hands still in his long grey trench coat as if nothing was bothering him before looking back to the city.

"Welcome to the city of angels dear boy," Jacob responds.

"Angels my ass, place is brimming with evil." Kyle bends over leaning on his knees as if ready to throw up.

"It's ok just give it a minute or two and it will fade." Jacob walks to his friend's side lifting him to a standing position and helping him walk on.

Moments later the feeling fades, Kyle's gestures to Jacob he can walk alone, looking at the sights Kyle begins to lighten up as he watches beautiful girls walking past, big signs and the busy city life engulf them.

"There's got to be a massive unnatural presence here for this amount of soul energy, and strong dark emotions huh JA?"

Most of what you're feeling is coming from the corruption and darkness of human nature!" Jacobs's responds as they run across a busy street.

Kyle stops dead in his tracks and looks to his friend in disbelief, Jacob smiles and shrugs as he continues to walk on.

Continuing on Kyle watches in disbelief as he watches the local people go about their life's, sometimes catching the sight of small crimes being committed and police officers working there trade under harassment from the locals.

Jacob watches as Kyle observes in disbelief, like a tour guide Jacob just stands and watches as Kyle witnesses more and more of the hatred, greed, and evil generated by this massive city.

The tour takes them finally to a familiar place, frank and Marie's dinner, Jacobs's heart fills with despair as windows are boarded up, some are kicked through as a huge sign reading foreclosure drops in front of the door.

Walking up closer to the dinner he had once known it seems beaten and aged, as if fifty years of age had ravaged it, Kyle runs up the small steps to the door and reads the details of the foreclosure sign.

"Closed back in 2003 due to unpaid rent." Kyle reads.

Walking back to Jacob who stands like a statue looking up into the boarded window as if he could see through it, remembering placing a similar board up over the window after he had disarmed an armed robber and sent him flying through it.

"You know this place?" Kyle asks.

"I used to, once." Jacobs tone was sorrowful.

Walking from the dinner down his old alley to where his home used to be only to be shocked further, the door is new and reinforced with a metal plate, the words beware the dog with a blown-up picture of steels snarling as a hound hangs on the door number 43.

Finally, Jacob smiles, satisfied not everything he knew is gone, taking comfort from the picture he walks down the small group of steps and knocks, Kyle remains up top and waits to look to what will come from the door.

Several knocks later leave Jacob unsatisfied again, deciding to check out the rest of his old neighbourhood they slowly take a look around.

Moving round familiar territory made Jacob a little uncomfortable as a lot had changed and for the worse, empty houses and buildings, burnt-out cars and people on the streets.

Jacobs mind started fearing the worse, thinking to himself steels would not have allowed this city to go to waste like this, praying nothing has happened to him they walk on.

Crossing a busy road and heading to another familiar place the two friends head towards the old library, where Jacob first met Steels.

Before reaching the steps up to the main the door both men stop as their senses attune to a presence, a huge unnatural presence looms nearby, Jacob and Kyle look around for their target but instead hear the sounds of battle echoing in the early evening night.

Following the battle cries and several screams followed by gunfire the presence grows.

"Wow, it's big whatever it is," Kyle states running behind Jacob.

The two find their destination, the back of the library is now a battle zone.

In the delivering area stands a huge towering beast, its stature is a huge muscular humanoid shape with grey skin, its head resembles that of a rhino with two huge horns protruding from the nose, it stands over twelve feet high.

As the two approaches, Jacob locates three terrified humans cowering in a small stairwell, the beast turns and its red cat-like eyes lock onto two new targets, with an almighty roar it lets Jacob and Kyle know it isn't happy.

Suddenly Jacobs and Kyle's gaze is caught by another shocking sight, a Hugh bald black man clad in leather jumps from behind the creature landing on its back and trying wrap his arms around its neck and latch on.

Kyle try's to rush forward to help only to be stopped by a smiling Jacob looking at the two combatants.

"Not so fast Kyle," Jacob states holding his arm out stopping Kyle going in.

Both men look on as the beast grabs the huge man with one hand and slams him into concrete smashing through several layers, lifting the man back out almost covering his head and upper body in one hand he slams him again and again.

Both Jacob and Kyle wince as the beast hits again and again.

"Err JA, don't you think we should do something?"

"Na, you'll only piss him off," Jacob replies looking back to his friend with a cocky cold look to his face.

After three more smashes into the concrete the beast releases his grip and turns to Jacob and Kyle, confident that the leather-clad man is no more, a devilish grin on its face it lowers its stance as if it were to charge.

From the hole in the floor, a pebble of broken concrete flies out and hits the beasts jaw catching his attention.

looking down into the hole he is suddenly smacked in the face by the man in black as he flies out the hole with a leap uppercutting the creature as he goes.

The man lands outside the hole and continues his assault, a left followed by a right slam into the lower body of the creature each one lifting it slightly as if the man were hitting well over his weight.

The beast tries to compensate by swinging his rather slow and bulky back fist at the man only to be avoided and the assault continues.

Finally, the beast interrupts the man's attack with a solid right cross sending the man hurtling back and landing hard on the floor, his body slides effortless along the floor stopping at Jacob and Kyle's feet.

Fresh blood pours from old scares and the man's mouth, but still, his eyes open and a look of shock and bewilderment fills his face.

Kyle bends down closer to the man.

"That had to hurt?"

"nice to see you Stanley," Jacob states looking down at him with a friendly smile.

"Son of a bitch!" Steels replies in shock.

"That's not very nice Stanley," Jacob replies with a cocky grin.

"No, it's not, you sure this your friend," Kyle adds, continuing the sarcastic joke.

Looking back at the creature Kyle is suddenly taken back at the sight of it charging horn first towards them, tapping Jacob on the shoulder rapidly trying to catch his attention.

"Err guys!"

Jacob looks to Kyle then to what he gestures at and he too is slightly shocked as the smile is wiped from his face.

Moving out the way rapidly Jacob pushes Kyle to safety Steels flips up to his feet and catches the beast mid-stride by the horn and slams on the breaks.

His large reinforced boots dig into the concrete tearing into the floor as he is pushed back several feet before stopping the towering beast in his tracks.

Both creature and man struggle shaking on the spot as neither seems able to win the feat of strength, Kyle's jaw drops in awe the sight of this vastly smaller man holding such a creature by the horns literally.

"Anytime, you wanna jump in, JA!" steels snarling voice creeps out as his struggle allows.

Jacob lets his cocky smile creep across his face and gestures as though he can't hear his friend properly holding his hand to his ear.

"Sorry what?" Jacobs tried to hide his smug grin.

"Ow fuc…" Steels curse is suddenly interrupted mid-sentence.

The beast lifts his head swiftly hurling him high into the air, timing it perfectly the creature slams his huge fist into steels body as he falls sending him into the wall of the library.

Once again both Jacob wince as if they knew the impact would hurt and by how much, Kyle bites his lip and holds his head as he turns away unable to watch.

"Ouch!" Jacob states trying to keep a straight face.

The creature watches as steels body falls out of the small crater in the wall to the floor in a heap, a deep husky laugh erupts from the creature.

Walking with a cocky swagger and cracking his mighty knuckles trying to intimidate Jacob and Kyle the beast walks towards his next targets.

Jacob puts on a fake smile and points behind the creature.

looking confused the beast looks behind only to see Steels stood and a look of anger on his face.

Reaching into his jacket his favourite weapon that of Betty a sawn-off modified 12 gauge is pulled from within and let loose.

Round after round slams into the beast only managing to cut partially into its skin, the force of each blast staggers it some.

as the rounds run dry steels runs at the creature using the side of the alley he jumps onto the wall and higher still to the head of the creature bringing his left hand down on the head of the creature.

The creature drops to one knee under the force of the attack, steels refuse to stop dropping betty back onto his retractable cord it flies back into the fold of his coat as his right hand smashed into the other side of the creatures face.

The attacks don't stop as steels left leg comes spinning around forming a fine hook kick as the heel hits the same target knocking the creature into a roll before lying flat on the floor.

Steels gather his strength and take a breath, cracking his neck with a sudden left tilt he walks towards the creature spitting out a small measure of blood, expecting it to be dazed he bends over the head.

"Had enough, you son of a bitch." Steels asked cockily.

From nowhere the creature grabs steels head, steels struggle to break free as the creature climbs to its feet, with a quick sharp move the creature lets his grip go and smash into steels head with his own, the horns make a solid thud.

Steels staggered back a few feet before falling back to the floor in a heap, the creature lets a grunt of approval out as he watches, walking up to his target he sniffs steels as if checking for life.

Realising he is still alive and combat-capable the creature grabs steels body and slams him into the wall, slowly applying all its strength it tries to crush him into the wall.

Steels fights against the strength of the attack with his own powerful body but fatigue is gaining on him, looking to Jacob and Kyle he gestures to their right revealing a large black weapons bag.

"Sword!" steel rasp as breath will allow.

Kyle goes into the back and finds a huge two-handed sword, retrieving it from the bag Kyle throws it towards steels only for it to land at the feet of the creature.

Steels look with pure disappointment at Kyle.

"Thanks!" he sarcastically states.

Jacob shakes his head still smiling as he walks forward slightly and empowers his body revealing the bright blue glowing aura, suddenly releasing a small telepathic jolt flying through the air it slams into the beast.

The creature releases steels and staggers sideways as if he were hit, holding his head he tried to shake off the effects.

Steels grasp his sword with a huge sigh, lifting the mighty weapon he charges wielding the sword in one hand he runs towards the creature leaping high into the air, lifting the blade above his head blade pointing to the ground.

As he falls back to earth the blade crashes down into the chest of the mighty beast, screaming in pain as the blade is pushed through with steels powerful strength.

Regaining his balance as the creature looks in shock and pain steels grasp the blade once more and pushes it further in and rams the beast into the alley wall.

Almost nailed to the wall the creature lets lose another right cross into steels face, only moving him slightly steel refuses to stop as the blade is pushed to the hilt within.

Letting the blade stay lodged deep into the chest of the creature and pinning him to the wall, steels steps back clenching his fists and closing his eyes, both Jacob and Kyle feel the ripple of bio-energy.

Watching his friend Jacob witnesses the bright blue energy swell from his hands and up to his arms, slamming first the left backhand followed by his right fist into the right knee of the creature the sound of bone smashing is heard.

The following procedure is followed on the left knee dropping the creature to its now destroyed knees, a final blow in the form a powerful right hook smashes into the beasts head knocking him unconscious.

The creature falls to is side on the floor, pulling the weapon from its chest and a swift kick rolling it to its back steels walks round it waiting for it to move again.

Steels nod in agreement as he reaches into his jacket and pulls a grenade, pulling the pin with his teeth he slams the weapon into the hole in its chest and turns away walking towards Jacob.

The explosion lifts the now-dead creature body off the floor slightly as its chest is splayed open and sprays the alley walls with its warm crimson, steels continue to walk on unaffected. Approaching his old friend steels lights a cigar, and smiles at Jacob.

"Subtle!" Jacob states sarcastically.

"Ja, good to see you." Steels states opening his arms still holding his sword.

Jacob is suddenly shocked by the speedy right cross from steels striking him in the jaw, Kyle jumps to his friend's defence and jumps in front of Jacob, steels looked on baffled by the young upstart, grabbing his jacket he throws him effortless aside a few feet.

"Cheers for the help man, appreciate it.!" Steels states annoyed slightly.

Jacob rubs his jaw and looks to steels.

The same look on steels face emerges as Jacob retaliates with his right cross, knocking his cigar to the floor.

"You're welcome, Stanley," Jacob replies.

"I told you not to call!" snarling at first steels looks at his smiling friend and forgets the rest of his sentence.

Both men erupt in laughter and embrace as old friend reunited after many years.

Kyle remains on the floor looking bewildered.

"God damn it's good to see you man, how longs it been?" steels asks.

"Err I don't know it errs 2007 isn't it?"

"yea." Steels replies.

"Then it's been eight years."

"Damn, eight years, long time without a word." Steels Still laughing suddenly stops and again strikes Jacob with a right cross.

Jacob once again looks back to his friend in shock, steels now stern face looks very serious.

"That's for not writing! Man, I gave you up for dead years ago! What the hell happened?" steels demands.

"It's a long story, my friend, ill fill you in over dinner, I trust you still been looking after my place?"

Steels face suddenly drops as if a memory suddenly fills his mind.

"JA err, you know the dinner?" steels tone now soft and sorrowful.

"Yea I saw, what happened?"

"Frank died four years ago, heart attack." Jacobs eyes close as his head drops, another friend lost he thinks to himself.

"After the funeral, Marie gave me the keys to your place said for me to keep it for you, then moved up north with franks family." Steels spoke with a heavy heart.

"But hey I still left everything the same in the house, except a few improvements, let's go eh?" steels voice now lighter trying to change the mood.

Suddenly the three trapped innocent's hiding down the stairwell scream at the sight of the dead creature rotting away to dust.

Jacob lifts Kyle to his feet and gestures for him to sort the people before they run, Understanding immediately what his mentor meant, placing a small telepathic command Kyle manages to wipe their minds clean of the event, and send them home safely with false memories.

"Who's the little pup?" steels asks as he watches the boy work.

"He's ok, he's with me, and he's a psychic." Jacobs's replies trying to push the pain of his friend death away.

Steels look to Jacob as if questioning him.

"I'll explain later."

Jacob grabs his pack and Kyle's and starts walking towards the old dinner, Kyle runs up behind and reaches for steels large weapon bag trying to help.

A large ripped and bloody leather glove grabs the straps first, looking up at a rather mean scarred and serious-looking steels, Kyle chooses to let him take it and just smile.

Steels raised his other hand and points at Kyle leaning in close.

"Ah-huh." Steel utters as he turns to follow Jacob.

Walking from the scene, the three men walk towards a haven for the night.

"JA, you better have a good excuse for being gone all this time boy." Steels states.

Jacob laughs as does steels as they walk home.

CHAPTER 13

Events In Motion

The apartment seems to be filled with ghosts of the past as if walking into a room full of memories playing themselves in Jacobs mind.

Steels changed little except a few of his personal belongings including the kitchen which is filled with gun parts and cleaning equipment as well as pans for cooking.

Both Jacob and Kyle are amazed by how clean and spotless the place is under Steels care, their shock is worsened by what appears to be a small indoor garden beautifully cared for and flourishing out of the living room.

"There goes the hard-ass image of you steels." Kyle jests.

"Say what!" Steels demands as he lifts head from the fridge and the cold beer he was about to neck.

"Well, I was expecting more like the movies you know big tough guy, guns and glory, too busy to clean the house with saving the world and all that." Kyle continues.

"He's joking Steels, he didn't mean anything by it." Jacob interrupts.

Steels swallow hard the beer from his can as he looks to Kyle with a disappointed unimpressed look.

"Uh-huh." He utters before turning to Jacob.

"Where you find this punk?" he asks.

Jacob walks into the kitchen turning to face his friend Steels in the fridge, leaning on the sink and folding his arms he too looks unimpressed by the turn of events of late.

"So how have you been Stanley?" Jacob asks knowing he is not going to like this conversation.

Steels offer Jacob one of the beers he currently holds in his hand as he leans on the fridge door, refusing his hospitality Jacob waits for a response.

"Ha, how have I been?" He mimics Jacobs question sarcastically.

Moving to the living room Steels starts spraying his small garden with a water sprayer shaking his head as if he couldn't believe the question.

"How did it get so bad?" Jacob follows his friend asking.

Suddenly stopping his watering he looks to his flowers not turning to face his friend as anger swells within him.

"How did it get so bad? You left! That's how!" repeating the question as if he couldn't believe he had to ask and then shouting steels turns to face his friend.

Jacob cannot help be feel hurt by his friend's remarks.

"You knew I had to leave, I can't stay in one place forever, I needed to find the others, and I needed answers," Jacob replies calmly.

Steels head lowers as he tried to contain his anger.

"What happened?" Jacob asks.

Steels dropped into his soft armchair, tears well in his eyes but as usual, he refuses to let them fall, Jacob lowers himself onto the chair opposite as does Kyle, Jacob looks to his friend knowing something horrible has happened to him.

"Their dead!" Steels rasps as his tears now flow down his cheeks.

"Who's dead?" Jacob asks.

"All of them, the hunters are gone."

Jacob's face drops into shock and fear.

"How? When?" he demands.

"Two years ago, I was requested by Simons to return to New York for our yearly meeting."
Wiping the tears from his eyes Steels tries once more to stop his tears.

"My flight was delayed, I was a day late when I got there, and it was too late."
Jacob rises in shock walking to the only window behind steels small garden, folding his arms and closing his eyes Kyle feels the ripple of sadness and fear coming from Jacob.

"When I arrived it was like a slaughterhouse in there, my brothers were ripped to pieces, blood was everywhere, some were burnt to ash were they stood." Steels mouth trembles as he speaks tears now flow freely from his eyes.

"Some of them were cut down by a blade, by a master swordsman too, some just laid there, and not a scratch on them but their eyes were pure white, no irises or pupils."

"Soulless" Jacob interrupts.

Walking to the sofa he flops onto it letting a sorrowful sigh as he looks to his friend.

"It's what happens to the body after the soul is taken." Jacob clarifies.

"The ones who were cut, the looks on the face was of pure shock as if they knew who did it."
Steels stated shaking his head as if he couldn't understand it.

"They can't all be gone surly?" Kyle interjects tying to join the conversation.

Moving around the room to face both Steels and Jacob.

"I watched you overpower that huge mountain of muscle earlier if their anything like you some of them must have survived." Kyle continues trying to instil a little hope into this dark tale.

Steel's shakes his head in disagreement before answering.

"No, they were all there save for Simons."

"You think he got out in time?" Jacob asks.

"I don't know, but when I find him am gonna find out." Steel's tone now harsh as he fights the tears once more.

"There's nothing you could have done Steel's if you were there you would likely have been killed too," Jacob adds.

"I should have been there, it was my duty to be there." Steels states.

Kyle fights the urge to jump in but cannot help his feelings and acts on them.

"You make it sound like you wish you had died with them." Kyle interrupts.

Jacob turns to Kyle as if he had hit a nerve, realising he is refereeing to both himself and Steels, Jacob remembers the conversation he had with Kyle two days ago about living on when others didn't.

"I know what you're feeling Steel's, you feel guilty because you're alive and their not, I feel the same, I have lost friends and still I go on," Jacob adds.

Snapping out of his sadness he turns back to the garden and watering the flowers.

"After that, I returned here, tried to carry on our work, I know it doesn't look like it but I tried, day in day out." Steels tone now angry as well as sorrowful.

"I knew you would Steel's." Jacob states.

Suddenly steels spun around looking to his friend, anger erupts from him but aimed at his failings.

"Did ya? You know I'd come back to this shit box! To fight, bleed and kill! Do you know what it's like to know nothing you've done is ever good enough? Steel's anger flows from him like an erupting volcano.

Collapsing back into his chair he lets out a heavy sigh as he calms down and looks at Jacob.

"Were losing Ja, Every time I kill one of those sons of bitchies, ten more jumps up to takes its place, every time I put a criminal in the hands of the cops they let them go again the next minute."

Steels lowered his head to his hand as if resting a heavyweight, Jacob walks to his friend placing a friendly hand on his shoulder.

"I do know what it's like Stanley, but we can't give up, the world is at stake." Jacob states.

Kyle looks at his new friends as he takes Jacobs old seat, his thoughts are for his two friends, their fight is never over, they will continue to lose friends and love ones till there is no one left, or they are dead.

Jacob walks back to the window, watching the city life buzzing as it normally does, the sad feeling that all those souls are in real danger and need of help, the cold feeling creeps up Jacobs's spine.

An evil twisted feeling starts to fill Jacob as if it is a wave of darkness pulsing outward infecting all within range, lowering his gaze saddened for a moment, Jacobs takes comfort from the beautiful flowers of Steels Garden.

Jacobs suddenly feels something stir within, looking out the window again to the dark grey life that seems to be merely existing, the corruption, the evil, the self-centred every man for himself attitude is suddenly lifted as he touches the flowers.

Like a fresh ray of sunshine erupts within him, he bends down and smells the flowers, taking in their sent and with it, a new sense of being content overwhelms him.

Jacobs mind erupts into images of his masters, of his friend Carl, and the promise he made to one day find him, strong feeling pulses through him, giving him the will to go on.

The thought such a delicate beautiful thing can bloom and be created in such a dark dismal city filled with hate and despair gave him hope.

Like a sudden shock to the system Jacob snaps out of the images of his mind and looks around, the darkness is still there reaching for him, Jacob opens his mind and feels the ebb and flow of a corrupting force washing over the city.

Turning to his friends, Jacob is suddenly taken back by the sight of steels laid asleep his head resting on the chair's head, Kyle sits stirring into space.

Anger now festers within Jacob, in his mind he knows there is more to just human greed and suffering at work here, something is offering a helping hand, Jacobs anger grows as he now knows he left Steels alone to fend this evil by himself.

The sudden crack of the wall as Jacobs's fist smashes a few inches into it awakes both Steels and Kyle from their previous states.

Both men look on with suspicion at their friend currently pulling his hand unaffected from the wall.

"I'm sorry Steels', I'm sorry I left you." Jacobs tone was angry, not sorrowful.

"I had no right to leave you to defend this city alone." He adds.

Steels looked to his friend still a little drowsy after his fight, Jacob turns to Kyle a stern look on his face.

"I'm sorry for you to Kyle."

Kyle looks at his mentor with a bewildered look.

"What for?"

"For bringing you into this war, for delaying your training and taking you to the masters."

"You didn't bring me into this war, the demon who attacked me did, and what you mean delaying me," Kyle asks curiously.

Jacob smiles and offers steels his hand, taking his friend by the hand he jerks him up to standing position, steels looked down to Jacob and puzzles at his smile.

"Are you done?" Jacobs tone harsh and mocking.

Steels bewildered look drops sharply as if he were just insulted or challenged.

"No," Steels tone Sharp and full of rage.

Turning to Kyle letting go of his friend's hand, Jacob places his hand on his student's shoulder and looks him in the eye.

"I will take you to the masters, you will become the greatest sentinel the order has known, but for now, I need you with me."

Turning away from both men back to the flowers Jacob feels his friend's strength growing as if the darkness seeps away from them.

"I'm always with you," Kyle responds.

"Good, because we're not done yet," Jacobs tone once more forceful and angry.

"What's the plan?" steels asks.

Jacob plucks one of Steels flowers and continues to smell its fragrance as if continually taking a hit of some happy juice.

"We're going to retake the city, piece by piece," Jacob replies.

Both steel's and Kyle smile, their determination returning their anxiety builds.

Turning back to Steels Jacob holds his friend's shoulder,

"You were outnumbered, outgunned, you had no idea what or were your enemy was coming from or what form its attack would be, still you fought, and fought well." Jacobs's proud voice instils respect from Steels.

"But now, we have an advantage." Jacob smiles and turns back to Kyle holding steels shoulder.

Kyle knows instantly he is referring to him and his abilities and returns his smile and confidence with a quick flash of his bright purple Bio-energy in his eyes.

"Humanity is going to start fighting back, one soul at a time."

Steel's watches Kyles display and looked a little shocked but agreed, any chance for payback is ok with him.

That very night the darkness takes a sudden and definite blow, multiple gangs are taken down harmlessly, merely falling to the floor unconscious.

Police officers witness the returns of their white and dark angels swoop into a barricaded building filled with gunmen, currently, in a shootout with the police, the sound of battle is heard as gunfire seems to range out in all directions before falling suddenly quiet.

The officers slowly enter only to see the entire gang unconscious or bound their weapons piled in a heap all empty before them.

Night after night the three ventured out, the crime rate fell dramatically, and the unnatural numbers dwindled, as did the darkness from the city.

During the day Steels and Kyle would rest, Jacob however was to full with anger at his failures to rest and sought out the corruption, tracking down corrupt officials, lawyers, judges, police offices, Jacob pushed the darkness from their minds and replaced their morals compass to how it should be with a little telepathic command.

Merely a week had gone past before the city was showing signs of improvement, people were returning work, taking care of their families paying bills, and occasional helping out a neighbour, the police were no longer lazy or fighting a losing war and were take pride in their work.

Small little victories Jacob thought to himself, but all contributed to the greater good.

***

Looking through the window on the people below from his high-rise office window the man Known as Daniel Lance looks out into the night.

Looking to the millions of people who live in his city of New York he cannot help to gloat to himself thinking of but one word.

"Cattle."

Turning from the window he unbuttons the expensive Armani suit jacket and sits in his large leather chair, a large oak desk spread before him has everything in a neat and tidy place, everything the now rich and powerful lawyer needs.

The roaring log and coal fire in the office illuminates the office as the flames flicking light shines of the black and white marble walls.

Leaning into his chair placing his elbows on his desk his hands together and resting on his chin, he expects a call any second.

The door opens slowly as a well-dressed man in a black and white suit and red tie enters, walking the long distance to his master's desk the man walks with a confident stride, to the trained eye, this man is a warrior in a suit, a wolf in sheep's clothing.

Stopping short of Daniel's desk, the man lowers his head in a slow bow.

"My lord, we have a problem in L A." the deep rattling voice too deep and powerful for a man of his stature.

Daniel refuses to move but just looks to his minion.

"Speak."

"The overlord of the city has lost control, he believes a sentinel to be the cause of the problem."

Daniel remains still at the news as if not phased in the slightest, although anger erupts within him.

"Send your horde!" his voice gives away his anger.

The minion in the suit lifts his gaze and turns to walk away, reaching halfway across the sixty-foot room he is stopped by his lord's voice.

"Bring me their souls."

The man turns and bows once more before leaving, turning his large leather chair to the window and looking out into the night Daniel's thoughts are worried.

"Finally the last sentinel surfaced, I knew you were still out there, nearly two years it took me to lure you out, but I have you now."

***

The three friends stand watch over their city, watching from a warehouse roof somewhere in the mess that is Los Angeles docks.

Selecting this area as it is the hive of criminal smuggling that Steel's knows off, gangs and thugs bring stolen goods here to sell to a crime boss using a scrap yard and delivery business as a front.

Kyle sits in a meditation posture and sends out his feelings in all direction as far as he can trying to locate thought patterns, not of this world, Steels looks out into the city with some binoculars trying to find a target.

Jacob stands leaning against the small roof wall folding his arms and waits patiently, his sense stretched out but not as far as Kyles.

"Ja this sucks! This past few weeks nothing's happening, the unnatural fled man am telling ya!" steels upset.

Both Jacob and Kyle smile as they go about their thoughts, Jacob starts to feel as fed up of waiting as Steels.

"Wow, I got something," Kyle says.

Both Steel's and Jacob turn to their friend as if waiting for him to continue with a description.

"Ok, now there's more than one, three of them, heading this way, and fast." Kyle states jumping from his sitting position looking out to their direction.

Steel's lifts his binoculars and tries to find something, Jacob focuses his senses in the same direction.

"He's right, three of them heading straight for us," Jacob adds.

"Where? I don't see shit." Steel's remarks.

Climbing from the roof the three friends stand under the street light looking to the open road before them as if phasing in and out of the world three well-dressed men in black suits and ties with white shirts appear and disappear and reappear several feet closer.

Jacobs mind suddenly remembers the encounter that sent him wandering again, the creature in the alley all those years ago, the creature he fought launched himself from the roof and smashed into a taxi releasing some demonic-looking creature from within.

"We have met these things before Steel's, the man on the taxi, eight years ago." Jacob states.

The three friends stand and watch as their enemies approach, stopping merely a few feet away the scene resembles an old western stir down.

The three dressed men's eyes flicker with hate and then flash red as their mouths flood with black sliver, black veins fill their now white skin as their teeth twist and sharpen.

Their stance changes to a beast-like in a combat position as the three in unison pull a short curved sword resembling a black stone-like material.

Kyle's eyes flare as does bio-energy aura, Steels grasps his jacket and pulls it behind him exposing his many guns, Jacob stands merely lowering his gaze slightly and waits.

The battle commences with the too outside men of the three suddenly disappear and reappear next to Kyle and Steels.

Kyle flinches as the man appears next to him, wasting no time the man thrusts the curved blade at Kyle only to be foiled by a flash of sparks as the blade hits the aura.

Thrusting his right arm forward and his mind into further action a pulse of bio-energy from his aura erupts and hurls the man flying backwards into the wall beyond.

Steel's grabs the man by the jacket as soon as he appeared, ramming his mighty scarred head into his opponent's followed by a right thrust kick to his enemies' chest sending the man flying backwards into a garbage bin, steel strolls after him.

"Paybacks a bitch isn't it!" Steel's adds following his prey.

Jacob watches as the man now creature before him twists his blade in his grip, reaching for his blade and readying it he waits for the charge.

Mere seconds later the creature before him disappears and reappears next to him with a strike with his blade, Jacob parries and counters but to thin air as the creature phases in and out of view away from strike after strike.

Several strikes later Jacob grows tired of this game, not one of the creatures attacks have landed but neither has Jacobs, parrying the last of his attacks Jacob empowers his mind, body and blade, in a single motion.

Twisting his blade in his grip to pointing to the floor Jacob slams the point into the ground a few centimetres releasing the energy out into the world.

The pulse from Jacobs's blade flies out in a sphere around him like a shockwave ever-growing, all though not enough to injure, the power from the blast last only a few feet but is enough to knock the creature of his game and reveal his presence.

Wasting no time Jacob spins his blade and position to attack, by the time his blade is raised it is fully charged with bright blue bio-energy, the blade crashes down passing through flesh, bone, and spirit.

The man stops suddenly and looks to Jacob in total shock, his curved stone blade drops to the floor, the blue energy appears in a diagonal line across his body pulsing with life, and Jacob lifts his blade ready to attack again.

With one more sudden strike, Jacobs's blade passes through the neck perfectly of his enemy as he continues to spin with the attack.

Continuing his turn as if he hit nothing but air stopping his movement facing the opposite way his mighty blade spins in his hand and up to be cleaned.

Stood behind Jacob the creature's neck also starts to glow with the same energy, as it starts to fall forward the head separates from the body, before hitting the deck the body is consumed by the blue Bio-energy and erupts into a large flash of light leaving nothing but ash to hit the floor.

Kyles fight ends a similar way, the creature attacks over and over but never able to penetrate the shield, Kyle pulls back his right hand and charges it with pure Bio-electricity, throwing his hand at the target the energy flies towards it.

Like something from a sorcery film the bright purple electricity zaps its target, continuing to apply the charge the creature convulses and jolts violently, several seconds later the creature also begins to glow before erupting in a flash of purplish light similar to Jacobs foe, Kyle stops and looks as the ash slowly falls to the floor.

Steel's conflict is slower, every attack is parried, every effort the creature has is foiled and retaliated, the pain Steel's has inside is being brought to bear on this creature.

Shots fired, betty released, even his blade is brought out for a taste as the creature takes every form of physical attack and keeps coming, finally Steel's is satisfied this creature has suffered enough and he will wait for the next one.

Charging his bio-energy to his hand and empowering his own body Steel's waits for the next attack, parrying the blade aside with his left hand Steel's forces his right into the chest of the creature, the sudden shock of a human overpowering him is all over his face.

Pulling his hand from the wound and with it his heart the creature falls back to the floor, stood over him Steels looks to the blackened heart in his hand as it beats its last.

Throwing the bloody mess to the ground next to his prey steel breathes a sigh of content.

The three friends walk from the battle sight as the last of the bodies' starts to decay into ash and blow away, Jacob places his hand on Kyle's shoulder and gives him an affirming look and grin.

Steel's heart a little lighter as Jacob nudges him as they walk, Steel's laughs and nudges back sending Jacob into Kyle, all three laugh as they return home.

The apartment is quiet, all three sit in silence, Jacob sits and meditates as his custom after combat, Steel's enjoys several beers while watering his flowers, Kyle just sits enjoying the moment, thinking to himself he is no longer a victim of this war, but one of its combatants.

The following morning the light shines through the only window in the apartment onto the flowers beside it, Kyle is the first to stir as the sofa is illuminated by light, groaning at first he blocks out the sun before letting the light fill his face warming him through to the core, taking in a deep breath he opens his eyes and climbs out of bed.

Jacob sits in his meditation posture, the light fills his face, slowly his breathing increases in depth and frequency, his eyes open and the morning greets him.

Steel's staggers through in nothing but his boxers, his muscular stature as impressive as his scars staggers to the fridge, cracking four raw eggs into a carton of milk he prepares to drink. "Breakfast of champions." Steel's states before the carton were poured down his neck.

Jacob never grew accustomed to Steel's morning routines and continues to shake his head in disbelief now. Kyle looks on and feels himself wanting to be sick.

A short time later dressed and ready for the day the three friend's break to do their own thing, Steels hits the weights in his mini gym, Kyle tries to copy at an extremely lower weight, Jacob ventures out into the world.

Finding a local newspaper stand he pays for the news and slowly walks on reading as he goes, nothing is mentioned of the fight last night as he expected, the city races buy always in a hurry.

Venturing into the park and sitting on a bench watching children playing brings a soothing feeling to Jacob.

"Safe for another day young ones." Jacob thinks to himself.

The soothing vanishes quickly as Jacobs senses suddenly pick up a presence approaching from behind, rising to his feet and turning to face the oncoming feeling Jacob is taken back by the sight.

A lone man walks towards him, his tall slim frame makes him look oddly familiar, and his long white hair placed in a ponytail his wide eyes barely hidden by large black sunglasses just peak over the edges, his pale silver skin gleams in the sunlight.

The man stops before Jacob looking at him with a smile and holds out his arm as you would expect from a handshake.

Jacob takes his arm just below the elbow and the tall man does the same.

"Grandmaster Shakarian," Jacob utters softly filled with surprise.

CHAPTER 14

How The Might Do Fall

Shakarian embraces Jacob in a huge bear hug like grip the grandmaster is pleased to see him, and Jacob returns the gesture before they both sit on the park bench overlooking the children playing.

Shakarian dressed in human clothing made Jacob feel a little weird, his slim powerful frame hid well under the pale green trench coat, black jeans and t-shirt.

"Master, not that am not over the moon to see you but why are you here?" Jacob asks curiously.

Shakarian looks to the children the same warm feeling Jacob had watching those fills his heart two.

"We have a problem, Jacob, the mages are here; well at least one flame lord is anyway." Shakarian states without removing his gaze from the children.

"A flame lord?" Jacob asks.

"One of the high ranking mages of fire, his name is Mirelock, lord Mirelock, we have crossed paths in the past." Shakarian states almost gritting his teeth at the end.

Jacob can feel the hatred coming from his master as he thinks of this mage.

"That's not all, we have found the ones responsible for master Takami and the attack," Shakarian says while turning his gaze back to Jacob a wicked smile creeps on his face.

Jacob feels like a bomb has gone off inside him, his anger and power swirls within wanting revenge.

"Who and where." Jacobs's voice was now stern and anxious.

"Easy my friend, the one in charge is in New York but the mage and two more of his generals are currently in L.A."

Turning back to the children Shakarian waits for Jacob to calm down slightly.

"Then were are the generals, I'll make them take me to the one in charge."

Jacob state's in anger.

"Calm yourself my friend, all in good time." Shakarian states while standing taken a breath and a last look at the children.

"Besides, I have not been back to this realm in over a thousand years I hear you have a wonderful drink called… coffee?" Shakarian asks trying to lighten Jacobs's mood.

Walking back to Jacobs's apartment below the old dinner Shakarian could feel the questions burning to come out of his friend, once they reached the apartment Shakarian stopped at the door sensing powerful presences within.

Looking to his friend sternly Shakarian opens his long green coat reading himself should he need his weapon.

"Friends of yours?" Shakarian asks curiously.

"Yes master, two friends, come ill introduce you." Shakarian put at ease at his friends trust in these people.

Kyle's head emerges from the bathroom his toothbrush still in his mouth his eyes wide with either shock or awe at the presence he felt entering the apartment.

Steels still oblivious to such power sits in front of the telly beer in hand watching sports and shout abuse at the telly.

Jacob walked in first locating Kyle half-naked with nothing but a towel and toothbrush he staggers from the bathroom as if a shy child looking at the magnificent creature before him. "Master this is Kyle, he's a...he's my student," Jacob states unsure how to introduce him to his grandmaster.

Shakarian looks this boy before him up and down sensing the pure power he possesses, both seem to be in shock and awe of each other, holding out his huge hand Kyle takes it in friendship.

"Student, you say, then why have you not brought him to the school?" Shakarian asks politely.

"There hasn't been a lot of time we have only been here a few weeks," Jacob replies.

Suddenly there is a flurry of abuse coming from the living room Steel unhappy with the way his team in whatever sport he is watching is losing.

Climbing to his feet and giving the TV a little friendly kick he struts to the kitchen ignoring all in the hallways and raids his fridge.

Finally, lifting his head above the fridge door beer can to his lips and emptying fast Steel's eyes suddenly lock onto Shakarian.

His eyes slowly widen as the can empties down his throat, he brings the can down throwing it in the bin without taking his eyes from his guest, shutting the fridge door he darts for his room and his weapons.

Jacob dashes after him quickly gaining on him knowing Steel's first instinct is to shoot first ask later.

"Here we go again," Kyle adds with an unimpressed look shaking his head.

Shakarian looks to his young host with a look of bewilderment on his face.

"Sorry about this," Kyle adds looking to his mentor's mentor. With an unhappy smile.

Suddenly emerging still wearing only his shorts and a vest Steel's pulls his trusty Betty from its hiding place muttering to himself he aims.

He is suddenly jolted to the side as Jacob charges his weapon pulling him into the living room. A single shot fires and suddenly absorbed by a hazy bright purple bioenergy shield Kyle quickly summoned before himself and Shakarian.

Shakarian suddenly taken back by this new technology is quick to learn that Steel's just tried to injure him. Suddenly walking with a purpose he pushes past Kyle towards the living room.

Kyle lowers his shield with a nod from Shakarian gesturing a thank you, the living room is now home to a wrestling match, Jacob is using all his strength minus his enhanced power to try and stop steels by pushing him against the wall.

Suddenly he is pulled away by a large silver-skinned friend pulling his collar as he walks before Steel's, steel's brought his betty to bear on his target.

The shock and rage on Steel's face are clear to all as Shakarian's takes hold of the barrel and suddenly bends it down rendering Betty obsolete.

"You son of a bitch!" Steel's screams after the trembling of his chin and tears in his eyes clear.

A sudden right cross is thrown to Shakarian, the attack is avoided as is several others, Jacob stands head in his hand shaking in disbelief, Kyle stands in the bathroom doorway toothbrush still in his mouth and towel wrapped around him watching.

Never able to strike Shakarian Steels pauses gasping for breath, he turns to Jacob still looking on in disbelief.

"You just gonna stand there J?" steel screams.

"This is my master Stanley, I tried to tell you before you went all gung-ho." Jacob replies a little sternly.

"Ow!" Steel seems to have come to his senses and suddenly feels a little awkward.

Shakarian still looks a little annoyed but seems willing to let things alone.

Kyle sniggers as he closes the door to the bathroom and continues to get changed, Jacob still stood in disbelief takes off his jacket and gestures for Shakarian to take his.

Without warning a firm right cross slams into Shakarian's face, steel's just remembered his pour, Betty.

A small stagger backwards as he was taking off his Jacket leaves Shakarian stood almost unscathed.

"That's for betty!" Steel's shouts clearly stating he is annoyed.

Shakarian's gaze slowly turns back to Steel's his jacket still half off he pulls his left arm out of the jacket and grabs hold of Steel's slamming him hard into the wall and pinning him there some few feet into the air.

Jacob shakes his head and flaps his arms once more in disbelief, finally brushing it aside he walked past his master taking off his jacket and walks off to hang up the coats muttering in disbelief as he goes.

"You attack me, then get annoyed as I render you weaponless, do you see any kind of normal reasoning here human!" Shakarian asks still pinning Steel's to the wall with ease.

"When you put it like that…no!" Steel's replied under the stress of his throat holding his entire body in the air.

"Good then follow that line of thought and stand down, before I turn this dwelling of yours into a battle zone, and you into a bloody mess." Shakarian states lowering him to the floor slowly.

Steel's rubs his neck and twists his head about checking for injury, as Shakarian turns away from him he looks to Betty and seems hurt inside.

"You still owe me a new gun." He quickly adds.

Shakarian stops for a second before continuing to find Jacob in the kitchen.

"Interesting friends you keep Jacob." Shakarian states entering the kitchen.

"I'm sorry master, Stanley can be very…stubborn, but he's a good friend." Jacob replies.

"I heard that!" Steel's shouts through from the living room.

Jacob finishes making the coffee and takes them through to the living room, steel sits in his armchair a bent Betty laid across his lap as if it were a dead pet.

The two friends sit on the sofa and other armchair Kyle emerges dressed from the bathroom and joins them, Shakarian's face after sipping some coffee suddenly lightens the mood, even steel's lets out a little snigger.

"So what brings you here master Shakarian?" Kyle asks.

"I'm hunting someone, and I'm here to warn you." Shakarian replies.

Both steel's and Kyle listen on with interest, while Jacob just sits and sips his coffee.

"There is a mage of high rank here in your realm, and I'm going to kill him."

"Ok, so what's the bad news?" Kyle asks.

Shakarian looks to Jacob as he speaks, expecting an outburst as he answers.

"I have traced the one responsible and his generals for the destruction of the hunters, and the attack on my school."

Jacob looks as shocked at this new news of the hunters as Steel's does.

"You just tell me who he is and where he is bright eyes and I'm on my way." Steels asked in anger.

"As much as I would like to let you go off and get yourself killed Stanley, I cannot," Shakarian says after taking another sip of the strong coffee.

"Why the hell not!" Steel's screams now standing up throwing Betty in his chair.

"Because I cherish all life, even one as misguided as yours, also you are Jacobs friend, therefor by default I'm also inclined to think of you as mine." Shakarian replies.

Steel's anger grows, but somehow manages to get a grip and sit back down holding his head in his hands he looks to the floor trying to calm down.

"The man responsible for wiping out the hunters was one of ours." Shakarian looks to Jacob as he spoke, Jacobs head rises and looks to his master in shock.

"He's also the man who killed master Takami in the school realm, that's how they managed to find us." Shakarian's voice now cold and full of anger itself.

"Who would...?" Jacob asks but unable to finish.

"I do not know, but I know his name to the hunters was Simon's he was the one who formed them." Shakarian states turning to Steels.

Steel's head rises pure anger and hatred run through him, he stands to look at his friends and back to Shakarian, unable to hold back the anger he walked with purpose to his room and his weapons.

Jacobs's eyes close unable to believe this turn of events, Shakarian continues with his news.

"A shadow lord has taken possession of a powerful lawyer and firm in New York he coordinates all attacks to his many minions from there."

"Shadow lord?" Kyle asks.

"An evil incorporeal spirit from the hell realm, capable of possessing a body and incredible powers, including summoning more of his lesser minions."

Kyle and Jacob suddenly flashback to the day Jacob rescued Kyle form the black Smokey ghost in New York.

"The ghost!" Kyle states.

Jacob nods in agreement.

"So that thing was a demonic spirit, and some of the things we have been fighting recently really are demons, from hell," Kyle asks.

"Yes, hell is just one of the many realms that exist, as doe's heaven, I would have thought Jacob to have told you that." Shakarian states turning to his friend.

Jacob looks back at the two men a shameful look on his face.

"You haven't told them?" Shakarian asks with a small amount of shock in his voice.

"Told us what Ja," Steels asks suddenly appearing full dressed and armed.

"They didn't need to know, hell even we don't know for sure." Jacob states rising to his feet and his defence.

"You call them friends, but yet you do not tell them what happened to you?" Shakarian asks slightly bewildered.

Kyle also rises to his feet now concerned, Steel' walked in front of Jacob looking intently down at his friend with a purpose, hands on his hips as if expecting an answer."

Jacob looks to his friends and turns away, looking back to the bed of flowers Steel's keeps for comfort.

"They don't need to know master, as I said we don't even know the truth of it yet." Jacob states.

"Something you wanna share with the group session JA, I thought were didn't have secrets here."Steels asked.

Jacob turns back to his friend tears in his eyes.

"the school realm was attacked I told you that, we were attacked by hordes of demonic creatures, a man with red hair in a suit commanded them and a single man in a black trench coat and hood killed my master." Jacob's voice was full of sorrow and regret as he recounts his story.

"Go on Jacob, tell the rest, they have a right to know." Shakarian states.

"During the attack I was... injured, I managed to kill my attacker with a single touch, it burnt the empty blackness that was its soul right out of him, then I..." Jacob seems unable to finish the last part of his story.

"he died... the wound he received pierced his heart, he died moments after destroying the creature, his master and I knew he was not fully human when we trained him, we suspected him to be a descendant of the fallen, an angel race from heaven."

All three look to their friend Jacob, Shakarian's looks on the same as he always does with respect but a little disappointed Jacob had not shared what happened with his closest friends, Steel's staggers back slightly at the news.

Kyle lowers his head and walks to his friend and mentor, no wonder you always win."

Kyle states with a smile holding his friend's shoulder, clearly unaffected by the news.

Steel's looks back to his old friend, a small shake of the head is all that is seen as he leans against the wall.

"I always knew there was more to you than just plain old sentinel training, I guess now I know why you want to try and save everyone... it's in your nature." Steel's replies calmly.

"So what now?" Kyle asks.

"We wait, the three generals consisting of the traitor Simon's, the mage and the red-haired man will no doubt have sensed my presence here, they are here in L.A."

Steels started cracking his knuckles a huge smile on his face, Kyle looks unimpressed he walks to his room removing his best clothes and changing into something he doesn't mind getting damaged.

Jacob looks to his friend Steels.

"I'm sorry didn't tell you, Stanley, I didn't know how to" Jacobs voice soft and filled with guilt.

"look Ja you tell me your angel, fine your and angel from heaven, you tell me you're an alien, fine I don't care, just don't keep shit like you dying and coming back a secret alright." Steel's smiles as he hugs his friend.

A quick jolt separates them as Steels grabs Jacobs's shoulders and looks at him seriously.

"Just don't be expecting me to be going all religious and shit and going to church on Sundays." Steels states with a mocking tone.

Both men erupting into a small amount of laughter.

Kyle emerges from his room with his fresh clothing on, he suddenly stops in the doorway his gaze falls to the floor as if looking into space.

Jacob and Steel's know this look well.

"Kyle, you feel something?" Jacob asks.

Kyle's eyes lift suddenly replaced by his bright purple bio-energy.

"They're here."

Jacob grabs the two blades from his and his master's jacket, throwing his blade to its owner they stand in the centre of the room gesturing Kyle to join them.

Steels grabbed Betty cocking the weapon his gaze works its way up to the now bent over barrel, he slowly turns his gaze to Shakarian a very unimpressed look on his face.

Throwing the gun away he pulls his sword.

"They will try and tender us up with their minions first before the general's come for the kill." Shakarian states.

"Same as before gentleman, Aim for the hearts or beheading, Kyle, fry them," steels informs his friends.

Both Jacob and Kyle smile at their orders, the four friends move back to back, as the lights start to flicker.

"Remember the mage is mine!" Shakarian states drawing his blade.

"All yours sparkle, I won't Simon's." Steel's states.

The lights continue to flicker as the very air in the apartment grows suddenly cold, the breath from the four friends creates steam from their lungs.

The lights finally fail, pure darkness fills the apartment for not but a second, a bright pulse and constant purple light suddenly erupts.

The sounds of battle rage out of the apartment from below the street, screams of pain are heard and sounds of powerful blasts striking solid walls.

The sounds of pain and battle last a few mere seconds, the three men stood looking onto the apartment from outside smirk to each other after sending in over half a dozen of the horde.

As the silence falls so does the bright purple light from the window and gaps in the door, another few seconds go before the door opens and four powerful friends emerge without a scratch.

Walking out into the street the friends take positions facing there selected enemies, Shakarian faces a red robe coat wearing fellow a black flame tattoo decorates his face his short bright red hair gelled back, his red silk shirt and black leather trousers give him a menacing look.

Steel's look to the hooded man, his hood hiding his face as his long black coat hides all other features, the hooded man bows his head slowly and then turns to Jacob.

The long red-haired man stands to look at Jacob anger festers in him, as this is sentinel who survived the attack on the school and has slaughtered yet more of his horde.

Kyle stands behind Jacob, the red-haired man senses the power from this boy and decides to increase their advantage, holding his arms out to his side slowly rising his teeth gritting a loud hum can be heard in the distance.

The shadows of the alley begin to twist and turn, like something from the movies, several tall demonic-looking creatures emerge, there frame a massive muscle-like structure with a reddish tone, black horns run across their foreheads and up out to the side there black claws massive as is there black eyes and mouths.

The red-haired man slowly lowers his arms the sounds stop as the shadows return to normal, his grin making him feel confident.

The three men now stand before the four friends, surrounded by a small army of demonic creatures behind them.

"Well, well Shakarian fancy meeting you here!" the tattooed man states mockingly.

"I knew you would find it irresistible to track me Mirelock, this was a ploy to draw you out." Shakarian replies smugly.

"The red-haired man steps forward abruptly.

"Enough of this twaddle, destroy them, now!"

The creatures behind start to close in as do the tattooed man and the hooded man.

"Remember my friends, there is no second place in this fight if you lose, you die, and you make them stronger, with your soul." Shakarian states as he walks towards the mage.

Jacob stands with his back to Kyle, never leaving his students side, he feels Kyles power erupt into life slightly jolting him forward, Kyle's power seems to have developed further his aura has grown and now his powers allow him to lift slightly from the ground hovering a few inches from the floor.

Steels walked with purpose towards the hooded man, his anger festers, and his body pumps with his bio-energy, taking off his jacket and throwing it aside he pulls his sword and waits.

The hooded man approaches and mocks Steel's gesturing him to come for him.

"How could you do it Simon's, how could you kill them all, we trusted you."

"Well you're all fools then ain't you?" a strangely faint Scottish accent replies.

Jacob hears this accents and sends out his senses trying to identify the hooded man, suddenly turning to Jacob the man's hood turns to him sensing the mental probe.

Slowly shaking his head and gesturing he is naughty to try he returns his attention to Steels.

Jacob returns his attention to the red-haired man.

"You were the one who led the attack on the school, for that I'll kill you." Jacob states.

The alley erupts into a massive power play for the realm, three generals serving there lord and master, supported by eight demonic creatures.

The tattooed man suddenly leaps into the air as if flying a wave of heat emanates from his feet as if he were stood on a rocket.

Propelled up and landing on a rooftop some six storeys up, Shakarian leaps into the air somersaulting onto window ledges and fire escapes he lands in front of his enemy.

The mage before him summons from his very hands two jets of fire hurling towards Shakarian, with ease the master swords evades them hiding behind an air duct.

Within seconds the air duct is melting rapidly, noticing this Shakarian leaps back into the fray somersaulting through the air evading sudden bolts of fire hurled at him.

****

The hooded man facing steels easily avoids all the attacks from his attacker, evading and dodging Steel's looks like a clumsy foul attacking widely.

In reality, each attack is precise and focused however his opponent is faster and better trained, running Steels left and right as his sword smashes both concrete flooring and walls alike.

Steel's grows tired of chasing him, slamming his massive blade into the floor burning the tip deep into the concrete holding it still he reaches for his two Glock pistols and opens fire.

****

The red-haired man opens his jacket and throws his sunglasses aside his blood-red eyes stir straight through Jacob, gritting his teeth he charges Jacob, still keeping his weapon in its scabbard, Jacob avoids much as the hooded man did with Steels.

Mimicking almost the same evade and doges and occasionally blocking attacks the red-haired man's physical power would match even Steel's.

Blow after blow the red-haired and eyed man throws, not one land, several punches smash into walls taking huge chunks from them as he chases Jacob.

"STAND AND FACE ME HUMAN!" the man shouts.

Jacob just smiles at the man.

****

Kyle looks to the eight creature before him, his powerfully bright purple aura now reaches out three to four feet from his body, and he floats off the ground by several inches. The creatures pay no attention and charge in all at once.

Pounding on his shield Kyle sniggers, their claws pounce off harmlessly, throwing his arms out to his side suddenly, a psychokinetic force wave flies from his shield.

The creatures fly backwards slamming into the walls and trashcans alike.

Choosing one of the creatures at random still on the ground shaking off his attack, Kyle thrusts out his hand and bio-electric energy, the creature jolts and convulses for mere seconds as Kyle focuses on the heart of the beast.

Falling suddenly quiet the creature begins to decompose rapidly before all to see.

****

Shakarian still dodging the hurled fireballs from his enemy approaches as suddenly changing to deflecting the blast with his blade allows him to summon a psychokinetic blast of his own in a counter-attack.

The blast smashes into the wall behind where the mage was stood, jumping through the air avoiding the attack the mage lands on a roof opposite and hurls a column of fire at his enemy.

Shakarian raises his bio-shield just in time as the flame deflects off the front blocking his view of his target.

Holding his ground the fire continues to pound the shield, looking for a way to attack Shakarian locates some melted debris from the mages onslaught of fireballs.

Using his telekinetic abilities Shakarian lifts the object and hurls it at his enemy, the piece of half-melted wall flies at speed towards its target, the mage suddenly changes targets and hurls his other hand forward releasing yet another fireball destroying the oncoming attack.

Shakarian uses the diversion and leaps for his attacker, landing but a few feet away he attacks, his blade a gleam in the night as the mage suddenly forces into being two blades made of flame to block Shakarian's sword.

****

Steel's fires round after round at his now hated master Simon's, two Glock pistols spew forth their hot metal rounds, the hooded man's blade suddenly appears from nowhere in his hand, a blur of moment flows as sparks erupt before him.

As the last round is deflected by the man's blade he enters a spinning technique charging his blade in red electrical energy and lets it rip through the air as his strike cuts from right to left sending a ripple of energy hurling towards Steel's.

The energy strikes Steel's in the chest hurling him through the air landing in a heap on the floor, the hooded man wastes no time, leaping through the air he falls blade pointing down as he aims for Steel's head.

Rolling out the way steels avoids the fatal blow swiftly, the man continues to attack this time keeping his blade at his side, punches and kicks are thrown each as powerful as if thrown by a demon lord himself.

Steel's is stuck by two punches and the hilt off his sword he takes the blows willingly.

Suddenly grabbing the hand holding the hilt of his weapon Steel's shakes off the blows and pulls one of his other pistols and fires point-blank into his old master's chest.

His body shakes as it is his hit, no screams of pain come from the man, a small amount of blood flies from the wounds as the bullets enter the flesh letting Steels know he has hit him.

****

Jacob continually evading each attack the red-haired man has thrown continuing to mock him, the man's takes of his jacket and loosens his tie, his size starts to grow, his skin reddens slightly his hands replaced by huge claws as teeth sharpen covered in black drool.

Jacob watches patiently as he draws his weapon from its scabbard, the red beast-man before him growls at Jacob then holds out his hand towards a nearby shadow, as if reaching for something.

From the ground, before him, a large black blade emerges from the shadows, covered in blood-red jewels decorating the hilt the massive two-handed sword is taken and wielded in one hand as if it were a twig.

Once again his attack commences, blade clashes against blade, the red beast-like man's strength now further increased knocks Jacob from side to side as he parries, allowing the overpowering attack to continue.

Jacob uses the power as it smashes into his blade ducking underneath the blade as it is deflected overhead as he brings the blade down on the now exposed back area of the beast.

****

Kyle's power still at full strength continues to protect him, the creatures rush him over and over, and finally, Kyle feels a little experiment is in order, suddenly reaching out with his telekinetic ability he gestures with one hand as he grasps all remaining seven creatures.

The creatures are lifted with ease into the air, they claw and sweep their arms and legs around trying to stop themselves moving, like a fish out of water the dangle helplessly.

Smirking how easy it now seems, his face grows cold as he things to the many innocent these creatures would kill and fest on, summoning back his rage, he thrusts his right hand out towards the creatures hanging in the air, bright purple lighting strobes erupt from his hand. The creatures once again jolt and convulse as raw electrical power courses through their bodies overloading their feeble minds and shorting out there organs.

Finally confident the creatures are now dead as their bodies start to decompose in his telekinetic grasp he releases them, the wind helps to eradicate any trace of them.

****

Shakarian now in a melee range engages the flame lord in a sword battle, strikes are thrown and deflected, and the mage seems very capable of defending himself with blades made of fire until Shakarian speed reaches unprecedented levels.

A block is used against one of his attacks, he suddenly empowers his body. Spinning on the spot around the back of the mage the blade is sliced through his leather coat and into his flesh across his shoulder area.

The mage howls in pain as he is flung forward, his blades vanish from existence as he lets go of his grip, holding onto the side of the building for support Shakarian watches slowly lowering form his last strike position.

The mage turns to him and starts to laugh still clearly in pain, regaining his stance he thrust his arms forward releasing several fire bolts hurling Shakarian back into the distance, suddenly the attacks stop as Shakarian uses yet another rooftop wall as cover.

Using his sense of energy he feels the mage building a huge amount of soul energy summoning it to his position, suddenly worried he looks over the edge of the wall to see the mage raising his arms looking to the sky his aura filled with pure fire as five small meteor-like strikes suddenly appear from nowhere slamming into the rooftop beside the mage.

The meteors made of lava-like rock twist and turn and form into humanoid figures no features emerge only there now large size, eyes and mouths made of fire look to Shakarian with hate.

****

Still holding the hooded Simon's hand which is wielding his sword the man now lowered to one knee as several rounds were fired point-blank into his chest steels looks on still filled with hate.

"I hope you rot in hell Simon's you son of a bitch." Steel's grunts as he thrust up with his left knee towards the man's face, Steels is shocked as the man evades it with ease and strikes his leg with an uppercut strike.

Jumping from his kneeling position high into the air two front kicks smash into steels face before he lands perfectly, steel's staggers back as the kicks hit there mark, the hooded man still using his blade pointing down in his grip blocks the gun to his left as he spins again bringing the blade down from collar to hip across Steel's chest and stomach.

Steel's drops his gun and holds his chest, clearly in shock that this man can still move and the fact he is now mortally injured stands and looks to his now open wound.

Falling to his knees before the hooded man shock and pain overpowering his instincts, steels watches as the hooded man approaches, he walks up to Steel's cockily as he lowers his hood, looking into the eyes and smiling to his former pupil.

Grabbing Steel's leather webbing lifting him slightly his short black hair and dark eyes look at him with nothing but discuss.

"Why did I waste my time…" pulling back his blade in an attempt to finish him he is suddenly interrupted by a sharp whistle.

"Hey, scumbag!"

Barely able to move his eyes to see the intrusion, Steel's watches as huge column of pure bright purple bio-energy slams into his attacker, Steel's falls to the floor holding his wound, the energy rip's through the man's body wracking him in pain and slams him through the old dinner's walls losing sight of him inside.

****

Jacobs last attack cut deep into the red-skinned man's back, the creature seems to shake off the attack as he would a pinprick, turning swiftly arm clenched in a back fist he swings blindly.

Jacob avoids the attack ducking underneath it and rising with a perfect uppercut under the creatures chin, the beast lifts slowly into the air as Jacobs now empowered body moves so fast it seems as though the creature is hovering in mid-air.

Taking hold of his magnificent blade he charges it and brings it swooping across the mid-section of the man floating in mid-air before him, time suddenly catches up as the new attacks slams into the man coursing bright blue bio-energy through his body and sends him hurtling through the air also landing into the old dinner beyond.

****

The lava creatures move with catlike grace as they attack, one after the other charges using the hands and feet as fiery weapons they press their advantage, the mage watches on waiting for his right moment.

Two or three would attack Shakarian at once forcing him to use his great unnatural speed and sword skill to deflect keeping his body basically in the same area, the mage anticipated this and hurls a mighty ball of flame into the area.

The blast strikes him in the back burning instantly his clothes and singing his silver skin, blocking out the pain he blocks three more attacks and manages to position himself behind one of the creatures.

As the lava-like creature is struck unharmed by the fireball Shakarian spins his blade to action charging it and severing it in two as it explodes in a bright burst of blue and white Bio-energy.

Another burst of attacks from the creatures forces Shakarian back into an open position as he defends four more attacks.

He howls in pains as another burst of fire smashes into his chest staggering him back against the wall of the roof.

The mage watches in delight as the attacks greatly weaken his enemy sapping his strength, Shakarian now kneeling on one leg and using his blade as support, looks to his enemies gasping.

The four remaining lava creatures rush towards him, taking a page from his finest student's book he suddenly enters a spin charging his blade entering a cut across his body as the blade cuts through the air it creates a huge bright blue energy wave hurling out at chest height towards the lava creatures.

The first two creatures avoid the attack the last two are struck and explode due to the force of the attack.

The mage manoeuvres himself behind Shakarian watching as the final two lava creature attack a now exhausted grandmaster.

Blocking and countering the creatures Shakarian's swords skill behead another one as yet another fireball slams into his body hurling him across the roof once more.

Barely able to stand Shakarian notices the mage moving across the rooftops ready to aim as the last lava creature rushes in once more. Defending himself but keeping the mage in sight Shakarian's tries to recuperate his energy.

The mage once more behind him waits for the attack, blocking the lava creature's last attack he senses the flames approaching from behind.

ducking the blast as it slams into the creature, Shakarian throws yet another energy strike through the air towards the mage striking him in the chest knocking him to a building roof closeby slightly lower than the one they were on.

Making short work of the last larva creature Shakarian walks to the building's edge, exhausted.

As he comes into clear view the sound of gunfire ripples through the air, bullets fly at Shakarian, the mage listening to the advice of his hooded friend found a liking to firearms. Defending as many as possible several hit their target as Shakarian is unable to move fast enough due to exhaustion.

Shakarian takes three rounds, one in the right arm his sword arm and two in the stomach, the grandmaster falls to the roof below in an ungraceful heap.

Rising to his feet holding his chest the mage gasps to breathe, he kicks Shakarian's blade aside and hurls a fireball point-blank into Shakarian's chest.

His howl of agony is not just of pain, but the realisation, he is about to fail, to leave his student alone.

The mage grabs Shakarian long hair lifting him and dragging him to the roof's edge, kicking his legs from under him Shakarian falls exhausted to his knees, his energies completely drained by the magic fire coursing through him.

Looking down to the fight below the mage watches as Kyle blasts the hooded man into the dinner followed by Jacob doing the same to the now enlarged red-haired man.

"Fools!" The mage shouts.

"ITS OVER!" the mage shouts to the men below as they run to Steel's side as he lay on the floor.

The two friends look up to the horrific sight before them, they watch is shock and despair as a flaming blade burst through Shakarian's chest piercing his heart.

The cry of pain and failure could be heard across the city, but city life is full of strange things people think as they continue on their way.

Jacob's heart seems to stop, his eyes wide with shock as his friend and master falls through the air, his scream seems to fall quiet.

The body falls lifeless towards the floor, taking what seems an eternity as it falls turning and twisting before a shallow thud is heard.

Jacob looks back to the mage on the roof and watches as he held out his hand a small white ball of light falls into his palm, his expression changed to pure delight at the trophy of the grandmaster's soul.

The man withdraws from the roof and sight, Jacob leaves his friend Steel's in Kyle's hands and runs to the body of his fallen friend.

Turning his lifeless body to face him his sadness is increased by the sight of his clear white eyes, the mighty soul of his master has gone, claimed by the flame lord who bested him.

A sudden Sharpe sound is heard as the blade of Shakarian falls to earth digging into the concrete besides Jacob and his fallen friend.

Jacob looks up to the mage saluting mockingly as he disappears once more, the hooded man and the red hair man climb from the debris that is the old dinner.

Jacob allows them to leave without further confrontation as they hold their wounds and retreat down the alley into the city.

***

The morning light erupts into the living room, the flower bed Steel's keeps now damaged and spread about the place after the attack. Jacob sits on the edge of the chair his fingers locked together supporting his head as he looks to his fallen master's body laid to rest on the table before him.

Kyle walks from steels room, a towel in his hands wiping blood from them as he looks to Jacob and his fallen friend.

"He's gonna be fine, I think he may actually be made of steel," Kyle says with a snigger trying to lighten the mood.

Jacob just sits not moving except a small head nod in agreement.

Jacobs's heart feels like it wants to explode, his mind wishing that his former master would suddenly open his eyes and rise from the dead as he did.

Kyle walks round to Jacobs's side holding his shoulder trying to comfort him.

Jacobs only response is his eyes closing as tears rush down his cheeks.

"I don't think that's in the vast repertoire of his abilities JA," Kyle states reading his friend's mind.

Jacob lets out a small snigger, as it reminded him of master Takami's trick back in the day.

"I'm sorry J, I'm sorry I couldn't help him." Jacob's head rises, his tears halting as he wipes his eyes.

"There's nothing you could have done Kyle, nothing any of us could have done," Jacob replies.

Rising to his feet and looking down to his friend once more, his beautiful blade laid down his body holding it as a funeral position of the knights of old.

"I wish I had the chance to know him better," Kyle says while looking to him and Jacob.

Jacob smiles and turns to his student fondly.

"He was a good friend, always having time for anyone, sometimes his small grasp of humour made for good times to," Jacob responds.

Wiping yet more tears away he sits next to Kyle and tells him of the time he and his fallen master first met, followed by fond stories of Shakarian's poor grasp on human humour and concepts.

A sudden moan from steel's room interrupts the two friends, they both jump up and run to his room, they look relieved to find him sitting on the bed wincing in pain as he tried to lift himself to his feet.

"Easy Stanley, even you can't take a deep cut across the chest like this and just walk away," Jacob states running to his side sitting him back down.

Helping him back to the bed Kyle keeps his distance a little hesitant to get to close after what happened in the fight earlier.

Jacob seems to have let his heartache lift for a while why he tends to Steel's, Kyle enjoys seeing the two friends together they seem to bounce off each other with compliments and insults.

Steel's holds his wound and winces as the memories flood back to him.

"That son of a bitch was too good JA, I couldn't ..." Steel's is unable to finish.

"We were all outmatched Stanley, there's no shame in it, just get some rest and heal we can talk about it later," Jacobs states as he tries to stand up and leave.

Steel's grabs Jacobs arm stopping him from moving, his eyes well with tears as he feels he failed his brothers.

"You got to promise me something JA, you got to kill that bastard for me, for my brothers, I'm not strong..." again Steel's seems unable to finish.

Taking hold of his hand firmly, Jacob looks to his friend sitting back down a stern look on his face.

"I promise, for all our brothers and sisters," Jacob replies.

Steel's nods in agreement swallowing his pride and tears he looks to Kyle and suddenly remembers his part in the fight.

Pointing a finger at him and trying to keep a stern face he looks to Kyle.

"Ok, ok am sorry, but I couldn't let that man kill you, we need you… and if it's a choice between losing you, or getting an ass-whooping… I'll take the whooping." Kyle utters out quickly before Steel's can speak.

Jacob looks to his young friend taking him by the shoulder he smiles at him as does Steels.

Kyle begins to relax realising Steel's was only teasing him.

"Thank you, Kyle, I'm grateful." Jacob states.

Kyle nods in agreement.

"Grateful, damn, I got to get me one of them, did you see the blast that kid did, whoa!"

Steel's continues to go on about the power Kyle released, going into detail of the attack Steel's finally accepts Kyle's place in the war.

Finishing with wishing he could put Kyle in a shell and use him as power cannon, bringing him out for big shots and special occasions.

Leaving the two friends alone Kyle walks back into the living room, gathering the cups ready to make a fresh batch of coffee, Kyles eyes catch Shakarian's pale green trench coat still hung up in the hallway.

Taking the coat and laying it over his fallen friend's body covering his face, a small object falls from his pocket, a small blue gem in the shape of a pyramid lies gleaming in the morning light.

Reaching for the gem a few images flash into kyles mind before he can block them out, taking it to his mentor he watches as Jacob rises to his feet looking at the gem.

"It's a message gem, Shakarian must have made it."

"Well, what's it say man?" Steel's asks.

Jacob looks to his friend lying in bed a curious but worried look creeps on his face, grasping the gem and empowering it with Bio-energy, Jacob focuses his telepathy on the gem.

Jacobs mind is thrown into the gem, a swirling blue energy whips around him in the distance, and he looks around the open space he is until he locks eyes with a friend.

His old friend and master Shakarian stands in his old samurai-like robes, his posture still with his arms laid in front of him grasping his other hand at the wrist.

"Shakarian?" Jacob speaks.

"Hello my friend, I'm sorry it has come to this." Shakarian replies.

A sudden realisation that Shakarian new he might lose his battle with the flame lord became apparent to Jacob.

"You knew…? You knew you would lose." Jacob asks.

"No, I did not, I knew there was a risk I would fail, but it was a risk I was willing to take to help you, to protect you."

"Protect me?"

"My friend you have more power within you than I have ever seen in any living being, but against the forces the shadow lord has accumulated you would fall."

"Then I fall…! And another takes my place! Kyle would be much more powerful than me if you had taught him instead of me." Jacob responds in anger.

"No, the boy's path is not yours, he has great power no question, but he lacks the will or the focus to control such gifts."

"But if you were there to teach him instead of fighting a battle you couldn't win, he would have."

"Jacob, my friend, listen to me." The Shakarian image distorts slightly as it walks forward placing his hands on Jacobs's shoulders.

"My time was over, my choice has allowed you a measure of information on your enemy so you can prepare, without this you would have failed, and the earth realm would have fallen to the shadow lord…"

"But why me, why am I always the one left behind, when others are taken, it's not fair." Jacobs's eyes well up with tears.

"No it is not, but it is your fate, you are an exceptional being among an incredible people, they will need a defender." Shakarian's smile warms Jacob slightly as he lowers his hands and turns to walk away from his friend.

"Master!" Jacob asks, stopping Shakarian in his tracks.

"I will free you, and master Takami, I promise."

Shakarian turns to his friend as if the last thought creeps into his head.

"Take my sword, it belongs to you now, use it, defend the realm, destroy the evil that threatens it, do not focus on just two souls, save them all."

Shakarian turns away again as he starts to walk once more.

"Master" Jacob shouts, stopping his friend again.

"Can I beat them?" Jacob asks.

Shakarian slowly turns to face his friend a confident smile creeps across his face and remains there as he begins once more to walk away.

CHAPTER 15

Let Slip The Dogs Of War

Daniel walks from around his desk and looks to his three generals, his anger under control the mere look from his dark eyes places fear within the men before him.

"Bring me their souls I said…I sent you to eradicate our last remnants of opposition, three mortal…" Daniel's voice echoes the anger he feels inside.

Walking closer to the men their head drop in shame, arriving first at the long red-haired man his glasses replaced and a new suit clean and tidy.

"Lord Varamont, you have failed me yet again."

"My lord I…" before the red-haired man can finish his response denials lifts his hand and flings it as if gesturing to flick something aside.

Varamont's body is suddenly flung in the directions of his master's hand, smashing into the marble wall he is suddenly thrown and smash into the opposite wall.

The other two generals just watch and pity there fellow general their heads never lifting from their position.

Finally, Varamont's broken and bloody body is sent hurtling towards his master's feet, again Daniel gestures with his hand sharply twisting his hand at the wrist the beaten body of Varamont flips over facing his lord.

Bending down to his general as he gasps for breath, Daniel rips open his shirt exposing his chest, suddenly a dark twisted look creeps on Daniels face as he holds his right hand over Varamont's chest, a dark humming sound like that heard during summoning's is heard.

Daniel's hand glows red as does Varamont's chest, the man howls in pain as small white and blue lights pulse into the room from Varamont's chest and into denials hand.

After several lights have left Varamont Daniel withdrawals, standing up and looking to his other two generals.

"Now…" Daniels tone was calmer and more relaxed as he thinks what to do with his other two generals, straightening up his attire.

"My lord, the encounter was not a total failure." The black tattooed man offers as the smug grin on his face appears.

"Ow really, do tell?" a mocking tone erupts from Daniel.

"Shakarian the soul reaper was present… and defeated!" again the tattooed man's confidence grows as he speaks the news.

"Really? And did you take your payment mage?" Daniel asks walking up to him.

"I did my lord." The tattooed man states with pride referring to the soul of Shakarian.

"I see, I expect you to fulfil our barging, lord Mirelock, or so help me your entire race will be next," Daniel states with anger as he walks away from the mage before turning back to the hooded man.

The mages smug grin turns to a snarl as he decides his next move is best to shut up and do as he is told.

Stood in front of the hooded man, Daniel just looks at him as if looking through him, the man lowers his hood looking to his master.

"And what of you master sentinel huh? Nothing to tell me?" Daniel's voice is mocking and angry.

"My lord there is." His faint Scottish accent rattles out as he keeps his head lowered.

"I know the last sentinel who stands against you my lord, his name is Jacob Rawn. I trained with him in the school realm." The man's voice smooth and unfeeling.

Daniel turns from him and walks back to his desk leaning on the front of it and gesturing for the man to continue.

"Masters Takami and Shakarian were convinced he wasn't fully human, that his abilities were too strong too quick, I did overhear a conversation between them referring to something called the fallen." Daniels eyes suddenly widen with shock as he looks to his general lying on the floor still clutching his chest in pain. with surprise.

"They think he is a descendant?" Daniels voice slightly on edge.

"Yes my lord." The man replies.

Daniel rises to his feet and walks to the window looking out into the night worried by this news.

Varamont finally climbs to his feet his now pale look gives him a weak appearance, adjusting his dress smarting himself up he takes his position at the head of the generals.

Finally, his colour returns as does his strength as he breaths normally again, clearly the souls taken from him were strong.

Daniels remains by the window, without turning to face them Daniels utters his commands.

"Lord Varamont, prepare the horde, get them into position in the shadow we shall attack at nightfall tomorrow."

The red-haired man bows without a word and withdrawals from the room.

"Lord Mirelock we are going to need some added security, summon your mages, they will provide us with some insurance."

The tattooed man gives a little head nod in the form of a cocky bow and turns to leave the room.

"Master Simon's, you will remain with me, just in case."

Suddenly sensing a small amount of fear from his master, the man known as simons cannot help but wonder how one creature could cause so much to change in their carefully laid plan.

"My lord, how is one man even a sentinel such a threat to you?" the man asks.

Daniel lowers his head but doesn't turn around.

"The fallen is the name given to a small group of my races immortal enemy, we have fought for millennia before this planet was even formed."

"I have never heard of them, my lord." The man states.

"Yes, you have… but by another name, they are the race known as the angels."

Daniels turns around his eyes burning red with rage.

***

The night was busy in the city of L.A as it always was, Steels now healed enough to move but not to fight helped to load master Shakarian's body into a truck and drive Jacob and Kyle out into the wilderness a few miles out of town.

The stars shone brightly in the night sky not hidden by the lights and buildings of the city, Kyle and Steel's carry the fallen master's body with respect laying it on the floor as Jacob kneels in the sand facing an open area.

Closing his eyes Jacob summons his exceptional powers from within, uttering a strange incantation in a language neither Kyle nor Steel's as ever heard, and the wind slowly picks up from no wear steadily building in strength it is enough to blow sand and debris all around.

Jacobs's eyes open revealing his bright blue bio-energy at work, still uttering the strange language he holds out his arms wide to the side and looks up at the stars.

A sudden eruption of noise and light bursts into being a few feet from Jacobs's position, a large twelve-foot diameter whirlpool of swirling colour.

Rising to his feet he walks through the porthole to the shadow, Steel's and Kyle follows carrying master Shakarian's body.

Travelling through the shadow was slow going, either Steel's or Kyle had felt anything like it and it took what seemed days to reach the door to the new school realm.

Steel's now almost fully healed carried Shakarian's body alone, carrying him like a groom would carry his bride over the threshold.

The last jolt of the porthole into the school realm allowed Steel's and Kyle to finally breath normally, they arrive in a sudden wall of shouts and screams as hundreds of young men and women rush to Jacob gathering around him trying to touch him like a rock star falling into a crowd of fans.

The screams stop suddenly as Jacob refuses to acknowledge them just stood still looking to the floor, the students turn to Steel's carrying their master's body, the gasps and sudden cries echo through the harsh quiet.

The students clear a path through the camp, lowering the heads and placing the right hand over their hearts they weep in silence.

Walking through the mass of students in front of his two friends Jacob walks to the main part of the camp housing all the Drakeions tents and huts.

Master Yevelle was the first to emerge from his tent walking over with a smile at first until his eyes focus on the fallen Shakarian behind him.

The Drakeions all surround the three friends and stand in silence, Jacob lifts from his jacket the magnificent sword of Shakarian the blade known as the soul reaper.

Holding the blade out in ceremonial fashion at shoulder height with both hands vertically with a bowed head Jacob waits with tears in his eyes for master Yevelle to take it.

Reluctantly Yevelle takes the blade placing a comforting hand of Jacob's shoulder, Jacob's eyes remain on the floor as he walks to Shakarian's tent Steel's and Kyle following.

Some hours later the entire camp is assembled, stood before them is a large funeral pyre, on top of it wrapped in his old samurai type garb the body of Shakarian looks at peace, his eyes closed as if asleep.

Jacob stood with his two friends beside him and the entire sentinel cast behind he joined them in his sentinel uniform but looks on with a heavy heart and tears in his eyes.

Master Yevelle facing the large pyre lights the wooden logs soaked in oil with a ceremonial metal torch resembling a dragon wrapping itself around a golden column.

Jacob's mind casts back to the last time the sentinels were assembled like this, his heart sinks further remembering the massive funeral they performed for all the fallen students and sentinel's in the attack.

The following morning in the school realm Jacob wakes much as he did in his time here, walking out into the training area as the blue sun rose, his blade in hand he would enter his kata, as time drew on several students would remember their training together and run out to join him.

Before long the camps entire student body was out practising mimicking Jacob, suddenly the serenity was broken a porthole erupted at the bottom of the training area and a single sentinel runs towards Jacob, his dress dusty and dirty.

Catching his breath as he arrives at Jacobs's side he pulls him aside away from the students before departing the horrific news.

"Master Rawn, I have just returned from one of our scouting positions a few miles from the earth realm door. We have a huge problem." The man's voice filled with fear and anxiety.

"What?" Jacob asks calmly.

"Demons, thousands of them, the same ones that attacked the school …heading for the earth realm door." The man watches as Jacobs's eye widen with fear and shock.

Jacobs's worse nightmare has arrived, the hordes of hell have been unleashed on the earth realm, and Jacob runs up the hill towards the Drakeion tents informing them of the situation. Jacob is enraged by the Drakeions response, they will not join in the defence of the earth realm, they do not have the resources and would mean pulling forces from elsewhere. Jacobs's anger is clear as he storms out the tent unimpressed, Yevelle strides after him informing him he will try and convince his people, but he must try and hold off the attack. Steel's and Kyle walk out their guest tents to see the camp full of life, sentinel's arming themselves alongside Jacob.

Walking up to their friend currently giving orders in haste to numerous people Steel's soon wishes he hadn't asked after what he is told.

Rushing to his weapons and gear Steels soon emerges with his large black weapons bag full of goodies as he puts it, Jacob turns to Kyle after assembling the sentinels.

"This is not exactly what I had in mind when I wanted to bring you here Kyle, I cannot ask you to come with me…"

"Am always with you." Jacob is unable to finish as Kyle jumps in.

Jacob smiles again looking to his friend.

"Kyle, I want you to remain here with the Drakeions, they have promised to keep you safe."

Kyle shakes his head as Jacob speaks in disagreement only to be silenced by Jacobs's speaking over him.

"Were not coming back, Kyle! We don't have the strength to stop them, eventually, they will break through and devour the earth realm, and at least on Drakeion you'll be alive."

Jacob is stunned by Kyle's persistence.

"No, I'm with you till the end, I'm not leaving you."

Jacob finally agrees as he throws his arm around Kyle's shoulders turning him towards the porthole and comes face to face with a smiling Steel's.

His cigar burning away in his mouth his large black bag hung off one shoulder, he stands before his friends, as if suddenly content.

"Time for some sweat and bad breath." Steels smile still holding the cigar in his teeth.

The shadow realm awaits them, travelling as fast as they can the sentinels reaching only sixty in number, leaving the students and a small guard behind run across the desert lands trying to reach the earth realm door before the horde.

The door remains closed, no sign of their enemy is in sight except for a large dust cloud several hills away possibly reaching as far back as three to five miles away.

Stood above the rock formation housing the hidden door Jacob addresses his fellow warriors.

"My brothers and sister, we must hold this door closed, once opened the beauty of our world will be desecrated and burnt, twisted into a slaughterhouse for the damned."

Jacob's voice echoes to the warriors below including his two friends.

Looking out across the wasteland the sky suddenly darkens as a wave of red demons comes over the hill, like blood washing over the landscape barely a gap can be seen between their numbers.

The sentinels stand firm, knowing they cannot win, they draw their weapons and turn to face the oncoming wave of demons.

"Stand fast brothers and sisters, make our masters proud, do yourselves proud, although their numbers will defeat us, I'll be damned if we don't make them pay dearly for the privilege."

Forming into a battle position spread out slight merely a few feet apart Kyle remains behind the main group ready to provide a helping hand, Steel's drops his jacket loading up out of his weapons bag.

Jacob runs to the front of the crowd-drawing his blade. And watches as the massive horde approach.

Stopping a mile or so away from the group of the sentinel's a single man walks from the horde, his black suit and red shirt and hair betrays his identity, walking towards the sentinel's alone Jacob walks towards him.

Meeting in the middle of the battlefield the two men converge.

"What's this, a last desperate stand? Are you insane?" Varamont asks mockingly.

"No... desperate yes, insane no... you won't take the realm without a fight." Jacob replies sternly.

"This isn't a fight you arrogant fool, you won't last a heartbeat, you've outnumbered hundreds to one." Varamont sniggers.

"Yes we are but, for every one of us who falls we shall take five of yours, enough to make your invasion a struggle, giving the realm a chance to defend themselves."

"You misguided, arrogant fool, your puny men won't kill five of my horde, they will swarm over you like locus feasting on crops."

Varamont begins to pace back and forth.

"I'll look for you on the field," Jacob states with anger pulsing from every pour in his body.

Varamont sniggers as he starts to walk away, stopping a few feet away he turns back to Jacob.

"I will enjoy watching you die, sentinel, I'll take your soul and feed on its essence as I will each of your friends." Varamont's sniggering as he speaks and walks back to his front lines.

Returning to his men Jacob can see each one ready to fight till the end, there will is set to the task at hand.

With a deafening roar, the horde of thousands charges forward its single gaze fixed on Jacobs small party.

"FIRST ROUND IN HEAVEN IS ON ME!" Jacob screams as the enemy approach.

The demons merely a few feet away ready to swipe there large black stone like blades and claws at their prey are suddenly stopped in the tracks.

A bright purple energy shield surrounds the Sixty sentinel's and the door to earth, several of the hordes are unable to stop and run full force into the shield, their bodies convulse and jolt rapidly as huge amounts of bioelectrical energy run through their bodies.

Jacob turns to see Kyle floating in the air his arms outstretched his aura and eyes flaring with power, his teeth gritting as he struggles to hold onto a shield of such size.

The demons attack the shield pounding on it as if there life depending on it, Steels walks to Jacob two mp5 assault rifles in hand he smiles, cigar lit and calmness to him.

The hordes push against those at the front adding more pressure to the shield.

Steel's nods to Jacob that it is time.

"FOR THE REALM" Jacob screams.

Steel's let's rip with his rifles they spray of bullets tearing into the heart or head of the creatures till there's nothing left of that organ, the sentinel's attack with precision and grace.

The demons surrounding the front of shield suddenly collapse as the sentinel's attack, either beheaded or their hearts run through in a single strike, their tactics resemble the phalanx of old.

As the first demons fall another wave tries to jump into its place only to be stuck down as well, Kyle's struggles, as the pressure builds on the shield is immense, blood begins to drip from his nose.

Wave after wave approaches the front of the shield only to be cut down, finally steel's changes to his sword and signals to Jacob once more with a nod.

"GO!" Jacob shouts.

The sentinel's team with another member strike into the Frey, first one sentinel would attack with enhanced speed, then the other would step forward and attack with speed, turning to their side both would attack to their picked side.

With the unison of attacks and great speed, the horde seems to stand still in time as the sentinels and steels with Jacob attack, in the blink of an eye the demon horde is greatly reduced, an entire wave almost gone as each sentinel in the group attack kill three demons before time catches up with their speed.

The area around the shield now clear Kyle has taken the brunt of the wave and relaxed the shield, wiping the blood from his nose he focuses on his second task, artillery.

Throwing his arms out supercharged with bio-electric energy he fires huge bolts into the ranks of the enemy incinerating sometimes four or five at once.

The attack of the sentinels continues, after each blink of the man known as Varamont eyes an entire section seems to fall and more due to Kyles attack.

Suddenly taken back at the amount of causality's his force has taken he staggers back slightly.

His anger builds as his form twists and turn, his size grows making him a towering twelve-foot red skin beast, two large black horns run across his brow up to the side of his head, his hands end in large black stone claws his teeth Sharpe hunger for blood.

Running towards the front lines he watches as his winged demons swoop in, trying to grab the sentinel's and interrupt there fighting advantage they are suddenly cut down or fried in mid-flight due to Kyles powers.

Jacob and Steel's continue their assault unwavering in the sight of demons about them, slowly they break away from their lines cutting far in front. With his enhanced skills Jacob manages to catch a glimpse at the situation, he can see the sentinel's tiring there enhanced speed will not last much longer and there advantage lost.

Giving Steel's the signal they retreat towards their lines keeping formation and waiting for the moment to come when the real fight would begin.

Kyle looks down to see the sentinel's moving, knowing there power is fading he fires into the horde a few feet in front of them giving them a chance.

Finally, the sentinel's power fails, some manage to hold on a little longer, but most fall back to normal speed, their superior fighting skills help them to brunt the sudden onslaught of demonic power for a short time before their ranks are broken.

The demons regain their forward moment separating sentinel's from each other, the battle now enters the brutal stage, screams of humans entre the sounds of battle,

Strikes from everywhere creep into their defence as hundreds of demons come down upon them in the space they have created amongst the fallen dead.

Jacob once again speeds up his body allowing him to watch the battle in slow motion as if they are barely moving, Kyle high in the air powers on through his fatigue, Jacob feels nothing but pride, and admiration for the young boy and future of humanity should it get the chance.

Steel's also enhanced by his speed smashes repeatedly with the butt of his sword into the face of a demon he is currently straddling the chest off as it falls to the floor.

Finally, Jacob looks to his brothers and sisters, fatigue has claimed them, some still managed to hold on to their speed and continue to attack, others were not so fortunate, their bodies litter the bodies of the fallen demons below them.

Jacob watches in horror as several more will fall once time catches up to Jacob, their bodies held in an agonising position as the demon's claw, bite of ripping them open.

Suddenly the battle catches up to Jacob the sounds rush back to him alerting him to its presence, several demons rush into his area next to Steel's, running towards them his enhanced speed pushes him faster than they can see.

Their bodies fall, either head or heartless, as his fine blade strikes true never halting for a moment.

After clearing an area of bodies from the earth realm door reaching out in all direction up to forty feet the demons pull back, there wave of red runs back to the hill, now loosing possibly a few hundred of their number they look a little fearful.

The sudden vacuum of red demons leaves several sentinel's left standing, clawing there way over the bodies they check to their fallen comrades checking them for life before returning to the door.

Gathering at the door gasping for breath, and holding their wounds and weapons they try to recuperate before they attack again, Kyle lowers himself down to the floor falling to his knees as he touches down.

His hands dig into the sand stopping himself from falling completely over, Steel's runs to him lifting his upper body back to a kneeling position, the boy looks exhausted his nose trickles with blood as does one of his ears.

Jacob looks to the battlefield, his heart drops at the sight of all this death, whether demon or human, Takami's words echo in his mind.

"All have a right to life."

Jacob turns to his friends and sentinel's, counting with a shocking discovery he counts less than twenty remains including Steel's and Kyle, his heart and mind sink, he looks back to the hordes gathered on the hill, a huge demon creature stands before them holding a massive black sword, it walks slowly out into the open once more alone.

Jacob walks to meet it halfway.

"And impressive feat master Rawn, but you are out of tricks now." The large twelve-foot demons deep rattling husky voice pounds.

"Maybe, but we're still standing," Jacob replies, as his breath will allow.

"You have lost human, surrender and I will make your deaths quick, and painless."

"Never, I will die where I stand, defending with my last breath the door to earth."

Varamont's anger grows and is getting the better of him.

"I heard it said, be proud of your enemy, and be proud of his accomplishments, when this is over, I'll be the proud one as I swallow your soul, feeding me, making me stronger."

Jacob turns from his tormentor towards his lines his calmness a guise for the anger within is pulsing for a life of its own.

"This time join your forces coward," Jacob states as he walks away.

Returning to his friends' Jacob looks and smiles at Kyle still kneeling gasping for breath, the remaining sentinel's huddle close to Jacob as if looking for another miracle tactic to help save them.

Another large horn echoes in the distance, Jacob stands as his eyes cannot believe the sight before him, Kyle's head drops as he looks on. Jacob swallows hard his shock, his eyes suddenly close after witnessing the red army of the horde reinforced with larger black demons and more enhanced by winged creatures flying overhead.

The now more massive horde army slowly works its way down towards the sentinels.

A hand takes hold of Jacob's arm gently, he looks to the man holding it, he could not be more than twenty years old, and a single wound across his chest of a large claw is the only wound he holds.

"Jacob, it's been an honour to serve with you master." The young boys spoke with a smile on his face as he looks on to the approaching horde and lets out a sigh and readies his weapon for combat.

"I'm no master my friend, but I am honoured to fight and die alongside you." Jacob returns the boys kind words, a sudden feeling lifts Jacobs fear as the boy's courage brings him peace.

Kyle lifts himself to Jacobs side, his bloody nose wiped clean he looks to his mentor and friend with a smile.

"I'm ready." Kyles tone was serious as he looks to his attackers.

Steel's cigar puffs with smoke as he looks happily at the sky above as he takes in the sights before looking to Jacob.

"Hell I'm ready, I'm just having fun." He states placing the cigar back in his mouth pulling his blade back out ready for action.

The hordes reach the bottom of the dune they ran down and suddenly stopped in their tracks. Several large bright whirlpools of colour erupt thirty to forty feet in front of the sentinel's. Rapidly with enhanced speed hundreds of tall slim figured creature's file out of the rifts like an army of ants emerging from there dens. forming ranks, there dress always in bright colours, their weapons raised and ready for battle.

The portholes flash once more disappearing into nothing, the whole army arriving in mere seconds before the oncoming horde over a thousand Drakeion warriors, a familiar master Yevelle stand at the front.

The Drakeions ranks take a single step forward and lower themself into an identical combat stance letting out a huge deafening roar at the demons.

Jacob looks on in disbelief and lighter heart, a welcoming sight indeed warms him through suddenly lifting his spirit.

Looking to the young sentinel beside him, Jacob is witness as the boy suddenly seems overwhelmed at the sight of an army of Drakeion warriors before him.

Jacob turns his attention to Kyle who just smiles and lets a huge a sigh emanate from him, Steel's looks on a little worried, he turns to Jacob looking rather upset.

"Aw hell no, they ain't taking all the fun." Steels mocking tone lifts there spirit further as he charged towards the Drakeions.

Following his friend Jacob and the sentinel's join there Drakeion brothers and sisters, moving through the ranks the survivors of the first wave are welcomed as heroes, pats on the backs and howls of encouragement are heard throughout the valley.

Emerging from the ranks of his people master Yevelle welcomes the sight of survivor's, but his heart is heavy at how few there are.

"Master Rawn, I'm sorry I could not get here sooner." The Drakeions voice heavy with guilt. Jacob cannot resist the urge and throws his arms around him hugging him intently, before releasing him with a smile.

Steel's looks unimpressed, as he loads his shotgun.

"You guys got some catching up to do!" Steel states as he starts to walk towards the enemy.

"Indeed, try and keep up Master Jackson." Yevelle draws his sword and joins the walk with him.

Lord Varamont looks on in disbelief at the sight before him, swallowing the small amount of fear he had he orders his horde to attack.

The black and red wave thrusts forwards, the winged devils swoop down on the numbers below, their attacks are thwarted by sudden eruptions of bright purple bio-energy as Kyle objects to their presence.

The two sides clash like a wave smashing against the rocks on the shore, several numbers on each side are killed instantly, the larger black demons although much stronger and harder to kill are still just as slow as the others, the Drakeions in union much as the sentinels did follow the same attack pattern.

Their enhanced speed enhances their movements dramatically striking in waves slicing through the ranks of the enemy, hundred die instantly as they are beheaded or their hearts are pierced with finely crafted weapons enhanced with bio-energy.

The larger black demons witnessed the fall of their lesser red brothers and have learned from this tactic, hundred decided to jump over the front wave into the rear of the Drakeion ranks and began attacking.

The attack breaks the lines of the Drakeions and separates them scattering the entire battlefield.

Jacob finds himself surrounded by four large black demons and four red ones, their tongues lashing around looking for blood and souls.

The first two black demons charge in reaching for him, empowering his body once more he flips through the air coming down blade first and charged through the heart of one oncoming red demon behind.

Using his body as a platform he pushes off somersaulting backwards and landing next to the first two oncoming black demons from the front, there posture unchanged as Jacobs enhanced speed as paused them in time.

Again his blade is charged as he swings his blade through the neck of one black demon and continues his spin thrusts up into the heart of the next.

Finally, time catches up with Jacob as one red demon and two black ones suddenly engulf in bright blue energy and explode leaving nothing but ash.

The remaining two black demons and one red one are suddenly shocked at this sight, their anger grows as they charge in, strikes fly at Jacob over and over, his blade either defecting or blocking until an opening presents its self.

Eventually the opening he was waiting for come in the form of an open-air swoop with a charged blade.

Striking through the air with an energy wave to the chest a black and red demon are slain as he turns and beheads the last black enemy.

Once more the bright blue energy envelops the creature and they burst to ash.

****

Steel's is suddenly charged by two black demons, one tackles him to the floor as if he were playing American football, Steel's flops to the ground and lifts the demons huge head and smashes repeatedly into it with the butt of his new shotgun.

Finally lifting his large body of Steel's shaking his head and reading his claws for a strike, Steel's let the shotgun present his dislike for being tackled.

The rounds slam into the creature barely entering the skin but manage to knock him back slightly, Steel's jumps into the air bringing him up to the creature head level before bringing his powerful right hand down into the creatures face.

As the creature falls to his hands and knees Steel's pulls out his trusty old faithful blade and readies to behead the creature.

Suddenly the blade is grabbed by the second creature from behind.

"Why you cheating son of a bitch!" Steel's states.

Suddenly pulling two pistols from his holsters on his legs the rounds fly into one knee repeatedly before dropping onto the floor, following the same procedure to the other leg Steel's slowly walks towards his target.

As the pistols run out of ammo Steel's repeatedly smashes the black demons face with his mighty right cross. Finally pulling from his weapon belt a grenade he pulls the pin with a finger in his right hand as he slams the grenade into the mouth of the beast.

Pulling his blade from the creatures grasp he turns back to the first demon, the head exploded on the creature he previously had behind him, Steel's lifts his weapon crashing down beheading the first.

****

Kyle's powers are at their peak, blast after blast he sends into the ranks of the oncoming horde, from an aerial view their numbers look endless, and lowering himself back to the ground into an open space he changes tactics.

Checking for friendly targets in his projected path he summons forth a huge blast of bio-energy, the trail of bright purple energy erupts forth, a large blast covers almost teen feet wide and far into the ranks of the enemy, and Kyle's power incinerates possible hundreds in a single blast, tearing up the grounds as it went.

This feat comes at a heavy price, Kyle's body suddenly weakens, and fresh blood pours from his nose and ears, hundreds of demons witness the eruption of power and slaver over a soul that can perform such acts.

Kyle is suddenly besieged, wave upon wave hurl themselves at him, summoning his shield to protect himself he desperately holds on falling to his knees trying to keep the shield alive.

Hurling demons away with smaller less effective strikes Kyle manages the storm, Jacob looks around in his moment of stillness, once more he is surrounded by bodies, his small wounds ache with pain but he ignores them, a small cut above his eyes seeps blood into his vision.

Jacobs's horror is once more realized, over sixty feet away he witnesses a failing bright purple shield surrounded by pounding demons attacking it.

Something inside Jacob snaps like a bomb going off, much like it did that day back in the war before the devourer, as it did after his mortal wound through the heart, and at his awakening. Jacob suddenly jolts slightly as his energy inside takes on a life of its own, his eyes flare a brilliant white with a haze of blue, and his fatigue lifts instantly as does his pain, his mindset clear, save Kyle.

Breaking into a run he leaps into the air, his body reaches some twenty feet in the air before coming back down Jacob lands on two large black demons backs his hands glows white as do the creatures eyes and heart, the energy burns through them, the sound of dull hum building to a climax can be heard close by as if Jacob were slowly building up to scream.

Like a man possessed Jacob evades attacks from the demons and closes the gap until he can get a grip on them, a mere touch and the same effect happens, demon after demon fall to Jacobs new power,

Smoking corpses follow Jacobs trail as he makes his way to Kyle, Jacobs blade now lost to war he recalls nothing of it as the white energy course through him, block and parry followed by touch and burn is all that he knows,

Varamont watches in disbelief at the sight of his forces being held back by the Drakeion warriors, and sentinels, many Drakeions have been slain and their souls claimed but it is not enough, he shouts, in his mind.

Finally, his gaze is caught by another spectacle, a single man twisting and turning with the graze of a cat and burning bright white light through his minions, shaking his head in disbelief once more he cannot believe the one man to be Jacob Rawn.

"A fallen, impossible!" Varamont shouts.

A sudden fear creeps over him, finally realising his master would wont to know the recent events he orders the retreat, the horde pulls away from the fight flooding back up the hill and over the dunes.

An overwhelming roar and cry of relief and success burst into the battle. The Drakeions cheer in success, watching their enemy retreat, Steel's climbs to his feet after a demon fell onto him as he ran it through the heart, his sigh is short-lived as he relights his cigar.

Kyles remains on the floor his eyes open as he peeks out to see his shield still burning bright just covering his body he looks up to see a calm and still Jacob stood looking down at him, his eyes were closed but a bright light shone from behind them just peeking through the gap in his eyelids.

Lowering his shield and rising to his feet gasping to try and breath he looks to his friend, the bright light under his eyes dies down as he turns to him and finally opens his eyes.

Jacob smiles with a worried look on his face, the last bit of bright white in Jacob's eyes die down as Steel's limps up and slaps Jacob on the back heavily, Jacob is jolted forward slightly as he Steel's smiles while smoking his cigar.

Kyle sighs heavily and relaxes wiping away the blood from his nose and ears.

"Who's got the beer?" Steel's shouts to the army of Drakeions.

Jacob looks to the battlefield aware of what just happened he looks to his hands as if questioning them in his mind, once more his fallen heritage has made an appearance.

Looking over the corpse of both Drakeion and demon alike several other bodies litter the field, more humans lie dead and soulless amongst the field.

Master Yevelle also walks up to Jacob, after seeing his wound Jacob runs to him helping him walk, sitting him on a smouldering corpse of a demon who Jacob had touched Yevelle thanks, Jacob.

"Your handy work I take it to master Rawn?" Yevelle asks as he rubs his wounded leg.

"I owe you an apology master Yevelle, I should have known the Drakeions would not abandon us, I had no right…" Yevelle holds up his hand stopping Jacob

"my people made a promise many thousands of years ago to help protect your beautiful realm, we forgot that promise, now we have corrected it, no more need be said, my friend."

Jacob nods in agreement as he helps his friend to his feet.

The school realm erupts in cheer as the survivor's return, a sudden silence falls on them as only nine sentinel's return, their injuries prevent them from interacting with the students as both Steel's and Jacob help carry one or two of them to the infirmary,

Multiple trips through the open porthole for the students, Steel's and Jacob as they help to carry the wounded Drakeions back to the infirmary to get aid.

Night falls on the camp Jacobs wounds are healed, but not his thoughts, his mind keeps flooding back to the time the white light took over the fall of the sentinel's, and the amount of death that happened today.

The camp is filled with Drakeions, and few humans, only a day ago the numbers were reversed Jacob thinks to himself looking out from the infirmary hut.

"Ouch…! Jesus…! Ok that will do just leave it ok." A rather angry and painful Steel's shouts to the doctor trying stitch yet another scar in his leg.

Jacob walks up smiling to his friend as he lays out on a bed sitting up slightly as the doc try's to sew.

"Ja I love your order but your gonna lose another one if he ain't bloody car…" Steel's sentence is interrupted by yet another scream of pain.

Jacob reaches for Steel's head with but a touch he urges his telepathy into action ushering Steel's to sleep.

Watching the huge black man suddenly grow groggy and collapse into sleep the Drakeion doctor smiles and thanks, Jacob.

Walking through the wounded Jacob manages to find Kyle laid flat out on one of the beds, clearly asleep, scanning his body injuries Jacob is relieved he found none.

The boy sleeps curled up slightly a relaxed almost smiling face as he dreams away, lowering himself to the bed opposite Jacob looks to this young boy with wonder.

Kyle's eyes slowly open and finds his friend watching over him, slowly trying to bring himself round slightly he smiles still.

"Wars over Ja, get some sleep." An exhausted Kyle states.

"You sleep, you earned it my boy, my god did you earn it, humanity's future is bright indeed if they are but a fraction of you," Jacob states still looking with amazement at his young student.

Jacobs's words fall on senseless ears as Kyle drifts off again, a small murmur of agreement is the only answer he gets as he snuggles into the bed.

"A wonder to behold master Rawn." A friendly voice echoes from behind.

Master Yevelle walks out of the night into the light of the infirmary, his wounded leg healing well is still giving him some trouble as he learns of the side of the open hut looking at Kyle.

"Yes he is, and not just his abilities, but his will," Jacob states walking up to his friend outside and resting against the wall next to master Yevelle.

"It bodes well for the future of your species, my friend, I witness the boy's power in the final moments." Yevelle shakes his head in disbelief.

"Incredible," Yevelle adds.

"Master, I want to thank you and your people for what happened today." Jacob is once again stopped in his sentence by Yevelle's hand.

"Jacob, I want to thank you, you gave me inspiration, I confess when I first came here I did not believe in the cause that much, I was hesitant, but I came all the same."

Jacob listens to his friend intently not understanding his need to thank him.

"But after seeing your people face an unimaginable force and drive them back with but a handful of men I..., consider me a believer my friend, I will give my life to defend such a people."

Yevelle smiles as Jacob now understands.

Another surprise befalls the two friends another porthole erupts swiftly and a small party of Drakeions makes its way up to the command area, four armed guards surround what looks like a female Drakeion.

Both Yevelle and Jacob look a little shocked and hurry after the party to the command tent, waiting outside giving the Drakeions time he lets Yevelle enter alone and get to grips with the situation.

The four-armed guards leave the tent, and bow to Jacob as they stand on guard a few feet from the entrance of the tent, entering the tent Jacob finds Yevelle talking something in draconic to the female, both suddenly fall silent as he enters.

Yevelle smiles at his friend and offers him a cheeky wink of the eye as he takes the hooded cloak from the woman.

Her long bright blond hair hangs down her back in a single long braid with silver and gold bands intertwined through the braids, her slim figure elegant, her dress that of an armoured warrior.

The golden and silver armour does little to hide her figure as the curves of her armour follow her body curves exactly, Jacob looks her up and down before he realises he is stirring like a schoolboy with a crush.

He bows his head as she turns around to face Jacob, her large cat-like eyes a brilliant green her skin glitters a pale blue and silver.

"Please master Rawn rise." A smooth soft tone emerges.

"It is us who should bow to you, for what you have accomplished here today." The woman adds.

"The sentinel's and the Drakeions are the ones that one the day my lady, not me," Jacob replies.

"Such modesty, my brother was right about you." The woman's comment suddenly baffled Jacob.

"This is the lady xwrens, she is Shakarian's younger sister," Yevelle adds.

Jacob's head drops as does his heart, he bows low holding his heart with his right hand.

"Please forgive me, my lady, your brother was my master and friend I would have given my life it meant he would live." Jacob quickly speaks before the lady darts in and lifts him from his bow looking into his eyes.

"Thank you, master Rawn, for your words, he told me how much you meant to him, and he cared a great deal for you and your realm," Xwrens speaks.

"Such power they have, and yet know nothing of how to use it, he would say, I see the first part is true at least." She adds.

"He was a great man my lady, and good friend, the universe is a darker place without him," Jacob replied.

"He spoke a great deal of you Jacob, he would talk endlessly of your achievements, even reviling master Takami, and replacing them both in time." Xwrens states.

"I'm not worthy of such compliments my lady, the two men you mentioned are my masters, and always will be, no one could replace them," Jacob states a little firmly.

"Am afraid someone has to replace them master Rawn, and that someone is you, I hereby promote you to grandmaster, master Yevelle will be your second in command," Xwrens stated firmly almost militaristic.

Jacob looks on puzzled at these turn of events.

"The lady xwrens is commander in chief of the Drakeions armed forces master Rawn, it was her I approached and requested the forces to help defend your realm," Yevelle states clearing up her authority.

Jacob nods in agreement but is still unhappy with this turn of events.

"With all due respect my lady, I must decline, I'm sentinel, I belong in the earth realm, and I shall be returning in the morning to finish the work I started and end the threat to my realm." Jacobs's voice filled with hate as he mentioned the threat to his world.

Xwrens looks at the creature before her, admiration fills her, and she cannot help but feel moved by this man's persistence and courage.

"You have just fought a war against impossible odds and survived, you have saved your realm from invasion, and you have saved what remains of your order, is that enough for one life." Xwren's asks almost knowing the answer.

"I won't the bastards holding my friend's souls." Jacobs's words cut the air like a knife.

Both Yevelle and xwrens smile as they look to each other, she turns back to Jacob holding out her arm to master Yevelle.

Pulled from a storage box a long object wrapped in red silk is passed to the lady she holds it vertically in both hands and holds it out for Jacob to take.

A look of confusion sweeps across his face as he moves to the object, slowly he uncovers the object, his eyes widen as the soul reaper appears before him, Shakarian's blade gleams in the light.

"Take it," Xwrens states forcibly.

"I cannot my lady that is your brother's sword." Jacob retreats slightly.

"My brother would have wanted his successor to wield it, and that's you, I can think of no one better." Xwrens tone was almost demanding.

Jacob walks forward again and claims the mighty weapon. Drawing the blade from its scabbard he looks the metal up and down, many times has he sparred against this incredible weapon but never held it.

"my brother would have been proud of you master Rawn, as am I, I shall leave our forces master Yevelle has stationed outside the earth realm door as a permanent garrison under his command," Xwrens states looking at Jacob holding her brother's blade.

"This will be my final command in the armed forces." The lady adds.

Both Yevelle and Jacob look at her in surprise and bewilderment.

"Someone has to train the sentinel's, and I shall, following in my brother's footsteps if you will have me, grandmaster?" Xwrens bows to Jacob awaiting his response.

Jacob cannot help but be moved by this woman's decision and love for her brother.

"My lady, you have given much for my realm and order, I have nothing to give you except my support and service," Jacob says.

"Master Rawn… Jacob, I do not require your service, only your friendship."

Jacob holds out his hand gesturing for the lady xwrens to take it, the two new friends shake a firm grip.

"I ask for one thing Jacob, free my brother's soul," Xwrens asks.

"My lady I don't know if I will return, I may not be strong enough," Jacob replies.

"If you are not master Rawn, no one is," Xwrens states harshly.

Jacob nods in agreement he turns away slightly as if to leave but yet more questions burn within him.

"My lady, I am eternally grateful for the help you and your people gave to my realm today, I shall not forget it if ever you need anything," Jacob states with conviction.

Xwrens suddenly jumps forward holding Jacobs hands as they grasp his new sword, she looks deep into his eyes.

"Bring me back my brother's soul, do not let the mage who took him live, bring him back to me so we can be together again." Xwrens voice now soft and pleading.

"I will my lady, or dye trying," Jacob replies before bowing to the new leaders of the school realm and leaving the tent.

Yevelle watches his friend leave, his gaze then turns to xwrens who still stood looking out at Jacob as he leaves, Yevelle cannot help but smile as thoughts run through his mind.

"You're quite taken with him are you not my lady?" Yevelle's voice is almost mocking.

Xwrens turns to her friend smiling.

"It's hard not to admire such a presence, after everything he's been through these last few years, still he goes on… there an incredible race."

Yevelle nods in agreement.

"I can see why my brother was so taken with him." Xwrens words betray her thoughts.

"Him or them my lady." Yevelle's cocky tone picks up on her mishap.

Xwrens lowers her head in a shy attempt to hide her eyes and thoughts.

CHAPTER 16

Vengeance Is Mine

Jacob after returning from the school realm alone hurries to the city known as New York. Leaving both Kyle and Steel's at the school to recuperate, Jacobs only thought was to keep them safe, he snuck out of the camp and into the shadow realm alone to hide his intentions of Facing the shadow lord alone.

In Jacobs mind he was doing the right thing, protecting the realm and his friends, he knew he could not bear to lose another so close to him, his heart ached at the thought.

Travelling the city streets using his senses to locate the place the shadow lord was using would not be hard, finally after but a few hours of searching Jacobs mind finds the tower building that houses the law firm of Daniel lance.

Standing opposite the building looking into the main foyer and up to the top floor his mind locates the creatures inside, the three generals and their master await him at the top.

Calming his fear and his mind Jacob pauses for a moment, he looks about the street watching commuters pass by without a thought that their world was just saved by a small hand of warriors giving their life to save them,

They have no incline that a war was fought merely days ago to prevent an invasion wiping all life from this world.

Jacobs mind remembers those famous words from his master some time ago,

"All have a right to life."

"That's right J, they do." A familiar but surprising voice echo's from behind him in the shadows.

Quickly turning round to face the voice Jacob lets out a comforting sigh.

"Kyle, Steel's, how did you…?"

"JA you may be able to fight an army of demons, you may be able to return from the dead, but you can't hide from me… or expect me to leave you to this alone." Kyle states.

"Or buy a train ticket punk!" Steel's states harshly as if extremely upset as Jacob tried to leave him out of the fun.

Jacob smiles as he drops his fear like you would a large weight from your back, suddenly relaxed at the arrival of his friends.

"I'm sorry guys, I wanted to handle this alone, you both have done and suffered enough of late, and I couldn't bear to lose either of you." Jacobs tone pleading almost.

"Ow but we could bear to lose you, or worse lose you and have to deal with a shadow lord with your soul as fuel… I don't think so" Kyle states mockingly with a smile.

"Yea, not like you ain't pulled your fair share of good deeds lately either now is it." Steel's adds with his smug grin holding on to his cigar.

Both Steel's and Kyles walk to their friend side and join him facing the building, Kyle senses reach inside and can sense the number of demons waiting for them inside.

Kyle's eyes widen as his face is filled with more than a little concern as he lets out a heavy sigh at what he senses.

"We got our hands full this time boys." Kyle states.

Jacob just stands smiling his fear now totally gone due to his friends stood beside him, suddenly feeling he can do anything.

"Good, hate to think I was over-prepared for the occasion." Steels states while pulling his two MP5 riffles out and reading them.

Both Jacob and Kyle look to their friend a sarcastic look on their face as if to question whether he just said what he did.

"What?" Steel's asks genuinely.

Jacob shakes his head with a smug grin not quite sure if Steel's knows how big his arsenal actual is when goes out hunting with him each time.

"Shall we finish this?" Kyle asks cockily.

"Ow hell ya!" Steel's says after spitting out his cigar.

The three friends approach the building confident in their abilities and the task at hand.

***

Daniel sits in his chair looking into his vast office, his three generals before him explaining the news of the defeat in the shadow realm.

His anger swelling within him his mind anxious for blood, he rises from his desk slowly his eyes now filled with bright red energy, his look dark and evil as he looks on his minions.

Suddenly his attention is caught, his gaze turns to the side as if someone were whispering something to him, his mind picks up three powerful presences entering his building.

Both Daniel and the man known as Simon's turns to look at each other confirming both their fears.

"He's here," Daniel says while still looking to the hooded man.

Lord Varamont's stomach and heart drop his fear building suddenly, the mage's smug grin remains thinking he is untouchable with the soul of Shakarian.

Daniel looks back to his generals.

"Lord Varamont reclaim your honour and destroy them." Daniel's voice was now forceful.

Varamont shoves his fear aside as he bows and turns to leave.

"You help him and your task here is done," Daniel speaks to the flame lord.

The mage again gives a head nod in agreement as using it as a bow he turns and walks after his colleague.

Daniel turns his attention to the hooded man.

"When they fail, you will be here waiting for him." Daniel states.

"My lord!" the hooded man Simons utters in agreement.

***

The main lobby is empty at this time of night, only a small security force sits in its security station a few feet from the main door.

Kyle walks in first sensing the three security officers Kyle knows they are only human, with a raised hand pushes telepathic commands into their minds without resistance.

The three friends pass the now sleeping officers harmlessly as they make for the elevators.

Steel's presses the top floor only to see from the diagram they need another lift once they reach level 34.

Waiting patiently as the lift rides up, Jacob and Kyle can sense numerous presence's waiting for them as they approach the level.

Standing before his two friends Jacob pulls from his grey trench coat the blade of Shakarian, standing ready to defend whatever they throw at them.

The lift reaches the level 34, the doors open and the three friends walk from the elevator, stood before them a large number of security officers with Tasers and nightsticks stand before lord Varamont.

Jacob's head lowers in disappointment, Kyles own face lets show his dislike, Steel's looks at his two friends realising their disappointment is because the security guards are completely human.

"Are you shitting me?" Steel's cocky tone erupts putting back his pistols back in there holsters.

Kyle stands at the back gesturing cockily that this one is down to Jacob and Steels.

Jacob shakes his head in disagreement, placing his sword back in the folds of his coat he walks towards the left side of the armed guards while Steel's goes to the right.

The guard's attack as they are paid to, trying to defend the building from a hostile force, their employers neglected to mention the invading force are more than capable of taking their security force to pieces with ease weather empowered or not.

Steel's takes his stance and waits for the guards to come charging in before rendering one unconscious before his body hits the deck with a quick right cross.

Guard after guard Steel's hits weather punch or kick, his mighty strength defeating them with a single strike, Jacob takes a more direct approach.

Walking up to them calmly they attack without hesitation, block and counter parry and counter Jacob moves amongst them, his blocks and parries exposing a weak point which he counters and moves to the next one.

Both men finish their side of the large hall-like room at the same time, neither one being struck in the process, both the men look to each other as they finish signalling they are done they meet each other in the middle.

A loud clapping noise is heard as lord Varamont walks from the far end in front of the second elevator they need, his oversized two-handed sword held under his arm as he claps for Steels and Jacobs show.

"Most impressive, for a bunch of humans, I do enjoy a good show." Varamont's cockiness has returned.

Jacob attempts to walk towards Varamont only to be stopped by Steels suddenly.

"This one is mine JA," Steel's serious tone lets Jacob knows he meant it.

A furious look covers Steel's face.

"Your boys took me in, treat me as an equal, and died beside me on that field, I'll be damned if I let that son of a bitch get away with taking them from me." Steel's states in anger tears well in his eyes as he looks to Varamont.

Jacob slowly nods in agreement, he places a comforting hand on his shoulder and gives a reaffirming smile before walking past him towards the elevator.

"Ja, kill simons for me." Steels states gritting his teeth still looking to Varamont.

Kyle walks up to Steel's looking to his prey.

"Kick his ass Steel's, give him one from me as well," Kyle adds before following Jacob.

Steel's gives Kyle a quick reaffirming tap on the back as he passes never taking his eyes from his enemy.

"Keep an eye on him, Kyle!" Steel refers to Jacob as he speaks.

"I will don't be long," Kyle adds.

Steel's waits till both his friends are in the elevator before slowly walking towards his enemy, Varamont walks up to him still holding his blade under his arm he smiles at the thought of defeating this petty human.

"Your either very brave… or very stupid human, you can't win." Varamont states in a cocky tone.

"ow shut the hell up you oversized bad breathed, skivvy, just draw your claws and let's get on with it fool!" Steel's responds in disgust.

***

The elevator rides up to the very top floor level 66, the doors open to a large lobby made of black marble with white inlays. A single desk sits on the right side for Daniels assistant who is absent.

Two large golden doors picturing some ancient tapestry dons the door, as the two men approach the doors open automatically, the massive hallway beyond reaches far back to the length of the building and a door at the far right leads into denials office.

Stood in the centre of the room stands the black tattooed mage his statue still as he crosses his arms in front of him, his gaze locks on Jacob and Kyle.

Jacobs anger grows before he pushes it away, slowly walking forward he draws his weapon increasing in pace towards his enemy.

Kyle reaches for his friend, grabbing his arm and turning him to face him suddenly.

Jacob spins to face his student and friend a serious look on his face, Kyle's sense reach out sensing everything in the building before looking to his master and friend.

"You can't!" Kyle states firmly.

"Like hell, I can't, he's…" Jacob tries to finish his objection.

"No, you can't, with Shakarian inside him he knows every move you'll make before you do and he'll be waiting for it, plus there something in the next room that needs your special attention."

Jacob looks back to the boy become a man before him, such pride runs through him as he looks to his student, smiling and agreeing Jacob reaffirms his friend with a gentle squeeze of his shoulder before turning away and walking past the mage to the doors beyond.

The mage looks a little stumped, his gaze turns to the mere boy before him.

"Is that it, the great sentinel leaves a boy to finish his task, is he afraid to face me?" the mage asks mockingly.

"No, I just want to kill you myself." Kyle states as the anger grow and the fear subsides.

The mage laughs as the boy's comments staggering forward trying to contain his laughter.

"Ha, and what can you possibly…?" the mages laugh and the sentence is suddenly interrupted.

First Kyle's eyes burst with bright purple bioelectrical energy followed by his aura pulsing out random strobes to close by structures.

"I see… you have power." The mage states sternly.

The mage stops his taunts and now focuses as the boy before has become a powerful threat indeed.

***

The two large double doors fly open as Jacob pushes them, inside lies the office of Daniel, disappointed at the sight of a lone hooded man stood facing him in the centre of the room with no sign of his master, Jacob walks in.

The doors shut behind him as the sound of a lock is heard clicking into place, Jacob is aware of the lock but pays little attention.

Walking closer to the hooded man slowly, Jacobs's senses scan the room trying to identify any other threats.

"We are alone." The hooded man's faint Scottish accent seeps outs.

Jacob continues to approach, a familiar feeling creeps over him, unable to place him he asks.

"I know you, don't I?" Jacob asked.

"Yes, you did… once." The man replies.

Reaching slowly for his hood the man lowers his guise and removes the black scarf covering his lower face allowing Jacob to see him for the first time.

Jacob's eyes widen in disbelief stopping him in his tracks, almost stunned, his old friend and instructor Carl stood before him, his now dark eyes covered in rage and hate, his face darker more twisted as if he bathed in evil.

"Carl!" Jacob shocked voice erupts.

"Been a long time boyo." His old mentor replies.

"Why?"

"Long story my boy, one I don't have time for, and neither do you now." The two men begin to circle each other as Jacob cannot believe the sight before him.

"You killed master Takami…! You brought the horde to the school…!" Jacobs's voice filled with disbelief and pain.

Carl's head lowers as the words shame him.

"I don't need a running commentary on my actions boy, I know what I did, and what am about to do."

Jacob stops motionless suddenly, looking to his old friend he shakes his head now in disappointment and regret

"Don't do this Carl," Jacob asks genuinely.

Carls face twists slightly as if he's in pain, his eyes flood over with a dull red colour as his composure returns, his smug grin returns as if he were suddenly possessed by evil confidence.

"I don't have a choice, now die!" Carl screams as he attacks.

***

The mighty black blade of Varamont wielded by this human looks so out of place as such a large weapon is wielded by such a small creature.

The blade smashes into solid steel columns either bending them or slicing through as Steel's avoids the attack.

Drawing his own blade Steel's starts fighting back, both men evenly matched in strength block and parry each other's attacks as an impressive amount of sword work erupts in the second lobby.

Steels blocks several attacks measuring his attacker up perfectly he makes his move, as he parries a last low thrust to his midsection with a low cut he stepped to his left as he slams his left fist into Varamont's face and follows through thrusting his blade into Varamont's stomach pushing right through him.

Both men seem to stop still for a moment before Steel's looks down to the man he has just killed, Varamont's shock is clear, as is the amount of pain he feels, which is none.

Steel's face drops his angry look for a bewildered one as Varamont's begins to snigger and laugh.

Stepping back slightly but still keeping a grip on his sword, Steel's watches as Varamont's body erupts into his true form.

The now twelve-foot muscular red skin demon stands before Steel's, with a jerk of his arm he grabs Steels by the throat bringing him close to his face and starts to laugh.

"You'll have to do better than that human." Varamont's voice was now deep and husky.

"ok, that's just cheating." Steels cocky attitude creeps out as he struggles to hold onto Varamont's grip around his neck.

Suddenly maddened by steel's comments Varamont hurls Steels up in the air with ease before throwing his mighty fist into Steel's falling body hurtling it away at speed into the wall.

The marble wall erupts into debris as Steels lands hard into it smashing a crater the size of his body in the wall.

His body flops to the floor with a heavy thud. Before rising climbing to his feet shaking off the attack.

"Ok guess that hit a nerve." Steel's mocks as he climbs to his feet.

Pulling from his wound, Varamont frees Steel's blade before throwing it on the floor and lifting his blade he charges for his prey.

Steel's lifts his two MP5s from inside his jacket and let's rip at Varamont's knees, the bullets bounce off him leaving no effect as Varamont slams his black blade towards Steel's trying to sever him in two at the hip, throwing away his rifles he summersault's over the attack and his enemy landing behind him.

Furiously hammering away with his enhanced strength Steel's pounds at his attackers back and spine, the creature known as Varamont's feels the blows hitting and jolt him slightly but they cause little damage.

Suddenly spinning back and catching Steel's with a back fist to the face he watches as his prey flies back across the room towards the elevator leading down to the bottom floor.

Flipping back to his feet Steel's brings his shotgun to play, firing round after round at Varamont's knees they manage to throw him off balance with each hit.

Steels walked to his blade to retrieves it as he fires his weapon, the beast attacks once more with his blade, as the swords clash once more.

Steel's knows he cannot overpower this creature and needs to use his head, as another low attack is thrust at Steel's stomach he changes stance blocking the blade away to his left.

Following his block and entering a small spin Steel's left leg comes round striking the creature in the face with his heel staggering it to the right slightly, finishing his attack as he jumps into the air bringing his now forward-facing left leg up and striking the creature on his face once more he is hurled backwards and away a few feet under steel's strength.

Landing with a thud Varamont shakes off the hits and looks in shock as Steel's in now in the elevator pressing the button for the doors to close.

Jumping to his feet forgetting his weapon he charges with all his speed as the doors begin to close, Steel's stands inside giving him the finger as the doors just manage to close before he shoulder barges through the steel doors.

Varamont slightly squashed inside such a small space looks about him trying to find his enemy, finally, his eyes look to the roof of the elevator and can see the escape hatch open. His anger builds as he punches through the roof making the hole big enough for his body to stand up in and looks into the elevator shaft.

Finally, he locks eyes with his target as Steel's pulls his grenade belt from his waist and pulls the pins in a single strip connecting them, throwing the belt into the lift he uses his speed and fires repeatedly at the capable holding the elevator in place.

Steel's watches as the elevator suddenly begins to hurl towards the floor some 34 levels below, Varamont reaches for Steel's knowing he can't reach him but tries out of instinct, all the same, a loud deafening roar can be heard as the elevator plummets.

The elevator shaft is suddenly illuminated from below as if hell itself had suddenly burst into the shaft, flames rush towards Steel's as he hung by the elevator cable in the wake of the explosions.

Jumping down to the bent melt doors of the elevator Steel's lands safely thanks to Varamont's body smashing through them, a sudden wave of heat and flame rush up the shaft past Steel's as he remains on the floor till it passes.

***

Kyle looks intently at the mage as he suddenly readies himself for combat, wasting no time the flame lord begins the attack with a column of fire erupting from his hand.

Kyle neglect's to move as the fire smashes harmlessly into his aura, the mage continues the assault for a few seconds before releasing the power and looking to its effect.

Suddenly taken back slightly as the blast had no effect he thrusts both arms forward erupting two columns of fire at his enemy, the bright purple aura just a few feet from Kyles skin shimmers slightly under the strain but once more no effect is seen.

The mage now looking worried slowly starts to walk backwards, Kyle smirks as he lifts slightly from the ground floating a few inches from the floor following his target.

The mage stops dead and lifts his hands to his side and focuses, the low hum of a summoning power can once more be heard as if a choir were waiting somewhere in shadows for its only verse.

As the hands of the mage reach the top over his head he thrusts them down to the floor as six columns of fire erupt around Kyle.

The columns of fire huge at first start to shrink and form human beings both men and woman wrapped in fire-themed clothing, each one summons some form of firepower, whether it's a weapon made of fire or a fireball its self.

Kyle looks to the mages in turn never losing his smug grin, he then looks to the flame lord who still has his doubts whether this will be enough right now.

The group of six fire mages attack, balls of fire erupt on Kyles shield as others attack with weapons made of flames, all hit the shield and deflect harmlessly, and Kyle lifts his gaze from the flame lord and back to the attacking mages.

"My turn." Kyles calm voice echoes.

Kyle's hands are suddenly pulsed with bio-energy as he points them towards the mages, pulse after pulse are fired from his hands as he keeps them positioned on his attacks.

The fire mages duck and weave, one raises a shield to take the blast, the shield suddenly erupts into a frenzy of sparks as it collapses saving its host from the first hit but not the second, third or fourth.

The mage jolts and jitters rapidly before his mind and organs give out in the overload dropping him to the floor dead.

The mages continue to attack, the blasts of fire strike his shield but are deflected still, and Kyle waits patiently for his moment, as one attacks he fires back, knowing his aura can take the hit he is confident they can't.

The mages fall one by one under the power of Kyle leaving the flame lord alone once more.

Finally, Kyle lets his aura drop as his mind struggles to hold, clearly he is not fully recovered from the battle a few days ago.

Gasping for a breather as he notices once more fresh blood dripping from his nose,

The mage moves from round the pillar littering the room to catch a glimpse of his enemy, finally finding Kyle leaning on a pillar for support and struggling for breath his anger builds.

Launching his fiery vengeance in the form of multiple fireballs for making him feel fear the mage attacks over and over.

Kyle leaps behind the pillar he was leaning on safe and protected while he catches a moment.

"Well done boy, it's not every day someone goes toe to toe a flame lord." The angry mage states still launching his attacks.

Kyle takes a last slow breath before erupting his power to life once more, his aura bright and strong he moves from the pillar into the open being struck by several large fireballs in the process.

The mage once more hurls a large column of fire using both hands joint together with the two flames intertwining making a large four-foot-wide column of pure flaming heat shoot towards Kyle.

Kyle also hurls his powers forwards forcing a bio-electric blast of the same size towards his enemy, the two forces strike in the middle as sparks and strobes of fire and lightning flare from the power struggle.

The mage leaning into the attack starts to feel the strain, as does Kyle, neither man backs down as the mage tries to use his entire power and focus and force it down the fire towards his enemy.

Kyle senses the added strength from the mage, looking to him his eyes still pulsating with his bright energy accepts the challenge, suddenly pulsing another blast followed by another and another down the column of bio-energy.

The extra waves follow the power line erupting to join the struggle smashing it further and further towards the mage before the last pulse envelops the entire flame and smashes into the mage hurling him through the air into the wall behind.

Kyle's aura fails as he drops to the floor once more his nose bleeding as he grabs his knees trying to support himself, the mage shakes off the last attacks as small amounts of bright purple electric shock through him, he looks with fear in his eyes to the small boy who just beat him.

"What are you?" the mages voice filled with fear and doubt.

"Vengeance," Kyle replies as his breath once more under control as he walks confidently towards his enemy.

Lifting himself to his feet steam emanates from his arms and shoulders, his black trench coat singed as is most of his clothes.

Examining his clothes and circumstance the mage tries to think of options, his powers almost drained he opts for a more primal method in hopes of winning.

Summoning two blades made of flame he takes up a position of combat in front of Kyle, Kyle looks at the blades and remains still, the mages fear and anger grows as he charges in waving the blades around towards his enemy.

With a simple gesture of Kyle's hand, the mage is stopped suddenly in his last position, the mages struggle to move but to no avail, only his head can move freely, he looks with fear and shock to Kyle.

Kyle's eyes open slowly revealing his powers are far from done he stands still his handheld out slightly in a relaxed position his look angry and full of hate, with a lift of his hand the mage is lifted with ease into the air stretching him out slightly.

"I won't my friend back you son of a bitch!" Kyle screams.

As his scream nears its end Kyle throws his hand away, the body of the mage follows Kyles gesture perfectly, the wall some thirty feet way objects strongly as the mage smashes into it creating a large crater within.

Walking slowly up to the flame lord unconscious on the floor Kyle sense life in him still, Kyle reluctant to carry on feels his powers suddenly weakening his eyes fail to focus, his head pounds, and his nose trickles fresh blood, shaking off the exhaustion Kyle summons his powers once more forming a small telepathic jolt in his hands.

Bending down to the body of the flame lord, he reluctantly places it in the mind of the mage, his body jolts furiously as if being riddled with bullets for a few seconds before falling silent and lifeless.

The synaptic impulses in his brain are fused out and dead, the flame lord's death was painless, far more than he deserved Kyle thought.

Collapsing to the floor beside the mage kyles relaxes as breath and pain will allow. His break in the calm is suddenly disturbed as he watches the body of the mages start to disintegrate before him. Several golf ball lights bursts from the remains like fireflies flying about erupt into being and flies towards the ceiling and phasing through leaving kyle alone once more.

Save for one, a larger size light hovers closer to kyle and flows about him steadily before slowly making a move for the ceiling, in his heart he knows it's the soul of Sharkarain.
The fatigue grows in Kyle he struggles for the second doorway towards Daniels office, his head spins as his dizziness builds, barely three or four steps later Kyle drops to the floor exhausted.
His mind shuts down, Kyle remains face down unconscious in the hallway, as his mind demands a break and his body obliges.

***

The former two friends erupt in conflict, both attack with the same technique's trained in the same way from the same masters.
Combinations blocks and parries are thrown into the Frey, the technique's from the ages show themselves as the two men clash, slowly as their battle settles into a rhythm a few strikes land on each man.
Refusing to feel the pain they continue, there empowered bodies hit with the same force as they were hit with a speeding car but neither gives, Jacob looks deep into the dark red eyes of carl, something inside him is gone, something that once made him who he was has been destroyed leaving the angry man before him.
Finally, the two break, wiping blood from their mouths and noses were struck they never remove their eyes from each other, both men pant heavily for breath as they circle each other once more.
Carl draws his sword, followed shortly by Jacob, they look to each other still panting.
"Goodbye Jacob." Carls tone angry and full of conviction.
"Goodbye carl, my friend," Jacob replies.
Carl seems angered by Jacobs sympathy and attacks, their enhanced speed makes their entire bodies an entire blur to the human eyes, each strike they throw is blocked or parried as the blades clash, carls powers reach their limit, his speed as fast as he can go.
Jacob senses his old friend's struggle and empowers his speed further, reducing Carl to a now slow-moving attacker, Jacob cannot help but feel for his friend, what must he have done to fall.
Shaking away his concern he recalls the actions this man has done, summoning back his anger he focuses as the blade of his enemy slowly comes creeping round towards him, Jacob pulls back his hand infused with bio-energy and slams it hard into carls chest.
The impact hits perfectly as Carls body now slowly takes the blow and slowly reacts to it as he starts to fly slowly backwards, his face slowly taking on a painful look.
Jacobs's eyes close as time catches up once more, Carl's body lets out a scream as it flies back swiftly smashing through the wall into the room beyond.
Opening his eyes he can see Carl laid holding his chest gasping for breath in pain as he climbs struggling to his feet.
Once to his feet, the cocky angry look is replaced by a concerned one.
"Impressive, you have improved in leaps and bounds boyo." Carls tone injured but firm.
"I was taught by the best," Jacob replies.
Carl steps off the rubble back onto the solid ground inside the room holding his chest, looking to Jacob now very seriously he attacks again, once more the former friend enhanced speed steadily build to carls limit.
Jacob reluctantly lets his blade strike across Carl's right thigh and right weapon arm, stopping in a ready position Jacobs releases his power allowing time to catch up and the pain to hit his enemy.

Carl's body wracks with pain as he staggeringly withdraws limping and holding his weapon arm, looking once more to his former friend Carl looks a little shocked.

"You could have killed me, instead you merely injure me, why?" he shouts.

"Who's knows… maybe I'm waiting for the real Carl to come to his senses." Jacob replies still in a ready position.

Once more Carl looks angry at this exchange, He attacks this time charging bio-energy in the form of a red haze with the electrical charge he hurls them like Kyle would at Jacob.

The blast smashes into the floor and walls as Jacob parries them or evades them, mixing the attacks with weapon strikes and bio-energy attack Carl once more charges in.

Finally under the pressure of constant attack Carls strike hits, slicing through Jacobs's upper weapon arm with his blade Carl follows up with a sudden kick to Jacobs's chest sending him flying back into the wall.

Carl's confidence begins to build as Jacob weakens, he attacks once more with a devious plan to cripple his former friend, with a blade attack being blocked by Jacob he thrusts his demonic powers into action and strikes Jacob with a bolt of pure hatred and energy.

The blast lands square in the chest of Jacob at point black range, the blast hurls his body through the air slamming hard into the wall dropping his blade aside and Jacob to the floor in a heap of debris.

Finally back to his normal self, he thinks to himself he walks slowly to his enemy and looks at him convulsing on the floor the red energy pulsing through him, clearly in pain Jacob slowly seems to fade, into blackness.

"You were once a good friend Jacob, I'm sorry it came to this…but I failed…I wasn't…" Carl softly speaks until the anger returns to regain control.

Lifting his blade into the air pointing it down at Jacobs's heart he looks to his friend, still convulsing, holding his position fighting the rage he lowers it quickly to his side as if fighting something inside.

Shaking away the softness he thinks he lifts the blade once more and brings it crashing down towards Jacobs's heart, the jolt from his blade stopping but a few centimetres from Jacobs's chest shocks him, unable to move his blade or his body he looks confused.

Jacobs's eyes open with their powerful bright blue energy flaring to life, knocking the weapon aside with his hand he suddenly climbs to his feet looking deep into Carl's eyes anger flaring within him.

Carls anger explodes Jacob was running a ruse, his sudden fatigue, his lack of defence, but Carl knows the blast he gave him could not be taken by anyone.

"How is this possible, that blast you took should have killed you or paralyzed you for life." Carl snarls.

Jacob looks him in the yes closely his stern face still not impressed.

"I've improved more than you know Carl, I'm not exactly normal now am I," Jacob adds forcibly reaching for his sword with his telekinetic ability's while still holding Carl on the pot.

Walking a few feet from his enemy and reading himself he releases carl, wasting no time he once again attacks, strike after strike he throws, Jacob easily avoids or parries them.

"Why did you fail Carl, tell me! Why wasn't you strong enough?" Jacob continues to question him at his as he defends himself easily and adds just a small amount of pain in the form of small telepathic jolts into his enemy.

Carl snarls under the pressure finally rushing at Jacob his arms held out to the sides open to attack, Jacob realises what is happening, and reluctantly charges the blade, twisting on the spot he lets the blade of energy slice through the air releasing both bio-energy and telepathic energy is a single electrical bright blue arc towards Carl.

The blast strikes true, the bio-energy hurls his body backwards some distance as the energy seems to pass through him knocking a dark shadow like version out of him screaming as it fades in the air, the telepathic jolt singes his mind paralyzing him.

His body lands hard his blade knocked aside he lays there gasping for breath unable to move.

Jacob walks up to Carl looking down at him in pity.

"What… did you, do to me?" Carl asks as breath will allow.

"The dragons breathe," Jacob replies calmly as if both men know this technique well.

Carl's eyes widen in shock.

"Impossible, no human…" Carl stops as he realises Jacob is not fully human.

Lowering himself to his former friend Jacob can sense the change in him as if the dark shadow knocked from him was the evil infecting him, his eyes now normal show his pride at Jacob and the pain he now feels.

"Well done boyo, bloody well done." Carl tries to snigger as the breath and paralysis will allow.

Jacob suddenly tries to hold onto his friend, as if trying to find a way to stop what is to happen, Carl looks to his friend fearful once more.

"Listen to me Ja while I have time," Carl utters as his breathing starts to become shallow.

Jacob lifts him onto his lap slowly shaking him trying to think of a way he can stop what's going to happen.

"I'm sorry my friend… forgive me, I wasn't strong enough to beat him…" carls last words were his last breath as his eyes suddenly fall away as he falls into darkness and death.

The dragon's breath technique overloads both mental and physical organs shutting them down bit by bit painlessly causing the creature it hits to die.

Jacob holds his friend corpse tightly, suddenly crying and in pain at what he has done, a hollowing scream echo from the room, the entire building hears the pain in the cry as it fades away.

slowly fighting back his pain he remembers the reason he is here, the shadow lord he now senses on the roof is the cause of all this pain and suffering.

Slowly lowering his friend to rest crossing his arms across his chest and closing his eyes Jacobs's tears run down his face.

The anger returns and is now added by the guilt he now carries for his fallen friend, taking his sword in hand he walks with a purpose for the roof.

The wind outside is gentle and the night skies are filled with stars, locating his enemy off to the right looking out to the city below he approaches cautiously.

Daniel dressed in his fine black suit turns to face Jacob his fiery eyes seem to look through him, his twisted evil grin remains despite him losing everyone around him.

"Just you and me now demon," Jacob states raising his sword to a ready position.

"Indeed, I believe our forces have cancelled each other out."

"A fact I shall repay you for momentarily," Jacob replies in anger.

Daniel smirk lets slip a small snigger.

"You can thank me now by lifting your chin just a little higher." Daniel jests as he pulls his finger across his throat simulating cutting it.

"I don't think so, you gonna pay for the death you have caused in this realm you twisted son of a bitch," Jacob adds.

Circling each other the men never take their eyes off each other, this does little to stop the sudden attack from Daniel as he reaches out with his grasp and telekinesis.

Avoiding the sudden grasp of telekinetic power Jacob hurls his psychokinetic jolt towards Daniel knocking his concentration.

Jacob charges in as Daniel staggers back some, summoning a small curved sword like the lesser demons used from the shadows around him, Daniel can parry a few blows from Jacob before he is struck.

The blade runs through his stomach cleanly, with a twist it is pulled away as Jacob readies the blade for a horizontal cut from head to toe.

The strikes pierce his body but no pain is felt just the push and pull of the blade momentarily shocking Daniel.

Daniel summons his psychokinetic ability's slamming a blast into Jacobs's chest hurling back through the air before his second strike can land.

Landing some ten feet away his body slides across the rooftop floor, as he comes to a halt Daniel reaches for him once more with his telekinesis.

Taking hold of Jacob by the throat he hurls him into the stairwell walls, the bricks smash as his body crashes into them.

Still not releasing him Daniel lifts him from the debris gasping for breath and from his new injuries and slams him shoulders first into the rooftop floor a few feet from him.

Jacobs's body smashes once more into the concrete creating a large crater some twelve feet in diameter

Blood jumps from his mouth as he coughs suddenly and roles to his side in agony, several ribs were broken along with his weapon arm and left leg, his head bleeds as several cuts emerge with fresh blood.

Trying to climb out the crater he locates Daniel laughing loudly watching him.

Forcing himself to function he reaches for his sword some distance away, his powers hesitate at first but finally obey.

Climbing out the crater and limping towards Daniel with injuries pulsing pain through his body Jacob refuses to give in.

Daniel still laughing summons a fine sword resembling Jacobs made of pure shadow.

Jacob attacks with his left arm wielding the blade, still a competent swordsman he is no match for the shadow lord in this condition.

Daniel parries several attacks before returning the favour slicing across Jacobs back as he over lunges due to injury, the shadow blade cuts into his skin releasing a small amount of dark energy into his system.

Falling once more to the floor landing on his knees, he lets out a scream of agony as the blackness works his way through his body.

Knocking the mighty blade of Shakarian away Daniel lets his weapon fade into the air before repeatedly striking Jacob in the face with a strong right cross.

Finally collapsing to the floor in a bloody heap Jacobs face is now a bloody lump of flesh, barely able to see out of cither eye due to blood and swelling.

"Ha, the mighty sentinel, defeats all in his path, save me!" Daniel rejoices jumping around excitedly.

Suddenly Daniels joy is interrupted, his body jolts violently, as several shotgun rounds slam into his chest, each one knocking him back slightly, the shots stop and Daniel regains his composure.

Looking out to the remains of the stairwell he can see Steel's walking towards him reloading his shotgun.

"Funs over asshole." Steel's states firmly finally letting his anger grow throwing the weapon down and slamming his right fist into Daniel's face.

Daniel once again jolts violently as Steel's pounds on him with strikes that could smash through concrete, punches kick knees and elbows, even a head butt is thrown into the mix.

Daniels face cuts open under the blunt force he received but he soon bursts into laughter as Steel's continues to hit him, finally stopping Steel's attack by grabbing his oncoming arm.

Steel's suddenly looks with surprise as Daniel looks to him his red eyes flare as Daniels now returns the blunt force trauma with more conviction.

Each strike lands on the steel's as expected and each one with the force of a freight train Steel's thinks as his mind allows, Steel's flops to the floor his body badly beaten and unable to stand let alone fight.

Looking down at the best the earth has to offer Daniel once more jumps around hysterically laughing, he looks up to the night sky his arms open wide as if mocking someone.

"Is this the best you can do?" Daniel shouts before bursting into laughter.

Once more his victory is interrupted, a small bright purple blast strikes him in the back knocking to the floor suddenly.

Turning back with an angry look he is shocked to see Kyle slowly climbing to his feet, a smile sudden creeps on his face as his first intended target on earth stands before him.

Rising to his feet and adjusting his suit as if the many holes slices and dirt stains on it are not there he walks towards Kyle stopping only a few feet away.

"Good to see you, Kyle, now you see what you have missed being hmm?" Daniel asks mockingly.

"Nothing but a cold lifeless lunatic who's about to be a bad memory," Kyle replies.

Kyle knows he is far from full strength, his mind pounds his nose still bleeding he needs rest and time to recuperate, but his friends need help.

"You don't honestly think you can win do, look at you, you're a mess," Daniel states sarcastically.

"Maybe, but I still got enough juice to finish you," Kyle adds.

Daniels face drops suddenly knowing the boy is serious, both men face each other as if back in the old west in a stare down on the quick draw.

Both men act at once, Daniel reaches out to Kyle with his telekinetic abilities trying to snap his neck instantly, Kyle releases a bio-energy bolt landing it in the chest of Daniel knocking him back several feet leaving a singed hole in his suit.

Jacobs eyes suddenly open, his body wracked with pain, he struggles to find his place in the battle looking around to the situation, and his body is healing rapidly but not quick enough as his weapon arm is still broken as are several ribs.

Daniel lifts his head and rolls to his side picking himself up and dusting himself off, Kyle runs to steel's checking he is alive and relieved to find he is.

"Nice move kid," Daniel states walking towards him.

Kyle looks up to him with hatred as he rises to his feet still exhausted he hides his lack in power.

Without warning Kyle's throat is squeezed through the air, Daniel lifts him off his feet into the air a few feet, summoning his powers once more Kyle fires several small telepathic jolts into Daniel, knocking him back slightly holding his head as did the shotgun shells.

Daniels anger grows once more, summoning a sphere of red and black energy in each hand he hurls them at Kyle, the bright aura of Kyles shield takes the blasts but strains under the pressure before giving in finally.

Steel's beginning to stir once more suddenly waking from his beating he turns to find his enemy in a power fight with Kyle.

Daniel opting to end this threat he hurls a black and red sphere of hatred infused with the shadow energy that infected Jacob towards his enemy, Kyle summons a small bio-energy shield in front of him blocking the blast.

The shield strains as denial continue to blast the shield with blast after blast, the shield erupts in a flurry of sparks as it shatters once more as a single blast hits Kyle hurling him backwards in pain.

Finally, Jacob manages to get to his knees, his arm and ribs still were broken and useless he manages to look across the debris and see what is happening.

Steel's manages to climb to his feet drowsy and beaten he looks as Kyle hits the deck in pain then to his attacker, pulling his twin pistols from there holster he opens fire releasing the hot lead at Daniel.

Daniel pulls back his hand and charges it with all his shadow might and telepathic power, hurling it at Steel's he is suddenly caught by surprise as Kyles body jumps in front of the blast with no defence.

The painful roar from Jacob is heard from miles away, his eyes wide in disbelief at the sight before him, although screaming his lungs out Jacob suddenly feels deaf and numb.

Jacob manages somehow to climb to his feet and limp towards his friends, moving slowly as his ribs are still broken he almost makes a crawl towards them.

Steel's also knocked to the floor as Kyle's body is hurled into his, shakes off the pain and realises what just happened, racing towards his friend he checks him for a pulse.

Steel's heart sinks as the boy's life is gone.

Steel's anger manages to block out the pain long enough for him to jump to his feet and charge Daniels, trying to tackle him to the floor, Daniel takes the brunt of the attack and is knocked back a few centimetres before slamming his hand down on Steel's head.

Steels once more unconscious Daniel turns and walks to Kyle's body, holding out his hand over the fallen boy's body, he pulls the soul from him leaving through the chest lifting the body for a moment as it pulls free into Daniel's hand.

As the light is absorbed it travels quickly up to his arm and disappears into his body, suddenly taking in the power from his fallen prey, Daniel starts to laugh.

Suddenly Daniel's laugh is interrupted once more, a presence behind him slowly gets closer, and spinning around to see this presence Daniel's is taken back slightly by the sight before him.

Stood but a few feet away in full health apart from a few small cuts and bruises stands Jacob with his eyes closed.

"You're supposed to be dead!" Daniel states in anger.

Jacobs smug grin creeps on his face, his eyes open suddenly revealing the bright white energy of the fallen.

Daniel steps back suddenly he is worried once more, reaching out with his telekinesis once more trying to reach for him, Jacob lifts his right hand as if telling him to stop, and Daniel's grasp is suddenly pushed aside.

Daniel's anger grows, summoning a large psychokinetic sphere infused with the shadow energy he hurls it at Jacob, crossing his hands in front of him and lowering his head the blast slams into him, his feet slide back but a few inches before the blast is gone.

The flurry of sparks subside as the bright blue and white shield shrinks and wraps it around Jacobs body, reaching out to his left the mighty blade of Shakarian flies to his hand.

Walking calmly once more towards his enemy, Daniel starts letting rip with several blots of pure shadow and pain as he did against Kyle, simple ducks evades and parries manage to deflect the blast never stopping his progress.

Using the knowledge from his latest soul he pulls back his arms and thrusts them forward hurling a massive blast of black bio-energy towards Jacob.

The wave of energy ranging from a five-foot-wide and five-foot height rips through the air tearing up the roof as it travels towards its target, Jacob still moving forwards jumping into the air he brings the blade down on the energy attack, his shield and blade covered in the bright blue and white energy slices through the blast splitting it in two.

Daniels eyes cannot believe what this man just did, the force of the blast would have incinerated a battleship and this man simply cut the blast in two dissipating it.

Finally in weapons range Jacob attacks, his moment to fast for Daniel to see he suddenly feels pain as he sliced across the midsection and sent hurtling back to the floor.

A Wound of bright blue and white energy appears refusing to heal, Jacob appears before him suddenly, reacting out of pure instinct Daniel lets loose the bio-energy he now has access to in the form of black lighting from his hand.

With a quick dash to his right away from the eruption of power Daniel struggles to find his enemy before sensing him behind him.

Turning to face him lifting himself to his feet he summons two curved shadow blades and attacks, the pain in his stomach affecting his performance.

Daniel's rage overwhelms his fear as he continues to attack once more and charges Jacob, with a simple, disarm and followed through with a deep cut through the mid-section Daniel howls in pain.

Jacob turns away from Daniel as he holds his body in pain, walking but a few feet away, the blade suddenly charges, Daniel knows what's coming and summons a shadow bio-energy shield to try and stop the oncoming attack.

A shield blocks everything in front of Daniel as he cowers behind it, Jacob suddenly springs back towards Daniel bringing the sword across his body releasing a mighty sweep of energy that arcs out towards Daniel.

The wave of bright blue and white swirls through the air, it smashes into the blackness that is Daniel's bio-energy shield and shatters it, the power continues through Daniel's body as it lifts him through the air slamming him hard down on his back some twenty feet away.

Jacob's eyes return to normal, suddenly the pain returns he grabs his rips as they are still broken and he struggles to breathe, completely aware of what he did he still has no idea how to summon such power again.

Walking towards his enemy he looks on as the black shadow creature erupts out of Daniel's dead body, its body releasing large amounts of black like smoke out of its body it tries to flee.

Once more the blade of Shakarian is brought to bear, jumping into the air ignoring his injuries Jacob hurls his body up and brings his charges to blade down on the ghost creature.

The bright blue and slightly white energy slices through the creature from collar to hip in a single stroke, the creature pains halting its retreat as it screams in agony a large rip appears in the form of the cut Jacob just performed before dispersing the creature in an explosion of blue and white.

Nothing remains of the creature but a shadowy pile of blackness twisting away on the floor the size of a football.

Looking to Shakarian's blade he smirks as he brings the blade down in yet another attack, twisting the blade in his grip he points the blade down and slams it into the blackness.

The blackness shrinks to that of a single golf ball-sized black dot and travels up the blade into the hilt, the sound of a dragon roaring in victory can be heard as the eyes of the dragon flare black then bright blue and then to the pummel stone at the end twists and turns before returning to normal.

Jacob sighs as he drops to his knees in exhaustion, his ribs suddenly click causing him pain but allowing him to breathe again properly.

CHAPTER 17

Life Goes On

Jacobs's body all though exhausted runs to his friend Kyle, checking one last time for life within him, his head drops in shame as he erupts in tears holding his students head dearly.
"I'm sorry Kyle, I'm so sorry." Jacobs weeping voice cries.
"Ahhhhh!" a deep husky voice cries from under some rubble.
Following the sounds and using his sense Jacobs finds his friends Steel's still alive and coming to.
Slowly placing Kyles head back to the ground respectfully, he runs to Steel's clearing the rubble before slowly and easy pulling him over on to his back.
Scanning his body Jacob can see damaged organs, broken ribs and internal bleeding, wincing at the news his mind feels him he comforts the now conscious and gasping Steel's.
"Did we win?" Steel's asks frailly.
"Yes…, yes we did Stanley…, but it cost us dearly," Jacob replies looking at his fallen friend.
Steel's lifts his head causing him more pain as he catches a glimpse of Kyle laying a few feet away.
"Son of a bitch!" Steel's anger erupts causing yet more pain as he slams his fist into the rooftop floor.
Jacob remains to hold Steel's up as his body slowly repairs itself, suddenly Steel's catches a glimpse of Daniels body occasionally jolting, turning his head to watch more intently his eyes watch as the body suddenly jolts from the chest as if something were trying to get out.
reaching for his gun he tries to aim, Jacob looks at his friend as if he is losing it before witnessing the same thing.
Slowly lowering Steel's down still aiming, Jacob walks forward to investigate. His blade ever readies the chest of Daniel begins to glow in a bright blue light before erupting, a solid column of bright blue energy reaching high into the night sky.
Spiralling up the column of light thousands of small white, blue and yellow lights fly upwards as if they were fireflies suddenly freed from a cage.
Two souls fly from the others and whip around Jacob almost tickling him lifting his saddened spirit.
They hover just a few feet from Jacob before a quick flash of bright light erupts from them like a pulse and leaves two pale transparent ghost images of Kyle and master Takami.
Jacob drops to his knees his eyes erupt in tears and he weeps knowing his friends are free, master Takami's spirit bows showing respect and a proud look on his face as he slowly turns from Jacob and returns to the column of light taking the small globe of the light form once more.
Looking up once more Jacob witness Kyle's spirit saluting his onlooking friend Steel's with a smile, finally looking back to Jacob his hand reaches out touching Jacobs chest gesturing to his heart, a simple slow head nod and smile follows as Kyle turns from him and follows master Takami's spirit.
The lights finally cease as the column of light shuts down and all is quiet in the night sky, the sounds of the city below erupt into being as Jacob follows the lights in the sky until they fade feeling his spirit lifted somehow.

Two days later Steel's awakens from his long sleep, his body aches but is well on the mend, he pulls himself around realising he is in his bedroom back home.

A note rests on the side of his bed, opening the letter he reads a message from Jacob.

Telling steel's he is taking Kyles body back to the school realm to be buried among the fallen heroes of the war were he would always be remembered.

The soul of Shakarian was freed from the dead mage by kyle, steels emotions let out a flare of joy at this news.

Jacobs next part touches Steel's as he refers to Stanley as a true brother one he will love always and should he ever need him, he needs but only think of him and Jacob would come running, but his road goes on forever and Steel's has earned a break.

Turning the page to read the final part Steel's anger builds to learn lord Varamont survived the elevator crash and fled, Jacob, vows to track him down and end him.

With a final goodbye and well wishes, Jacobs note ends.

Steel's lets a sigh go as looks around his apartment, walking to his living room he is taken back the sudden bloom of flowers in his little garden, knowing Jacob must have done this he looks out as if looking through the walls of his apartment out into the world.

"Give em hell Ja."

***

Paul's eyes run with tears, as does Jacobs as he looks to the roaring fire, Paul never took his eyes from Jacob the entire time listening to his story and seeing in his mind thanks to his host.

"Did you ever see him again?" Paul asks referring to his friend Steels.

Jacob shakes his head as he states he hasn't.

"But I will..., one day," Jacob replies wiping his tears.

Jacob takes in a deep breath before rising his feet and walking once more to the door and looking out into the grey mists that surround this cabin.

Paul looks to his host confusion on his face and filling his mind.

"So...what happens now? I mean you have stopped the invasion you stopped the shadow lord, and killed Varamont what else is out there?" Paul asks.

Jacob lets a small snigger creep out as he turns back to Paul.

"There's always something else out there, just waiting."

Paul nods as if agreeing, he watches as Jacob walks to his coat and pack, donning them both suddenly Paul is afraid.

"Where are you going?" Paul asks.

Jacob smiles at his new friend, as he finishes getting ready.

"But that's not all surly? I mean you must know more... what about your fallen heritage, what about the school realm, and what about the other things out there."

"Paul I have no answers for you, I have told you my story, it's your job now to spread the word... and as for the rest, I'll learn as I go." Jacob smiles as he starts to leave.

Stopping just outside the door, he turns back to Paul as if remembering something.

"When you want to leave just head straight out the door, till you can't see the cabin no more wait for the winds to drop then turn around and you'll be back in the park." Jacob states.

Turning to leave once more Paul walks to the doorway watching this incredible man leave.

"Will, I ever see you again?" Paul shouts.

Jacob stops and turns back to his new friend a cocky smile on his face as if he knew the answer to the future already.

"Who knows, maybe in a year or two ill have more stories to tell you," Jacob adds with a mocking tone.

Walking into the mists this lone soldier continues on his path, boldly accepting his fate not knowing what tomorrow brings, after narrowly avoiding one apocalypse he walks out into the future looking for the next one.

Printed in Great Britain
by Amazon